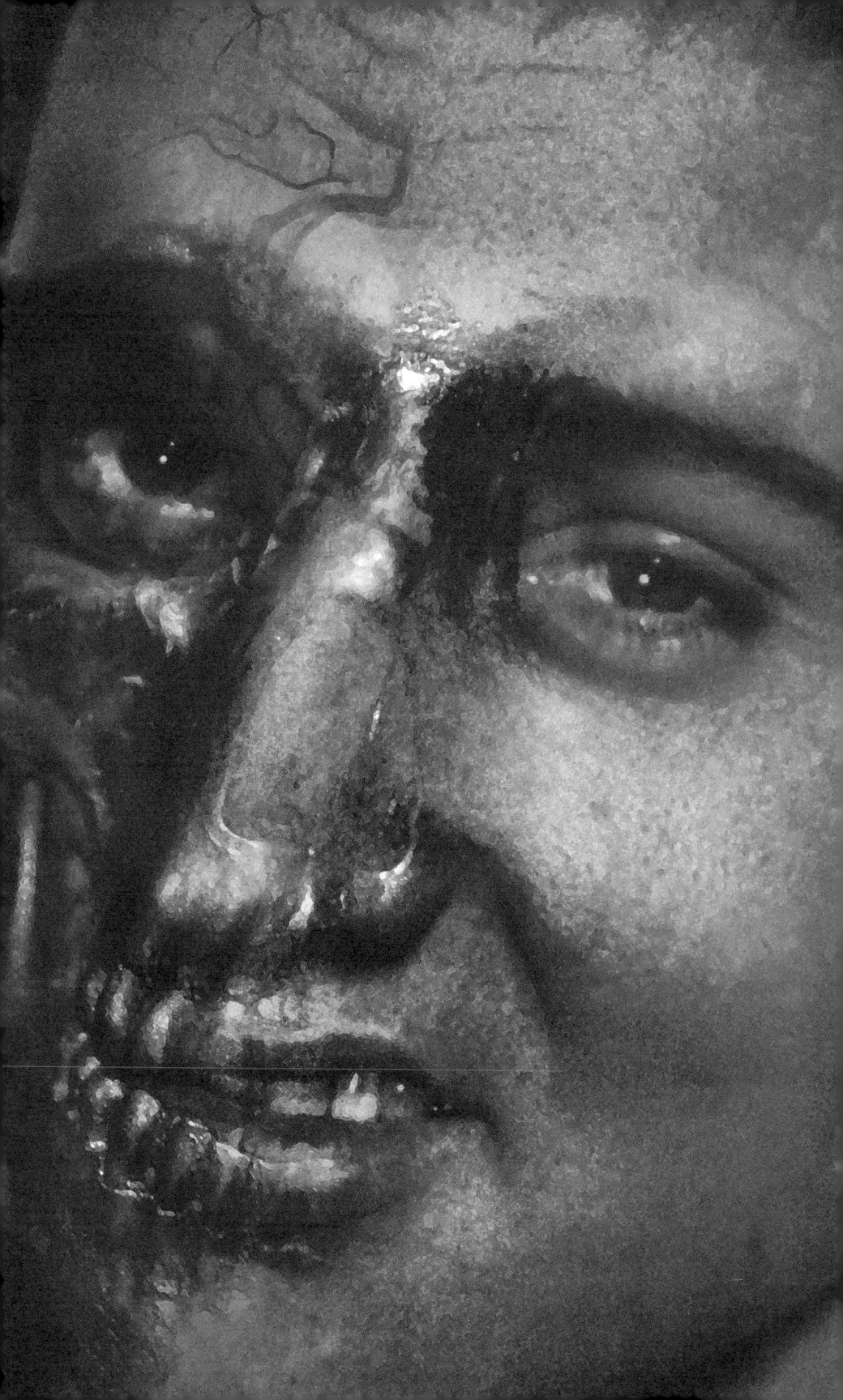

Walk on the Wild Side
The Best Horror Stories of
Karl Edward Wagner, Volume 2

Edited by Stephen Jones
Illustrated by J.K. Potter
Introduction by Peter Straub
Afterword by David Drake
Published by Centipede Press

This is a Centipede Press Book
Published by Centipede Press
2565 Teller Court, Lakewood, Colorado 80214

Walk on the Wide Side:
The Best Horror Stories of Karl Edward Wagner, Volume 2
edited by Stephen Jones
Published by arrangement with the Estate of Karl Edward Wagner

Copyright © 2011 by The Estate of Karl Edward Wagner
Introduction © 21011 by Peter Straub
Afterword © 2011 by David Drake
Cover and interior artwork © 2011 by J.K. Potter
Page 359 constitutes an extension of this copyright page.
All rights reserved.

ISBN 978-1-933618-98-2 (hc.: alk. paper)
Printed and bound in the United States of America.

April 2012
www.centipedepress.com

Contents

Introduction: Various Encounters with Karl,
 by Peter Straub, 7

The Last Wolf, 21
Into Whose Hands, 31
More Sinned Against, 53
Shrapnel, 69
Silted In, 79
Lost Exits, 89
Endless Night, 97
An Awareness of Angels, 107
But You'll Never Follow Me, 123
Cedar Lane, 129
The Kind Men Like, 139
The Slug, 153
Did They Get You to Trade?, 167
Little Lessons in Gardening, 187
A Walk on the Wild Side, 201
Passages, 215
In the Middle of a Snow Dream, 227
Gremlin, 245
Prince of the Punks, 253
The Picture of Jonathan Collins, 257
Locked Away, 277
I've Come to Talk with You Again, 293
Final Cut, 299
Brushed Away, 307
Old Loves, 319
Lacunae, 335

Afterword: The Truth Insofar As I Know It by David Drake, 349
Acknowledgements, 359

Introduction:
Various Encounters with Karl
by Peter Straub

I remember the place where it happened and my impressions of the person better than the circumstances which brought about my first meeting with that good soul, Karl Edward Wagner. Even the year is unhappily vague, but it must have been 1975 or 1976, because the education in horror literature I had begun in 1974 under the instruction of Thomas Tessier, my tour guide, reference librarian and seminar leader, had progressed at least far enough beyond its initial stages so that I was already trying to write it.

Thomas Tessier and I had been friends since meeting one another at a 1970 poetry reading in the cellar of a Dublin pub called Sinnot's, and our literary conversations had taken an unusual course. In 1970 and '71, we talked about Geoffrey Hill (a modernist English poet), Derek Mahon (a not very modernist but anyhow wonderful Irish poet who was a friend of Thom's), Wallace Stevens, John Berryman, John Ashbery and Yeats. In 1972, we were on to Sylvia Plath, Ted Hughes, Mark Strand, Bill Knott (who called himself St. Geraud, "virgin and suicide," and

Left Dennis Etchison, Jeff Conner and Karl Edward Wagner at the 1984 World Fantasy Convention, Ottawa, Canada. Photograph by J.K. Potter.

wrote brief poems seemingly from the point of view of someone recently deceased), Greg Kuzma (another now-forgotten oddity whose poems we found hilariously inept), Thomas Mann, Henry James, Federico García Lorca, Virginia Woolf and Iris Murdoch, along with all of our earlier enthusiasms.

By 1974, we were still gabbing about these same people some of the time, but more often, before and after the endless hours frittered away in front of low-rent horror movies at the equally low-rent Kilburn Odeon, we obsessed about H.P. Lovecraft, Clark Ashton Smith, Arthur Machen, Robert Bloch, Ira Levin and James Hadley Chase. I'm almost certain that I had already written my first excursion into horror, a novel called *Julia*. If I had not, Tessier would have had little reason to invite me along to his own first meeting with an American fantasy and horror writer of about our age named Karl Edward Wagner, who had just arrived in London.

Thom was at this time the Managing Director of Millington Books, a delightful publishing house located on the western fringes of Bloomsbury and not far from the British Museum in a structure with a curved, glass-brick exterior which bore an odd resemblance to a public convenience. Across Southampton Row from Millington's offices were the Russell Hotel, always filled with Americans in new Burberrys, and, a little way south, another, humbler hotel memorable only because directly inside its entrance a wide, comfortable staircase led down to the congenial Peter's Bar. After I joined Thom at Millington, we walked across the street, entered the hotel and went down the stairs to meet Karl in the chiaroscuro of the pub, as I did twice later, once when he was in the company of his dear friends, Mr. and Mrs. Manly Wade Wellman, and once with Ramsey Campbell.

On all of these occasions, Karl was accompanied by his wife, Barbara Wagner. Barbara and Karl were nothing if not a striking couple. In an ironic moment, a celestial dating bureau had arranged the conjunction of an unusually thoughtful Hell's Angel and a Playmate of the Month with big granny glasses and a wide-open smile. He looked like someone you would mess with,

Panel on "Horror in Literature." L-R: Charles L. Grant, Dennis Etchison, Robert Bloch, Douglas E. Winter, Karl Edward Wagner, Paul Sammon, Hugh B. Cave, Ramsey Campbell. DeepSouthCon 25, Huntsville, Alabama, June, 1987. Photograph by John L. Coker, III.

were you stupid enough to think about messing with him, at some risk to your health. She looked like someone you had conjured up in a fantasy during your sophomore year in high school, except for being even nicer and more sociable. The combination of two such particular and disparate types was immediately appealing. I am representing, I rush to add here, a point of view shaped by what was already a lengthy time spent in England, and the Wagners might have, very likely would have, seemed less anomalous to anyone who had lived through the first half of the 1970s in the United States. Yet even then Barbara and Karl must have seemed to many who knew them well a couple whose great appeal had at least something to do with the utterly amiable anomaly they presented.

Then, at the time I first met him, Karl required only a couple of minutes to dispel the associations brought to mind by his cascading red-blond hair, his impressive beard, his equally impressive bulk. His sly, subtle, witty mind, the unexpectedness of his thoughts, almost instantly took care of that. I guess he did have a motorcycle, I'm not sure, but it was just a possession, not a definition. What did define him was an instinctive generosity, a native compassion, his sense of humor, his capacity for observation, his alertness and the way it lay in wait, also the way these capacities very quickly declared themselves above the conventional forms of judgement. The other essentially defining

Introduction: Various Encounters with Karl · 9

Robert Bloch & Karl Edward Wagner. DeepSouthCon 25, Huntsville, Alabama, June, 1987. Photograph by John L. Coker, III.

matter, one which nearly always permeated and aerated Karl's conversation, was the astonishing, dazzling, unprecedented, quantity of what he knew.

Karl was an enormously informed human being, and the range of his knowledge had several sources. During our first encounter in Peter's Bar, I learned that he had finished medical school and qualified as a psychiatrist, which already meant that he was smarter than most people, as well as being more dedicated to those tasks he had decided were worthwhile. To pause for a moment in which to state what should be obvious, it is not possible to advance through college, medical school, the demanding requirements of internship, residency and psychiatric training without a degree of application, intelligence, determination and sheer savvy not only beyond the comprehension of most people but actually unimaginable to them. Karl was entirely uninterested in claiming the recognition ordinarily due these achievements, and as far as I knew, never alluded to their intellectual or emotional cost. He simply wanted you to know what he had done on his journey toward becoming a writer because he knew that it informed his work.

Another aspect of his knowledge was made up of what he had

Karl Edward Wagner. DragonCon, Atlanta, Georgia, July 1994. Photograph by John L. Coker, III.

read. Somehow, and here we must invoke those same capacities for intelligent, determined, savvy application which had seen him through his medical training, Karl had managed to read almost everything related to fantasy and horror literature published in the past three centuries. His erudition was extraordinarily profound and precise. A few years later, Karl did everyone the favor of sharing in his *Fantasy Newsletter* column some of what he knew about the European variants of horror's tropes, forgotten writers, overlooked early stories, the publishing history and bibliographic information pertinent to these writers and their stories, and a lot more of the same. One knew there was a lot more where that came from, that Karl was drawing upon a deep well of such information.

It is almost impossible to suggest how impressive all of this was to anyone who had the good luck to come across Karl's columns or provoke him into conversation about arcane horror literature. Anything but a show-off and a great deal more interested in talking about matters closer to hand, such as the merits of the beer in our pint glasses, the labyrinthine thought processes excited in him by whatever he had happened to have been doing that day, his entertaining fantasies about the strangers visible

Julius Schwartz and friend with Karl Edward Wagner at the 1993 World Fantasy Convention, Minneapolis, Minnesota. Photograph by John L. Coker, III.

from his chair, the current state of Carcosa and its manifold sagas, the ever-fascinating subject of food, anecdotes about friends and recent visitors, animadversions about North Carolina and his curiosity as to these new people he was meeting, he had to be prodded into talking about the subject he undoubtedly knew in greater detail and breadth than anyone I've ever known.

But the most crucial, most central part of his knowledge had nothing to do with what he had learned during medical school, his psychiatric training or his unprecedented command of the history of supernatural and fantasy literature. To an extent well beyond the usual human capacity, even as represented by most fiction-writers, and it now seems to me to an extent so drastically uncomfortable as to be painful, Karl was able to see what was actually before him. This ability is nothing if not rare. Most people move through a fog of preconceptions, unconscious fantasies, Oedipal plots and ideational patterns that distorts the tiny portion of available reality they allow themselves to see into a form they already know. Karl wasn't like that. In the days before he succeeded in numbing himself into something like a perpetual state of grumpy, amused, self-medicated ease, he was

Karl Edward Wagner at the 1992 World Fantasy Convention, Pine Mountain, Georgia. Photograph by John L. Coker, III.

one of those people who take in the undercurrents and meanings of what is going on around them. He didn't miss anything. You could see it in his eyes, in the movements of the face hidden beneath the heroic beard, and you could hear it in every word he said. Truly observant and insightful human beings often strike everyone else as approaching daily life from an eccentric angle, and Karl must have accustomed himself early on to this sort of witless marginalization. I am tempted to ascribe the flowing hair and beard, the entire physical solidity of the self he presented in adulthood, to his reaction against such reflexively thoughtless opposition, but Karl was more complicated than that. In any case, the stories collected in *In a Lonely Place* demonstrate in paragraph after paragraph how closely he attended to the nuances of ordinary, daily behaviors, how much he observed and took into himself.

I mention the collection called *In a Lonely Place* because of all his books it was the only one I was able to read. By the time I met Karl, nearly all of contemporary fantasy literature, except for its capacious subgenre known as horror and the work of extraordinary wild cards like Angela Carter and a very few

Introduction: Various Encounters with Karl · 13

others, had come to seem so unrelated to my own concerns as to belong to another world, like that of science fiction, another field I had long ago found unreadable. That I saw Tolkien as a miraculous storyteller of enduring importance did not make the work of his imitators compelling, and heroic fantasy written under the influence of Robert E. Howard was so distant from what interested me as to be unapproachable. I didn't get it, and I still don't. The adventures of muscular heroes in ahistorical but presumably ancient times equipped with invented cultures and landscapes struck me as belonging to a variety of literature best suited to adolescents. I realize that this is a limitation, a kind of flaw, but it is not one I can correct. Like jazz musicians, painters, dancers, composers, poets and every other sort of artist, writers are subject to those specific blind spots inevitably caused by their continuous investigations of the seams they find richest. What Karl found most suited to his particular talent never spoke to me, which does not mean that I dismissed it—the work of many wonderful writers forbids me entry, and I don't dismiss them either, I just can't read them. This is not a matter of choice. Karl must have known that I was not likely to be attuned to his Kane fictions, and one demonstration of his great awareness was that he never pressed the issue. However, when his collection of contemporary horror stories was accepted by Warner Books, he asked me if I would write an introduction, and I was delighted to do so.

The overture first came through Kirby McCauley, who was our mutual agent and friend through the end of the 1970s and all of the 1980s and a great supporter of Karl's work. By then, my respect for Karl was such that I would have agreed to do an introduction for a sword-and-sorcery collection from the point of view of a one-eyed cat and written in rhymed couplets if the stories had his name on them (come to think of it, as long as he could keep himself sufficiently entertained, Karl could probably have pulled it off!), but of course *In a Lonely Place* was nothing like that. Neither was it very much like anything else, either—I mean, the stories resembled no one else's. Their radical originality was largely a matter of structure, the way the narratives kept breaking out of themselves, shifting ground and relocating themselves in entirely unforeseen territory. At some point after Kirby had sent along the manuscript, Karl telephoned to thank me for taking on the job, and he listened to my effusions with his usual good-humored grace. The same quality came into play after the book was published, when it became obvious that my admiration had not rescued me from overlooking a crucial, explanatory detail in one of the stories.

I was blissfully unaware of my mistake until the Wagners and I met at a vast, hectic party in a suite the size of a bowling alley that Kirby had rented during a World Fantasy Convention not long after the book came out. Barbara eventually drifted off deeper into the throng, and Karl thanked me for what I had written about him. Then he mentioned one of the stories I had liked most and asked if I had noticed the moment in its beginning paragraphs when the protagonist catches sight of his reflection in a window. Yes, I said, I did remember that section…and suddenly understood what it meant. Oh, I said, Yes. I see. He nodded, and, satisfied that I had seen the point at last, went on to talk about something else. If that was a rebuke, it was certainly the most diplomatic I've ever been given.

For a long time, I saw Karl and Barbara once or twice a year in the heightened, swirling atmosphere of the party suites and bars in the hotels where World Fantasy and World Horror Conventions were held. The Wagners, especially Karl, were one of the reasons I went to conventions—like Bob Bloch, Fritz Leiber, Charles Grant, Chelsea Quinn Yarbro, Jim French, Steve Jones, Dennis Etchison and a number of others, the Wagners were people of whom I was extremely fond and thought of as friends but saw only at these massive gatherings. I met them, I think, in all of these cities: Providence (twice), Nashville, Knoxville, Baltimore, Chicago, New York (twice), New Haven, Berkeley, Ottawa and Seattle. I often fantasized about visiting Karl in Chapel Hill, but we never managed to arrange it. What we managed to arrange instead was some time for private

Karl Edward Wagner at the 1987 World Fantasy Convention, Nashville, Tennessee. Photograph by John L. Coker, III.

conversation at each of the conventions we both attended, itself no easy feat. Almost all of these deeply enjoyable conversations took place in bars.

We almost always had drinks in our hands, and another one was almost always in the offing. I know something like sixty or seventy writers of one kind or another, and only three of them do not drink alcohol. Some of them drink too much for their own good, but very few of them seem at all impaired. In the mid-1980s, many of the people I knew took drugs of one kind or another, and only a few of them experienced serious difficulties. By 1990, nearly everyone had stopped using drugs, and almost everyone had cut back on their drinking, Karl invariably seemed in command of himself, at least to me, his colleague at the bar. He did not slur his words, forget what he was talking about in mid-sentence, tell stupid jokes, get glassy-eyed, become incoherent, fall off the stool or lurch when he walked. I assumed that he had once used some kind of drug or drugs, or maybe still did now and again, because he occasionally talked about them and, anyhow, they were hardly uncommon in our shared world. (Two people came up to me separately at the same horror-related party in

1988 to ask if I had any coke. When I said no, they both glared at me in disbelief because they thought I was holding out on them. I suppose that after me they tried the bathrooms, where from behind the locked doors of the stalls you could hear what sounded like the snorting of horses.) In any case, a lot of Karl's drug conversation had to do with what he and his fellow MDs had obtained from medical laboratories, and therefore had a retrospective cast. He struck me as far too purposeful and aware to get into trouble with substance abuse.

    The picture darkened in 1989, when within fifteen minutes of my arrival at a convention in Seattle someone told me that the Wagners had separated and Karl was taking it badly. Only a few minutes after that, Barbara appeared before me, in radiant bloom as ever, and with her new lover in tow. I don't remember anything about the man except that he was well-dressed (Karl made the idea of being well-dressed seem like a joke, no matter what he was wearing), dark-haired and slender (no comment is necessary), and rather good-looking (as impressive as his appearance was, Karl rendered the concept of "good looks" as irrelevant as he did "well-dressed"). They lived on the beach in Venice, California, which seemed entirely appropriate to Barbara, and she was in fine good humor, as happy as I'd ever seen her. Karl, she said, was fine—I'd run into him sooner or later, I'd see.

    Not fine, Karl loomed into view moments after Barbara left me. He seemed thoroughly depressed. He looked wounded. His eyes sagged, and his face was puffier than I remembered it. He immediately began talking about Barbara. Although he was angry, there was little rancor in what he said. He was still reeling from his loss. He loved her, and he wished that she would come back to him. It must have been extraordinarily painful for him to see her there, and I still wonder why he put himself in such an agonizing trap. He must have wanted to demonstrate that he was still a functioning presence, and he probably also wanted to see his friends. The second goal was successful, but the first one completely failed. Karl met a great many friends who one and all thought he was falling apart. Nearly all of his conversation focused on Barbara, and his inability to talk about anything else wore you out. During that convention, drink eventually did erode his speech, to the point where it became difficult to understand. After enough alcohol, he developed a gnomic twinkle which indicated that the vanity of human folly could still amuse him, but it was a sad echo of his former wit. He wandered through the convention like an unhappy ghost, visibly encased in his sorrow and isolated by it. Everyone who cared for him hoped he would soon come to terms with the end of his marriage and return to his best self.

Instead, at least from what I saw, he increasingly succumbed to his sense of loss. The Karl I met two years later at another convention in another city, this one forgotten, moved in a shuffle like an upright bear, was almost completely incomprehensible and existed within a profound, self-imposed isolation. His voice emerged in a dark brown, tarry rumble which obliterated individual words. Whatever he was taking kept him on his feet and ignited the gnomic twinkle, but the object of his amusement was incommunicable. He was glad to see me, and I to see him, and we embraced in our usual fashion. After that came only dismay. He was like a walking ruin.

Others closer to him, those who saw Karl on a daily basis or at least more frequently than I did, must have witnessed happier and more intact versions of the man. He continued to write and to edit, he travelled, he got out and did things. I wish I could have been with him at those times when he gathered himself together and again became something like that amazing person, the Karl Wagner I had the privilege of knowing for so many years. That person was splendidly one of a kind, and I miss him enormously. Karl's degree of perception and the whole arduous, dedicated, observant balancing act it demanded of him during the course of his life could not but exact a cruel payment, whatever the conditions and terms by which it was rendered.

—Peter Straub

The Last Wolf

The last writer sat alone in his study.

There was a knock at his door.

But it was only his agent. A tired, weathered old man like himself. It seemed not long ago that he had thought the man quite young.

"I phoned you I was coming," explained his agent, as if to apologize for the writer's surprised greeting.

Of course…he had forgotten. He concealed the vague annoyance he felt at being interrupted in his work.

Nervously the agent entered his study. He gripped his attaché case firmly before him, thrusting it into the room as if it were a shield against the perilously stacked shelves and shelves of musty books. Clearing a drift of worn volumes from the cracked leather couch, he seated himself amidst a puff of dust from the ancient cushions.

The writer returned to the chair at his desk, swivelling to face his guest. His gnarled fingers gripped the chair arms; his black eyes, bright beneath a craggy brow, bored searchingly into the agent's face. He was proud and wary as an aging wolf. Time had weathered his body and frosted his hair. No one had drawn his fangs.

The agent shifted against the deep cushions and erased the dusty film on his attaché case. His palm left sweat smears on the vinyl. He cleared his throat, subconsciously striving to clear his thoughts from the writer's spell. It would be easier if he could see him just as another client, as nothing more than a worn out old man. Just another tired old man, as he himself had become.

"I haven't had any success with your manuscripts," he said softly. "No luck at all."

There was pain in his eyes, but the writer nodded stiffly. "No, it was obvious from your manner that you hadn't been successful this time." He added: "This time either."

"Your last seven novels," the agent counted. "Nothing."

"They were good books," the writer murmured, like a parent recalling a lost child. "Not great books, for all my efforts, but they were good. Someone would have enjoyed reading them."

His eyes fell upon the freshly typed pages stacked on his desk, the newest page just curling from his ancient mechanical typewriter. "This one will be better," he stated.

"That's not the problem," his agent wearily told him. He had told him before. "No one's saying that you haven't written well—it's just…Who's going to print them?"

"There are still one or two publishers left, I believe."

"Well, yes. But they don't publish books like this anymore."

"What do they publish then?" The writer's voice was bitter.

"Magazines, mostly—like these." The agent hurriedly drew a pair of flimsy periodicals from his case.

The writer accepted them with a wry smile and thumbed through the pages of bright photographs. He snorted. "Pretty pictures, advertisements mostly, and a few paragraphs of captions. Like the newspapers. Not even real paper anymore."

He gestured toward the shelves of age-yellowed spines. "Those are magazines. *Saturday Review. Saturday Evening Post. Playboy. Kenyon Review. Weird Tales. Argosy.* And the others that have passed. Do you remember them? They contained stories, essays, articles, criticism. A lot of garbage, and a lot of things worthwhile. They contained thoughts."

"Still, there's some writing in the few periodicals that we have left," the agent pointed out. "You could do that sort of thing."

"That sort of thing? That's not writing! Since the learned journals all went to computerized tapes, the only excuse for a periodical that's left are these mindless picture brochures the ad companies publish. Damned if I'll write copy for Madison Avenue!

"But what are you trying to get to?" he scowled.

The plastic pages of smiling young consumers fluttered back into the attaché case. "I'm trying to say it's impossible to sell your books. Any books. No one publishes them. No one reads this sort of thing anymore."

"What do they read instead?"

The agent waved his hands in a vague gesture. "Well, there's these magazines. One or two newspapers are still around."

"They're just transcripts of the television news," the writer scoffed. "Pieced together by faceless technicians, slanted and censored to make it acceptable, and then gravely presented by some television father image. What about books?"

"Well, there are a few houses that still print the old classics—for school kids and people who still go to libraries. But all that's been made into movies, put on television—available on cassettes to view whenever you like. Not much reason to read those—not when everybody's already seen it on TV."

The writer made a disgusted noise.

"Well, damn it, man!" the agent blurted in exasperation. "Marshall McLuhan spoke for your generation. You must have understood what was coming."

"He didn't speak for my generation," the writer growled. "What about those last three novels that you did sell? Somebody must have read those."

"Well, maybe not," explained the other delicately. "It was pure luck I found a publisher for them anyway. Two of them the publisher used just as a vehicle for Berryhill to illustrate—he has quite a following, you know. Collectors bought them for his artwork—but maybe some read the books. And the last one I sold… Well, that was to a publisher who wanted it for the nostalgia market. Maybe somebody read it while that fad lasted."

Beneath his white mustache, the writer's lips clamped tightly over words that would be ill-bred to use to a guest.

"Anyway, both publishers are defunct now," his agent went on.

The Last Wolf · 23

"Printing costs are just too high. For the price of half a dozen books, you can buy a TV. Books just cost too much, take too much time, for what you can get out of them."

"So where does that leave me?"

There was genuine sympathy, if not understanding, in the agent's voice. He had known his client for a long while. "There just doesn't seem to be any way I can sell your manuscripts. I'm sorry—truly sorry. Feel free to try another agent, if you want. I honestly don't know one to recommend, and I honestly doubt that he'll have any better success.

"There just isn't any market for books in today's world. You're like a minstrel when all the castles have fallen, or a silent film star after the talkies took over. You've got to change, that's all."

More than ever the writer seemed a wolf at bay. The last wolf. They were all gone too. Just the broken-spirited creatures born in cages to amuse the gawking, mindless world on the other side of the bars.

"But I do have some other prospects for you," the agent announced, trying to muster a bright smile.

"Prospects?" The writer's shaggy brows rose dubiously.

"Sure. Books may have outlived their day, but today's writers still have plenty to keep them busy. I think a few of your old crowd may even still be around, writing for television and the movies."

The writer's face was dangerous.

"I've talked with the producers of two new shows—one of them even remembered that best-seller you had years back. They both said they'd take a close look at anything you have to show. Quite a break, considering you've never written a script before. Ought to be right in your line though—both shows are set back in your salad days.

"One's a sitcom about a screwball gang of American soldiers in a POW camp back in the Indo-China wars. Dorina Vallecia plays the commandant's daughter, and she's a hot property right now. The other's a sitcom about two hapless beatnik drug pushers back in the Love Generation days. This one looks like a sure hit for next season. It's got Garry Simson as the blundering redneck chief of police. He's a good audience draw, and they've got a new black girl, Livia Stone, to play the bomb-throwing activist girl friend."

"No," said the writer in a tight voice.

"Now wait a minute," protested the agent. "There's good money in this—especially if the show hits it off. And it wasn't easy talking to these guys, let me tell you!"

"No. It isn't the money."

"Then what is it, for Christ's sake! I'm telling you, there's a bunch of old-time writers who've made it big in television."

"No."

"Well, there's an outside chance I can get you on the script team for a new daytime Gothic soaper. You've always had a fondness for that creepy stuff."

"Yes. I always have had. No."

The agent grimaced unhappily. "I don't know what I can do for you. I really don't. I tell you there's no market for your stuff, and you tell me you won't write for the markets that are there."

"Maybe something will come up."

"I tell you, it's hopeless."

"Then there's nothing more to say."

The agent fidgeted with the fastenings of his attaché case. "We've been friends a long time, you know. Damn it, why won't you at least try a few scripts? I'm not wanting to pry, but the money must look good to you. I mean, its been a long dry spell since your last sale."

"I won't say I can't use the money. But I'm a writer, not a hired flunky who hacks out formula scripts according to the latest idiot fads of tasteless media."

"Well, at least the new social security guarantees an income for everyone these days."

The writer's lined face drew cold and white. "I've never bothered to apply for the government's dole. Turning my personal life over to the computers for a share of another man's wages seems to me a rather dismal bargain."

"Oh." The agent felt embarrassed. "Well, I suppose you could always sell some of these books—if things got tight, I mean. Some

The Last Wolf · 25

of these editions ought to be worth plenty to a rare book collector, wouldn't they?"

"Good night," said the writer.

Like a friend who has just discharged his deathbed obligations, the agent rose to his feet and shook hands with the writer. "You really ought to keep up with today's trends, you know. Like television—watch some of the new shows, why don't you? It's not so bad. Maybe you'll change your mind, and give me a call?"

"I don't think so."

"You even got a television in this house? Come to think, I don't remember seeing a screen anywhere. Does that antique really work?" He pointed to an ancient fishbowl Stromberg-Carlson, crushed in a corner, its mahogany console stacked with crumbling comic books.

"Of course not," said the writer, as he ushered him to the door. "That's why I keep it here."

The last writer sat alone in his study.

There was a knock at his door.

His stiff joints complained audibly as he left his desk, and the cocked revolver that lay there. He swung open the door.

Only shadows waited on his threshold.

The writer blinked his eyes, found them dry and burning from the hours he had spent at his manuscript. How many hours? He had lost all count of time. He passed a weary hand over his face and crossed the study to the bourbon decanter that stood, amber spirits, scintillant crystal, in its nook, as always.

He silently toasted a departed friend and drank. His gaze fell upon a familiar volume, and he pulled it down with affection. It was a tattered asbestos-cloth first of Bradbury's *Fahrenheit 451*.

"Thank God you're dead and gone," he murmured. "Never knew how close you were—or how cruelly wrong your guess was. It wasn't government tyranny that killed us. It was public indifference."

He replaced the yellowed book. When he turned around, he was not alone.

A thousand phantoms drifted about his study. Spectral figures in a thousand costumes, faces that told a thousand stories. Through their swirling ranks the writer could see the crowded shelves of his books, his desk, substantial.

Or were they? When he looked more closely, the walls of his study seemed to recede. Perhaps instead he was the phantom, for through the ghostly walls of books, he began to see strange cities rising. Pre-Babylonian towers washed by a silent sea. Medieval castles lost within thick forests. Frontier forts standing guard beside unknown rivers. He recognized London, New York, Paris—but their images shimmered in a constant flux of change.

The writer watched in silence, his black eyes searching the faces of the throng that moved about him. Now and again he thought he glimpsed a face that he recognized; but he could not call their names. It was like meeting the brother of an old friend, for certain familiar lines to these faces suggested that he should know them. But he had never seen their faces before. No one had.

A heavy-set man in ragged outdoor clothing passed close to him. The writer thought his virile features familiar. "Don't I know you?" he asked in wonder, and his voice was like speaking aloud from a dream.

"I doubt it," replied the young man. "I'm Ethan Blackdaw. You would know me only if you had read Jack London's *Spell of the Snows*."

"I'm not familiar with that book, though I know London well."

"He discarded me after writing only a fragment."

The writer called to another visitant, a powerful swordsman in antediluvian armor: "Surely I've met you."

"I think not," the barbarian answered. "I am Cromach. Robert E. Howard would have written my saga, had he not ended his life."

A lean-faced man in dirty fatigues nodded sourly. "Hemingway doomed me to limbo in the same way."

"We are the lost books," murmured a Berber girl, sternly beautiful in medieval war dress. "Some writer's imagination gave us our souls, but none of us was ever given substance by his pen."

The writer stared in wonder.

A young girl in the dress of a flapper smiled at him wistfully.

"Jessica Tilman wanted to write about me. Instead she married and forgot her dream to write."

"Ben Pruitt didn't forget about me," growled a tall black in torn fieldhand's overalls. "But no publishers wanted his manuscript. The flophouse owner tossed me out with the rest of Pruitt's belongings that night when he died."

A slim girl in hoopskirts sighed. "Barry Sheffield meant to write a sonnet about me. He had four lines completed when a Yankee bullet took him at Shiloh."

"I was Zane Grey's first book," drawled a rangy frontier marshal. "Or at least, the first one he tried to write."

A bleary-eyed lawyer adjusted his stained vest and grumbled, "William Faulkner always meant to get started on my book."

"Thomas Wolfe died before he started me," commiserated a long-legged mountain girl.

The walls of his study had almost vanished. A thousand, ten thousand phantoms passed about him. Gothic heroines and brooding figures in dark cloaks. Cowboys, detectives, spacemen and superheroes in strange costumes. Soldiers of a thousand battles, statesmen and explorers. Fat-cheeked tradesmen and matrons in shapeless dresses. Roman emperors and Egyptian slaves. Warriors of an unhistoried past, children of a lost future. Sinister faces, kindly faces, comic and tragic, brave men and cowards, the strong and the weak. There seemed no end to their number.

He saw a fierce Nordic warrior—a companion to Beowulf, had a war-axe not ended his stave. There were countless phantoms of famous men of history—each subtly altered after the conception of a would-be biographer. He saw half-formed images of beauty, whose author had died heartbroken that his genius was insufficient to transform his vision into poetry. A Stone Age hunter stalked by, gripping his flint axe—as if seeking the mammoth that had stolen from mankind its first saga.

And then the writer saw faces that he recognized. They were from his own imagination. Phantoms from uncounted fragments and forgotten ideas. Characters from the unsold novels that yellowed in his files. And from the unfinished manuscript that lay beside his typewriter.

"Why are you here?" the writer demanded. "Did you think that I, too, was dead?"

The sad-eyed heroine of his present novel touched his arm. "You are the last writer. This new age of man has forgotten you. Come join us instead in this limbo of unrealized creation. Let this ugly world that has grown about you sink into the dull mire of its machine imagination. Come with us into our world of lost dreams."

The writer gazed at the phantom myriads, at the spectral cities and forests and seas. He remembered the dismal reality of the faceless, plastic world he had grown old in. No one would mark his passing…

"No." He shook his head and politely disengaged her hand. "No, I'm not quite ready for limbo. Not now. Not ever."

And the book-lined walls of his study rose solid about him once more.

The last writer sits alone in his study.

His eyes glow bright, and his gnarled fingers labor tirelessly to transform the pictures of his imagination into the symbolism of the page. His muscles feel cold, his bones are ice, and sometimes he thinks he can see through his hands to the page beneath.

There will be a knock at his door.

Maybe it will be death.

Or a raven, knelling "Nevermore."

Maybe it will be the last reader.

Into Whose Hands

Originally, back during the War (which Marlowe understood to be World War II), Graceland State Psychiatric Hospital had been an army base, and some of the old-timers still referred to the center as Camp Underhill. Marlowe was never certain whether there had been a town (named Underhill) here before the base was built, or whether the town had grown about the periphery of the base (named Underhill) at the time when it was carved out of the heart of the scrub and pine wilderness. Marlowe probably could have found out by asking one of the old-timers, had he ever thought to do so, or had he even cared to know. It was more to the point that no wing of the red brick hospital was of more than two stories; further, that each wing was connected to the next by a long corridor. This, so Marlowe had been told upon coming here, had been a precaution against an air raid—an enemy sneak attack could not annihilate the outspread base with its absence of central structures and its easy evacuation. Marlowe was uncertain as to the means by which an Axis blitzkrieg might have struck this far inland, but it was a fact that the center contained seven miles of corridors. This Marlowe had verified through many a weary weekend of walking to and fro and up and down through the complex, making rounds.

On this weekend Marlowe was feeding dimes into the slot of a vending machine, chained to the tile wall of one labyrinthine corridor. After judicious nudges and kicks, the packet of crackers was spat from its mechanical womb in a flurry of crumbs. Marlowe eyed the tattered cellophane sourly. An industrious mouse had already gnawed across the pair on the end. He should have tried the machines in the staff lounge, but that meant another quarter of a mile walk.

At his belt, the beeper uttered a rush of semi-coherent static. Marlowe, shaking the nibbled crackers onto the tile floor, thumbed the beeper to silence with his other hand and plodded for the nearest nursing station. He swiped a cup of virulent coffee from the urn there, washed the crackers from his throat with a gulp of boiling fluid, and dialed the number to which he had been summoned.

"This is Dr Marlowe."

"You have an involuntary admission on South Unit, Dr Marlowe."

"I'll be down once I finish one on North."

The voice persisted. Marlowe sensed the speaker's anxiety.

"The patient is combative, Doctor. He's delusional, obviously hallucinating. If you could give us an order…"

"What's the problem? Do we know anything about this one?"

"This is his first admission here, and all we have are the commitment papers the deputies brought. He's obviously psychotic. He says he's Satan."

"Hell, that's my third this month. All right, seclude and restrain. I'm coming right down, and I'll sign the order when I get there."

Marlowe glanced at his watch. It was past ten, he still hadn't eaten dinner, and the deputies from Beacon City were due to arrive on East with that adolescent runaway who'd slashed her wrists. Best take care of South Unit quickly. The coffee was sour in his stomach, and he regretted discarding the mouse-chewed crackers.

He was in North Unit, which was actually Central, since the northernmost unit was the Alcoholic Rehab Unit, but the walk was going to be a brisk five minutes in addition to the time lost in unlocking sectional doors. Marlowe, who showed a footsore limp under the best of circumstances, knew better than to wear himself out this early in the weekend. It was Friday night. Until 8:00 Monday morning he would be the only doctor on the grounds at Graceland. In that time he might have twenty to thirty admissions, on an average, in addition to the task of overseeing the well-being of some five hundred patients within the state hospital complex. A demanding situation under the best of circumstances, and impossible without a capable staff. Marlowe often wished for a capable staff.

He was tall and lean, with a profile that might have made a good Holmes if the haphazardly trimmed beard and randomly combed black hair hadn't more suggested Moriarty. His eyes were so deep a blue as to seem almost black; one patient had told him he looked like Lord Byron, but many patients had called him many names. In a three-piece suit Marlowe would have fit the TV-romantic ideal of the distinguished young physician; however, around the hospital he favored open-necked sport shirts of imaginative pattern, casual slacks, and scuffed Wallabies. The crepe soles of these last were generally overworn to one side, giving him almost a clubfooted stance, but tile corridors are not kind to feet, and Marlowe liked such comforts as were permitted.

He unlocked an outside door, stepped out to cut across a courtyard. The summer night was hot and still. Behind electrified grates, ultraviolet lamps lured nocturnal insects to their doom; harsh crackles made the only sound other than the soft crunch of gravel beneath Marlowe's crepe soles. There was a full moon, hot and electric itself, and Marlowe knew he would get little rest this weekend.

There was sound again when he unlocked the door to South Unit's admission ward. The door to a seclusion room stood open, and inside three attendants were just fastening the padded cuffs. Spread-eagled on the bed, a young black man struggled against the wrist and ankle restraints and screamed curses. At the end of the hallway, several of the ward patients hovered anxiously, until a nurse's assistant shooed them back to bed.

An attendant handed Marlowe the commitment papers. He glanced through them: 23-year-old black male, combative and threatening to life and person of family and neighbors since last night, apparently hallucinating, claimed to be Satan released from

Hell. Today fired shotgun at neighbor's house, subdued by officers; involuntary commitment papers signed by family, no previous history of mental disorders.

Marlowe entered the seclusion room, studying his patient. His dress was flamboyant, his appearance well-groomed; he was lean but not emaciated, with prominent veins standing out from the straining muscles of his arms. Marlowe's initial impression was psychotic drug reaction, probably angel dust or amphetamines.

"Mr Stallings, my name is Dr Marlowe. I'm your physician, and I'd like to ask you a few questions."

"I am His Satanic Majesty, Lucifer God, Son of the Sun, Prince of Darkness and Power! Ye who seek to chain me in the Pit shall be utterly cast down! Bow down to me and worship, or feed the flames of my wrath!"

Marlowe played his stethoscope across his heaving chest. "Anyone able to get a blood pressure?"

The ward nurse handed him a sheet. "Don't know how good these vital stats are—he's been abusive and combative since the deputies brought him in. He's strong as a horse, I can tell you."

"These are about what they recorded at Frederick County when they examined him," Marlowe said. "We still don't have a chart on him?"

"First admission to Graceland, Dr Marlowe."

The patient shouted obscenities, ignoring Marlowe's efforts to examine him. Verbal content was a jarring mixture of street slang and religious phrases, frankly delusional. There seemed little point in continuing with the examination at this point.

Marlowe turned to the ward nurse, who was showing anger despite her experience with abusive patients. "Thorazine, 100 mgm IM."

Two attendants held the patient on his side, pants drawn down, while she gave him the injection. The graveyard shift would be coming on shortly, and they had work to finish before they could go off. Marlowe observed the familiar ritual in silence, studying his patient's reactions.

"Just make sure his blood pressure doesn't drop out," he told them. "I'll write out orders for another 100 IM PRN q 4 hours, if this doesn't do it. I'll finish my examination once he's quiet."

"Thank you, Doctor."

Marlowe's beeper summoned him while he was writing orders. "That's North Unit. Could you dial that for me, please?" He took the phone from the attendant and wedged it under his chin; one hand holding a Styrofoam coffee cup, the other scribbling an admission note.

"Dr Marlowe, we have an unauthorized absence from North Unit. The patient is Billy Wilson. He is an involuntary admission."

Marlowe sipped his coffee. "Chronic schiz from Jefferson County? I've had him on my service a couple times. Better call the family and local sheriff. He usually hitches a ride home and tells people he's on the run from the CIA."

"We also have a voluntary admission here to see you."

"What's his problem?"

"He says he's depressed."

"I'll get over to see him when I can."

Marlowe finished his coffee and the conversation, placed cup and receiver in appropriate niches. His beeper wondered if he might phone the ARU. Marlowe thought he might.

"Dr Marlowe, we have three unauthorized absences."

"These are...?"

"Two voluntary, one involuntary. Jimmy Roberts and Willy Wilbertson from Adams County are voluntary; Freddie Lambert from Tarpon is involuntary."

"Those first two always check back in together as soon as they've gone through their Social Security checks. Lambert usually winds up under a bridge with a gallon of skull-rot; better notify family and sheriff on him."

He finished his admission notes, looked in on Stallings. The new admission was still raging against his restraints; shrill obscenities penetrated the seclusion room door. "Another 100 mgm Thorazine IM stat, I think," Marlowe decided. "I'd like a quiet night."

It was past midnight when Marlowe made it back to North Unit to interview the voluntary admission. As he sought to leave the nurse's aide on South Unit had delayed him with a question about Dr Kapoor's medication orders; the Pakistani resident had been eight weeks in the US and six weeks on South Unit, and still hadn't discovered the distinction between *q.i.d.*, *q.d.*, and *q.o.d.* when writing medication orders. Marlowe made hasty corrections, ordered stat lithium levels on one patient, and swore a little.

The graveyard shift came on at eleven, and no one knew anything about his voluntary on North. The same, seated beside a flight bag in the office area, regarded Marlowe with politely contained anger.

He wore Nike running shoes, Levi jeans, and an Izod knit shirt, all of it just starting to slide past the comfortably well-worn stage. His beard had reached that scraggly sort of seediness that usually breaks the resolve of its wearer and brings the razor back out of the medicine cabinet. The black hairline was beginning to recede, but there were no flecks of grey. He had a complex digital watch toward which he pointedly glanced. The eyes behind the designer frames were red-rimmed and puffy, despite the effort of the tinted lenses to mask them. Marlowe guessed him to be a grad student or junior faculty from the state university campus at Franklin, some thirty miles to the north, and he wondered why the patient had not availed himself of the posh psychiatric unit at the medical school there.

"Hello, I'm Dr Marlowe. Sorry to keep you waiting."

"Frank Carnell." The handshake was accepted, but weak.

"Would you care to step into my office, Mr Carnell?"

Each unit included an interview room for the on-call physician; however, as North Unit's attending, Marlowe had an office of his own on the unit. He ushered his patient into the cheap vinyl-upholstered chair beside his desk and eased himself into the often treacherous swivel chair behind the expanse of pea-grey enameled metal littered with manila chart folders. The office furnishings were state-purchase, some of them going back to Graceland's army camp days. A filing cabinet and a pair of unlovely metal bookcases of brownish-grey enamel housed a disarray of books, journals and drug company handouts. There was also a couch of cracked brown Naugahyde, a coffee table, two folding chairs, and a spindly rubber tree leaning against the Venetian blinds. Overhead fluorescent lamps hummed behind acoustic ceiling tiles and made all too evident the yellow wax-stains on the uncarpeted floor of worn asbestos tile. One wall boasted a plastic-framed imitation oil of a mountain landscape that might have been discarded by a Holiday Inn, but Carnell was devoting his attention to the framed diplomas and certificates that completed the room's decoration.

"Impressive credentials, Dr Marlowe. I had the impression that our state hospitals were staffed entirely by foreign medical school graduates."

"An exaggeration. I'm not the only American-educated psychiatrist here at Graceland." There were, in fact, two others.

"From what I've seen, it makes me wonder what a psychiatrist of your training is doing here at Graceland State?"

"I think the question more properly, Mr Carnell," said Marlowe evenly, "is why are you here?"

Carnell's eyes, behind the tinted glasses, shifted to his chewed fingernails. He fidgeted with the flight bag on his lap. "I suppose you could say I'm depressed."

"Depressed?"

"I haven't been sleeping well. Can't fall asleep until the late late show and half a bottle of vodka; sometimes I need pills. I wake up before dawn, just lie awake thinking about things that keep running through my mind. Tired all the time. No appetite. No energy. Used to jog to my classes; now I just cut them and lie about the apartment. Haven't been able to study in weeks." Carnell spoke slowly, and Marlowe sensed tears.

"When did all this begin?"

"This spring. I'm in journalism at State, trying to complete work on my doctorate before the funds all dry up. My wife said she'd had enough of floating around the secretarial pool to pay the bills while I played the eternal student. She's shacked up with her old boss from central accounting, and the divorce is pending. I haven't been able to adjust to that. My performance has been on the skids—I'm supposed to teach a class during summer session, but I've missed so many my students don't bother either. I've been called on the carpet by the department twice. I'm broke, in debt, and now my fellowship has been canceled. It's just that no matter how hard I try, it just keeps getting worse."

Marlowe waited while Carnell worked to control his voice. "Mr Carnell, I certainly understand that you have good reason to be undergoing a great deal of anxiety and depression. However, since this appears directly related to your present life situation, I feel confident that this disturbance is a transient one. This is a painful crisis in your life, and I appreciate the profound distress you are experiencing. Under the circumstances, I definitely agree that you need professional counseling; however, I believe you would far better benefit from outpatient counseling rather than hospitalization at this time."

Carnell fumbled with his flight bag. "Am I to understand that you are refusing me psychiatric care?"

"Not at all!" Marlowe had seen patients produce knives and an occasional handgun from unscreened personal belongings, but he doubted that Carnell was likely to turn violent. "I very strongly urge you to accept professional counseling. In my opinion you will derive considerably greater benefits through outpatient therapy than as a hospitalized patient here at Graceland."

"In other words, in your opinion I'm better off seeing a shrink on the outside than I'd be if I entered Graceland State as a patient." There was a certain triumph in Carnell's voice. "Well, it happens that I'm broke. I can't afford to be psychoanalyzed by some hundred-bucks-an-hour private shrink."

"That isn't necessary, Mr Carnell. If you wish, I can make an appointment for you to be seen on a priority basis this Monday at your community mental health clinic in Franklin; Dr Liebman there is an excellent therapist. Or if you prefer, I can make an appointment for you at the medical school to be seen by the psychiatric outpatient service."

"I'm a tax-paying citizen of this state, Dr Marlowe. Why are you refusing me treatment in a state facility?"

"I'm not refusing you treatment, Mr Carnell. I frankly do not believe that hospitalization would be beneficial to you. If you would prefer to receive treatment at Graceland rather than in your local community, I will gladly make an appointment for you to be seen Monday in our outpatient clinic."

"Suppose I don't care to wait until Monday for medical attention."

"Mr Carnell, you must understand that our facilities here are limited. Our primary task is to care for the severely disabled patient, the chronically ill. Patients whose problems can best be dealt with without hospitalization are directed toward more appropriate community programs."

"Dr Marlowe, I can't wait until next week for you to shuffle me off to some community agency. I can't keep going on like I have these last weeks. If I don't get help now I'm afraid…"

He paused to make certain Marlowe was giving his undivided attention.

"Well, I have quite a collection of sleeping pills. Tonight I feel like taking them all."

"I have some papers you'll need to sign," Marlowe said.

After 2 am Marlowe let himself into the employees' snack bar. It was nothing more than a cinder-block room, walled with vending machines, furnished with plastic tables and chairs about the color of tomato soup that's been left too long to cool. It differed from the patients' snack bar in that the plastic tables and chairs were not bolted to the tiled floor, spectators did not gape at the machines in slack-jawed hopefulness, and the drugs that changed hands were of better quality. There was also a microwave oven.

The oven was Marlowe's solace during hungry nights on call. Underhill was a town too small to support a single fast-food franchise—something of a blessing in that otherwise Allen's Eat Good Food would no longer be serving home-cooked meals at family prices (the last Blue Plate Special known to Marlowe), nor would the Ski-Hi Drive-Inn still be making malts out of real ice cream and frying greasy hamburgers made of hand-shaped patties (all in a decor that left Marlowe humming medleys of Andrews Sisters Hits). Underhill was also a town small enough to retain a blue law, and on Sundays even the Fast Fare convenience store was closed. The employees' cafeteria, in any event, closed for the weekend, and the outer world was closed to Marlowe beyond range of his beeper. On occasion Marlowe might escape Graceland long enough to grab a meal at Allen's or the Ski-Hi, but on Sunday, the day Marlowe hated above all days, if he were to have a hot meal, he must cook it himself.

There was a stove and refrigerator for staff in North Unit's administrative section, but Marlowe was one of those bachelors for whom cooking was a forbidden art. Marlowe had only hazy memories of a youth before college and medical school, and whether the food put upon his plate was doled out or paid for, Marlowe regardless had had no thought to spare as to its conception. In his office Marlowe kept a hotplate and various cans, the sins of whose preparation were concealed by virtue of a large bottle of Tabasco sauce. With the microwave oven, Marlowe felt a competence somewhat akin to the laboratory.

For this weekend, Fast Fare's frozen foods counter (Marlowe understood two classes of foods: canned or frozen) had supplied him with a carton of Western Steer's Hungry Cowhand Rib-Eye Filets. These Marlowe had retrieved from North Unit's refrigerator and now fed to the microwave. He punched buttons at random, drawing tired satisfaction as the blocks of frozen beef stuff turned a pallid grey and began to steam. A clatter of quarters excerpted the last two Reel-Keen Cheez-Burgers from a vending machine. Marlowe filled each stale bun with a partially thawed segment of Hungry Cowhand, placed his mutant creations within the microwave. The cheese-food was just starting to melt when his beeper interrupted.

Marlowe ignored its summons until the microwave's buzzer announced the perfection of his cooking artistry, then picked up the snack bar phone and dialed. It was North Unit, and he'd just made the seven-minute walk from there.

"Dr Marlowe, this is Macafee on the admissions ward. I'm afraid we're having some problems with that patient you just admitted."

"Which one is that?" Marlowe had had eight admissions tonight, and they began to blur together.

"Frank Carnell, sir. The suicide attempt from Franklin."

"What's the difficulty?"

Macafee was a Nam vet and continued to regard doctors as officers. "Sir, this patient is noncooperative and abusive. He's objecting to the suicide precautions you ordered, he claims someone has stolen a cassette recorder he had with him on admission, and he demands to speak with you immediately."

"*Did* he have a cassette recorder when he was admitted?"

"No sir. Only a small canvas bag containing clothing and personal articles."

Marlowe tried a mouthful of steaming steakburger, decided it needed catsup. "I need to stop in at the med unit, then do an admission at the ARU. I'll try to look in on you in between. Meanwhile it might be best to place Carnell under sedation and seclude if necessary. I believe I wrote a PRN for p.o. Valium?"

"Yes sir, you did. However, Mr Carnell has refused medication."

"Then write an order for Valium 10 mgm IM stat, then Valium 5 mgm IM q 3-4 hours times 48 hours PRN agitation and anxiety. I'll sign it when I stop by. You already have a PRN seclusion order with the suicide precautions."

"Dr Marlowe, Mr Carnell claims that as a voluntary patient he should not be on a locked ward and that we have no right to force him to take medications."

"An argument the patient advocates have often raised," Marlowe said. "However, Mr Carnell is an involuntary admission. I suggest you observe him carefully for further signs of delusional behavior."

Late at night Marlowe owned the corridors. They stretched in fifty-yard sections from brick unit to brick unit. After 11:00 pm only every third fluorescent ceiling fixture was left on, leaving the corridors hung with darkness in between the flickering islands of light. The corridors were entirely of tile: discolored acoustic tiles for the ceiling, glossy ceramic tiles for the walls, stained asbestos tiles for the floor. Marlowe wondered how such a manufactured environment could still stink of human filth and hopelessness.

Marlowe paused, not breathing. It was 4 in the morning, the hour of the cockroach, an hour before the keepers of the graveyard shift began to prompt their cares into a semblance of reality to greet their breakfast and the day shift at 7. He listened.

The roaches here were larger than any Marlowe had seen since an age when dinosaurs were but a fanciful gleam in a tree fern's eye. He could hear them as they scuttled along the worn tiles of the long long corridor. Some, intent upon a smear of feces lodged within a missing bit of broken floor tile, were reluctant to flee his approach.

Marlowe stomped at them, withheld his foot at the last instant. The roaches scattered halfheartedly. It was, perhaps, an old game. Marlowe heard the silky rustle of their reconvergence as he silently passed by.

As he passed a snack vending machine, he could hear a mouse feasting within.

"Dr Marlowe never sleeps."

"Can't spare the time, Mr Habberly. Surely you've heard that there's no rest for the wicked."

Habberly chuckled. "Never going to sleep long's you keep drinking my coffee." He handed Marlowe his cup—a gift from the Sandoz rep, featuring a smiling yellow Happyface and the wish to "Have a Happy Day" from "Mellaril." Pudgy and greying, Habberly was nearing state retirement age; he had been an orderly and later ward supervisor at Graceland since it opened. He and an aging male nurse, occasionally joined by a ward attendant on break, were the only inhabitants of North Unit's administrative section during the graveyard shift.

"Careful, Doctor—that's fresh poured!"

Marlowe ignored his warning and swallowed without looking up from his admissions notes. "Thank you, Mr Habberly."

"Never could understand how some folks can drink coffee when it's hot enough to scald your hand carrying it."

"Practice deadens all feeling, Mr Habberly, and because there's too little time to wait for it to cool. But I can still taste: you brew the best cup of coffee in Graceland."

"Thank you, sir. Well, now, that's practice again. I don't fool with that big urn the day shifts use. Got me a three-four cup percolator just right for night shift. Been using it for years. And I don't fool with state-purchase coffee."

Marlowe finished his coffee and handed Habberly a sheaf of triplicate forms. "Here's the commitment papers for tonight's involuntaries. With luck you won't have any more admissions until day shift comes on in an hour."

Habberly thumbed through the forms, making certain that all had been signed and notarized as the law required. A patient could only be committed involuntarily if he constituted an immediate threat to others or to himself in the opinion of local magistrates and the admitting physician. Marlowe had had three involuntaries on North Unit tonight.

Habberly paused over the commitment papers for Frank Carnell. "Is this the patient who was causing the fuss about someone stealing his suitcase?"

Marlowe craned his neck to see which patient Habberly meant. "Yes. Which reminds me that I told Macafee I'd look in on him. By the way, you didn't happen to notice whether Carnell had any sort of bag or anything with him when he was admitted, did you?"

"Why, no sir. He didn't have any personal belongings with him at all. The deputies carried him up here straight from the emergency room at Franklin Memorial. I let them into the ward when they brought him here 'long about midnight."

The admitting ward for each unit was a locked ward, and it was hospital policy that every patient admitted after hours or on weekends must be kept on the admissions ward until such time as the psychiatrist to whose service he was assigned had had an opportunity to interview him. The rule applied to voluntary and involuntary patients alike. Patient advocates complained that this rule was only intended to discourage voluntary admissions after office hours, but hospital administration pointed out that the rule had come into being after a Korean resident blithely admitted a seemingly depressed voluntary patient to an open ward one night, who quietly strangled and raped the retarded teenage boy who shared his room and passed it off the next morning as the work of Mafia hitmen.

Marlowe let himself into North Unit Admission Ward. It was, he reflected, a bit of a misuse of terms in that patients judged not suitable for the open wards might linger in a unit's admission ward for weeks until proper disposition could be made. Graceland did not treat dangerous psychotics in theory; the state maintained a hospital for the criminal insane, now euphemized as a forensic psychiatric facility, in conjunction with the state penitentiary at Russellville. A patient who required long-term hospitalization at Graceland was either found suitable for an open ward or transferred to a chronic care ward, where long-term hospitalization usually meant lifetime.

Macafee nodded to him through the glass of the nurses' station, unlocked the door to let him enter. "Good morning, sir. Almost 600 hours; we'll be waking them soon. Care for some coffee, sir?"

"Yes, thank you." Marlowe looked through the glass. The nurses' station was a locked cubicle placed along one wall to give an aquarium resident's view of the communal ward. Already several of the patients were beginning to shuffle about between the close-spaced beds; it was close enough to breakfast, which arrived with the day shift, that minimal activity was permitted.

"Any problems?" Marlowe signed his telephone orders in the ward orders book.

"No sir. Not after we put Mr Carnell to bed." Macafee sometimes confused the ward with training barracks, but it was usually quiet when he was on night shift, and Marlowe disliked disturbances.

"How is Mr Carnell?"

"Quiet, sir. Sawyer's checking on him just now."

"I'll just take a look myself."

A short hallway led from the communal ward to the outside corridors. Connected by a door to the nursing station was a small room for supplies and medications. There was an examining and treatment room farther along the hallway, then toilets, showers, a patients' lounge, and several seclusion rooms. Carnell was lying on the bed within one of these; a wooden night stand was the only other furnishing. Sawyer was just coming out of the room.

"Good evening, Dr Marlowe—or good morning, it's getting to be."

"And let's hope it will be a good day, Mr Sawyer. How is Mr Carnell?"

"He's been resting quietly. Starting to wake up now." Sawyer had had ambitions of a pro-football career before a high school knee injury scrubbed that as well as hopes for a college scholarship. He was ten years younger than Macafee and a good audience.

Carnell was muttering to himself when Marlowe bent over him. "Good morning, Mr Carnell," Marlowe said, since his eyes were open. "How do you feel?"

"Damn you, Marlowe!" Carnell sat up sluggishly. "I've been locked up, robbed, drugged, I don't know what! Do you think you're running some sort of prison camp? I demand to be released from this zoo right now!"

"I'm sorry, Mr Carnell. Have you forgotten why you came here?" Marlowe's voice was patient. "Try to remember."

Carnell's face showed anger, then growing indecision. His eyes began to widen in fear.

"Mr Sawyer, could we have that IM Valium order stat?"

"Yes sir. Five mgm, was it, Dr Marlowe?"

"Better make it ten."

The chronic care wards were always on the second story of Graceland's far-flung units. Marlowe supposed this was because Graceland had no cellars. Presumably, had there been cellars, the temptation to wall them off would have been irresistible. Marlowe supposed Graceland had never had cellars.

There were two basic divisions among the chronics: the ambulatory and the nonambulatory. The ambulatory could be trusted to leave their locked wards, perform acceptably under controlled situations, and return to their locked wards. The nonambulatory could not be trusted to function within acceptable guidelines. They remained in their wards, often in their beds, often only a dream from the chronic med care unit; spoon-fed gobs of pasty slop, when they could no longer handle spoons; moved to the chronic med unit when they could only be fed through tubes and IV's.

They fed the ambulatory chronics three times a day—breakfast, lunch, and dinner—the same as living souls. This meant they were herded from their wards three times a day, down the stairs (there was an elevator for each unit, and those who could walk, but not negotiate stairs, were granted this), and along the tiled corridors to the patients' cafeteria. They moved along docilely enough, each regimented segment of quasi-humanity, herded along the long, long corridors by nurses and attendants.

Their clothes were shapeless garments that fit their shapeless bodies: not uniforms, only styleless wads of clothing donated by middle-class patrons who found salve for their consciences in charity bins for flotsam their guilt would not allow them to fling into trashcans. Some, who were habitually incontinent, might wear rubber (now vinyl) underpants, although it had been established with chronics that floors and clothing were more easily washed than could dermatitis and pustulant sores be cured; and so many, by chance or by choice, wore no underwear at all.

Marlowe, a microcassette recorder in one hand, a Powerhouse candybar in the other, alternately dictating and chewing, stood against one wall as the chronics shuffled past him on their way to be fed. Their faces were as shapeless as their bodies: some smiling, some grimacing, some frozen from the effects of too many shock treatments, too many drugs. A few seemed to recognize Marlowe, and waved or winked or muttered. Some, Marlowe thought, had been in Graceland longer than Marlowe, and that was forever. A grey-mustached grandmother in a shapeless polyester sack dribbled excrement as she shuffled past. The corridor stank of urine and feces and unwashed living dead, and no antiseptic nor disinfectant would ever cleanse it. Marlowe finished his candybar breakfast, waiting for them to pass before resuming dictation.

"If God exists," a patient had once told Marlowe, "then what sort of sadist is he to curse the elderly with the indignity of loss of sphincter control?"

"An angry god," Marlowe had replied with bitterness. "And vengeful."

By midmorning Saturday Marlowe decided he had completed Friday's tasks and it was time to recognize Saturday. He had contemplated napping on his couch, but there were two voluntary admissions waiting on West Unit, and the adolescent runaway on East had pulled her stitches out.

Marlowe dragged a toilet kit from his filing cabinet and paid a visit to the staff restroom, where he washed his face in cold water, brushed his teeth, gargled mouthwash, brushed his hair and beard. Returning to his office, he pulled off his red Hawaiian shirt, sprayed on deodorant, and changed into a blue Hawaiian shirt, also from his filing cabinet. Sleeping quarters were provided for on-call physicians in a cinder-block horror known as married residents' housing, but this was detached from the hospital unit, and after a night when it took Marlowe twelve minutes to respond to a cardiac arrest from there, he decided to take calls from his office.

East and West Units cared for women patients, North and South Units for the men. Whatever symmetry had been intended by this plan had been completely obscured by the addition of the Adolescent Unit, the Med Unit, the Alcoholic Rehab Unit (again segregated by sexes and separated by a five-minute walk), and Central Administration—not to mention the semi-automonous Taggart Center for Special Children (once known as the State Home for the Mentally Retarded), the Crawford Training School (the state had seen fit to include a center for juvenile offenders within Camp Underhill's disused facilities), and the P. Everett Amberson Clinic (a former hotel refurbished as a drying-out spot for the less shabby class of alcoholics and pill addicts). It took new psychiatric residents a few months to find their way around, and a car was necessary to reach the outlying centers—a complication in that many of the foreign residents had licenses to practice medicine but not to drive.

Marlowe, who was not moved by tears and found them a bit bothersome, considered East and West Units more than a little bothersome. Granted that tears were nonverbal communication, women patients tended to use them as dramatic expression or as means to terminate an interview. A generalization, but an accurate one, for Marlowe had timed things. Even allowing for the additional time entailed by a pelvic exam on new admissions, as opposed to a quick grope and cough to check for inguinal hernia, it took half again as long on the average to complete any task on the women's wards as on the men's. Marlowe compared notes with several of the women psychiatrists and found their experience to be the same. Marlowe saw the basis of an article for the journals in this business of tears, but he left it unwritten as he hated the journals. The crucial point was that, given too many tasks and too little time to accomplish them, East and West Units demanded a disproportionate share of that nonexistent time.

Marlowe spent most of the day between East Unit and West Unit. It was a pleasant day, and families liked to carry their senile grandmothers and Valium-addicted aunts to the hospital on weekends. Everyone was off work, the children could come along, and it was a nice outing for Grannie or Noonie or Auntie or maybe Mom or Sis, who had begun to wander into traffic or seduce the paperboy after two bottles of vodka. Major holidays were worst of all, for then families liked to rid themselves of unwanted and incontinent organic old ladies, so they could enjoy Christmas or Easter without the pressure of an invalid. Graceland was cheaper than a rest home, and afterward, if conscience troubled, they could always take a drive and reclaim her. Best of all, on weekends they could drop a patient off and be miles away before the lone on-call physician had a chance to interview her. The worse the weather, the better Marlowe liked it: involuntary commitments might come in at any time, but it was unlikely that the family would decide to haul off Grandma when it looked like it might pour down all day.

By midnight Marlowe limped back to his office and collapsed on his couch. He had had fourteen admissions since morning, with more on the way. Most of the usual problems he had been able to deal with over the phone—too much medication, too little medication, extra-pyramidal reactions to the medications. Marlowe titrated and adjusted, switched from phenothiazines to Haldol or

Navane or vice versa, dispensed Artane and Cogentin as required. Metal chains and straitjackets had required no such artistry, but the old-timers told Marlowe of how they used to scream and howl on nights of the full moon in the days before major tranquilizers, and Marlowe kept it quiet the nights he was on call.

Marlowe's eyes stung. A Philippino resident had admitted a patient Thursday night and not noticed that he was a severe alcoholic; nor had the resident who inherited him in the morning and who transferred him to an open ward. When the patient went into DT's with paranoid delusions, it took security two full cans of Mace to convince him to drop the table leg he was swinging like a club at anything, real or delusional, that came within reach. Marlowe had had to examine the patient once subdued, and Mace was still running like sweat off the man's blistering skin.

The familiar coffee burn in his stomach reminded Marlowe that he hadn't eaten anything except a candybar and a large tomato one of the nurses had carried in from her garden. Fast Fare had closed, even had Marlowe felt up to a short drive. Red-eyed ("Remember—*don't* rub your eyes," security had warned him.), Marlowe pawed through his filing cabinet and uncovered a can of ravioli. He managed to open it without cutting himself, found a plastic spoon and fed himself cold ravioli from the can. He considered heating it on his hotplate, but lacked the time or ambition. He almost fell asleep while chewing, but his beeper reminded him who and where he was.

At 3 in the morning Willy Winslow on South Unit smashed the salt shaker he had stolen earlier and sawed at his wrists with the jagged glass. He was quite pleased when he flailed his bleeding wrists against the nurses' station window, but neither the ward attendants nor Marlowe shared his amusement.

Winslow was a regular at Graceland, one of an undefined group of patients who enjoyed staying in state institutions, constantly admitted and readmitted, either voluntarily or involuntarily, and constantly discharged again. Winslow was well known to all the staff at Graceland; if he could not con a resident into a voluntary admission, he would gash his wrists and gain an involuntary commitment thereby. During this, his seventeenth admission to Graceland, a concerned resident from one of the better private medical schools had devoted three months toward helping Winslow re-enter the community. Bolstered by an extensive outreach program, Winslow was to be discharged next week.

Marlowe, selecting from the suture tray, gazed at the masses of scar tissue upon each wrist and shook his head. "Mr Winslow, you managed to do this without anesthetic, and I don't see why I should waste any in sewing you back together."

Winslow's eyes glittered, but he didn't reply. It was, perhaps, an old game.

"And how many times do I have to tell you," said Marlowe, drawing the curved needle with difficulty through the layers of scar, "cut lengthwise down your wrist, just here below the thumb—not crosswise."

Frank Carnell was still in seclusion when Marlowe made rounds through North Unit on Sunday evening, but the ward attendants reported that he had been quiet throughout the day, and he appeared to be ready to come out into the ward. Marlowe found him sitting up on the edge of his bed, staring dazedly at his hands.

"Good evening, Mr Carnell. How are you feeling today?"

"I'm sorry—I'm bad about names. You're Dr…?"

"Dr Marlowe. Dr Chris Marlowe."

Carnell struggled to recall. "I remember seeing you, of course. When I was…upset. And when they brought me here from the hospital."

"Do you remember coming here from the hospital?"

"I must have been completely irrational." Carnell smiled sheepishly at the memory. "I seemed to believe I had come here as a voluntary patient. I had a cassette recorder, and I was going to take firsthand notes for my dissertation on the inadequacies of our state mental hospitals. I'm a journalism student at State, but then you know all that."

"I'm sure there's more than sufficient material there for a

number of dissertations," Marlowe agreed. "And was that actually your topic?"

"One of them," Carnell confessed. "I had plenty of ideas, just never followed up on them. Guess that was just another of the things that helped my life slide downhill, until…"

He struggled to control his voice. "Well, until I finally pulled out all the pills I had on hand and gobbled them down like M&M's. I remember getting sick and passing out, and then I guess I woke up there in the emergency room."

"You *guess*?"

Carnell frowned, trying to recall. "To tell the truth, my memory is pretty hazy for the last day or so—all those pills, plus whatever medications you've been giving me. There must have been a time there in the emergency room when they were bringing me around after I took all those pills…"

Marlowe waited patiently while he tried to remember.

Carnell's face began to twist with fear. "Dr Marlowe, I can't remember anything from the time I blacked out until when I was sitting there in your reception room and…Wait a minute, I was never brought here! I came voluntarily!"

"Indeed, you did," Marlowe's smile was almost sympathetic. "And voluntarily, I'm afraid, is unforgivable."

Carnell started to rush for the door, but it was blocked by Macafee and Sawyer, and he was too weak to put up much of a struggle.

"Don't worry, Mr Carnell," said Marlowe soothingly, as the needle plunged home. "It does take time at first to understand, and you have plenty of time."

It was past 5 am when Marlowe made rounds through South Unit. The sun would be creeping out soon, signaling the dawn of what Marlowe knew would be another Friday, and he would be on call.

"Dr Marlowe," suggested Wygul, the ward attendant on South, "maybe when you finish signing those ECT orders, could you take a look in on Mr Stallings? He's been a lot calmer tonight, and we haven't had to restrain him since Saturday afternoon. I think he's ready to be let out of seclusion now so we can see how he does on the ward."

"Mr Wygul," Marlowe finished his coffee, "I've never known your judgment to fail yet. Is the patient awake yet?"

"Yes, Doctor. He was sitting up in bed half an hour ago, and we'll be waking everybody up in just a minute."

"All right then, I'll talk to him."

Stallings gazed at Marlowe expectantly when he entered the seclusion room. He made no hostile moves.

"Good morning, Mr Stallings. I'm Dr Marlowe."

"How do you do, Dr Marlowe." Stallings' manner was courteous, but in a friendly way, rather than cautious.

"Do you remember me from the night you came here, Mr Stallings?"

"Yes sir, I sure do." Stallings laughed and shook his head. His hand seemed to want a cigarette to complete the gesture. "Man, I sure was out of my skull on something that night!"

"What do you remember?"

"Well, I remember being carried in here by the deputies, and being tied down and all, and I was cussing and telling the whole world that I was Satan."

"And did you believe that?"

Stallings nodded in embarrassment, then looked earnestly into Marlowe's eyes. "Yes sir, I sure did. And then you came into the room, and I looked into your face, and I knew that I was wrong, because I knew that *you* were Satan."

"Mr Stallings," Marlowe smiled sadly, "you appear to have made a rapid recovery."

More Sinned Against

Theirs was a story so commonplace that it balanced uneasily between the maudlin and the sordid—a cliché dipped in filth.

Her real name was Katharina Oglethorpe and she changed that to Candace Thornton when she moved to Los Angeles, but she was known as Candi Thorne in the few films she ever made—the ones that troubled to list credits. She came from some little Baptist church and textile mill town in eastern North Carolina, although later she said she came from Charlotte. She always insisted that her occasional and transient friends call her Candace, and she signed her name Candace in a large, legible hand for those occasional and compulsive autographs. She had lofty aspirations and only minimal talent. One of her former agents perhaps stated her *mot juste*: a lady with a lot of guts but too much heart. The police records gave her name as Candy Thorneton.

There had been money once in her family, and with that the staunch pride that comes of having more money than the other thousand or so inhabitants of the town put together. Foreign textiles eventually closed the mill; unfortunate investments leeched the money. Pride of place remained.

By the time that any of her past really matters, Candace had graduated from an area church-supported junior college, where she was homecoming queen, and she'd won one or two regional beauty contests and was almost a runner-up in the Miss North

Carolina pageant. Her figure was good, although more for a truckstop waitress than suited to a model's requirements, and her acting talents were wholehearted, if marginal. Her parents believed she was safely enrolled at U.C.L.A., and they never quite forgave her when they eventually learned otherwise.

Their tuition checks kept Candace afloat as an aspiring young actress/model through a succession of broken promises, phony deals, and predatory agents. Somewhere along the way she sacrificed her cherished virginity a dozen times over, enough so that it no longer pained her, even as the next day dulled the pain of the promised break that never materialized. Her family might have taken back, if not welcomed, their prodigal daughter, had Candace not begged them for money for her first abortion. They refused, Candace got the money anyway, and her family had no more to do with her ever.

He called himself Richards Justin, and there was as much truth to that as to anything else he ever said. He met Candace when she was just on the brink of putting her life together, although he never blamed himself for her subsequent crash. He always said that he was a man who learned from the mistakes of others, and had he said "profited" instead, he might have told the truth for once.

They met because they were sleeping with the same producer, both of them assured of a part in his next film. The producer failed to honor either bargain, and he failed to honor payment for a kilo of coke, after which a South American entrepreneur emptied a Browning Hi-Power into him. Candace and Richards Justin consoled one another over lost opportunity, and afterward he moved in with her.

Candace was sharing a duplex in Venice with two cats and a few thousand roaches. It was a cottage of rotting pink stucco that resembled a gingerbread house left out in the rain. Beside it ran a refuse-choked ditch that had once been a canal. The shack two doors down had been burned out that spring in a shoot-out between rival gangs of bikers. The neighborhood was scheduled for gentrification, but no one had decided yet whether this should entail restoration or razing. The rent was cheaper than an apartment, and against the house grew a massive clump of jade plant that Candace liked to pause before and admire.

At this time Candace was on an upswing and reasonably confident of landing the part of a major victim in a minor stalk-and-slash film. Her face and teeth had always been good; afternoons in the sun and judicious use of rinses on her mousy hair had transformed her into a passable replica of a Malibu blonde. She had that sort of ample figure that looks better with less clothing and best with none at all, and she managed quite well in a few photo spreads in some of the raunchier skin magazines. She was not to be trusted with a speaking part, but some voice and drama coaching might have improved that difficulty in time.

Richards Justin—Rick to his friends—very studiously was a hunk, to use the expression of the moment. He stood six foot four and packed about 215 pounds of health club-nurtured muscle over wide shoulders and lean hips. His belly was quite hard and flat, his thighs strong from jogging, and an even tan set off the generous dark growth of body hair. His black hair was neatly permed, and the heavy mustache added virility to features that stopped just short of being pretty. He seemed designed for posing in tight jeans, muscular arms folded across hairy chest, and he often posed just so. He claimed to have had extensive acting experience in New York before moving to Los Angeles, but somehow his credentials were never subject to verification.

Candace was a type who took in stray animals, and she took in Richards Justin. She had survived two years on the fringes of Hollywood, and Rick was new to Los Angeles—still vulnerable in his search for the elusive Big Break. She was confident that she knew some friends who could help him get started, and she really did need a roommate to help with the rent—once he found work, of course. Rick loaded his suitcase and possessions into her aging Rabbit, with room to spare, and moved in with Candace. He insisted that he pay his share of expenses, and borrowed four hundred bucks to buy some clothes—first appearances count everything in an interview.

They were great together in bed, and Candace was in love. She recognized the sensitive, lonely soul of the artist hidden beneath his macho exterior. They were both painfully earnest about their acting careers—talking long through the nights of films and actors, great directors and theories of drama. They agreed that one must never compromise art for commercial considerations, but that sometimes it might be necessary to make small compromises in order to achieve the Big Break.

The producer of the stalk-and-slash flick decided that Candace retained too much Southern accent for a major role. Having just gone through her savings, Candace spent a vigorous all-night interview with the producer and salvaged a minor role. It wasn't strictly nonspeaking, as she got to scream quite a lot while the deranged killer spiked her to a barn door with a pitchfork. It was quite effective, and a retouched still of her big scene was used for the posters of *Camp Hell!* It was the high-water mark of her career.

Rick found the Big Break even more elusive than a tough, cynical, street-wise hunk like himself had envisioned. It discouraged the artist within him, just as it embarrassed his virile nature to have to live off Candace's earnings continually. Fortunately coke helped restore his confidence, and unfortunately coke was expensive. They both agreed, however, that coke was a necessary expense, career-wise. Coke was both inspiration and encouragement; besides, an actor who didn't have a few grams to flash around was as plausible as an outlaw biker who didn't drink beer.

Candace knew how discouraging this all must be for Rick. In many ways she was so much wiser and tougher than Rick. Her concern over his difficulties distracted her from the disappointment of her own faltering career. Granted, Rick's talents were a bit raw—he was a gem in need of polishing. Courses and workshops were available, but these cost money, too. Candace worked her contacts and changed her agent. If she didn't mind doing a little T&A, her new agent felt sure he could get her a small part or two in some soft-R films. It was money.

Candace played the dumb Southern blonde in *Jiggle High* and she played the dumb Southern cheerleader in *Cheerleader Super Bowl* and she played the dumb Southern stewardess in *First Class*

Only and she played the dumb Southern nurse in *Sex Clinic* and she played the dumb Southern hooker in *Hard Streets*, but always this was Candi Thorne who played these roles, and not Candace Thornton, and somehow this made the transition from soft-R to hard-R films a little easier to bear.

They had their first big quarrel when Candace balked over her part in *Malibu Hustlers*. She hadn't realized they were shooting it in both R- and X-rated versions. Prancing about in the buff and faking torrid love scenes was one thing, but Candace drew the line at actually screwing for the close-up cameras. Her agent swore he was through if she backed out of the contract. Rick yelled at her and slapped her around a little, then broke into tears. He hadn't meant to lose control—it was just that he was so close to getting his break, and without money all they'd worked so hard together for, all they'd hoped and prayed for…

Candace forgave him, and blamed herself for being thoughtless and selfish. If she could ball off camera to land a role, she could give the same performance on camera. This once.

Candace never did find out what her agent did with her check from *Malibu Hustlers*, nor did the police ever manage to find her agent. The producer was sympathetic, but not legally responsible. He did, however, hate to see a sweet kid burned like that, and he offered her a lead role in *Hot 'n' Horny*. This one would be straight X—or XXX, as they liked to call them now, but a lot of talented girls had made the big time doing their stuff for the screen, and Candi Thorne just might be the next super-X superstar. He had the right connections, and if she played it right with him…

It wasn't the Big Break Candace had dreamed of, but it was money. And they did need money. She worried that this would damage her chances for a legitimate acting career, but Rick told her to stop being a selfish prude and to think of their future together. His break was coming soon, and then they'd never have to worry again about money. Besides, audiences were already watching her perform in *Malibu Hustlers*, so what did she have left to be shy about?

The problem with coke was that Rick needed a lot of it to keep him and his macho image going. The trouble with a lot of coke was that Rick tended to get wired a little too tight, and then he needed downers to mellow out. Smack worked best, but the trouble with smack was that it was even more expensive. Still, tomorrow's male sex symbol couldn't go about dropping 'ludes and barbs like some junior high punker. Smack was status in this game—everybody did coke. Not to worry: Rick had been doing a little heroin ever since his New York days—no needle work, just some to toot. He could handle it.

Candace could not—either the smack or the expense. Rick was gaining a lot of influential contacts. He had to dress well, show up at the right parties. Sometimes they decided it would be better for his career if he went alone. They really needed a better place to live, now that they could afford it.

After making *Wet 'n' Willing* Candace managed to rent a small house off North Beverly Glen Boulevard—not much of an improvement over her duplex in Venice, but the address was a quantum leap in class. Her biggest regret was having to leave her cats: no pets allowed. Her producer had advanced her some money to cover immediate expenses, and she knew he'd be getting it back in pounds of flesh. There were parties for important friends, and Candace felt quite casual about performing on camera after some of the things she'd been asked to do on those nights. And that made it easier when she was asked to do them again on camera.

Candace couldn't have endured it all if it weren't for her selfless love for Rick, and for the coke and smack and pills and booze. Rick expressed concern over her increasing use of drugs, especially when they were down to their last few lines. Candace economized by shooting more—less waste and a purer high than snorting.

She was so stoned on the set for *Voodoo Vixens* that she could barely go through the motions of the minimal plot. The director complained; her producer reminded her that retakes cost money, and privately noted that her looks were distinctly taking a shopworn plunge. When she threw up in her costar's lap, he decided that Candi Thorne really wasn't star material.

Rick explained that he was more disappointed than angry with her over getting canned, but this was after he'd bloodied her lip. It wasn't so much that this financial setback stood to wreck his career just as the breaks were falling in place for him, as it was that her drug habit had left them owing a couple thou to the man, and how were they going to pay that?

Candace still had a few contacts to fall back on, and she was back before the cameras before the bruises had disappeared. These weren't the films that made the adult theater circuits. These were the fifteen-minute-or-so single-takes shot in motel rooms for the 9-mm. home projector/porno peepshow audiences. Her contacts were pleased to get a semi-name porno queen, however semi and however shopworn, even if the films seldom bothered to list credits or titles. It was easier to work with a pro than some drugged-out runaway or amateur hooker, who might ruin a take if the action got rough or she had a phobia about Dobermans.

It was quick work and quick bucks. But not enough bucks.

Rick was panic-stricken when two large black gentlemen stopped him outside a singles bar one night to discuss his credit and to share ideas as to the need to maintain intact kneecaps in this cruel world. They understood a young actor's difficulties in meeting financial obligations, but felt certain Rick could make a substantial payment within forty-eight hours.

Candace hit the streets. It was that, or see Rick maimed. After the casting couch and exotic partners under floodlights, somehow it seemed so commonplace doing quickies in motel rooms and car seats. She missed the cameras. It all seemed so transient without any playback.

The money was there, and Rick kept his kneecaps. Between her work on the streets and grinding out a few 9-mm. films each month, Candace could about meet expenses. The problem was that she really needed the drugs to keep her going, and the more drugs she needed meant the more work to pay for them. Candace knew her looks were slipping, and she appreciated Rick's concern for her health. But for Rick the Big Break was coming soon. She no longer minded when he had other women over while she was on the streets, or when he stayed away for a day or two without calling her.

She was selling her body for his career, and she must understand that sometimes it was necessary for Rick, too, to sleep around. In the beginning, some small compromises are to be expected.

A pimp beat her up one night. He didn't like freelance chippies taking johns from his girls on his turf. He would have just scared her, had she agreed to become one of his string, but she needed all her earnings for Rick, and the truth was the pimp considered her just a bit too far gone to be worth his trouble. So he worked her over but didn't mess up her face too badly, and Candace was able to work again after only about a week.

She tried another neighborhood and got busted the second night out; paid her own bail, got busted again a week later. Rick got her out of jail—she was coming apart without the H, and he couldn't risk being implicated. He had his career to think about, and it was thoughtless of Candace to jeopardize his chances through her own sordid lifestyle.

He would have thrown her out, but Candace paid the rent. Of course, he still loved her. But she really ought to take better care of herself. She was letting herself go. Since her herpes scare they seldom made love, although Candace understood that Rick was often emotionally and physically drained after concentrating his energy on some important interview or audition.

They had lived together almost two years, and Candace was almost twenty-five, but she looked almost forty. After a client broke her nose and a few teeth in a moment of playfulness, she lost what little remained of her actress/model good looks. They got the best cosmetic repair she could afford, but after that neither the johns nor the sleaze producers paid her much attention. When she saw herself on the screen at fifth-rate porno houses, in the glimpses between ducking below the rows of shabby seats, she no longer recognized herself.

But Rick's career was progressing all the while, and that was what made her sacrifice worthwhile. A part of Candace realized now that her dreams of Hollywood stardom had long since washed down the gutter, but at least Rick was almost on the verge of big things. He'd landed a number of modeling jobs and already had made some commercials for local TV. Some recent roles in what Rick termed "experimental theater" promised to draw the attention of talent scouts. Neither of them doubted that the Big Break was an imminent certainty. Candace kept herself going through her faith in Rick's love and her confidence that better times lay ahead. Once Rick's career took off, she'd quit the streets, get off the drugs. She'd look ten years younger if she could just rest and eat right for a few months, get a better repair on her nose. By then Rick would be in a position to help her resume her own acting career.

Candace was not too surprised when Rick came in one morning and shook her awake with the news that he'd lined up a new film for her. It was something about devil worshipers called *Satan's Sluts*—X-rated, of course, but the money would be good, and Candace hadn't appeared even in a peepshow gangbang in a couple months. The producer, Rick explained, remembered her in *Camp Hell!* and was willing to take a chance on giving her a big role.

Candace might have been more concerned about filming a scene with so small a crew and in a cellar made over into a creepy B&D dungeon, but her last films had been shot in cheap motel rooms with a home video camera. She didn't like being strapped to an inverted cross and hung before a black-draped altar, but Rick was there—snorting coke with the half-dozen members of the cast and crew.

When the first few whip lashes cut into her flesh, it took Candace's drugged consciousness several moments to be aware of the pain, and to understand the sort of film for which Rick had sold her. By the time they had heated the branding iron and brought in the black goat, Candace was giving the performance of her life.

She passed out eventually, awoke another day in their bed, vaguely surprised to be alive. It was a measure of Rick's control over Candace that they hadn't killed her. No one was going to pay much attention to anything Candace might say—a burned out porno star and drug addict with an arrest record for prostitution. Rick had toyed with selling her for a snuff film, but his contacts there preferred anonymous runaways and wetbacks, and the backers of *Satan's Sluts* had paid extra to get a name actress, however faded, to add a little class to the production—especially a star who couldn't cause problems afterward.

Rick stayed with her just long enough to feel sure she wouldn't die from her torture, and to pack as many of his possessions as he considered worth keeping. Rick had been moving up in the world on Candace's earnings—meeting the right people, making the right connections. The money from *Satan's Sluts* had paid off his debts with enough left over for a quarter-ounce of some totally awesome rock, which had so impressed his friends at a party that a rising TV director wanted Rick to move in with her while they discussed a part for him in a much-talked-about new miniseries.

The pain when he left her was the worst of all. Rick had counted on this, and he left her with a gram of barely cut heroin, deciding to let nature take its course.

Candace had paid for it with her body and her soul, but at last this genuinely was the Big Break. The primetime soaper miniseries, *Destiny's Fortune*, ran for five nights and topped the ratings each night. Rick's role as the tough steelworker who romanced the millowner's daughter in parts four and five, while not a major part, attracted considerable attention and benefited from the huge success of the series itself. Talent scouts saw a new hunk in Richards Justin, most-talked-about young star from the all-time hit, *Destiny's Fortune*.

Rick's new agent knew how to hitch his Mercedes to a rising star. Richards Justin made the cover of *TV Guide* and *People*, the centerfold of *Playgirl*, and then the posters. Within a month it was evident from the response to *Destiny's Fortune* that Richards Justin was a hot property. It was only a matter of casting him for the right series. Network geniuses juggled together all the ingredients of recent hits and projected a winner for the new season—*Colt Savage, Soldier of Fortune*.

They ran the pilot as a two-hour special against a major soaper and a TV-movie about teenage prostitutes, and *Colt Savage* blew the other two networks away in that night's ratings. *Colt Savage* was The New Hit, blasting to the top of the Nielsen's on its first regular night. The show borrowed from everything that had already been proven to work—"an homage to the great adventure classics of the '30s" was how its producers liked to describe it.

Colt Savage, as portrayed by Richards Justin, was a tough, cynical, broad-shouldered American adventurer who kept busy dashing about the cities and exotic places of the 1930s—finding lost treasures, battling spies and sinister cults, rescuing plucky young ladies from all manner of dire fates. Colt Savage was the protégé of a brilliant scientist who wished to devote his vast fortune and secret inventions to fighting Evil. He flew an autogiro and drove a streamlined speedster—both decked out with fantastic weapons and gimmickry rather in advance of the technology of the period. He had a number of exotic assistants and, inevitably, persistent enemies—villains who somehow managed to escape the explosion of their headquarters in time to pop up again two episodes later.

Colt Savage was pure B-movie corn. In a typical episode, Colt would meet a beautiful girl who would ask him for help, then be kidnapped. Following that there would be fights, car chases, air battles, captures and escapes, derring-do in exotic locales, rescues and romance—enough to fill an hour show. The public loved it. Richards Justin was a new hero for today's audiences—the new Bogart, a John Wayne for the '80s. The network promoted *Colt Savage* with every excess at its command. The merchandising rights alone were bringing in tens of millions.

Rick dumped the director who had given him his start in *Destiny's Fortune* long before he moved into several million bucks worth of Beverly Hills real estate. The tabloids followed his numerous love affairs with compulsive and imaginative interest.

Candace blamed it all on the drugs. She couldn't bring herself to believe that Rick had never loved her, that he had simply used her until she had no more to give. Her mind refused to accept that. It was she who had let Rick down, let drugs poison his life and destroy hers. Drugs had ruined her acting career, had driven her onto the streets to pay for their habit. They could have made it, if she hadn't ruined everything for them.

So she quit, cold turkey. Broken in body and spirit, the miseries of withdrawal made little difference to her pain. She lived ten years of hell over the next few days, lying in an agonized delirium that barely distinguished consciousness from unconsciousness. Sometimes she managed to crawl to the bathroom or to the refrigerator, mostly she just curled herself into a fetal pose of pain and shivered beneath the sweaty sheets and bleeding sores. In her nightmares she drifted from lying in Rick's embrace to writhing in torture on Satan's altar, and the torment of either delirium was the same to her.

As soon as she was strong enough to face it, Candace cut the heroin Rick had left her to make five grams and sold it to one of her friends who liked to snort it and wouldn't mind the cut. It gave her enough money to cover bills until Candace was well enough to go back on the streets. She located the pimp who had once beat her up; he didn't recognize her, and when Candace asked to work for him, he laughed her out of the bar.

After that she drifted around Los Angeles for a month or two, turning tricks whenever she could. She was no longer competitive, even without the scars, but she managed to scrape by, somehow making rent for the place on North Beverly Glen. It held her memories of Rick, and if she let that go, she would have lost even that shell of their love. She even refused to throw out any of his discarded clothing and possessions; his toothbrush and an old razor still lay by the sink.

The last time the cops busted her, Candace had herpes, a penicillin-resistant clap, and no way of posting bail. Jail meant losing her house and its memories of Rick, and there would be nothing left for her after that. Rick could help her now, but she couldn't manage to reach him. An old mutual friend finally did, but when he came to visit Candace he couldn't bear to give her Rick's message, and so he paid her bail himself and told her the money came from Rick, who didn't want to risk getting his name involved.

She had to have a legitimate job. The friend had a friend who owned interest in a plastic novelties plant, and they got Candace a factory job there. By now she had very little left of herself to sell in the streets, but at least she was off the drugs. Somewhat to the surprise of all concerned, Candace settled down on the line and turned out to be a good worker. Her job paid the bills, and at night she went home and read about Richards Justin in the papers and magazines, played back video cassettes of him nights when he wasn't on live.

The cruelest thing was that Candace still nurtured the hope that she could win Rick back, once she got her own act together. Regular meals, decent hours, medication and time healed some wounds. That face that looked back at her from mirrors no longer resembled a starved plague victim. Some of the men at the plant were beginning to stare after her, and a couple of times she'd been asked to go out. She might have got over Richards Justin in time, but probably not.

The friend of a friend pulled some strings and called in some favors, and so the plant where Candace worked secured the merchandising rights to the Colt Savage, Soldier of Fortune Action Pak. This consisted of a plastic Colt Savage doll, complete with weapons and action costumes, along with models of Black Blaze, his supersonic autogiro, and Red Lightning, the supercar. The merchandising package also included dolls of his mentor and regular assistants, as well as several notable villains and their sinister weaponry. The plant geared into maximum production to handle the anticipated rush of orders for the Christmas market.

Candace found herself sitting at the assembly line, watching thousands of plastic replicas of Richards Justin roll past her.

She just had to see Rick, but the guards at the gate had instructions not to admit her. He wouldn't even talk to her over the phone or answer her letters. The way he must remember her, Candace couldn't really blame him. It would be different now.

His birthday was coming up, and she knew he would be having a party. She wrote him several times, sent messages via old contacts, begging Rick to let her come. When the printed invitation finally came, she'd already bought him a present. Candace knew that her confidence had not been a mistake, and she took a day off work to get ready for their evening together.

The party had been going strong for some time when Candace arrived, and Rick was flying high on coke and champagne. He hugged her around the shoulders but didn't kiss her, and half carried her over to where many of the guests were crowded around a projection television.

Ladies and gentlemen here she is — our leading lady, the versatile Miss Candi Thorne.

All eyes flicked from the screen to Candace, long enough for recognition. Then the cheers and applause burst out across the room. Rick had been amusing his guests with some of her films. Just now they were watching the one with the donkey.

Candace didn't really remember how she managed to escape and find her way home.

She decided not to leave a note, and she was prying the blade out of Rick's old razor when the idea began to form. The razor was crudded with dried lather and bits of Rick's whiskers, and she wanted to get it clean before she used it on her wrists. A scene from another of her films, *Voodoo Vixens*, arose through the confusion of her thoughts. She set the razor aside carefully.

Candace made herself a cup of coffee and let the idea build in her head. She was dry-eyed now and quite calm — the hysterical energy that had driven her to suicide now directed her disordered thoughts toward another course of action.

She still had all of her mementos of Rick, and throughout the night she went over them, one by one, coolly and meticulously. She scraped all the bits of beard and skin from his razor, collected hair and dandruff from his brush and comb, pared away his toothbrush bristles for the minute residues of blood and plaque. She found a discarded handkerchief, stained from a coke-induced nosebleed, and from the mattress liner came residues of their former lovemaking. Old clothes yielded bits of hair, stains of body oils and perspiration. Candace searched the house relentlessly, finding fragments of his nails, his hair, anything at all that retained physical residues of Rick's person.

The next day Candace called in sick. She spent the day browsing through Los Angeles' numerous occult bookshops, made a few purchases, and called up one or two of the contacts she'd made filming *Voodoo Vixens*. It all seemed straightforward enough. Even those who rationalized it all admitted that it was a matter of belief. And children have the purest belief in magic.

Candace ground up all her bits and scrapings of Richards Justin. It came to quite a pile and reminded her of a bag of Mexican heroin.

Candace returned to work and waited for her chance. When no one was watching, she dumped her powdered residue into the plastic muck destined to become Colt Savage dolls. Then she said a prayer of sorts.

Beneath the Christmas tree, Joshua plays with his new Colt Savage doll. *Pow!* An electron cannon knocks Colt out of the sky, crashes him to the rocks below!

Jason pits Colt Savage against his model dinosaurs. *Yahhh!* The dinosaur stomps him!

David is racing Colt Savage in his car, Red Lightning. *Ker-blam!* Colt drives off the cliff at a hundred miles an hour!

Billy is still too young to play with his Colt Savage doll, but he likes to chew on it.

Mark decides to see if Colt Savage and Black Blaze can withstand the attack of his atomic bomb firecrackers.

Jessica is mad at her brother. She sees his Colt Savage doll and stomps on it as hard as she can.

Tyrone is bawling. He pulled the arms off his Colt Savage doll, and he can't make them go back on.

Richards Justin collapsed on set, and only heavy sedation finally stilled his screams. It quickly became apparent that his seizures were permanent, and he remains under sedation in a psychiatric institution. Doctors have attributed his psychotic break to long-term drug abuse.

Nothing excites the public more than a fallen hero. *Richards Justin: The Untold Story*, by Candace Thornton, rose quickly on the best-seller charts. Reportedly she was recently paid well over a million for the film rights to her book.

3501

Shrapnel

It looked like the wreckage of a hundred stained glass windows, strewn across a desolate tangle of wasteland in a schizophrenic kaleidoscope.

The hood of the '78 Marquis buckled in protest as Harmon shifted his not inconsiderable weight. He smeared sweat from his face with a sweatier arm and squinted against the piercing sunlight. Even from his vantage point atop the rusting Mercury, it was impossible to achieve any sense of direction amidst these thousands of wrecked cars.

At some point this had been farmland, although such was difficult to envision now. Whatever crops had once grown here had long ago leeched the red clay of scant nutrients. Fallow acres had lapsed into wild pasture where enough soil remained; elsewhere erosion scourged the slopes with red gashes, and a scrub-growth of pine, sumac, honeysuckle and briar grudgingly reclaimed the dead land. Grey knobs of limestone and outcroppings could almost be mistaken for the shapeless hulls of someone's tragedy.

Harmon wished for a beer—a tall, dripping can of cold, cold beer. Six of them. He promised himself a stop at the first convenience store on the highway, once he finished his business here. But first he needed a fender.

"Left front fender. 1970 or '71 Montego."

"I think it will interchange with a '70–'71 Torino," Harmon had offered—too tired to explain that the fender was actually needed for a 1970 Cyclone Spoiler, but that this was Mercury's muscle car version of the Montego, which shared sheet metal with Ford's Torino, and anyway the woman who ran Pearson's Auto Yard probably knew all that sort of stuff already.

She had just a dusting of freckles, and wheat-colored hair that would have looked striking in almost anything other than the regulation dyke haircut she had chosen. The name embroidered across the pocket of her freshly washed but forever grease-stained workshirt read *Shiloh*. Shiloh had just finished off a pair of redneck truckers in quest of certain axle parts incomprehensible to Harmon, and she was more than capable of dealing with him.

"Most of the older Fords are off along the gully along the woods there." Shiloh had pointed. "If they haven't been hauled to the crusher. There's a row of fenders and quarter panels just beyond that. You wait a minute and Dillon or somebody'll be here to look for you."

The thundering air conditioner in the window of the cramped office might have been able to hold the room temperature at 80 if the door weren't constantly being opened. Harmon felt dizzy, and he further felt that fresh air, however searing, was a better bet than waiting on an office stool for Dillon or somebody.

"You watch out for the dogs," Shiloh had warned him. "If one of them comes after you, you just jump on top of something where they can't get at you until Dillon or somebody comes along."

Hardly comforting, but Harmon knew his way around junkyards. This was an acquaintance that had begun when Harmon had decided to keep the 1965 Mustang of his college days in running order. It had become part hobby, part rebellion against the lookalike econoboxes or the Volvos and BMWs that his fellow young suburban professionals drove each day from their energy-efficient homes in Brookwood or Brookcrest or Crestwood or whatever. Harmon happened to be an up-and-coming lawyer in his own right, thank you, and just now his pet project was restoring a vintage muscle car whose string of former owners had not been overly concerned with trees, ditches, and other obstacles, moving or stationary.

It was a better way to spend Saturday morning than on the tennis court or golf course. Besides, and he wiped his face again, it was good exercise. Harmon, over the past four years and at his wife's insistence, had enrolled in three different exercise programs and had managed to attend a total of two classes altogether. He kept telling himself to get in shape, once his schedule permitted.

Just now he wished he could find Dillon or somebody. The day was too hot, the sun too unrelenting, for a comfortable stroll through this labyrinth of crumbled steel and shattered glass. He rocked back and forth on the hood of the Marquis, squinting against the glare.

"Yoo hoo! Mister Dillion! There's trouble brewin' on Front Street!"

Christ, enough of that! He was getting light-headed. That late-night pizza had been a mistake.

Harmon thought he saw movement farther down along the ravine. He started to call out in earnest, but decided that the general clatter and crash of the junkyard would smother his words. There was the intermittent mutter of the machine shop, and somewhere in the distance a tractor or towtruck, innocent of muffler, was dragging stripped hulks to their doom in the jaws of the yard's crusher. Grunting, Harmon climbed down from the wreck and plodded toward where he thought he'd glimpsed someone.

The heat seemed worse as he trudged along the rutted pathway. The rows of twisted sheet metal effectively stifled whatever breeze there might have been, at the same time acting as grotesque radiators of the sun's absorbed heat. Harmon wished he had worn a hat. He had always heard that a hat was a good thing to wear when out in the sun. He touched the spot on the top of his head where his sandy hair was inclining to thin. Unpleasant images of frying eggs came to him.

It *smelled* hot. The acres of rusted metal smelled like an unclean oven. There was the bitter smell of roasting vinyl, underscored by the musty stench of mildewed upholstery basted in stagnant rainwater. The palpable smell of hot metal vied with the noxious fumes of gasoline and oil and grease—the dried blood of uncounted steel corpses. Underlying it all was a sickly sweet odor that Harmon didn't like to think about, because it reminded him of his small-town childhood and walking home on summer days through the alley behind the butcher shop. He supposed they hosed these wrecks down or something, before putting them on the yard, but nonetheless...

Harmon's gaze caught upon the sagging spiderweb of a windshield above a crumpled steering wheel. He shivered. Strange, to shiver when it was so hot. He seemed to feel his intestines wriggle like a nest of cold eels.

Harmon supposed he had better sit down for a moment.

He did.

"Morris?"

Harmon blinked. He must have dropped off.

"Hey, Morris—you OK?"

Where was he?

"Morris?" The voice was concerned and a hand was gently shaking him.

Harmon blinked again. He was sitting on a ruined front seat in the shade of an eviscerated Falcon van. He jerked upright with a guilty start, like a junior exec caught snoring during a senior staff meeting. Someone was standing over him, someone who knew his name.

"Morris?"

The voice became a face, and the face a person. Arnie Cranshaw. A client. Former client. Harmon decided to stop blinking and stand up. On the second try, he made it to his feet.

Cranshaw stared reproachfully. "Jesus! I thought maybe you were dead."

"A little too much sun," he explained. "Thought I'd better sit down in the shade for a minute or two. I'm OK. Just dozed off is all."

"You sure?" Cranshaw wasn't so certain. "Maybe you ought to sit back down."

Harmon shook his head, feeling like a fool. "I'll be fine once I get out of this heat. Christ, I'd kill for a cold beer right now!"

Not a well-chosen remark, he suddenly reflected. Cranshaw had been his client not quite a year ago in a nasty sort of thing: head-on collision that had left a teenaged girl dead and her date hopelessly crippled. Cranshaw, the other driver involved, had been quite drunk at the time and escaped injury; he also escaped punishment, thanks to Harmon's legal talents. The other car *had* crossed the yellow line, no matter that its driver swore that he had lost control in trying to avoid Cranshaw, who had been swerving all over the road—and a technicality resulted in the DUI charges being thrown out as well. It was a victory that raised Harmon's stock in the estimation of his colleagues, but it was not a victory of which Harmon was overly proud.

"Anyway, Morris, what are you doing here?" Cranshaw asked. He was ten years younger than Harmon, had a jogger's legs, and worked out at his health club twice a week. Nonetheless, the prospect of lugging a semiconscious lawyer out of this metal wasteland was not to Cranshaw's liking.

"Looking for a fender for my car."

"Fender-bender?" Cranshaw was ready to show sympathy.

"Someone else's, and in days gone by. I'm trying to restore an old muscle car I bought back in the spring. Only way to find parts is to dig through junkyards. How about you?"

"Need a fender for the BMW."

Harmon declined to press for details, which spared Cranshaw any need to lie about his recent hit-and-run encounter. He knew a country body shop that would make repairs without asking questions, if he located some of the parts. A chop shop wasn't likely to respond to requests for information about cars with bloodstained fenders and such grisly trivia. They'd done business before.

Cranshaw felt quite remorseful over such incidents, but he certainly wasn't one to permit his life to be ruined over some momentary lapse.

"Do you know where we are?" asked Harmon. He wasn't feeling at all well, and just now he was thinking only of getting back into his little Japanese pick-up and turning the air conditioner up to stun.

"Well. Pearson's Auto Yard, of course." Cranshaw eyed him suspiciously.

"No. I mean, do you know how to get out of here?"

"Why, back the way we came." Cranshaw decided the man was maybe drunk. "Just backtrack is all."

Cranshaw followed Harmon's bewildered gaze, then said, less confidently: "I see what you mean. Sort of like one of those maze things, isn't it. They ought to give you a set of directions or something—like, 'Turn left at the '57 Chevy and keep straight on till you pass the burned-out VW bug.'"

"I was looking for one of the workers," Harmon explained.

"So am I," Cranshaw said. "Guy named Milton or something. He'll know where to find our fenders, if they got any. Sort of like a Chinese librarian, these guys got to be."

He walked on ahead, tanned legs pumping assertively beneath jogging shorts. Harmon felt encouraged and fell in behind him. "I thought I saw somebody working on down the ravine a ways," he suggested to Cranshaw's back.

They seemed to be getting closer to the crusher, to judge by the sound. At intervals someone's discarded dream machine gave up its last vestiges of identity in great screams of rending, crumpling steel. Harmon winced each time he heard those deathcries. The last remaining left front fender for a '70 Cyclone might be passing into recycled oblivion even as he marched to its rescue.

"I don't think this is where I want to be going," Cranshaw said, pausing to look around. "These are pretty much stripped and ready for the crusher. And they're mostly Ford makes."

"Yes. Well, that's what I'm trying to find." Harmon brightened. "Do you see a '70 or '71 Montego or Torino in any of these?"

"Christ, Morris! I wouldn't know one of those from a Model T. I need to find where they keep their late-model imports. You going to be all right if I go on and leave you here to poke around?"

"Sure," Harmon told him. The heat was worse, if anything, but he was damned if he'd ask Cranshaw to nursemaid him.

Cranshaw was shading his eyes with his hand. "Hey, you were right. There *is* somebody working down there. I'm going to ask directions."

"Wait up," Harmon protested. He'd seen the workman first.

Cranshaw was walking briskly toward an intersection in the rows of twisted hulks. "Hey, you!" Harmon heard him call above the din of the crusher. "Hey, Milton!"

Cranshaw turned the corner and disappeared from view for a moment. Harmon made his legs plod faster, and he almost collided with Cranshaw when he came around the corner of stacked cars.

Cranshaw was standing in the middle of the rutted pathway, staring at the mangled remains of a Pinto station wagon. His face looked unhealthy beneath its tan.

"Shit, Morris! That's the car that I…"

"Don't be ridiculous, Arnie. All burned-out wrecks look alike."

"No. It's the same one. See that porthole window in back? They didn't make very many of that model. Shit!"

Harmon had studied photos of the wreck in preparing his defense. "Well, so what if it is the car. It had to end up in a junkyard somewhere. Anyway, I don't think this is the same car."

"Shit!" Cranshaw repeated, starting to back away.

"Hey, wait!" Harmon insisted.

A workman had materialized from the rusting labyrinth. His greasy common-placeness was initially reassuring—faded work clothes, filthy with unguessable stains, and a billed cap too dirty for its insignia patch to be deciphered. He was tall and thin, and his face and hands were so smeared and stained that Harmon wasn't at first certain as to his race. The workman carried a battered tool box in one hand, while in the other he dragged a shapeless bag of filthy canvas. The eyes that stared back at Harmon were curiously intent above an expressionless face.

"Are you Dillon?" Harmon hoped they weren't trespassing. He could hear a dog barking furiously not far away.

The workman looked past Harmon and fixed his eyes on Cranshaw. His examination of the other man seemed frankly rude.

"Are you Milton?" Cranshaw demanded. The workman's name

across his breast pocket was obscured by grease and dirt. "Where do you keep your late-model imports?"

The workman set down his tool box and dug a limp notebook from a greasy shirt pocket. Licking his fingers, he paged through it in silence. After a moment, he found the desired entry. His eyes flicked from the page to Cranshaw and back again.

"Yep," he concluded, speaking for the first time, and he made a checkmark with a well-chewed pencil stub. Returning notebook and pencil to shirt pocket, the workman knelt down and began to unlatch his tool box.

Harmon wanted to say something, but his mouth was too dry to speak, and he knew he was very much afraid, and he wished with all his heart that his legs were not rooted to the ground.

Ahead of him, Cranshaw appeared to be similarly incapable of movement, although from the expression on his face he clearly seemed to wish he were anyplace else but here.

The tool chest was open now, and the workman expertly made his selection from within. The tool chest appeared to contain mainly an assortment of knives and scalpels, all very dirty and showing evidence of considerable use. If the large knife that the workman had selected was a fair sample, their blades were all very sharp and serviceable.

The canvas bag had fallen open, enough so that Harmon could get a glimpse of its contents. A glimpse was enough. The arm seemed to be a woman's, but there was no way of telling if the heart with its dangling assortment of vessels had come from the same body.

Curiously, once Harmon recognized that many of the stains were blood, it seemed quite evident that much of the dirt was not grease, but soot.

The sound of an approaching motor was only a moment's cause for hope. A decrepit Cadillac hearse wallowed down the rutted trail toward them, as the workman tested the edge of his knife. The hearse, converted into a work truck, was rusted out and so battered that only its vintage tailfins gave it identity. Red dust would have completely masked the chipped black paint, if there hadn't been an overlay of soot as well. The loud exhaust belched blue smoke that smelled less of oil than of sulfur.

Another grimy workman was at the wheel. Except for the greasy straw cowboy hat, he might have been a double for the other workman. The doors were off the hearse, so it was easy to see what was piled inside.

The hearse rolled to a stop, and the driver stuck out his head.

"Another pick-up?"

"Yeah. Better get out and give me a hand here. They want both right and left leg assemblies, and then we need to strip the face. You got a three-inch flaying knife in there? I left mine somewhere."

Then they lifted Cranshaw, grunting a little at the effort, and laid him out across the hood.

"Anything we need off the other?" the driver wondered.

"I don't know. I'll check my list."

It was very, very hot, and Harmon heard nothing

Someone was tugging at his head, and Harmon started to scream. He choked on a mouthful of cold R.C. and sputtered foam on the chest of the man who was holding the can to his lips. Harmon's eyes popped open, and he started to scream again when he saw the greasy workclothes. But this black face was naturally so, the workman's eyes showed kindly concern, and the name on his pocket plainly read *Dillon*.

"Just sip on this and take it easy, mister," Dillon said reassuringly. "You had a touch of the sun, but you're going to be just fine now."

Harmon stared about him. He was back in the office, and Shiloh was speaking with considerable agitation into the phone. Several other people stood about, offering conflicting suggestions for treating heat stroke or sun stroke or both.

"Found you passed out on the road out there in the yard," Dillon told him. "Carried you back inside here where we got the air conditioner running."

Harmon became aware of the stuttering howl of an approaching siren. "I won't need an ambulance," he protested. "I just had a dizzy spell is all."

"That ambulance ain't coming for you," Dillon explained. "We had a bad accident at the crusher. Some customer got himself caught."

Shiloh slammed down the phone. "There'll be hell to pay!" she snapped.

"There always is," Harmon agreed.

Silted In

The pain in his chest was back again. Perhaps it was worse this time, but he couldn't remember.

He leaned against the sink, trying to belch. The kitchen counter was stacked high with dishes: to his right dirty ones; to his left clean ones, waiting to dry themselves. He rinsed the suds from his hands, staring at them as the suds peeled away. Were the wrinkles from the dishwater, or had he grown that much older?

He sat down heavily at the kitchen table, remembered his cup of coffee. It had grown cold, but he sipped it without tasting. That was enough of the dishes for today; tomorrow he'd make a fresh start.

He hated the dishes. Each one was a memory. This was her coffee cup. This was her favorite glass. They drank together from these wine glasses. They'd picked out this china pattern together. This casserole dish was a wedding present. This skillet was the one she used to make her special omelets. This was the ash tray she always kept beside her favorite chair.

Her chair. He shuffled into the living room, collapsed across the swaybacked couch. Her chair waited there for her, just as she had left it. He wouldn't sit in it. A guest might, but he never had guests now.

A broken spring pressed into his consciousness, and he shifted his weight. Not much weight now. Once he had enjoyed cooking for her. Now every meal he fixed reminded him of her. He left his food untasted. When he cleaned out the freezer, her dog had grown plump on roasts and steaks and chops, stews and soups and etouffées, fried chicken and roast goose and curried duck. After her dog died, he simply scraped the untouched food into the dog's old bowl, left it on the back porch for whatever might be hungry. When his stomach gave him too much pain, he made a sandwich of something, sometimes ate it.

The mail truck was honking beside his mailbox, and he remembered that he hadn't checked his mail all week. Once he had waited impatiently each day for the mail to come. Now it was only bills, duns, letters from angry publishers, some misdirected letters for her, a few magazines whose subscriptions still ran.

He was out of breath when he climbed back up the steps from the street. He stared at his reflection in the hallway mirror without recognition, then dumped the armload of unopened mail onto the pile that sprawled across the coffee table.

The phone started to ring, but his answering machine silently took charge. He never played back the messages, used the phone only now and again to order a pizza. No one comes up into the hills at night.

"Why don't you answer it?" Bogey asked him. He was working his way through a bottle, waiting for Ingrid to show up.

"Might be my agent. He's been stalling my publishers as long as he can. Now I owe him money, too."

"Maybe it's her."

He ignored the poster and found the bathroom. He took a long piss, a decidedly realistic touch which was the trendiest verism in horror fiction this season. So inspired, he groped his way into his study, dropped into the leather swivel chair she had bought him for his last birthday. He supposed it was a gift.

He brought up the IBM word processor and hit the command for global search and replace, instructed it to replace the phrase "make love" with "piss on" throughout the novel. Yes, go ahead and replace without asking.

While the computer sorted that out, he fumbled with the bank of stereo equipment, tried to focus his eyes on the spines of a thousand record albums. He reached out to touch several favorites, pulled his hand away reluctantly each time. Every album was a memory. The Blues Project album he'd played while they made love for the first time. The Jefferson Airplane album she loved to dance to: Don't you need somebody to love? And not the Grateful Dead—too many stoned nights of sitting on the floor under the black lights, passing the pipe around. Hendrix? No, too many acid trip memories.

"You're burning out, man," Jimi told him.

"Better to burn out than to fade away," he answered. "You should know."

Jimi shrugged and went back to tuning his Fender Stratocaster.

He left the stereo on, still without making a selection. Sometimes a beer helped him get started.

The dishes were still waiting in the sink, and Jim Morrison was looking in the refrigerator. He reached an arm in past Jimbo and snagged the last beer. He'd have to remember to go to the store soon.

"Fucking self-indulgent," Jim said.

"What was? Oh, here." He offered Jimbo the beer can.

Jim shook his head. "No. I meant changing 'fuck' to 'piss on' in the novel."

"It's the same thing. And anyway, it's so New Wave."

"How would you know? You're past forty."

"I was New Wave back in the '60s."

"And you're still stuck in the '60s."

"And so are you."

"Maybe so. But I *know* that I'm dead."

"You and all my heroes."

Back in his study he sipped his beer and considered his old Royal portable. Maybe go back to the roots: a quill pen, or even clay tablets.

He rolled in a sheet of paper, typed 1 at the top of the page. He sipped the rest of his beer and stared at the blank page. After a while he noticed that the beer can was empty.

The battery in his car was dead, but there was a 7-11 just down the hill. His chest was aching again by the time he got back. He chugged a fresh brew while he put away the rest of the six-pack, a Redi-Maid cheese sandwich, a jar of instant coffee and a pack of cigarettes. The long belch made him feel better.

James Dean was browsing along his bookshelves when he returned to the living room. He was looking at a copy of *Electric Visions*. "I always wondered why you dedicated this book to me," he said.

"It was my first book. You were my first hero—even before Elvis. I grew up in the '50s wanting to be like you."

James read from the copyright page: "1966." He nodded toward the rest of the top shelf. "You write these others, too?"

"Fourteen hardcovers in ten years. I lived up to your image. Check out some of the reviews I stuck inside the books: 'The New Wave's brightest New Star.' 'Sci-fi's rebellious new talent.' 'The angriest and most original writer in decades.' Great jacket blurbs."

James Dean helped himself to a cigarette. "I don't notice any reviews more recent than 1978."

"Saving reviews is the mark of a beginner." There hadn't been many since 1978, and those had been less than kind. The last had pronounced sentence: Tired rehash of traditional themes by one of the genre's Old Hands. He hadn't finished a book since then.

James French-inhaled. "Don't see many books since 1978 here either."

"Whole next shelf."

"Looks like reprints mostly."

"My books are considered classics. They're kept in print."

"What a load of bull."

"Why don't you go take a spin in your Porsche?"

The remark was in poor taste, and he decided to play his tape of *Rebel Without a Cause* by way of apology. And then he remembered how she had cried when the cops gunned down Sal Mineo. Maybe he should get some work done instead.

The stereo and the word processor were both still on when he returned to his study, and there was a sheet of paper in his typewriter with *1* typed across the top. He studied all of this in some confusion. He cut power switches; cranked out the blank sheet of paper, carefully placed it in a clean manila folder and dated the tab.

He sat down. Maybe he should listen to a tape. Something that wouldn't remind him of her. He turned his stereo back on. The tapes were buried under a heap of unanswered correspondence, unread magazines, unfinished manuscripts on the spare bed. He sat back down.

It might be best to make a fresh start by tackling an unfinished manuscript. There were a few, several, maybe a dozen, or more. They were all somewhere on the spare bed, hidden beneath one overturned stack or another. He'd paid fifteen bucks for the brass bed when he'd moved in, twenty years ago. Spent two days stripping the multi-layered paint, polishing with Brass-O. Five bucks to Goodwill for the stained mattress and box springs. They'd slept together on it their first year together, until he pulled down a big enough advance to convert his former housemate's room into their bedroom, pay for a proper double bed. He'd always meant to sell the single brass bed, put in proper shelves instead.

He never slept in their bedroom now. It held her clothes, her pictures, her scent, her memories.

It would be an all-day chore to sort through all the mess to find just the right manuscript whose moment had come. Best to tackle that tomorrow.

He pulled out an abused legal pad, wrote *1* across the first yellow page.

His stomach was hurting now. That made it hard to choose which pen to write with. He thought there might still be some milk left.

He drank a glass of milk and then a cup of coffee and smoked three Winstons, while he waited for his muse to awaken. The living room walls were hung with the same black-light posters they had put there when they'd first moved in together, back in the late '60s. He supposed that the black lights still worked, although it had been years since he had switched them on. About all that had changed over the years were occasional new bookshelves, growing against the walls like awkward shelf-fungus. They were triple-stacked with books he really meant to read, although he hadn't been able to finish reading a book in years.

I can't see you because of your books, she had warned him on occasion, from her chair across the room from his. And then he would stick together another shelf, try to clear away the confusion of books and magazines piled in the middle of the living room, try to explain the necessity of keeping copies of *Locus* from 1969. In another year the pile would grow back.

My books are my life, he would tell her. Now that she was gone, he had grown to hate them almost as much as he had grown to hate himself. They were memories, and he clung to them while hating them, for memories were all he had left of his life.

It was getting dark. He glanced toward the front door, thinking it was about time for the cat to show up to be fed. He remembered that he hadn't seen the cat in weeks.

Time to get back to work. He would write all night.

The cigarettes started him coughing again. She had nagged him to see a doctor about that cough. He treasured the cough for that memory of her concern.

He drank a glass of water from the tap, then remembered that her plants needed watering. She had left him with her plants, and he tried to keep them watered. He was crying again by the time he completed his rounds with the watering can. That made the cough worse. His chest ached.

"What you need is to stop feeling sorry for yourself," Elvis advised him. "Stop moping around this dump. Go out and get yourself a new woman."

"Too old for chasing tail at the singles bars," he protested, reaching around Elvis to select some pills from the medicine cabinet. Shitty street speed they sold now only made him long for the good old days of Dex and Ritalin and black beauties.

"Never too old to make a comeback," The King said.

"Who says I need to make a comeback?"

"Shit. Look at yourself."

"You look at yourself, dammit! You've got an extra chin and

sleeping bags under your eyes. Try to squeeze that stomach into one of those black leather jackets you slouched in back when I was trying to grow sideburns like yours."

"But I'm not getting any older now."

"And I won't grow up either."

"It's not the same thing."

Street speed always made him hungry. He ate half of the cheese sandwich, felt vaguely nauseated, and had a swallow of Maalox with several aspirin.

He really ought to take a break before getting back to work. There was nothing on television that interested him at all, and he wondered again why he paid for all the cable channels that were offered. Still, best to have access; there might be something that would inspire him—or at least fill the empty hours of pain.

He could watch a tape. The trouble was that the tapes were unsorted and unlabeled, stuffed away into boxes and piled together with all the other debris of his life. He could dig through it all, but then he would run the risk of pulling out a cassette of a film that was special to her. He would never watch *To Have and Have Not* again. Best just to turn on Cable News and let it run.

He put the rest of the cheese sandwich out for the cat, in case he came back during the night. His stomach was hurting too much to finish eating. Despite the Maalox, he felt like vomiting. Somehow he knew that once he started vomiting, he would never stop—not until all that he spewed out was bright blood, and then not until he had no more blood to offer. A toilet bowl for a sacrificial altar.

There was inspiration at last. Vomiting was back in vogue now—proof that great concepts never die.

While the fire was in him, he brought up the IBM, instructed global search to replace "kiss" with "vomit on."

That was more than enough creativity for one day. He felt drained. It was time to relax with a cold beer. Maybe he could play a record. He wondered if she had left him a little pot, maybe hidden away in a plastic film canister.

But film canisters reminded him of all the photographs they had taken together, frozen memories of the two of them in love,

Silted In · 85

enjoying their life together. He was too depressed to listen to a record now. Best just to sit in the darkness and sip his beer.

Janis Joplin was trying to plug in one of the black lights, but she needed an extension cord. Giving it up, she plopped down onto the couch and grinned at him. She was wearing lots of beads and a shapeless paisley blouse over patched and faded bell-bottoms. From somewhere she produced a pint of Southern Comfort, took a pull, offered the bottle to him.

"Good for that cough," she urged in her semi-hoarse voice.

"Thanks," he said. "I got a beer."

Janis shook back her loose waves of hair, looked around the room. "Place hasn't changed."

"It never does."

"You're stuck in the past, man."

"Maybe. It sure beats living in the future."

"Oh wow." Janis was searching for something in her beaded handbag. "You're buried alive, man."

"Beats just being buried."

"Shit, man. You're lost among your artifacts, man. I mean, like you've stored up memories like quicksand and jumped right in."

"Maybe I'm an artifact myself. Just like you."

Janis laughed her gravelly cackle. "Shit, man. You're all left alone with the pieces of your life, and all the time life is passing you by. Buried alive in the blues, man."

"Since she left me, all I have left to look forward to is my past."

"Hey, man. You got to let it go. You got to let her go. You know how that old song goes."

Janis began to sing in her voice that reminded him of cream sherry stirred into cracked ice:

> Look up and down that long lonesome road,
> Where all of our friends have gone, my love,
> And you and I must go.
> They say all good friends must part someday,
> So why not you and I, my love,
> Why not you and I?

"Guess I'm just not ready to let it all go," he said finally. But now he was alone in the darkness, his chest hurt, and his beer was empty.

She shouldn't have left him.

He tossed the beer can into the trash, turned off the kitchen light. One thing to do before sprawling out across the couch to try to sleep.

He opened the upright freezer. It had only been a matter of removing the shelves.

"Goodnight, my love," he whispered to her.

Lost Exits

Every morning she would wake him with a kiss and a sleepy vow, "I love you," and he would smile and echo, "I love you," and he never saw the hatred behind her eyes.

Mercedes O'Brien slipped her feet into blue pumps, smoothed her skirt, and stepped up to the cheval glass to give final inspection to her mascara. She adjusted the bow at the throat of her silk blouse, fussed with the lapels of her business suit, and agreed with herself that muted blues enlivened the greys without softening the crisp projection of competence.

She was long-legged, her figure drew second and third looks, and at 30 she could still wear clothes she'd worn at 20. Her hair was bright and black and coiffured atop her head. She had a straight nose which she thought too large, full lips which she thought were rather sensual, and a firm jawline which she thought connoted determination. Her teeth were white and straight and strong. Most of all she approved of her eyes, which were dark and flashing and a mask.

She trusted mirrors, distrusted windows—agoraphobia, one therapist had said—and once she had lost control when she sensed another presence beyond the two-way mirror of a boutique dressing room.

Sean O'Brien had struggled into an old pair of blue jeans and was frying bacon when Mercedes strode into the kitchen. She heard him cuss as hot grease spat onto his bare belly.

"I'll just have juice and toast," she told him. "I'm in a rush. Big presentation."

"Then you'd better stoke up."

"May run late."

"All the more reason."

He was half a head taller than she and maybe had gained a pound for each of the ten years of their marriage. Back then he was strung out on crystal meth, and he could still gain ten pounds without showing love handles. Friends attributed it to good diet, exercise, and a loving wife.

They had met at the Filmore when he was opening before Cactus. She was an aspiring groupie. He was lead singer for Broken Bridges. He wrote most of their material himself, and they had great hopes for their first album. All they needed was a break—and maybe a little polish.

She knew from the start that he was singing to her. She told him so backstage, and at the motel, and the next morning. She would still tell him so after a dozen years and as many faded dreams.

Their marriage had been orchestrated with the release of the first album of his then-current group, Clouded Skies. While neither marriage nor album had generated the anticipated attention, the marriage endured—to the wonder and envy of all who knew them.

Sean O'Brien had been born in Cobble Hill, Brooklyn, claimed second- or fourth-generation Irish descent, had never visited that island, but refused to change his name to something trendier. He had rust-colored hair, which he sometimes allowed to be cut in the prevailing style—but he would make no further concessions. His eyes were green, his temper was moody, and his face was neither pretty nor sneering. His voice was very good, but he lacked the charisma of a successful lead singer. His songs were very good, but his guitar could only be called "bad" in the original sense of the word.

Sean had managed half a dozen albums with half a dozen groups on half a dozen labels. Sean had not found fame, but he was not entirely forgotten, and some of his crib-death albums now sold for more than he'd eventually been paid to record them.

This did not pay the bills. To cover the dry spells, Mercedes had found a part-time job as receptionist for one of Sean's disappointed record companies, whose junior vice-president they had met at a party. When Mercedes became executive secretary, Sean simply felt pride that her organizational skills had compensated for her inability to type.

She was his muse, an inspiration to him, a reason to fight on against all odds. She understood his artistic frustrations, believed in the validity of his work, proudly protected him from slings and arrows. He loved her. She loved him. All else was secondary and transient.

Sean was pouring orange juice.

Mercedes was executive assistant to the junior-most partner of Arrow Records Productions.

"One O.J."

"Thank you."

"Toast on its way."

Standing, she sipped her juice.

He popped out the toast and buttered it for her. "Take your vitamins?"

"Of course. Did you?"

"Soon as I've had my morning workout."

"I want you to stay healthy," she said with real concern.

"Count on it."

She bit her toast with lips drawn back, not to muss them. "I said I'd be late."

Sean was having vodka with his orange juice. "Probably be late myself. Got to see some people. Maybe we can do a late dinner around St Mark's Place tonight."

"You buying, or just carrying the Mace?"

"Cockroaches aren't that big. Not at Nero's, anyway."

"I'm not going in there again."

"You name the place. Price no object. We'll get a cab."

Mercedes eyed him over her toast. "So what are you trying to tell me?"

Sean sipped his screwdriver. "Phone call before you got in last night. Nicki's putting something together. Something big. They want to talk about it, and I said, 'Maybe, if the money's right,' and Nicki said, 'It's right, my man.' So, we'll talk."

Mercedes lunged to hug him. Toast crumbs and lipstick smeared his mouth. "Do you think…?"

Sean was nonchalant. "Nicki owes me. I've written some fucking good stuff since that mess with Nuked Mutants. We'll see."

"I know you can do it. I've always known it."

"Hey, wait till we sign!"

She gave him a long kiss, then released him. "I got to run."

"Hey, let's both be late to work."

"Celebrate after." She blew him another kiss. "Good luck—and I love you."

"Love you too, Mercy. Don't be too late."

"He's got so much talent," Mercedes explained to three of her subordinates around the coffee urn. "He just won't compromise. That's what's held him back."

"Well, I think it's just wonderful that you've stood by him for so long," said one. "So may couples these days…"

"It isn't easy," Mercedes confessed. "Rock stars—well, you know…"

They nodded, waiting to know more.

"Drugs and booze," confided Mercedes. "Wild parties in hotels. Teenaged groupies. All that backstage sort."

"And you put up with Sean despite all this?"

"I have to—because I love him," Mercedes said tragically. "I know what he does, and I don't care."

"That's life in the fast lane, for sure," said someone, as Mercedes returned to her office. "Sort of makes you wonder."

"She loves him," concluded someone else. "That's all that matters to her. Poor kid."

Twice each week she took a long lunchbreak in order to see her latest therapist. Trafford knew about it, of course, and, of course, he approved. She kept it a secret from Sean.

Dr Ruckerman was a fiftyish and heavyset woman who looked as if she ought to be wearing tweeds and decimating grouse, but she favored pastel polyester pantsuits, and she was listening to Mercedes instead.

Mercedes shifted squeakily upon the leather chair, wishing for a mirror so she might evaluate her composure.

"It's hard to say," she said with difficulty, "but I hate him."

She cast her eyes downward, almost blushing. She'd practiced.

"I understand that it's hard to say," prompted Dr Ruckerman. "I also understand that you feel this need to express such feelings."

"I love him, but he's changed—changed from what I loved. He's lost all ambition, given up his dreams. He's a stranger to me now. Sometimes he frightens me."

"Has he threatened you?"

"Several times—whenever he's drunk."

"Is that often?"

"Every night. He's so typically Irish."

"Have you tried to urge him to seek help?"

"That's when he becomes abusive."

"Does he have a job?"

"I support him. He used to perform in rock bands, but he never made it. I guess it was because of the drugs."

Dr Ruckerman checked her watch and her notes. "I think next time we should talk less about him and more about you."

Nicki opened another bottle of French champagne and started to pour. "Sean—where's your glass?"

"Two's my limit tonight," Sean begged off. "I got to get home to the wife and kids."

"Shit! You and Mercy got kids?"

"Soon, I hope. We're working on it. But she's expecting me. Working late herself."

The studio was crowded and just a bit sweaty, and the party was ready to break up. Billy Spree and entourage were trying to sort out limos, the media were finishing notes and caviar, and tomorrow an interested public would know that Billy Spree was reforming The Terminators with Sean O'Brien doing lead vocals. Billy Spree could raise the dead with his guitar, but there his genius ended, and by now even he knew it.

"Where's she at?" Nicki poured champagne onto his foot. "We'll take a limo and go pick her up."

"Got a presentation to finish. Mercy's turned yuppie on us."

"Shit." Nicki missed his nose with his coke spoon, passed the phial to Sean. "That woman sure loves you. Can't think of anybody else who've kept together so long. Been...?"

"Married for over ten." Sean returned the phial.

"Oldest married couple on earth. What's your secret?"

"Vitamin E."

"Yeah? Really?"

"For sure. You squish the suckers open, and then you spread the oil..."

Mercedes wiped her cunt once more, then held some folded tissues there until she snugged the cotton-lined crotch of her panties securely in place. No wet seat on the cab ride back to the East Village.

Trafford remained sprawled across his office couch, watching her dress, smoking a cigarette, his cock limp upon his right thigh.

"What's the rush?"

"My husband, remember?"

"So what?"

"He'll start to raise shit if I'm not back."

"So what?"

"I told you what he's like." Mercedes fitted her breasts into her bra. "He's a drunken jealous sadist."

"Word is that you have a perfect marriage."

"Whose word? Sean's? I let him believe that. I have to. He'd hang me up by my thumbs if he thought I was in love with someone else. In love with you."

Trafford sat up on the couch. "Hey, lover. Pull off that brassiere and come back here."

He gripped her head and pushed her face onto his cock.

She readily accepted its familiar length deep into her throat. She could identify a dozen past and potential bosses purely by taste.

It was really getting late, and Mercedes was starting to feel anxious as the elevator descended from Trafford's office. The door opened, and she strode briskly across the lobby, hoping for a quick cab. Not even Sean could always be so trusting, so dense.

As Mercedes pushed into the revolving door, she saw her reflection in the glass. Somehow something seemed wrong with her image there, and then she realized that she was not looking at her reflection, but at another person confined within the glass chambers of the revolving door.

Her twin gaped back at her as they spun past. There was a shock of panic, a feeling of vertigo, and then a sense of some wrenching, of deep tearing.

And Mercedes was through the door, stumbling across the sidewalk, frantically hailing the cab that waited there.

Mercedes lay back against the seat cushions, as the feeling
Mercedes lay back against the seat cushions, as the feeling of lightheadedness began to fade. She really had been working
of lightheadedness began to fade. She really ought to cut-back too hard lately, but the response to her presentation made
on the coke and 'ludes, but it helped to get her through the all the hard work worthwhile. The senior staff were taking
living hell with Sean. At least Trafford was a good fuck, and note of her abilities, and there was a lot of talk of a major
office gossip indicated she could ride him to a senior vice- promotion.
presidency.
Sean would be so proud of her, and she'd work even harder
Sean *would be a problem, and it was time she left the drunken Irishman* to support their life together. Mercedes hoped his sessions
He was a washed-up loser, and Mercedes with Nicki had gone OK. Sean was a genius, and it hurt her to
rejoiced with each predictable failure. She liked wielding see his work ignored. Probably by now he was worried sick
the financial whiphand over him. Probably by now he was drunk about her. At least he knew that she was faithful to him,
and passed out in his vomit. At least he never guessed that just as she knew Sean was faithful to her.

she was fucking around, not that Sean could get it up anymore.

Mercedes was reaching for her key when Sean opened the door—relief and excitement in his face. He held a dozen red roses out to her, and he was kissing her while she tried to take them.

Mercedes let herself into the apartment and found Sean sprawled on the couch, his face bloated and angry. He had a near-empty bottle of vodka in his fist, and he staggered toward her.

"Nicki came through!" Sean told her, trying to hug her and dance at the same time. "Billy Spree picked me for his new lead with The Terminators!"

"Who you been fucking tonight, you goddamn slut!" Sean shouted, trying to hit her with the bottle. "I been waiting here all night for some dinner!"

"Sean! I knew it'd happen!"

"Sean! Keep away from me!"

Mercedes sorted out purse, roses, and Sean—kissing the latter.

Mercedes dodged the bottle, screaming at him.

"Keep your purse," Sean said. "I'm taking us out on the town."

"You're gonna pay for fucking around on me!" Sean yelled.

"Let's just stay here," Mercedes said.

"You drunken son of a bitch!" Mercedes shouted back.

Then they were together on the couch, laughing and kissing like giggling teenagers, and the roses scattered a red pattern across the rug.

Then he knocked her to the floor, where they wrestled and screamed like animals, until Sean began to bash her face with the bottle, *and a red pattern sprayed across the rug.*

Endless Night

> I runne to death, and death meets me as fast,
> And all my pleasures are like yesterday.
> —John Donne, *Holy Sonnet I*

The dream landscape always stretched out the same. It had become as familiar as the neighborhood yards of his childhood, as the condo-blighted streets of his middle years. Dreams had to have some basis in reality—or so his therapists had tried to reassure him. If this one did, it was of some unrecognized reality.

They stood upon the edge of the swamp, although somehow he understood that this had once been a river, and then a lake, as all became stagnant and began to sink. The bridge was a relic, stretched out before them to the island—on the far shore—beyond. It was a suspension bridge, from a period which he could not identify with certainty, but suspected was of the early 1930s judging by the Art Deco pylons. It seemed ludicrously narrow and wholly inappropriate for its task. As the waters had risen, or the land mass had sunk, its roadway, ridged and as gap-toothed as a railway trestle, had settled into the water's surface—so that midway across one must slosh through ankle-deep water, feeling beneath the scum for the solid segments of roadway. Spanish moss festooned the fraying cables; green lichens fringed the greener verdigris of bronze faces staring out from the rotting concrete pylons. Inscriptions, no doubt explaining their importance, were blurred beyond legibility.

It was always a breathless relief to reach the upward-sloping paving of the far end, scramble toward the deserted shoreline beyond. His chest would be aching by then, as though the warm, damp air he tried to suck into his lungs were devoid of sustenance. There were ripples in the water, not caused by any current, and while he had never seen anything within the tepid depths, he knew it was essential not to linger in crossing.

His companion or guide — he sometimes thought of her as his muse — always seemed to know the way, so he followed her. Usually she was blonde. Her bangs obscured her eyes, and he only had an impression of her face in profile — thin, with straight nose and sharp chin. He sensed that her cheekbones would be pronounced, her eyes large and watchful and widely spaced. She was barefoot. Sometimes she tugged up her skirt to hold its hem above the water, more often she was wearing only a long T-shirt over what he assumed was a swimsuit. He realized that he knew her, but he could never remember her name.

He supposed he looked like himself. The waters gave back no reflection.

It — the building — dominated the shoreline beyond. From the other side he often thought of it as an office building, possibly some sort of apartment complex. He was certain then that he could see lights shining from its many-tiered windows. It appeared to have been constructed of some salmon-hued brick, or perhaps the color was another illusion of the declining sun. It was squat, as broad as its dozen-or-more stories of height, and so polyhedral as to seem almost round. Its architecture impressed him as featureless — stark walls and windows, Bauhaus utilitarian. Either its creator had lacked any imagination or else had sacrificed external form to unguessable function.

The features of the shoreline never impressed themselves upon his memory. There was a rising of land, vague blotches of trees, undergrowth. The road dragged slowly upward toward the building. Trees overhung from either side, reaching toward one another, garlanded with hanging vines and moss—darkening skies a leaden ribbon overhead. The pavement was cracked and broken—calling to mind orphaned segments of a WPA-era two-lane highway, bypassed alongside stretches of the interstate, left to decompose into the wounded earth. Its surface was swept clean. Not disused; rather, seldom used.

Perhaps too frequently used.

If there were other structures near the building, he never noticed them. Perhaps there were none; perhaps they were simply inconsequential in comparison. Sometimes he thought of an immense office building raised out of the wilderness of an industrial park or a vast stadium born of the leveled wasteland of urban renewal, left alone and alien in a region where the *genius loci* ultimately reconquered. A barren space, encroached upon by that which was beyond, surrounded the building—sometimes grass-latticed pavement (parking lot?), sometimes a scorched and eroded barrier of weeds (ground zero?).

Desolation, not wholly dead.

Abandoned, not entirely forgotten.

The lights in the windows, which he was certain he had seen from across the water, never shone as they entered.

There was a wire fence, sometimes: barbed wire leaning from its summit, or maybe insulated balls of brown ceramic nestling high-voltage lines. No matter. All was rusted, corroded, sagging like the skeletal remains that rotted at its base. When there was a fence at all.

If there was a fence, gaps pierced the wire barrier like the rotted lace of a corpse's mantilla. Sometimes the gate lay in wreckage beneath its graffitied arch: Abandon Hope. Joy Through Work. War Is Peace. Ask Not.

My Honor Is Loyalty.

One of his dreams is a fantasy of Nazis.

He knows that they are Nazis because they are all wearing Jack boots and black uniforms, SS insignia and swastika armbands, monocles and Luger pistols. And there are men in slouch-brim hats and leather overcoats, all wearing thick glasses—Gestapo, they have to be. White-clad surgeons with button-up-the-back surplices, each one resembling Lionel Atwill, suck glowing fluids into improbable hypodermics, send tentative spurts pulsing from their needles.

Monocles and thick-lensed spectacles and glass-hard blue eyes peer downward. Their faces are distorted and hideous—as if he, or they, someone, is viewing this perspective through a magnifying glass. The men in black uniforms are goose-stepping and Heil-Hitlering in geometric patterns behind the grinning misshapen faces of the doctors.

The stairway is of endless black marble, polished to a mirror-sheen, giving back no reflection. The SS officers, alike as a thousand black-uniformed puppets, are goose-stepping in orderly, powerful ranks down the polished stairway. Toward them, up the stairway, a thousand blonde and blue-eyed Valkyries, sequin-pantied and brass-brassiered, flaxen locks bleached and bobbed and marcelled, are marching in rhythm—a Rockette chorus line of Lorelei.

Wir werden weiter marschieren,
wenn alles in Sherben fällt,
denn heute gehört uns Deutschland
und morgen die ganze Welt!
Needles plunge downward.
Inward.
Distancing.

Der Führer leans and peers inward. He wipes the needles with his tongue and snorts piggishly. *Our final revenge*, Hitler promises, in a language he seems to understand. The dancers merge upon the stairway, form a thousand black-and-white swastikas as they twist their flesh together into DNA coils.

Sieg Heil!
Someday.

A thousand bombs burn a thousand coupled moths into a thousand flames.

A thousand, less one.

Distance.

While he hated and feared all of his fantasies, he usually hated and feared this one worst of all. When he peered through the windows of the building, he saw rows of smokestacks belching uncounted souls into the recoiling sky.

But often there was no fence. Only a main entrance.

A Grand Entrance. Glass and aluminum and tile. Uncorroded, but obscured by thin dust. A receptionist's desk. A lobby of precisely arranged furniture—art moderne or coldly functional—nonetheless serving no function in the sterile emptiness.

No one to greet him, to verify an appointment, to ask for plastic cards and indecipherable streams of numbers. He always thought of this as some sort of hospital, possibly abandoned in the panic of some unleashed plague virus.

He always avoided the lifts. (Shouldn't he think of them as elevators?) Instead he followed her through the deserted (were they ever occupied?) hallways and up the hollow stairwell that gave back no echo to their steps.

There is another fantasy that he cannot will away.

He is conscious of his body in this fantasy, but no more able to control his body than to control his fantasy.

He is small—a child, he believes, looking at the boyish arms and legs that are restrained to the rails of the hospital bed, and examining the muted tenderness in the faces of the white-clad supplicants who insert the needles and apply the electrodes to his flesh.

Electric current makes a nova of his brain. Thoughts and memories scatter like a deck of cards thrown against the sudden wind. Drugs hold his raped flesh half-alert against the torture. Smoke-stacks spew forth a thousand dreams. All must be arranged in a New Order.

A thousand cards dance in changing patterns across his vision. Each card has a face, false as a waxen mask. His body strains against the leather cuffs; his scream is taken by a soggy wad of tape on a wooden paddle.

The cards are telling him something, something very essential. He does not have time to read their message.

I'm not *a fortune-teller!* he screams at the shifting patterns of cards. The wadded tape steals his protests.

The rape is over. They are wheeling him away

The cards filter down from their enhanced freedom, falling like snowflakes in a dying dream.

And then he counts them all.

All are there. And in their former order.

Order must be maintained.

The Old Order is stronger.

But he knows—almost for certain—that he has never been a patient in any hospital. Ever.

His health is perfect. All too perfect.

She always led him through the maze within—upward, onward, forward. The Eternal Female/Feminine Spirit-Force. Goethe's personal expression of the ultimate truth of human existence—describing a power that transcended and revoked an informed commitment to damnation—translated awkwardly into pretentious nonsense in English. He remembered that he had never read Goethe, could not understand a word of German.

His therapists said it was a reaction to his adoption in infancy as a German war orphan by an American family. The assertive and anonymous woman represented his natural mother, whom he had never known. But his birth certificate proved that he had been born to unexceptional middle-class American parents in Cleveland, Ohio.

And his memories of them were as faded and unreal as time-leached color slides. Memories fade before light, and into night.

False memories. Reality a sudden celluloid illusion.

Lightning rips the night.

Doctor! It's alive!

Another fantasy evokes (or is invoked by, say his therapists) visions of *Macbeth*, of scary campfire stories, of old films scratched and eroded from too many showings. His (disremembered) parents (probably) only allowed him to partake of the first, but Shakespeare knew well the dark side of dreams.

Sometimes he is on a desolate stretch of moor, damp and furred with tangles of heather. (He supposes it is heather, remembering Macbeth.) Or perhaps he is on a high mountain, with barren rocks thrusting above dark forest. (He insists that he has never read *Faust*, but admits to having seen *Fantasia*.) Occasionally he stands naked within a circle of standing stones, huge beneath the empty sky. (He confesses to having read an article about Stonehenge.) And in this same Gothic context, he has another such fantasy, and he never speaks of its imperfectly remembered fragments to anyone — not to lovers, therapists, priests, or his other futile confidants.

It is, again (to generalize), a fantasy in which he is the observer. Passive, certainly. Helpless, to be sure. But the restraints hold a promise of power to be feared, of potential to be unleashed.

Hooded figures surround him, center upon his awareness. Their cloaks are sometimes dark and featureless, sometimes fantastically embroidered and colored. He never sees their faces.

He never sees himself, although he senses he stands naked and vulnerable before them.

He is there. In their midst. *They* see him.

It is all that matters.

They reach/search/take/give/violate/empower.

There is no word in English.

His therapists tell him this is a homosexual rape fantasy.

There is no word in any language.

There is only the power.

The stairway climbed inexorably as she led him upward into the building. Returning — and they always returned, he knew now — the descent would be far more intolerable, for he would have his thoughts to carry with him.

A stairwell door: very commonplace usually (a Hilton or a Hyatt?), but sometimes of iron-bound oak, or maybe no more than a curtain. No admonition. No advice. On your own. He would have welcomed *Fire Exit Only* or *Please Knock*.

She always opened the door — some atavistic urge of masculine courtesy always surfaced, but he was never fast enough or certain enough—and she held it for him, waiting and demanding.

Beyond, there was always the same corridor, circling and enclosing the building. If there was any significance to the level upon which they had emerged, it was unknown to him. She might know, but he never asked her. It terrified him that she might know.

There is innocence, if not guiltlessness, in randomness.

He decided to look upon the new reality beyond the darkened windows of the corridor. She was impatient, but she could not deny him this delay, this respite.

Outside the building he saw stretches of untilled farmland, curiously demarcated by wild hedgerows and stuttering walls of toppled stone. He moved to the next window and saw only a green expanse of pasture, its grassy limitlessness ridged by memories of ancient fields and villages.

He paused here, until she caught at his arm, pulled him away. The next window—only a glimpse—overlooked a city that he was given no time to recognize, had he been able to do so through the knowledge of the fire that consumed it.

There were doors along the other side of the corridor. He pretended that some might open upon empty apartments, that others led to vacant offices. Sometimes there were curtained recesses that suggested confessionals, perhaps secluding some agent of a higher power—although he had certainly never been a Catholic, and such religion that he recalled only underscored the futility of redemption.

She drew aside a curtain, beckoned him to enter.

He moved past her, took his seat.

Not a confessional. He had known that. He always knew where she would lead him.

The building was only a façade, changing as his memory decayed and fragmented, recognizing only one reality in a dream-state that had consumed its dreamer.

A stadium. A coliseum. An arena.

Whatever its external form, it inescapably remained unchanged in its function.

This time the building's interior was a circular arena, dirt-floored and ringed by many tiers of wooden bleachers. The wooden benches were warped and weathered silver-gray. Any paint had long since peeled away, leaving splinters and rot. The building was only a shell, hollow as a whitened skull, encircled by derelict rows of twisted benches and sagging wooden scaffolding.

The seats were all empty. The seats had been empty, surely, for many years.

He sensed a lingering echo of "Take Me Out to the Ball Game" played on a steam calliope. Before his time. Casey at the bat. This was Muddville. Years after. Still no joy.

He desperately wished for another reality, but he knew it would always end the same. The presentations might be random, might have some unknowable significance. What mattered was that he knew where he really was and why he was here.

Whether he wanted to be here was of no consequence.

She suggested, as always. *The woman at the bank who wouldn't approve the car loan. Send for her.*

She was only doing her job.

But you hated her in that moment. And you remember that hatred.

Involuntarily, he thought of her.

The numberless windows of the building's exterior pulsed with light.

A window opened.

Power, not light, sent through. And returned.

And the woman was in the arena. Huddled in the dirt, too confused to sense fear.

The unseen crowd murmured in anticipation.

He stared down at the woman, concentrating, channeling the power within his brain.

She screamed, as invisible flames consumed her being. Her scream was still an echo when her ashes drifted to the ground.

He looked for movement among the bleachers. Whatever watched from there remained hidden.

Another, she urged him.

He tried to think of those who had created him, this time to send for them. But the arena remained empty. Those he hated above all others were long beyond the vengeance of even his power.

Forget them. There are others.

But I don't hate them.

If not now, then soon you will. There is an entire world to hate.

And, he understood, too many nights to come.

> Some are Born to sweet delight,
> Some are Born to Endless Night.
> —William Blake, *Auguries of Innocence*

An Awareness of Angels

He surrendered so meekly. It was over so quietly. It was anticlimactic.

Sheriff Jimmy Stringer certainly thought so. "Please." And there were tears quavering his voice, but his hand with the .357 was steady. "Please. Just try something. Please try something."

But the killer just stood there placidly in the glare of their lights, blood-smeared surgical gloves raised in surrender.

In the back of his van they could see the peppermint-stripe body of the fourteen-year-old hooker, horribly mutilated and neatly laid out on a shower curtain. Another few minutes, and all would be bundled up tidily—destined shortly thereafter for a shallow grave in some pine-and-scrub wasteland, or perhaps a drop from a bridge with a few cinder blocks for company. Like the other eleven they had so far been able to find.

"Please. Do it," begged Stringer. One of the eleven had been an undercover policewoman, and that had been Stringer's idea. "Come on. *Try* something."

But already there were uniformed bodies crowding into the light. Handcuffs flashed and clacked, and someone began reading the kid his rights.

"Steady on there, Jimmy. You're not Clint Eastwood." Dr Nathan Hodgson's grip on his shoulder was casual, but surprisingly strong.

His own hand suddenly shaking, Stringer slowly lowered his Smith & Wesson, gently dropped its hammer, and returned the revolver to the holster at his side. His belt was a notch tighter now, needed one more. He'd lost fifteen of his two hundred pounds during the long investigation, despite a six-pack every night to help him sleep.

More sirens were curdling the night, and camera flashes made grotesque strobe effects with the flashing lights of police and emergency vehicles. They'd already shoved the killer—the suspect—into one of the county cars.

Stringer let out a shuddering breath and faced the forensic psychiatrist. Dr Hodgson looked too much like a television evangelist for his liking, but Stringer had to admit they'd never have nailed this punk tonight without the shrink's help. *Modus operandi* was about as useful as twenty-twenty hindsight; Hodgson had been able to study the patterns and to predict where the psycho most likely would strike again. Like hunting a rabbit with beagles: wait till it runs around by you again—then, *bang*.

"Suppose now that we caught this little piece of shit, you'll do your best to prove he's crazy, and all he needs is some tender loving care for a couple of months."

Stringer's freckled face was sweaty, and he looked ready to hit someone. "Dammit, Nate! They'll just turn the fucker loose and call him a responsible member of society. Let him kill and kill again!"

Dr Hodgson showed no offense. "If he's guilty, then he'll pay the penalty. I don't make the laws."

An old excuse, but works every time. Stringer tried to spit, found his mouth too dry. The bright flashes of light hurt his eyes. Like kicking over a long-dead dog on the side of the road. Just a bunch of wriggling lumps, all bustling about a black Chevy van and the vivisected thing in its belly. Lonely piece of two-lane blacktop, an old county road orphaned by the new lake. Old farm fields overrun with cedar and briar and a couple years' growth of pine and sumac. Probably a good place to hunt rabbits. He had half a beer in his car.

"Neither do I," Stringer said heavily "I just try to enforce them."

Right off the TV reruns, but he was too tired to be clever. He hoped some asshole deputy hadn't used his beer can for an ashtray.

His name was Matthew Norbrook, and he wanted to make a full confession. So they'd only found a dozen? He'd show them where to look for the rest. If he could remember them all. The ones in this end of the state. Would they like to know about the others? Maybe the ones in other states?

Too easy, and they weren't taking chances on blowing this case due to some technicality. The judge ordered a psychiatric examination for the next morning.

Dr Nathan Hodgson was in charge.

There were four of them in the observation room, watching through the two-way mirror as Dr Hodgson conducted his examination. Morton Bowers was the court-appointed defense attorney—a gangling black man cleanly dressed in an off-the-rack mill-outlet suit that didn't really fit him. Cora Steinman was the local D.A., and her businesswoman's power suit fit her very well indeed. Dr something Gottlieb—Stringer hadn't remembered her first name—was wearing a shapeless white lab coat and alternated between scribbling notes and fooling with the video recording equipment. Stringer was wearing his uniform for a change—none too neat, and that wasn't a change—partly to show that this was official business, but mainly to remind these people that he was in charge here, at least for now. A further reminder, two of Stringer's deputies were standing just outside in the hallway. In charge for now: the state boys would be crowding in soon, and probably the FBI next.

Stringer sipped on his coffee. It reminded him of watching some bad daytime drama on the big projection TV they had in the bar at the new Trucker's Heaven off I-40—actually their sign read "Haven," but try to tell that to anyone. Stringer wished for a smoke, but they'd all jumped on his case when he'd earlier pulled out a pack. It had all been boring thus far: preliminaries and legal technicalities. Stringer supposed it all served some purpose.

Trouble was, you could be damn sure that the purpose was to make certain this murdering little pervert got off scot-free. Stringer just wished they'd leave him alone in a room with the filthy creep—two-way mirrors or not. He might be pushing fifty, but...

An Awareness of Angels · 109

"Before we go any further," Norbrook was saying, "I want it perfectly understood that I consider myself to be entirely sane."

He was wearing orange county-jail coveralls—Dr Hodgson had insisted that they remove the handcuffs—but he still managed the attitude of having kindly granted this interview. His manner was condescending, his speech pedantic to the point of arrogance.

Some bright little college punk, Stringer judged—probably high on drugs most of the time. About thirty, and tall, dark, and handsome. Just like they say. He'd have no problem picking up girls: Let's climb into my van and snort a little coke. Here, try on this gag while I get out my knives. Stringer knotted his heavy fists and glared at that TV-star nose and smiling mouth of toothpaste-ad teeth.

"Are you sometimes concerned that other people might not think that you are entirely sane?" Dr Hodgson asked him.

The psychiatrist was wearing a three-piece suit that probably cost more than Stringer's pickup truck. He was almost twice the age of the suspect—of his patient—but had the distinguished good looks and gray-at-the-temples pompadour that seemed to turn on women from teeny-boppers to golden-agers. Stringer had heard enough gossip to know that Hodgson was sure no fairy, and maybe there was a dent or two in the old Hippocratic Oath back up North that had made the doc content to relocate here in a rural Southern county.

Norbrook's smile was supercilious. "Please, Dr...Hodgson, is it? We can dispense with the how-do-you-feel-about-that? routine. My concern is that the story I propose to tell may at first sound completely mad. That's why I asked for this interview. I had hoped that a psychiatrist might have the intelligence to listen without preconception or ignorant incredulity. All Sheriff Andy of Mayberry and his redneck deputies here seem capable of understanding is a body count, and that rather limits them to their ten fingers."

Stringer dreamed of sharing Norbrook's ten fingers with a sturdy brick. Afterward they'd slip into those surgical gloves just like Jell-O going into a fancy mold.

"This story you want to tell me must seem very important to you," Dr Hodgson said.

"Important to the entire human race," Norbrook said levelly. "That's why I decided to surrender when I might have escaped through the brush. I didn't want to risk the chance that a bullet would preserve their secrets."

"Their secrets?"

"All right. I'm perfectly aware that you're fully prepared to dismiss everything I'm about to tell you as paranoid fantasy. And I'm perfectly aware that paranoid schizophrenics have no doubt sat here in this same chair and offered this same protest. All I ask is that you listen with an open mind. If I weren't able to furnish proof of what I'm about to tell you, I'd never have permitted myself to be captured. Agreed?"

"Suppose you begin at the beginning."

"It began a hundred years ago. No, to be precise, it began before history—perhaps at the dawn of the human race. But my part of the story begins a century ago in London.

"My great-grandfather was Jack the Ripper."

Norbrook paused to study the effect of his words.

Hodgson listened imperturbably. He never made notes during an interview; it was intrusive, and it was simpler just to play back the tape.

Stringer muttered, "Bullshit!" and crumpled his coffee cup.

"I suppose," continued Norbrook, "that many people will say that madness is inherited."

"Is that how you sometimes feel?" Hodgson asked.

"My great-grandfather wasn't mad, you see—and that's the crux of it all."

Norbrook settled back in his chair, smiling with the air of an Agatha Christie detective explaining a locked-room murder.

"My great-grandfather—his identity has defied discovery all these years, although I intend to reveal it in good time—was a brilliant experimental surgeon of his day. Because of his research, some would have condemned him as a vivisectionist."

"Can you tell me how all of this was revealed to you?"

"Not through voices no one else can hear," Norbrook snorted. "Please, Doctor. Listen and don't interrupt with your obvious ploys.

An Awareness of Angels

My great-grandfather kept an extensive journal, made careful notes of all of his experiments.

"You see, those prostitutes—those creatures—that he killed. Their deaths were not the random murders of a deranged fiend. On the contrary, they were experimental subjects for my great-grandfather's early researches. The mutilation of their corpses was primarily a smoke screen to disguise the real purpose for their deaths. It was better that the public know him as Jack the Ripper, a murderous sex fiend, rather than a dedicated scientist whose researches were destined to expose an unsuspected malignancy as deadly to humanity as any plague bacillus."

Norbrook leaned forward in his chair—his face tense with the enormity of his disclosure.

"You must understand. They aren't *human*."

"Prostitutes, do you mean—or women in general?"

"Damn you! Don't mock me!"

Stringer started to head for the door, but Norbrook remained seated.

"Not all women," he continued. "Not all prostitutes. But *some* of them. And they're more likely by far to be hookers or those one-night-stand easy lays anyone can pick up in singles bars. Liberated women! I'm certain that *they* engineered this so-called sexual revolution."

"They?"

"Yes, *they*. The proverbial *they*. The legendary *they*. They really are in legend, you know."

"I'm not certain if I follow entirely. Could you perhaps…?"

"Who was Adam's first wife?"

"Eve, I suppose."

"*Wrong.*" Norbrook leveled a finger. "It was Lilith, so the legend goes. Lilith—a lamia, a night creature—Adam's mate before the creation of Eve, the first woman. Lilith was the mother of Cain, who slew Abel, the first child born of two human parents. It was the offspring of Lilith that introduced the taint of murder and violence into the blood of mankind."

"Do you consider yourself a Creationist, Mr Norbrook?"

Norbrook laughed. "Far from it. I'm afraid I'm not your textbook religious nut, Dr Hodgson. I said we were speaking of legends—but there must be a basis for any legend, a core of truth imperfectly interpreted by the minds of those who have experienced it.

"There's a common thread that runs through legends of all cultures. What were angels really? Why are they generally portrayed as feminine? Why was mankind warned to beware of receiving angels unawares? Why are witches usually seen as women? Why was mankind told not to suffer a witch to live? Why were the saints tormented by visions of sexual lust by demonic temptresses? What is the origin of the succubus—a female demon who copulates with sleeping men?"

"Do you sometimes feel threatened by women?"

"I've already told you. They aren't *human*."

Norbrook leaned back in his chair and studied the psychiatrist's face. Hodgson's expression was impassively attentive.

"Not *all* women, of course," Norbrook proceeded. "Only a certain small percentage of them. I'm aware of how this must sound to you, but consider this with an open mind.

"Suppose that throughout history a separate intelligent race has existed alongside mankind. Its origin is uncertain: parallel evolution, extraterrestrial, supernatural entities—as you will. What is important is that such a race does exist—a race that is parasitic, inimical, and undetectable. Rather, was undetectable until my great-grandfather discovered their existence.

"They are virtually identical to the human female. Almost always they are physically attractive, and always their sexual appetites are insatiable. They become prostitutes not for monetary gain, but out of sexual craving. With today's permissive society, many of them choose instead the role of a hot-to-trot pickup: two beers in a singles bar, and it's off to the ball. Call them fast or easy or nymphos—but they won't be the ones complaining about it on your couch, Doctor."

Dr Hodgson shifted himself in his chair. "Why do you think these women are so sexually promiscuous?"

An Awareness of Angels · 113

"The answer is obvious. Their race is self-sterile. Think of them as some sort of hybrid, and you'll understand a hybrid of human form and alien intelligence. To reproduce they require human sperm, and constant inseminations are required before the right conditions for fertilization are met. It's the same with other hybrids. Fortunately for us, reproduction is difficult for them, or they'd have reduced humanity to mere breeding stock long ago.

"They use mankind as cuckoos do other birds, placing their eggs in nests of other species to be nurtured at the expense of natural hatchlings. This is the truth behind the numerous legends of changelings—human-appearing infants exchanged in the crib for natural offspring, and the human infant carried away by malevolent elves or fairies. Remember that elves and fairies are more often objects of fear in the older traditions, rather than the cutesy cartoon creatures of today. It's hardly coincidence that elves and fairies are usually thought of as feminine."

"This is a fucking waste of time!" Stringer muttered—then responded, "Beg pardon, ladies," to Dr Gottlieb's angry "Shh!"

To Stringer's disgust, Dr Hodgson seemed to be taking it all in. "Why do you think they only take the shape of women?"

"We've considered that," Norbrook said. "Possibly for some reason only the female body is suited for their requirements. Another reason might be a genetic one: only female offspring can be produced."

"When you say 'we' do you sometimes feel that there are others who have these same thoughts as you do?"

"All right, I didn't really expect you to accept what I've told you as fact. I asked you to keep an open mind, and I ask that you continue to do so. I am able to prove what I'm telling you.

"By 'we' I mean my great-grandfather and those of our family who have pursued his original research."

"Could you tell me a little more about what you mean by research?"

"My great-grandfather made his initial discovery quite by accident—literally. A prostitute who had been run over by a carriage was brought into his surgery. She was terribly injured; her pelvis was crushed, and she was unconscious from skull injuries. Her lower abdomen had been laid open, and he worked immediately to try to stop the profuse bleeding there. To his dismay, his patient regained consciousness during the surgery. His assistant hastened to administer more ether, but too late. The woman died screaming under the knife, although considering the extent of her injuries, she could hardly have noticed the scalpel.

"Her uterus had been ruptured, and it was here that my great-grandfather was at work the moment of her death. His efforts there continued with renewed energy, although by now his surgical exploration was clearly more in the nature of an autopsy. When his assistant set aside the ether and rejoined him, my great-grandfather described a sort of lesion which he characterized as an 'amoeboid pustulance' that had briefly appeared under his blade at the moment of her death agony. The lesion had then vanished in the welter of blood—rather like an oyster slipping from the fork and into the tomato sauce, to use his expression—and subsequent diligent dissection could reveal no trace of it. His assistant had seen nothing, and my great-grandfather was forced to attribute it to nervous hallucination.

"He might have dismissed the incident had not he been witness to a railway smashup while on holiday. Among the first to rush to the aid of the victims, he entered the wreckage of a second-class carriage where a woman lay screaming. Shards of glass had virtually eviscerated her, and as he tried to staunch the bleeding with her petticoats, he again saw a glimpse of a sort of ill-defined purulent mass sliding through the ruin of her perineum just at the instant of her final convulsion. He sought after it, but found no further trace—these were hardly ideal conditions—until other rescuers drew him to the aid of other victims. Later he conducted a careful autopsy of the woman, without success. It was then that he learned the victim had been a notorious prostitute.

"Despite my great-grandfather's devotion to medical research, he was a man of firm religious convictions. In deliberating over what he had twice seen, he considered at first that he had witnessed physical evidence of the human soul, liberated in the instant of death. I won't bore you with details of the paths he followed with his initial experiments to establish this theory; they are all recorded in his journals. It soon became evident that this transient mass—this entity—manifested itself only at the moment of violent death.

"Prostitutes seemed natural subjects for his research. They were easily led into clandestine surroundings; they served no good purpose in the world; they were sinful corrupters of virtue—undeserving of mercy. Moreover, that in both cases when he had witnessed the phenomenon the victims had been prostitutes was a circumstance not lost upon my great-grandfather—or Jack the Ripper, as he was soon to be known.

"He was unsuccessful in most of his experiments, but he put it down to imprecise technique and the need for haste. Fortunately for him, not all of his subjects were discovered. Mary Ann Nichols was his first near-success, then nothing until Catherine Eddowes. With Mary Jane Kelly he had time to perform his task carefully, and afterward he was able to formulate a new theory.

"It wasn't the human soul that he had glimpsed. It was a corporeal manifestation of evil—a possession, if you prefer—living within the flesh of sinful harlots. It was an incarnation of Satan's power taken seed within woman—woman, who brought about mankind's fall from grace—for the purpose of corrupting innocence through the lure of wanton flesh. This malignant entity became fleetingly visible only at the instant of death through sexual agony—rather like rats fleeing a sinking ship, or vermin deserting a corpse."

Norbrook paused and seemed to want to catch his breath.

"I use my great-grandfather's idiom, of course. We've long since abandoned that Victorian frame of reference."

Dr Hodgson glanced toward the two-way mirror and adjusted his tie. "How did you happen to come into possession of this journal?"

"My great-grandfather feared discovery. As quickly as discretion allowed, he emigrated to the United States. Here, he changed his name and established a small practice in New York. By then he had become more selective with his experimental subjects—and more cautious about the disposal of their remains.

"He was, of course, a married man—Jack the Ripper was, after all, a dedicated researcher and not a deranged misogynist—and his son, my grandfather, grew up to assist him in his experiments. After my great-grandfather's death shortly before the First World War, my grandfather returned to England in order to serve as an army field surgeon in France. The hostilities furnished ample opportunity for his research, as well as a cover for any outrage that may have occurred. Blame it on the Hun.

"It was my grandfather's opinion that the phenomenon was of an ectoplasmic nature, and he attempted to study it as being a sort of electrical force. He married an American nurse at the close of the war and returned to New York, where my father was born. By now, my grandfather's researches had drifted entirely into the realm of spiritualism, and his journals, preserved alongside my great-grandfather's, are worth reading only as curiosa. He died at the height of the Depression—mustard gas had damaged his lungs—discredited by his peers and remembered as a harmless crank.

"It was intended that my father should follow the family tradition, as they say. He was working his way through medical school at the time of Pearl Harbor. During his college days, his pro-Nazi sentiments had made him unpopular with some of his classmates, but like many other Americans he was quick to enlist once bombs and tanks replaced political rhetoric. His B-17 was shot down over France early on, and he spent the remainder of the war in various prison camps. After the fall of Berlin, my father was detained for some time by the Russians, who had liberated the small prison camp where he was assisting in the hospital. There was talk of collaboration and atrocities, but the official story was that the Russians had grabbed him up along with all the other German scientists engaged in research there. My father was a minor Cold War hero when the Russians finally released him.

"He left the Army and resettled in southern California, where he married my mother and spent his remaining reclusive years on her father's citrus farm. His manner was that of a hunted fugitive, and he had a great fear of strangers—eccentricities the locals attributed to the horror of German and Russian prison camps. His journals recounting his wartime experiences, fragmentary as they are, show that he had good reason to feel hunted. By the time I was born, a decade after the war, there were rumors of newly declassified documents that linked my father to certain deplorable experiments regarding tests for racial purity—performed under his direction. I'm afraid my father was rather obsessed with the concept of Aryan superiority, and his research was vitiated by this sort of tunnel vision. It was about the time they got Eichmann when they found him hanging in the orange grove. They ruled it suicide, although there was talk of Nazi hunters. I know better.

"So did my mother. She sold the farm, bundled me up, and left for Oregon. I heard that afterward the whole place was burned to the ground. My mother never told me how much she knew. She hardly had the chance: I ran off to San Francisco early in my teens to join the Haight-Ashbury scene. When I hitched my way home five years later, I found that my mother had been murdered during a burglary. There was insurance money and a trust fund—enough for college and a medical education, though they threw me out after my third year. Her lawyers had a few personal items as well, held in trust for my return. My great-grandfather's Bible didn't interest me, until I untied the cord and found the microfiche of the journals tucked into a hollow within.

"I suppose they got the originals and didn't concern themselves with me. In any event, I covered my tracks, got a formal education. Living on the streets for five years had taught me how to survive. In time I duplicated their experiments, avoided all the blind alleys their preconceptions had led them down, formed conclusions of my own.

"It's amazing just how really easy it is these days to pick up a woman and take her to a place of privacy—and I assure you that they all came willingly. After the first it was obvious that the subjects had to want to be fucked. No, kidnapping was counterproductive, although I had to establish a few baselines first. They're all the same wherever you go, and I should know. Over the past few years

I've killed them all across the country—a few here, a few there, keep on moving. In all this time I've been able to establish positive proof in about one case out of twenty"

"Proof?"

"Portable VCRs are a wonderful invention. No messy delays with developing film, and if you draw a blank, just record over it on the next experiment. You have to have the camera exactly right; the alien presence—shall we consider it an inhuman ovum?—exudes from the uterus only in the instant of violent death, then dissipates through intracellular spaces within the dead tissue. I've come to the conclusion that this inhuman ovum is a sentient entity on some level, seeking to escape dissolution at the moment of death. Or is it trying to escape detection? I wonder."

"There were videocassettes found in your van."

"Useless tapes. I've put the essential tapes in a safe place along with the microfiches."

"A safe place?"

"I've already told my attorney how to find them. The judge tried to appoint a woman attorney to defend me, you know, but I saw the danger there."

"You say you allowed yourself to be captured. Wasn't some part of you frightened?"

"I have the proof to expose them. My forebears lacked the courage of their misguided convictions. Personal safety aside, I feel that I have a duty to the human race."

"Do you see yourself as handing this trust on to your son?"

"I have no children, if that's what you mean. Knowing what I do, I find the idea of inseminating any woman totally abhorrent."

"Tell what you remember most about your mother?"

Norbrook stood up abruptly. "I said no psychiatric games, Dr Hodgson. I've told you all I need to in order to establish my sanity and motives. That's all a part of legal and medical record now. I think this interview is terminated."

The door opened as Norbrook arose. He turned, with cold dignity permitted the deputies to cuff his wrists.

Stringer stopped the psychiatrist as he followed the others into the hallway. The sheriff scowled after Norbrook as his deputies led him away to the car.

"Well, Doc—what do you think?"

"You heard it all, didn't you?"

Stringer dug out a cigarette. "Craziest line of bullshit I ever listened to. Guess he figures he can plead insanity if he makes up a load of crap like that."

Dr Hodgson shook his head. "Oh, Matthew Norbrook's insane—no doubt about it. He's a classic paranoid schizophrenic: well-ordered delusional system, grandiosity, feelings of superiority, sense of being persecuted, belief that his actions are done in the name of a higher purpose. On an insanity scale of one to three, I'd have to rate him as four-plus. He'll easily be found innocent by reason of insanity."

"Damn!" Stringer muttered, watching Norbrook enter the elevator.

"The good news, at least from the patient's point of view," Hodgson went on, "is that paranoid schizophrenia so easily responds to treatment. Why, with the right medication and some expert counseling, Matthew Norbrook will probably be out of the hospital and living a normal life in less than a year."

Stringer's hand shook as he drew on the cigarette. "It isn't *justice*, Nate!"

"Perhaps not, Jimmy, but it's the way the law works. And look at it this way—the dead don't care whether their murderer is executed or cured. Norbrook may yet live to make a valuable contribution to society. Give me one of those, will you?"

Stringer hadn't known the doctor smoked. "The dead don't care," he repeated.

"Thanks, Jimmy." Hodgson shook out a Marlboro. "I know how you must feel. I saw a little of what was on that one videocassette—the one where he tortured that poor policewoman, Sherri Wilson. Hard to believe she could have remained conscious through it all. Guess it was the cocaine he used on her. Must have really been tough on you, since you talked her into posing as a hooker to try and trap him. It's understandable that you're feeling a lot of guilt about it. If you'd like to come around and talk about it sometime..."

Hodgson was handing back the cigarettes, but already Stringer had turned his back and walked off without another word.

Cora Steinman, the district attorney, stepped out from the doorway of the observation room. She watched the elevator doors close behind Stringer.

"I hope you know what you're doing," she said finally.

Dr Hodgson crushed his unsmoked cigarette into the sand of a hallway ash can. "I know my man."

From the parking lot, the report of the short-barreled .357 echoed like cannon fire against the clinic walls.

"Morton, you've taken care of the journals?" Hodgson asked.

The black defense attorney collected his briefcase. "I took care of *everything*. His collection of evidence is now a couple of books on Jack the Ripper, a bunch of S&M porno, and a couple of snuff films."

"Then it's just a matter of the tape from the interview."

"I think there's been a malfunction in the equipment," Dr Gottlieb decided.

"It pays to be thorough," Steinman observed.

A deputy flung open the stairway door. He was out of breath. "Norbrook tried to escape. Had a knife hidden on him. Jimmy had to shoot."

"I'll get the emergency tray!" Dr Hodgson said quickly.

"Hell, Doc." The deputy paused for another breath. "Just get a hose. Most of the sucker's head is spread across your parking lot."

"I'll get the tray anyway," Hodgson told him.

He said to the others as the deputy left, "Must keep up appearances."

"Why," Steinman wondered, as they walked together toward the elevator, "why do you suppose he was so convinced that we only exist as females?"

Dr Hodgson shrugged. "Just a male chauvinist *human*."

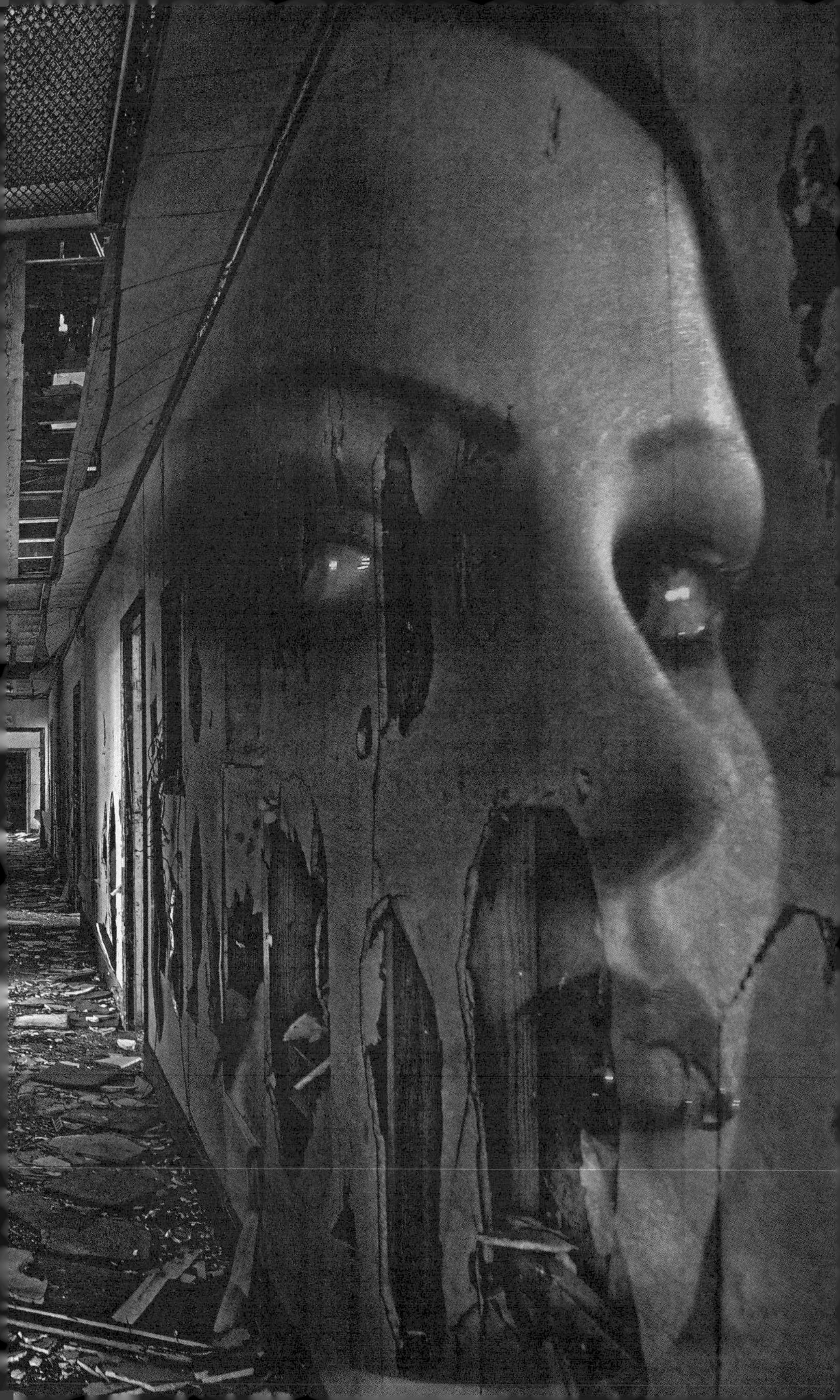

But You'll Never Follow Me

It wasn't the smell of death that he hated so much. He'd grown used to that in Nam. It was the smell of dying that tore at him. Slow dying.

He remembered his best buddy stuck to the paddy mud, legless and eviscerated, too deep in shock to cry out, just gulping air like a beached fish, eyes round with wonder and staring into his. Marsden had closed those eyes with his right hand and with his left he put a .45 slug through his friend's skull.

After that, he'd made a promise to himself never to kill again, but that was as true a promise as he'd ever made to anyone, and never-intended lies rotted together with never-realized truths of his best intentions.

Marsden found a moment's solitude in the slow-moving elevator as it slid upward to the fourth floor. He cracked a zippered gash into his bulky canvas flight bag, large enough to reach the pint bottle of vodka on top. He gulped down a mouthful, replaced the stopper and then replaced the flask, tugged down the zipper—all in the space of four floors. Speed was only a matter of practice. He exhaled a breath of vodka as the elevator door opened.

Perhaps the middle-aged couple who waited there noticed his breath as he shouldered past them with his bag, but Marsden doubted it. The air of Brookcrest Health Care Center was already choked with the stench of bath salts and old lady's perfume, with antiseptics and detergents and bouquets of dying flowers, and underlying it all was the veiled sweetness of urine, feces and vomit, physically retained in bedpans and diapers.

Marsden belched. A nurse in the fourth floor lounge scowled at him, but a blue-haired lady in a jerrycart smiled and waved and called after him, "Billy Boy! Billy Billy Boy!" Michael Marsden shut his eyes and turned into the hallway that led to his parents' rooms. Somewhere along the hall a woman's voice begged in feeble monotone, "Oh Lord, help me. Oh Lord, help me. Oh Lord, help me." Marsden walked on down the hall.

He was a middle-aged man with a heavy-set frame that carried well a spreading beer-gut. He had mild brown eyes, a lined and long-jawed face, and there were streaks of grey in his short beard and in his limp brown hair where it straggled from beneath the Giants baseball cap. His denim jacket and jeans were about as worn as his scuffed cowboy boots.

"You'd look a lot nicer if you'd shave that beard and get a haircut," Momma liked to nag him. "And you ought to dress more neatly. You're a good-looking boy, Michael."

She still kept the photo of him in his uniform, smiling bravely fresh out of bootcamp, on her shelf at the nursing home. Marsden guessed that that was the way Momma preferred to hold him in memory—such of her memory as Alzheimer's Disease had left her.

Not that there was much worth remembering him for since then. Certainly the rest of his family wouldn't quarrel with that judgment.

"You should have gone back to grad school once you got back," his sister in Columbus had advised him with twenty-twenty and twenty-year hindsight. "What have you done with your life instead? When was the last time you held on to a job for more than a year?"

At least she hadn't added, "Or held on to a wife?" Marsden had sipped his Coke and vodka and meekly accepted the scolding. They were seated in the kitchen of their parents' too-big house in Cincinnati, trying not to disturb Papa as he dozed in his wheelchair in the family room.

"It's bad enough that Brett and I keep having to drive down here every weekend to try to straighten things out here," Nancy had reminded him. "And then Jack's had to come down from Detroit several times since Momma went to Brookcrest, and Jonathan flew here from Los Angeles and stayed two whole weeks after Papa's first stroke. And all of us have jobs and families to keep up with. Where were you during all this time?"

"Trying to hold a job in Jersey," Marsden explained, thinking of the last Christmas he'd come home for. He'd been nursing a six-pack and the late-night movie when Momma drifted into the family room and angrily ordered him to get back to mowing the lawn. It was the first time he'd seen Momma naked in his life, and the image of that shrunken, sagging body would not leave him.

"I'm just saying that you should be doing more, Michael," Nancy continued.

"I was here when you needed me," Marsden protested. "I was here to take Momma to the nursing home."

"Yes, but that was after the rest of us did all the work—finding a good home, signing all the papers, convincing Papa that this was the best thing to do, making all the other arrangements."

"Still, I was here at the end. I did what I had to do," Marsden said, thinking that this had been the story of his life ever since the draft notice had come. Never a choice.

They hadn't wanted to upset Momma, so no one had told her about the nursing home. Secretly they'd packed her things and loaded them into the trunk of Papa's Cadillac the night before. "Just tell Momma that she's going for another check-up at the hospital," they'd told him to say, and then they had to get home to their jobs and families.

But despite her advanced Alzheimer's, Momma's memory was clear when it came to remembering doctors' appointments, and she protested suspiciously the next morning when he and Papa bundled her into the car. Momma had looked back over her shoulder at him as they wheeled her down the hall, and her eyes were shadowed with the hurt of betrayal. "You're going to leave me here, aren't you," she said dully.

The memory of that look crowded memories of Nam from his nightmares.

After that, Marsden had avoided going home. He did visit Momma briefly when Papa had his first stroke, but she hadn't recognized him.

Papa had survived his first stroke and, several months later, had surprised them all again and survived his second stroke. But that had been almost a year ago from the night Marsden and his sister had sat talking in the kitchen while Papa dozed in his wheelchair. That first stroke had left him weak on the one side; the second had taken away part of his mind. The family had tried to maintain him at home with live-in nursing care, but Papa's health slowly deteriorated, physically and mentally.

It was time to call for Michael.

And Michael came.

"Besides," Nancy reassured him, "Papa only wants to be near Momma. He still insists on trying to get over to visit her every day. You can imagine what a strain that's been on everyone here."

"I can guess," said Michael, pouring more vodka into his glass.

"Where are we going, son?" Papa had asked the next morning, as Marsden lifted him into the Cadillac. Papa's vision was almost gone now, and his voice was hard to understand.

"I'm taking you to be with Momma for awhile," Marsden told him. "You want that, don't you?"

Papa's dim eyes stared widely at the house as they backed down the driveway. He turned to face Michael. "But when are you bringing Momma and me back home again, son?"

Never, as it turned out. Marsden paused outside his mother's room, wincing at the memory. Over the past year their various health problems had continued their slow and inexorable progress toward oblivion. Meanwhile health care bills had mushroomed, eroding insurance coverage, the last of their pensions, and a lifetime's careful savings. It was time to put the old family home on the market, to make some disposal of a lifetime's possessions. It had to be done.

Papa called for Michael.

"Don't let them do this to us, son." The family held power of attorney now. "Momma and I want to go home."

So Michael came home.

The white-haired lady bent double over her walker as she inched along the hallway wasn't watching him. Marsden took a long swig of vodka and replaced the pint bottle. Momma didn't like to see him drink.

She was sitting up in her jerrycart staring at the television when Marsden stepped inside her room and closed the door. They'd removed her dinner tray but hadn't cleaned her up, and bits of food littered the front of her dressing gown. She looked up, and her sunken eyes showed recognition.

"Why, it's Michael!" She held out her food-smeared arms to him. "My baby!"

Marsden accepted her slobbery hug. "I've come for you, Momma," he whispered, as Momma began to cry.

She covered her face with her hands and continued weeping, as Marsden stepped behind her and opened his flight bag. The silencer was already fitted to the Hi-Standard .22, and Marsden quickly pumped three hollow-points through the back of his mother's head. It was over in seconds. Little noise, and surely no pain. No more pain.

Marsden left his mother slumped over in her jerrycart, picked up his canvas bag, and closed the door. Then he walked on down the hall to his father's room.

He went inside. Papa must have been getting up and falling again, because he was tied to his wheelchair by a bath towel about his waist.

"Who's that?" he mumbled, turning his eyes toward Marsden.

"It's Michael, Papa. I'm here to take you home."

Papa lost sphincter control as Marsden untied the knotted towel. He was trying to say something—it sounded like "Bless you, son"—then Marsden lovingly shot him three times through the back of his skull. Papa would have fallen out of the wheelchair, but Marsden caught him. He left him sitting upright with Monday Night Football just getting underway on the tube.

Marsden finished the vodka, then removed the silencer from the pistol and replaced the clip. Shoving the Hi-Standard into his belt, he checked over the flight bag and left it with Papa.

He heard the first screams as the elevator door slowly closed. Someone must have finally gone to clean Momma's dinner off her.

A uniformed security guard—Marsden hadn't known that

Brookcrest employed such—was trying to lock the lobby doors. A staff member was shouting into the reception desk phone.

"Hold it, please! Nobody's to leave!" The guard actually had a revolver.

Marsden shot him through the left eye and stepped over him and through the glass doors. Marsden regretted this, because he hated to kill needlessly.

Unfortunately, the first police car was slithering into the parking lot as Marsden left the nursing home. Marsden continued to walk away, even when the car's spotlight pinned him against the blacktop.

"You there! Freeze!"

They must have already been called to the house, Marsden thought. Time was short. Without breaking stride, he drew his .22 and shot out the spotlight.

There were still the parking lot lights. Gunfire flashed from behind both front doors of the police car, and Marsden sensed the impact of buckshot and 9 mm. slugs.

He was leaping for the cover of a parked car, and two more police cars were hurtling into the parking lot, when the twenty pounds of C4 he'd left with Papa went off.

The blast lifted Marsden off his feet and fragged him with shards of glass and shattered bricks. Brookcrest Health Care Center burst open like the birth of a volcano.

Two police cars were overturned, the other on fire. The nursing home was collapsing into flaming rubble. No human screams could be heard through the thunder of disintegrating brick and steel.

Marsden rolled to his feet, brushing away fragments of debris. He retrieved his pistol, but there was no need for it just now. His clothes were in a bad state, but they could be changed. There was no blood, just as he had known there would not be.

They couldn't kill him in Nam, that day in the paddy when he learned what he was and why he was. They couldn't kill him now.

Was it any easier when they were your own loved ones? Yes, perhaps it was.

Michael Marsden melted away into the darkness that had long ago claimed him.

Cedar Lane

He was back at Cedar Lane again, in the big house where he had spent his childhood, growing up there until time to go away to college. He was the youngest, and his parents had sold the house then, moving into something smaller and more convenient in a newer and nicer suburban development.

A rite of passage, but for Garrett Larkin it truly reinforced the reality that he could never go home again. Except in dream. And dreams are what the world is made of.

At times it puzzled him that while he nightly dreamed of his boyhood home on Cedar Lane, he never dreamed about any of the houses he had lived in since.

Sometimes the dreams were scary.

Sometimes more so than others.

It was a big two-story house plus basement, built just before the war, the war in which he was born. It was very solid, faced with thick stones of pink-hued Tennessee marble from the local quarries. There were three dormer windows thrusting out from the roof in front, and Garrett liked to call it the House of the Three Gables because he always thought the Hawthorne book had a neat spooky title. He and his two brothers each had his private hideout in the little dormer rooms—just big enough for shelves, boxes of toys, a tiny desk for making models or working jigsaw puzzles. Homework was not to intrude here, relegated instead to the big desk in Dad's never-used study in the den downstairs.

Cedar Lane was an old country lane, laid out probably at the beginning of the previous century along dirt farm roads. Now two narrow lanes of much-repaved blacktop twisted through a narrow gap curtained between rows of massive cedar trees. Garrett's house stood well back upon four acres of lawn, orchards, and vegetable garden—portioned off from farmland as the neighborhood shifted from rural to suburban just before the war.

It had been a wonderful house to grow up in—three boys upstairs and a sissy older sister with her own bedroom downstairs across the hall from Mom and Dad. There were two flights of stairs to run down—the other leading to the cavernous basement where Dad parked the new car and had all his shop tools and gardening equipment, and where dwelt the Molochian coal furnace named Fear and its nether realm, the monster-haunted coal cellar. The yard was bigger than any of his friends had, and until he grew old enough to have to mow the grass and cuss, it was a limitless playground to run and romp with the dogs, for ball games and playing cowboy or soldier, for climbing trees and building secret clubhouses out of boxes and scrap lumber.

Garrett loved the house on Cedar Lane. But he wished that he wouldn't dream about it *every* night. Sometimes he wondered if he might be haunted by the house. His shrink told him it was purely a fantasy—longing for his vanished childhood.

Only it wasn't. Some of the dreams disturbed him. Like the elusive fragrance of autumn leaves burning, and the fragmentary remembrance of carbonizing flesh.

Garrett Larkin was a very successful landscape architect with his own offices and partnership in Chicago. He had kept the same marvelous wife for going on thirty years, was just now putting the youngest of their three wonderful children through Antioch, was looking forward to a comfortable and placid sixth decade of life, and had not slept in his bed at Cedar Lane since he was seventeen.

Garrett Larkin awoke in his bed in the house on Cedar Lane, feeling vaguely troubled. He groped over his head for the black metal cowboy-silhouette wall lamp mounted above his bed. He found the switch, but the lamp refused to come on. He slipped out from beneath the covers, moved through familiar darkness into the bathroom, thumbed the light switch there.

He was filling the drinking glass with water when he noticed that his hands were those of an old man.

An old man's. Not his hands. Nor his the face in the bathroom mirror. Lined with too many years, too many cares. Hair gray and thinning. Nose bulbous and flecked with red blotches. Left eyebrow missing the thin scar from when he'd totaled the Volvo. Hands heavy with calluses from manual labor. No wedding ring. None-too-clean flannel pajamas, loose over a too-thin frame.

He swallowed the water slowly, studying the reflection. It *could* have been him. Just another disturbing dream. He waited for the awakening.

He walked down the hall to his brothers' room. There were two young boys asleep there. Neither one was his brother. They were probably between nine and thirteen years in age, and somehow they reminded him of his brothers—long ago, when they were all young together on Cedar Lane.

One of them stirred suddenly and opened his eyes. He looked up at the old man silhouetted by the distant bathroom light. He said sleepily, "What's wrong, Uncle Gary?"

"Nothing. I thought I heard one of you cry out. Go back to sleep now, Josh."

The voice was his, and the response came automatically. Garrett Larkin returned to his room and sat there on the edge of his bed, awaiting daylight.

Daylight came, and with it the smell of coffee and frying bacon, and still the dream remained. Larkin found his clothes in the dimness, dragged on the familiar overalls, and made his way downstairs.

The carpet was new and much of the furniture was strange, but it was still the house on Cedar Lane. Only older.

His niece was bustling about the kitchen. She was pushing the limits of thirty and the seams of her housedress, and he had never seen her before in his life.

"Morning, Uncle Gary." She poured coffee into his cup. "Boys up yet?"

Garrett sat down in his chair at the kitchen table, blew cautiously over the coffee. "Dead to the world."

Lucille left the bacon for a moment and went around to the stairway. He could hear her voice echoing up the stairwell. "Dwayne! Josh! Rise and shine! Don't forget to bring down your dirty clothes when you come! Shake a leg now!"

Martin, his niece's husband, joined them in the kitchen, gave his wife a hug, and poured himself a cup of coffee. He stole a slice of bacon. "Morning, Gary. Sleep well?"

"I must have." Garrett stared at his cup.

Martin munched overcrisp bacon. "Need to get those boys working on the leaves after school."

Garrett thought of the smell of burning leaves and remembered the pain of vaporizing skin, and the coffee seared his throat like a rush of boiling blood, and he awoke.

Garrett Larkin gasped at the darkness and sat up in bed. He fumbled behind him for the cowboy-silhouette wall lamp, couldn't find it. Then there was light. A lamp on the nightstand from the opposite side of the king-size bed. His wife was staring at him in concern.

"Gar, are you okay?"

Garrett tried to compose his memory. "It's all right...Rachel. Just another bad dream is all."

"Another bad dream? Yet another bad dream, you mean. You sure you're telling your shrink about these?"

"He says it's just nostalgic longing for childhood as I cope with advancing maturity."

"Must have been some happy childhood. Okay if I turn out the light now?"

And he was dreaming again, dreaming of Cedar Lane.

He was safe and snug in his own bed in his own room, burrowed beneath Mom's heirloom quilts against the October chill that penetrated the unheated upper story. Something pressed hard into his ribs, and he awoke to discover his Boy Scout flashlight was trapped beneath the covers—along with the forbidden E.C. horror comic books he'd been secretly reading after bedtime.

Gary thumbed on the light, turning it about his room. Its beam was sickly yellow because he needed fresh batteries, but it zigzagged reassuringly across the bedroom walls—made familiar by their airplane posters, blotchy paint-by-numbers oil paintings, and (a seasonal addition) cutout Halloween decorations of jack-o'-lanterns and black cats, broomriding witches, and dancing skeletons. The beam probed into the dormer, picking out the shelved books and treasures, the half-completed B-36 "Flying Cigar" nuclear bomber rising above a desk strewn with plastic parts and tubes of glue.

The flashlight's fading beam shifted to the other side of his room and paused upon the face that looked down upon him from beside his bed. It was a grown-up's face, someone he'd never seen before, ghastly in the yellow light. At first Gary thought it must be one of his brothers in a Halloween mask, and then he knew it was really a demented killer with a butcher knife like he'd read about in the comics, and then the flesh began to peel away in blackened strips from the spotlit face, and bare bone and teeth charred and cracked apart into evaporating dust, and Gary's bladder exploded with a rush of steam.

Larkin muttered and stirred from drunken stupor, groping beneath the layers of tattered plastic for his crotch, thinking he had pissed himself in his sleep. He hadn't, but it really wouldn't have mattered to him if he had. Something was poking him in the ribs, and he retrieved the half-empty bottle of Thunderbird. He took a pull. The wine was warm with the heat of his body, and its fumes trickled up his nose.

Larkin scooted further into his cardboard box to where its back propped against the alley wall. It was cold this autumn night—another bad winter, for sure—and he wondered if he maybe ought to crawl out and join the others around the trash fire. He had another gulp of wine, letting it warm his throat and his guts.

When he could afford it, Larkin liked to drink Thunderbird. It was a link to his boyhood. "I learned to drive in my old man's brand-new 1961 Thunderbird," he often told whoever was crouched beside him. "White 1961 Thunderbird with turquoise-blue upholstery. Power everything and fast as shit. Girls back in high school would line up to date me for a ride in that brand-new Thunderbird. I was ass-deep in pussy!"

All of that was a lie, because his father had never trusted him to drive the Thunderbird, and Larkin instead had spent his teenage years burning out three clutches on the family hand-me-down Volkswagen Beetle. But none of that really mattered in the long run, because Larkin had been drafted right after college, and the best part of him never came back from Nam.

V.A. hospitals, treatment centers, halfway houses, too many jails to count. Why bother counting? Nobody else gave a damn. Larkin remembered that he had been dreaming about Cedar Lane again. Not even rotgut wine could kill those memories. Larkin shivered and wondered if he had anything left to eat. There'd been some spoiled produce from a dumpster, but that was gone now.

He decided to try his luck over at the trash fire. Crawling out of his cardboard box, he pocketed his wine bottle and tried to remember if he'd left anything worth stealing. Probably not. He remembered instead how he once had camped out in the huge box from their new refrigerator on Cedar Lane, before the rains melted the cardboard into mush.

There were half a dozen or so of them still up, silhouetted by the blaze flaring from the oil drum on the demolition site. They weren't supposed to be here, but then the site was supposed to have been cleared off two years ago. Larkin shuffled over toward them—an identical blob of tattered refuse at one with the urban wasteland.

"Wuz happnin', bro?" Pointman asked him.

"Too cold to sleep. Had dreams. Had bad dreams."

The black man nodded understandingly and used his good arm to poke a stick into the fire. Sparks flew upward and vanished into the night. "About Nam?"

"Worse." Larkin dug out his bottle. "Dreamed I was a kid again. Back home. Cedar Lane."

Pointman took a long swallow and handed the bottle back. "Thought you told me you had a happy childhood."

"I did. As best I can remember." Larkin killed the bottle.

"That's it," Pointman advised. "Sometimes it's best to forget."

"Sometimes I can't remember who I am," Larkin told him.

"Sometimes that's the best thing, too."

Pointman hooked his fingers into an old shipping crate and heaved it into the oil drum. A rat had made a nest inside the packing material, and it all went up in a mushroom of bright sparks and thick black smoke.

Larkin listened to their frightened squeals and agonized thrashing. It only lasted for a minute or two. Then he could smell the burning flesh, could hear the soft popping of exploding bodies. And he thought of autumn leaves burning at the curbside, and he remembered the soft popping of his eyeballs exploding.

Gary Blaze sucked in a lungful of crack fumes and fought to hold back a cough. He handed the pipe to Dr Syn and exhaled. "It's like I keep having these dreams about back when I was a kid," he told his drummer. "And a lot of other shit. It gets really heavy some of the time, man."

Dr Syn was the fourth drummer during the two-decades up-and-down career of Gary Blaze and the Craze. He had been with the band just over a year, and he hadn't heard Gary repeat his same old stories quite so many times as had the older survivors. Just now they were on a very hot worldwide tour, and Dr Syn didn't want to go back to playing gigs in bars in Minnesota. He finished what was left of the pipe and said with sympathy, "Heavy shit."

"It's like some of the time I can't remember who I am," Gary Blaze confided, watching a groupie recharge the glass pipe. They had the air conditioner on full blast, and the hotel room felt cold.

"It's just all the years of being on the road," Dr Syn reassured him. He was a tall kid half Gary's age, with the obligatory long blond hair and heavy-metal gear, and getting a big start with a fading rock superstar couldn't hurt his own rising career.

"You know"—Gary swallowed a lude with a vodka chaser—"you know, sometimes I get up onstage, and I can't really remember whether I can play this thing." He patted his vintage Strat. "And I've been playing ever since I bought my first Elvis forty-five."

"'Hound Dog' and 'Don't Be Cruel,' back in 1956," Dr Syn reminded him. "You were just a kid growing up in East Tennessee."

"And I keep dreaming about that. About the old family house on Cedar Lane."

Dr Syn helped himself to another hit of Gary's crack. "It's all the years on the road," he coughed. "You keep thinking back to your roots."

"Maybe I ought to go back. Just once. You know—see the old place again. Wonder if it's still there?"

"Make it sort of a bad-rocker-comes-home gig?"

"Shit!" Gary shook his head. "I don't ever want to see the place again."

He inhaled forcefully, dragging the crack fumes deep into his lungs, and he remembered how his chest exploded in a great blast of superheated steam.

Garrett Larkin was dreaming again, dreaming of Cedar Lane.

His mother's voice awoke him, and that wasn't fair, because he knew before he fell asleep that today was Saturday.

"Gary! Rise and shine! Remember, you promised your father you'd have the leaves all raked before you watched that football game! Shake a leg now!"

"All right," he murmured down the stairs, and he whispered a couple of swear words to himself. He threw his long legs over the side of his bed, yawned and stretched, struggled into blue jeans and high school sweatshirt, made it into the bathroom to wash up. A teenager's face looked back at him from the mirror. Gary explored a few incipient zits before brushing his teeth and applying fresh Butch Wax to his flattop.

He could smell the sausage frying and the pancakes turning golden-brown as he thumped down the stairs. Mom was in the kitchen, all business in her apron and housedress, already serving up his plate. Gary sat down at the table and chugged his orange juice.

"Your father gets back from Washington tomorrow after

church," Mom reminded him. "He'll expect to see that lawn all raked clean."

"I'll get the front finished." Gary poured Karo syrup over each pancake in the stack.

"You said you'd do it all."

"But, Mom! The leaves are still falling down. It's only under those maples where they really need raking." Gary bolted a link of sausage.

"Chew your food," Mom nagged.

But it was a beautiful October morning, with the air cool and crisp, and the sky cloudless blue. His stomach comfortably full, Gary attacked the golden leaves, sweeping them up in swirling bunches with the rattling leaf-rake. Blackie, his aged white mutt, swayed over to a warm spot in the sun to oversee his work. She soon grew bored and fell asleep.

He started at the base of the pink marble front of the house, pulling leaves from under the shrubs and rolling them in windrows beneath the tall sugar maples and then onto the curb. Traffic was light this morning on Cedar Lane, and cars' occasional whizzing passage sent spirals of leaves briefly skyward from the pile. It was going faster than Gary had expected it to, and he might have time to start on the rest of the yard before lunch.

"There's really no point in this, Blackie," he told his dog. "There's just a lot more to come down."

Blackie thumped her tail in sympathy, and he paused to pat her head. He wondered how many years she had left in her, hoped it wouldn't happen until after he left for college.

Gary applied matches to the long row of leaves at the curbside. In a few minutes the pile was well ablaze, and the sweet smell of burning leaves filled the October day. Gary crossed to the front of the house and hooked up the garden hose to the faucet at the base of the wall, just in case. Already he'd worked up a good sweat, and he paused to drink from the rush of water.

Standing there before the pink marble wall, hose to his mouth, Gary suddenly looked up into the blue sky.

Of course, he never really saw the flash.

There are no cedars now on Cedar Lane, only rows of shattered and blackened stumps. No leaves to rake, only a sodden mush of dead ash. No blue October skies, only the dead gray of a long nuclear winter.

Although the house is only a memory preserved in charcoal, a section of the marble front wall still stands, and fused into the pink stone is the black silhouette of a teenaged boy, looking confidently upward.

The gray wind blows fitfully across the dead wasteland, and the burned-out skeleton of the house on Cedar Lane still mourns the loss of those who loved it and those whom it loved.

Sleep well, Gary Larkin, and dream your dreams. Dream of all the men you might have become, dream of the world that might have been, dream of all the people who might have lived—had there never been that October day in 1962.

In life I could not spare you. In death I will shelter your soul and your dreams for as long as my wall shall stand.

> What we see,
> And what we seem,
> Are but a dream,
> A dream within a dream.
> — From the Peter Weir film of
>   Joan Lindsay's novel *Picnic at Hanging Rock*

The Kind Men Like

"She was better than Betty Page," said Steinman. "We used to call her Better Page!"

He laughed mechanically at his own tired joke, then started to choke on his beer. Steinman coughed and spluttered, foam oozing down his white-goateed chin. Chelsea Gayle reached across the table and patted him urgently on his back.

"Thanks, miss. It's these cigarettes." Morrie Steinman dabbed at his face with a bar napkin, blinking his rheumy eyes. He gulped another mouthful of beer and continued: "Of course, that always made her mad. Kristi Lane didn't like to be compared to any other model—didn't matter if you told her she was ten times better. Kristi'd just pout her lips that way she'd do and tell you in a voice that'd freeze Scotch in your mouth that there was *no one* like her."

"And there wasn't," Chelsea agreed. "How long did you work with her?"

"Let's see." Steinman finished his beer and set down the empty glass with a deep sigh. Chelsea signaled to the barmaid, who was already pouring another. She guessed Steinman was a regular here. It was an autumn afternoon, and the tired SoHo bar was stagnant and deserted. Maybe soon new management would convert it into something trendy; maybe they'd just knock it down with the rest of the aging block.

"I was working freelance, mostly. Shooting photo sessions

sometimes for the magazines, sometimes for the mail-order pin-up markets, sometimes for the private photo clubs where you could get away with a lot more. Of course, 'a lot more' back in the fifties meant 'a lot less' than you can see on TV these days.

"Thank you, miss." Steinman sipped his fresh beer, watching the barmaid walk away from their booth. "I remember doing a few pin-up spreads of Kristi for Harmony Publishing back about '52 or '53—stuff for girlie magazines like *Wink* and *Eyeful* and *Titter*. They'd seem tame and corny now, but back then…"

The paunchy photographer rolled his eyes and made a smacking sound with his lips. Chelsea thought of a love-stricken geriatric Lou Costello.

"After that I shot several of her first few cover spots—magazines like *Gaze* and *Satan* and *Modern Sunbathing*. That must have been the mid-fifties. Of course, she was also doing a lot of work for the old bondage-and-fetish photo sets, same as Betty Page. I heard once that Kristi and Betty did a few sessions together, but if that's true no one I know's ever seen them."

"Did Kristi Lane do any work for Irving Klaw?"

"Not a lot that I can recall. I remember introducing them sometime about 1954, or was it 1953? I think they may have shot a few sessions—high heels and black lingerie, pin-up stuff. No bondage."

"Why not?"

"Word was that Kristi Lane was a little too wild for Klaw, who was really pretty straightlaced." Steinman wheezed at his joke. "People said that Kristi could get a little too rough on the submissive model when she had the dominant role. I know some of the girls wouldn't work with her unless they played the mistress."

"Where did she get all her work, then?"

"Mostly from the private photo clubs. And from the mail-order agencies who'd change their dropbox number every few months. You know, the ones with the ads in the back of the girlie mags for comics and photos—'the kind men like.' They could get away with murder, and poor Irving got busted and never showed so much as a bare tit in his photo sets."

While Steinman sucked down his fresh beer, Chelsea opened her attaché case and withdrew several manila envelopes. She handed them to Steinman. "What can you tell me about these?"

Each envelope contained half a dozen black-and-white four-by-fives. Steinman shuffled the photo sets. "That's Kristi Lane, all right."

The first set showed the model in various pin-up poses. The white bikini would have been too daring for its day, and Kristi Lane's statuesque figure seemed about to burst its straps. Her hair was done in her characteristic short blond pageboy, her face held her familiar pout (Bardot's was a careful copy), and her wide blue eyes were those of a fallen angel.

In the next set Kristi was shown dressed as a French maid. Her short costume exposed ruffled panties and lots of cleavage as she bent over to go about her dusting.

"I shot this one," Steinman said, licking his lips. "About 1954. She said she was twenty. Anyway, they ran it in *Beauty Parade*, I think."

Kristi was tied to a chair in the next set. She was wearing high heels, black stockings and garter belt, black satin panties and bra. A black scarf was knotted around her mouth, and her eyes begged for mercy. She was similarly clad in the next set, but this time she was lying hog-tied upon a rug. In the next, she was tied spread-eagled across a bed.

"All shot the same afternoon," Steinman judged. "Do a few costume changes, give the girl a chance to stretch between poses, and you could come up with maybe a hundred or so good stills."

The next series had Kristi wearing thigh-high patent leather boots and a matching black corset. Her maid, attired in heels, hose, and the inevitable skimpy uniform, was having trouble lacing up Kristi's boots. Over the subsequent poses, the maid was gagged and bound facedown across a table by Kristi, who then applied a hairbrush to the girl's lace-clad bottom.

"Could have been done for Klaw," said Steinman, "but none of these were. The numbers at the bottom aren't his numbering system. There were a lot of guys doing these back then. Most, you never heard of. It wasn't my thing, you gotta understand, but a buck was a buck, then same as now."

Chelsea pulled out another folder. "What about these?"

Steinman flipped through a selection of stills, color and black-and-white, four-by-fives and eight-by-tens. In most of them, Kristi Lane was completely nude, and she was obviously a natural blonde.

"Private stock. You couldn't do that over the counter back then. Even the nudist magazines had to use an airbrush."

"Here's some more."

Kristi Lane was wearing jackboots, a Nazi armband, an SS hat, and nothing else. The other girl was suspended by her wrists above the floor and wore only a ball gag. Kristi wielded her whip with joyous zeal, the victim's contorted face hinted at the screams stifled by the rubber ball, and the blood that oozed from the welts across her twisting body looked all too real.

"No. I never did any of this sort of stuff." Steinman seemed affronted as he handed her back the folder.

"Who did?"

"Lot of guys. Lot of it amateur. Like I say, it wasn't sold openly. Hey, I'm surprised a girl like you'd even want to know about this kind of stuff, Miss...uh..." He'd forgotten her name since her phone call yesterday.

"Ms. Gayle. Chelsea Gayle."

"Miss Gayle. I thought all modern girls were feminists. Burning their bras and dressing up like men. I guess you're not one of them." His stare was suddenly professional, and somewhere in his beer-soaked brain he was once again focusing his 4 × 5 Speed Graphic camera.

Chelsea tasted her rum and flat cola and tried not to look flustered. After all, she was wearing her wide-shouldered power suit with a silk blouse primly gathered at the neck by a loose bow, and there was no nonsense about her taupe panty hose or low-heeled pumps. Beneath the *New Woman* exterior, she was confident that her body could as easily slither into a *Cosmopolitan* party dress. Her face took good close-ups, her blond hair was stylishly tousled, and she wore glasses more for fashion than necessity. Let the old fart stare.

"It's for an article on yesterday's pin-up queens," she said, repeating the lie she had told him over the phone. "Sort of a nostalgic look back as we enter the nineties: The women men dreamed of, and where are they now?"

"Well, I can't help you there on Kristi Lane." Steinman waved to the barmaid. "I don't know of anyone who can."

"When did you last work with her?"

"Hard to say. She was all over the place for those few years, then she moved out of my league. I'd guess the last time I shot her would have been about 1958. I know it was a cover for one of those *Playboy* imitations, but I forget the title. Didn't see much of her after that."

"When did you last see her?"

"Probably about 1960. Seem to recall that's about when she dropped out of sight. A guy told me once he'd run into her—at a hippie party in the Village late in the sixties, but he was too strung out to know what he was seeing."

"Any ideas?"

"Nothing you haven't heard already. Some said she got religion and entered a convent somewhere. There was some talk that she got pregnant; maybe she married some Joe from Chillico and settled down. There was one story that she was climbing in bed with JFK, and the CIA snuffed her like they did Marilyn Monroe."

"But what do *you* think happened to her?"

Steinman chugged his beer. "I think maybe she got a little too wild."

"Too wild?"

"You know what I mean. Maybe got in too deep. Had to drop out of sight. Or somebody made sure she did."

Chelsea frowned and dug into her case. "This one is pretty wild."

It was a magazine, and on the front it said, *Her Satanic Majesty Requests*, and below that, *For Sale to Adults Only*. The nude woman on the cover was wearing a sort of harness about her hips with a red pointed tail in back and a monstrous red dildo in front. Her face was Kristi Lane's, blond pageboy and all.

Steinman flipped to the centerfold. A writhing victim was tied to a sacrificial alter. Kristi Lane was astride her spread-eagled body, vigorously screwing her with the dildo.

Steinman slapped the magazine shut, shoved it back to Chelsea. "Not my bag, baby. I never shot any porno."

Chelsea replaced the magazine. "Was that Kristi Lane?"

"Maybe. It sure looked like her."

"But that magazine has a 1988 copyright. Kristi Lane would have looked a lot older—she'd be in her fifties."

"You can't tell about that sort of smut. Maybe it was bootleg stuff shot years before. You don't worry about copyrights here."

"The publisher is given as Nightseed X-Press, but their post office box now belongs to some New Age outfit. They weren't helpful."

"The old fly-by-night. Been gone for years."

"Who was shooting stuff like this back then? This looks fresh from the racks on 42nd Street."

"So it's a Kristi Lane lookalike. Hey, I saw Elvis singing at a bar just yesterday. Only, he was Jewish."

Steinman reached again for his empty glass, gave it a befuddled scowl. "Look. It's all Mob stuff now. The porno racket. Don't ask. Forget it. But—you *really* interested in the old stuff, the pin-up stuff? I got all my work filed away at my studio. No porno. Want to come up and see it?"

"Come up and see your etchings?"

"Hey, on the level. I could be your grandfather."

"Do you have any shots of Kristi Lane?"

"Hundreds of them. Say, have you ever posed professionally? Not pin-ups, I mean—but you have a wonderful face."

Chelsea smiled briskly and closed her case. "Tell you what, Morrie. Here's my business card. See what you've got on Kristi Lane, and then phone me at work. Could be I'll come by and take off my glasses for you."

She gathered up her things and the bar tab, and because he looked so much like a gone-to-seed gnome, she kissed him on top of his balding head.

"Hey, Miss Gayle!" he called after her. "I'll ask around. Look, doll, I'll be in touch!"

Chelsea played back the messages on her answering machine, found nothing of interest, and decided on a long, hot bath. Afterward, she slipped into a loose T-shirt and cotton boxer shorts, and she microwaved the first Lean Cuisine dinner she found in her freezer. A dish of ice cream seemed called for, and she curled up with her cat to consider her day.

The old geek at the used books and magazines dump off Times Square had given her Morrie Steinman's name after she had purchased an armload of Kristi Lane material from him. Apart from adding to her collection, she had really gained nothing from it at all—although it was a thrill to talk with someone who had actually photographed Kristi Lane back at the start of her career.

Chelsea gave her cat the last of the ice cream and hauled the heavy coffee-table book on Kristi Lane onto her lap. It had recently been published by Academy Editions, and she had lugged it back to New York from the shop in Holland Street, Kensington, certain that there was not likely to be a U.S. edition. Its title was *Kristi Lane: The Girl of Men's Dreams*, but Chelsea had already been dreaming of her for years.

She turned through the pages, studying photo after photo of Kristi Lane. Kristi Lane in stripper's costumes, Kristi Lane in high heels and seamed tights and pointed bras and lacy panties and bulky girdles and all the clumsy undergarments of the fifties. Kristi Lane decked out in full fetish gear—boots and corsets and leather gloves and latex dresses and braided whips. Kristi Lane tied to chairs, lashed to tables, spread-eagled over wooden frames, chained and gagged, encased in leather hoods and body sheaths. Kristi Lane tying other women into stringent bondage positions, gagging them with tape and scarves and improbable devices, spanking them with hairbrushes and leather straps.

Chelsea already had many of the photos in her own collection. However familiar, she kept paging through the book. Perhaps this time she might find a clue.

Of course, there was nothing new to be learned: Kristi Lane. Real name unknown. Birthplace and date of birth unknown. Said to be from Ohio. Said to be a teenager when she began her modeling career in New York. Much in demand as pin-up and bondage model during the 1950s. Dropped out of sight about 1962. End of text. Nothing left to do but look at the pictures.

Chelsea shoved the book aside and plopped her cat onto her vacated warmth on the couch. It was bedtime for the Chelsea girl.

Her dream was not unexpected. Nor surprising.

She was wearing one of those funny conical bras that made her breasts stick out like Dagmars on a fish-tail Cadillac—that was her first impression. After that came the discomfort of the boned white corset that pinched her waist and the tight girdle that squeezed her hips and gartered her seamed hose. She tottered on six-inch-high heels, as her mistress scolded her for some imagined offense. Her mistress looked very stern in her black corselet and spike-heeled boots, and it was only the flip of a page before she was punishing her clumsy maid.

There was a wall-length mirror, so Kristi could watch herself being tied across a coffee table. Her ankles were tied to the table legs at one end, her wrists bound to the legs at the other end, forcing her to support her weight with her flexed legs and arms. Another rope secured her waist to the tabletop, and a leather gag stifled her pleas. Kristi wriggled in helpless pain in her cramped position, rolling her eyes and whimpering through the leather strap. Her thighs were spread wide by her bondage, and she flushed as she saw her mistress smiling at the dampening crotch of her girdle. Her cunt was growing hotter and wetter the harder she struggled...

Chelsea awoke with the pulse of her orgasm. After a moment she decided that, in the morning, she would try to search out the photo set and make a notation. She had made hundreds of such notations.

Her secretary told her, "Your grandfather phoned while you were at lunch."

"What?" Chelsea studied the memo. "Oh, that has to be Morrie."

"Said he has some new etchings to show you. Your grandfather is quite the kidder."

"He's a randy old goat. I'll see what he wants."

Chelsea returned the call from her office. Morrie's answering machine said that Mr Steinman was at work in the darkroom just now and to please leave a message and number at the tone. Chelsea started to speak, and Steinman picked up the phone.

"Hey, doll! Got something for you."

"Like what?"

"Nightseed X-Press. The porno mag you showed me."

"Yes?"

"Most of them aren't really models. Just hookers doing a trick in front of a camera. I had a friend ask around. Discreetly. Found a girl who says she did some work for Nightseed about a year ago, gave me the address."

"Did she say anything about Kristi Lane?"

"The bimbo's maybe eighteen. She wouldn't know Kristi Lane from Harpo Marx. No phone number, but it's a loft not far from here. Want I should check it out?"

"I can do that."

"I don't think so. Not a job for a lady. Why don't you come by here sometime after five, and I'll make a full report. I got some photos you might like to see as well."

"All right. I'll come by after work."

Chelsea hung up and opened her shoulder bag. Yes, the can of Mace was right on top.

Steinman's studio was a second-floor walk-up above a closed-down artists' supply shop a few blocks from the bar where they'd met. The stencil on the frosted glass read *Morris Steinman Photography*, and Chelsea tried to imagine what sort of business he might attract.

The door was unlocked, and the secretary's desk had probably been vacant since Kennedy's inauguration. It was going on six, so Chelsea rapped on the glass and walked inside. The place was surprisingly neat, if a bit faded, and the wastebasket contained only a beer can. A row of filing cabinets had been recently dusted.

Chelsea let herself into the studio beyond the front office. She smelled coffee. There was a green davenport, a refrigerator, a hot plate, and an electric percolator, which was steaming slightly. There was a large empty room with a lot of backdrops and lighting stands and camera tripods. In the back there was a darkroom with a red light glowing above the DO NOT ENTER sign on the door. As she watched, the light winked out.

"Morrie?" Chelsea crossed the darkroom. "It's Chelsea Gayle."

The door of the darkroom slowly opened. Morrie Steinman shuffled out into the studio. He was holding a still-damp print, but he wasn't looking at it or at Chelsea. His face was a pasty mask, his eyes staring and unfocused. Steinman stumbled past Chelsea, moving dreamily toward the couch. He was a puppet whose strings were breaking, one by one. By the time he collapsed onto the davenport, there were no more strings to break.

Chelsea pried the photograph from his stiff fingers. Blood was trickling from beneath the frayed sleeve of his shirt, staining the four-by-five print as she tore it free. The photo was smeared, but it was a good pose of Kristi Lane in a tight sweater with a bit of stocking-top laid bare by her hiked-up skirt. She was seated with her knees crossed on the green davenport.

"Morrie always did good work," Kristi Lane said, stepping out of the darkroom. "I thought I owed him one last pose."

She closed her switchblade and pouted—teenage bad girl from the 1950s B-movies. In face and figure, Kristi Lane hadn't changed by so much as a gray hair from the pin-up queen of 1954. Chelsea reflected that her pageboy hairstyle was once again high fashion.

"Why kill him?"

Kristi slowly walked toward her. "Not too many left from the old days who could recognize me. Now there's one less. You shouldn't have prodded him into looking for me."

"There's thousands of photographs. You're a cult figure."

"Honey, if you passed Marilyn Monroe jogging in Central Park, you'd know she was just another lookalike."

Chelsea reached for the can of Mace as Kristi stepped close to her. Kristi's hand closed like steel over her wrist before she could work the spray. The can flew from her grasp, as Kristi effortlessly flung her across the studio. She crashed heavily against the wall opposite and slid down against it to her knees.

Kristi reached down for her throat, and the switchblade clicked. "We can make this as rough as you want, honey."

Chelsea lunged to her feet and caught Kristi beneath her arms, lifting the other woman and hurtling her through a backdrop. Kristi lost her switchblade as she crashed down amidst a tangle of splintering wood.

Struggling free, she swung a heavy light-stand at Chelsea's head. Chelsea caught the blow with her forearms and wrenched the bent metal stand away from her. Diving forward as Kristi stumbled back, she tackled the other woman—pinning her as the two smashed through the wreckage of another backdrop.

Kristi Lane suddenly stopped struggling. She stared in wonder at the woman crouched on top of her.

"*Who are you?*"

"I'm your daughter," Chelsea panted. "Now tell me *what* I am!"

Kristi Lane laughed and pushed Chelsea off her. "Like mother, like daughter. You're a succubus."

"A succubus!"

"Dictionary time? A demon in female form—a temptress who haunts men's dreams, who draws youth and strength from their lust. Surely by now you've begun to wonder about yourself."

"I'd found out from agency records that you were my mother. I thought that if I could find you, you might explain things—like why I'm unnaturally strong, and why I look like I'm still twenty, and why I keep having dreams about being you."

"I think it's time we had our mother-daughter chat," Kristi said, helping her to her feet. "Let's go home."

"Chelsea Gayle," Kristi murmured. "I gave you the name, Chelsea."

"Why did you give me up?"

"No place for a baby in my life. The social agency had no problems with that, although they hardly could have guessed the full reasons. Most offspring never survive infancy. You've been feeding off my energy all these years—and you turned out very well."

Chelsea tugged off the remains of her blouse and slipped into a kimono. She couldn't decide whether her mother's gaze held tenderness or desire.

"Who was my father?"

"All men. The thousands who fucked me in their wet-dream fantasies, who jacked off over my pictures. Their seed is our strength. Sometimes the combined energy of their lust is strong enough to create a child. It happens only rarely. Perhaps someday you'll bear another of us."

"I work in advertising."

"Selling false dreams. Already you were becoming one of us."

Kristi took away Chelsea's kimono and unhooked her bra. Chelsea did not resist.

"You shouldn't hide your beauty," Kristi told her. "We need to feed from their secret lusts. Both of us. Now it's time you were weaned. Get rid of those clothes, and I'll find you something better to wear."

Chelsea was naked when Kristi returned from another corner of the loft. Her mother had changed into spike-heeled boots and a studded leather bikini. Her arms were loaded with leather gear.

"I'll teach you," she said. "They need stronger stimulation now than they did when I began. I almost waited too long; I'd become nostalgia to them, no longer their sexual fantasy. My comeback will also be your coming out."

Kristi Lane led her over to a small stage area. Lights were coming on, and Chelsea sensed cameras and presences behind them in the encircling darkness, but she couldn't see beyond the lights.

"Now then, dear." Kristi set down her bondage paraphernalia and picked up a riding crop. "I am mistress here, and you must obey me in every way. Do you promise?"

"Yes, mistress. I promise."

"After all," her mother said softly, "this is what you've always known you wanted." Then, sharply: "Now then! Let's get you into these!"

Meekly Chelsea put on the leather corselet and thigh-high boots, then submitted to having her arms laced tightly behind her back in a leather single-glove. By then it was pointless to struggle when Kristi strapped a phallus-shaped gag deep into her mouth, then brought out what at first glance had looked like a leather chastity belt. Choking on the gag, Chelsea moaned as the twin dildos penetrated her vagina and rectum, stretching her as they pushed inward to rub together against the thin wall that separated their bulbous heads.

Her mother leaned forward to kiss her face as she padlocked the belt securely into place. "You'll stay like me, Chelsea—forever young and beautiful."

Kristi helped her lie down on top of a long leather sheath. As Chelsea writhed on her belly, Kristi began to lace together the two edges of the leather sleeve, tightly encasing her daughter within a leather tube from her ankles to her neck.

Kristi kissed her face again, just as she fitted the leather hood over Chelsea's head and laced it across the back of her neck. "Their lust is our strength. I'll help you."

Chelsea lay helpless, blinded and gagged, barely able to wriggle so much as her fingers. She felt her ankles being strapped together. Then slowly, she was lifted into the air by her ankles until she was completely suspended above the stage.

Hanging upside down, tightly wrapped in her leather sheath, Chelsea could sense the gloating touch of the cameras. She writhed helplessly, beginning to experience the warmth that flowed into her from the hard rubber penises swollen inside her mouth and cunt and ass. She did not feel violated. Instead she felt the strength that she was drawing from an unseen prey.

Suspended and satisfied, Chelsea Gayle waited to be released from her cocoon, and wondered what she had become.

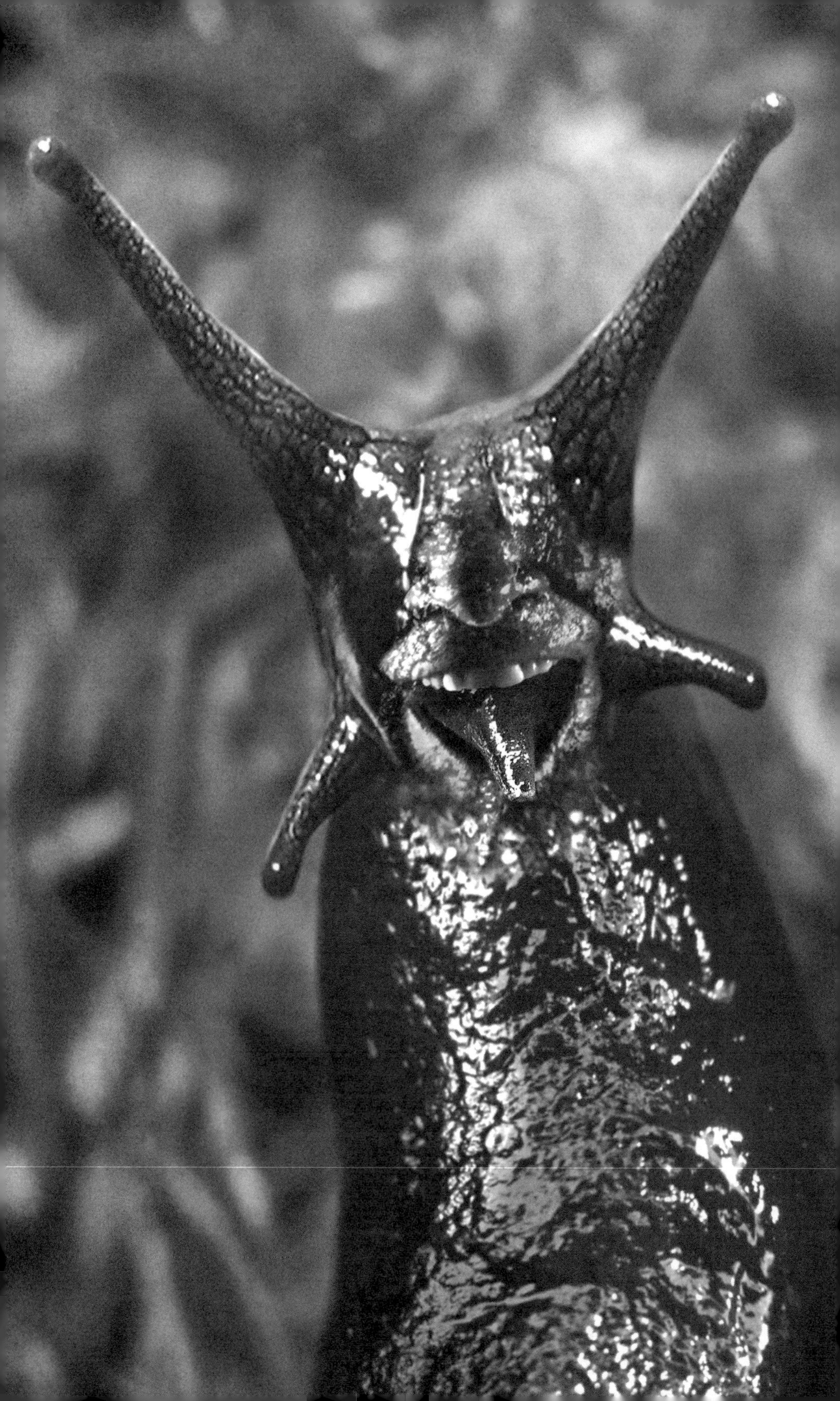

The Slug

Martine was hammering away to the accompaniment of Lou Reed, tapedeck set at stun, and at first didn't hear the knocking at her studio door. She set aside hammer and chisel, put Lou Reed on hold, and opened the door to discover Keenan Bauduret seated on her deck rail, leaning forward to pound determinedly at her door. The morning sun shone bright and cheery through the veil of pines, and Keenan was shit-faced drunk.

"Martine!" He lurched toward her. "I need a drink!"

"What you need is some coffee." Martine stood her ground. At six feet and change she was three inches taller than Keenan and in far better shape.

"Please! I've got to talk to someone." Keenan's soft brown eyes implored. He was disheveled and unshaven in baggy clothes that once had fit him, and Martine thought of a stray spaniel, damp and dirty, begging to be let in. And Keenan said, "I've just killed someone. I mean, something."

Martine stepped inside. "I can offer gin and orange juice."

"Just the gin."

Keenan Bauduret collapsed onto her wooden rocking chair and mopped at his face with a crumpled linen handkerchief, although the morning was not yet warm. Now he reminded her of Bruce Dern playing a dissolute Southern lawyer, complete with out-of-fashion and rumpled suit; but in fact Keenan was a writer, although dissolute and Southern to be sure. He was part of that sort of artist/writer colony that the sort of small university town such as Pine Hill attracts. Originally he was from New Orleans, and he was marking time writing mystery novels while he completed work on the Great Southern Novel. At times he taught creative writing for the university's evening college.

Martine had installed a wet bar complete with refrigerator and microwave in a corner of her studio to save the walk back into her house when she entertained here. She sculpted in stone, and the noise and dust were better kept away from her single-bedroom cottage. While Keenan sweated, she looked for glasses and ice.

"Just what was it you said that you'd killed?"

"A slug. A gross, obscene, mammoth, and predatory slug."

"Sounds rather like a job for Orkin. Did you want your gin neat?"

"Just the naked gin."

Martine made herself a very light gin screwdriver and poured a double shot of Tanqueray into Keenan's glass. Her last name was still McFerran, and she had her father's red hair, which she wore in a long ponytail, and his Irish blue eyes and freckled complexion. Her mother was Scottish and claimed that her side of the family was responsible for her daughter's unexpected height. Born in Belfast, Martine had grown up in Pine Hill as a faculty brat after her parents took university posts here to escape the troubles in Northern Ireland. Approaching the further reaches of thirty, Martine was content with her bachelorhood and her sculpture and had no desire to return to Belfast.

"Sure you don't want orange juice?" She handed the glass to Keenan.

Keenan shook his head. "To your very good health." He swallowed half the gin, closed his eyes, leaned back in the rocker and sighed. He did not, as Martine had expected, tip over.

Martine sat down carefully in her prized Windsor chair. She was wearing scuffed Reeboks, faded blue jeans, and a naturally torn university sweatshirt, and she pushed back her sleeves before tasting her drink.

"Now, then," she said, "tell me what really happened."

Keenan studied his gin with the eye of a man who is balancing his need to bolt the rest of it against the impropriety of asking for an immediate refill. Need won.

"Don't get up." He smiled graciously. "I know the way."

Martine watched him slosh another few ounces of gin into his glass, her own mood somewhere between annoyance and concern. She'd known Keenan Bauduret casually for years, well before he'd hit the skids. He was a few years older than she, well read and intelligent, and usually fun to be around. They'd never actually dated, but there were the inevitable meetings at parties and university town cultural events, lunches and dinners and a few drinks after. Keenan had never slept over, nor had she at his cluttered little house. It was that sort of respectful friendship that arises between two lonely people who are content within their self-isolation, venturing forth for nonthreatening companionship without ever sensing the need.

"I've cantaloupe in the fridge," Martine prompted.

"Thanks. I'm all right." Keenan returned to the rocker. He sipped his gin this time. His hands were no longer shaking. "How well do you know Casper Crowley?"

"Casper the Friendly Ghost?" Martine almost giggled. "Hardly at all. That is, I've met him at parties, but he never has anything to say to anyone. Just stands stuffing himself with chips and hors d'oeuvres—I've even seen him pocket a few beers as he's left. I'm told he's in a family business, but no one seems to know what that business is—and he writes books that no one I know has ever read for publishers no one has heard of. He's so dead dull boring that I always wonder why anyone ever invites him."

"I've seen him at your little gatherings," Keenan accused.

"Well, yes. It's just that I feel sorry for poor boring Casper."

"Exactly." Keenan stabbed a finger and rested his case. "That's what happened to me. You won't mind if I have another drink while I tell you about it?"

Martine sighed mentally and tried not to glance at her watch.

His greatest mistake, said Keenan, was ever to have invited Casper Crowley to drop by in the first place.

It began about two years ago. Keenan was punishing the beer keg at Greg Lafollette's annual birthday bash and pig-picking. He was by no means sober, or he never would have attempted to draw Casper into conversation. It was just that Casper stood there, wrapped in his customary loneliness, mechanically feeding his face with corn chips and salsa, washing it down with great gulps of beer, as expressionless as a carp taking bread crumbs from atop a pool.

"How's it going, Casper?" Keenan asked harmlessly.

Casper shaved his scalp but not his face, and he had bits of salsa in his bushy orange beard. He was wearing a tailored tweed suit whose vest strained desperately to contain his enormous beer gut. He turned his round, bland eyes toward Keenan and replied, "Do you know much about Aztec gods?"

"Not really, I suppose."

"In this book I'm working on," Casper pursued, "I'm trying to establish a link between the Aztecs and Nordic mythology."

"Well, I do have a few of the usual sagas stuck away on my shelves." Keenan was struggling to imagine any such link.

"Then would it be all right if I dropped by your place to look them over?"

And Casper appeared at ten the following morning, while Keenan was drying off from his shower, and he helped himself to coffee and doughnuts while Keenan dressed.

"Hope I'm not in your way." Casper was making a fresh pot of coffee.

"Not at all." Keenan normally worked mornings through the afternoon, and he had a pressing deadline.

But Casper plopped down on his couch and spent the next few hours leafing without visible comprehension through various of Keenan's books, soaking up coffee, and intermittently clearing his throat and swallowing horribly. Keenan no longer felt like working after his guest had finally left. Instead he made himself a fifth rum and Coke and fell asleep watching *I Love Lucy*.

At ten the following morning, Keenan had almost reworked his first sentence of the day when Casper phoned.

"Do you know why a tomcat licks his balls?"

Keenan admitted ignorance.

"Because he can!"

Casper chuckled with enormous relish at his own joke, while Keenan scowled at the phone. "How about going out to get some barbecue for lunch?" Casper then suggested.

"I'm afraid I'm really very busy just now."

"In that case," Casper persisted, "I'll just pick us up some sandwiches and bring them on over."

And he did. And Casper sat on Keenan's couch, wolfing down barbecue sandwiches with the precision of a garbage disposal, dribbling gobbets of sauce and cole slaw down his beard and belly and onto the upholstery. Keenan munched his soggy sandwich, reflecting upon the distinction between the German verbs *essen* (to eat) and *fressen* (to devour). When Casper at last left, it was late afternoon, and Keenan took a nap that lasted past his usual dinnertime. By then the day had long since slipped away.

He awoke feeling bloated and lethargic the next morning, but he was resolved to make up for lost time. At ten-thirty Casper appeared on his doorstep, carrying a bag of chocolate-covered raspberry jelly doughnuts.

"Do you know how many mice it takes to screw in a light bulb?" Casper asked, helping himself to coffee.

"I'm afraid I don't."

"Two—but they have to be real small!" Jelly spurted down Casper's beard as he guffawed. Keenan had never before heard someone actually guffaw; he'd always assumed it was an exaggerated figure of speech.

Casper left after about two in the afternoon, unsuccessful in his efforts to coax Keenan into sharing a pizza with him. Keenan returned to his desk, but inspiration was dead.

And so the daily routine began.

"Why didn't you just tell him to stay away and let you work?" Martine interrupted.

"Easy enough to say," Keenan groaned. "At first I just felt sorry for him. OK, the guy is lonely—right? Anyway, I really was going to tell him to stop bugging me every day—and then I had my accident."

A rain-slick curve, a telephone pole, and Keenan's venerable

VW Beetle was grist for the crusher. Keenan fared rather better, although his left foot would wear a plaster sock for some weeks after.

Casper came over daily with groceries and bottles of beer and rum. "Glad to be of help," he assured Keenan as he engulfed most of a slice of pepperoni-and-mushroom pizza. Sauce obscured his beard. "Must be tough having to hobble around day after day. Still, I'll bet you're getting a lot of writing done."

"Very little," Keenan grudgingly admitted. "Just haven't felt up to it lately."

"Guess you haven't. Hey, do you know what the difference is between a circus and a group of sorority girls out jogging?"

"I give up."

"Well, one is a cunning array of stunts," Casper chortled and wiped red sauce from his mouth. "Guess I better have another beer after that one!"

Keenan missed one deadline, and then he missed another. He made excuses owing to his accident. Deadlines came around again. The one novel he did manage to finish came back with requests for major revisions. Keenan worked hard at the rewrite, but each new effort was only for the worse. He supposed he ought to cut down on his drinking, but the stress was keeping him awake nights, and he kept having nightmares wherein Casper crouched on his chest and snickered bad jokes and dribbled salsa. His agent sounded concerned, and his editors were losing patience.

"Me," said Casper, "I never have trouble writing. I've always got lots of ideas."

Keenan resisted screaming at the obese hulk who had camped on his sofa throughout the morning. Instead he asked civilly, "Oh? And what are you working on now?"

"A follow-up to my last book—by the way, my publisher really went ape-shit over that one, wants another like it. This time I'm writing one that traces the rise of Nazi Germany to the Druidic rites at Stonehenge."

"You seem to be well versed in the occult," observed Keenan, repressing an urge to vomit.

"I do a lot of research," Casper explained. "Besides, it's in my blood. Did I ever tell you that I'm related to Aleister Crowley?"

"No."

"Well, I am." Casper beamed with secret pride.

"I should have guessed."

"Well, the name, of course."

Keenan had been thinking of other similarities. "Well, I really do need to get some work done now."

"Sure you don't need me to run you somewhere?"

"No, thank you. The ankle is a little sore, but I can get around well enough."

At the door, Casper persisted: "Sure you don't want to go get some barbecue?"

"Very sure."

Casper pointed toward the rusted-out Chevy wagon in Keenan's driveway. "Well, if that heap won't start again, just give me a call."

"I put in a new battery," Keenan said, remembering that the mechanic had warned him about the starter motor. Keenan had bought the clunker for three hundred bucks—from a student. He needed wheels, and wheels were about all that did work on the rust-bucket. His insurance hadn't covered replacement for his antique Beetle.

"Heard you had to return your advance on that Zenith contract."

"Where'd you hear that?" Keenan wanted to use his fists.

"My editor—your old editor—brought it up when we were talking contract on my new book the other day. She said for me to check out how you were getting along. Sounded concerned. But I told her you were doing great, despite all the talk."

"Thanks for that much."

"Hey, you know the difference between a sorority girl and a bowling ball?"

Keenan did not trust himself to speak.

"No? Well, you can't stuff a sorority girl into a bowling ball!"

After the university informed Mr Bauduret that his services would no longer be required as instructor of creative writing at the evening college, Keenan began to sell off his books and a few antiques. It kept the wolves at arm's length, and it paid for six-packs. Editors no longer phoned, and his agent no longer answered his calls.

Casper was sympathetic, and he regularly carried over doughnuts and instant coffee, which he consumed while drinking Keenan's beer.

"Zenith gobbled up *Nazi Druids*," he told Keenan. "They can't wait for more."

The light in Keenan's eyes was not the look of a sane man. "So, what's next?"

"I got an idea. I've discovered a tie-in between flying saucers and the Salem witch burnings."

"They hanged them. Or pressed them. No burnings in this country."

"Whatever. Anyway, I bought a bunch of your old books on the subject at the Book Barn the other day. Guess I won't need to borrow them now."

"Guess not."

"Hey, you want some Mexican for lunch? I'll pay."

"Thank you, but I have some work to do."

"Good to see you're still slugging away."

"Not finished yet."

"Guess some guys don't know when they're licked."

"Guess not."

"Hey"—Casper chugged his beer—"you know what the mating cry of a sorority girl is?"

Keenan gritted his teeth in a hideous grin.

Continued Casper in girlish falsetto, "Oh, I'm so-o-o drunk!" His belly shook with laughter, although he wasn't Santa. "Better have another beer on that one!"

And he sat there on the couch, methodically working his way through Keenan's stock of beer, as slowly mobile and slimy gross as a huge slug feasting its way across the garden. Keenan listened to his snorts and belches, to his puerile and obscene jokes, to his pointless and inane conversation, too drained and too weak to beg him to leave. Instead he swallowed his beer and his bile, and fires of loathing stirred beneath the ashes of his despair.

That night Keenan found the last bottle of rum he'd hidden away against when the shakes came at dawn, and he dug out the vast file of typed pages, containing all the fits and starts and notes and revisions and disconnected chapters that were the entirety of his years' efforts toward the Great Southern Novel.

He had a small patio, surrounded by a neglected rock garden and close-shouldering oak trees, and he heaped an entire bag of charcoal into the barbecue grill that rusted there. Then Keenan sipped from the bottle of Myers's, waiting for the coals to take light. When the coals had reached their peak, Keenan Bauduret fed his manuscript, page by crumpled page, onto the fire; watched each page flame and char, rise in dying ashes into the night.

"That was when I knew I had to kill Casper Crowley."

Martine wasn't certain whether she was meant to laugh now. "Kill Casper? But he was only trying to be your friend! I'm sure you can find a way to ask him to give you your space without hurting his feelings."

Keenan laughed instead. He poured out the last of her gin. "A friend? Casper was a giant grotesque slug! He was a gross leech that sucked out my creative energy! He fed off me and watched over me with secret delight as I wasted away!"

"That's rather strong."

"From the first day the slug showed up on my doorstep, I could never concentrate on my work. When I did manage to write, all I could squeeze out was dead, boring, lifeless drivel. I don't blame my publishers for sending it back!"

Martine sighed, wondering how to express herself. She did rather like Keenan; she certainly felt pity for him now. "Keenan, I don't want to get you upset, but you have been drinking an awful lot this past year or so…"

"Upset?" Keenan broke into a wild grin and a worse laugh, then suddenly regained his composure. "No need for me to be upset now, I've killed him."

"And how did you manage that?" Martine was beginning to feel uneasy.

"How do you kill a slug?"

"I thought you said he was a leech."

"They're one and the same."

"No they're not."

"Yes they are. Gross, bloated, slimy things. Anyway, the remedy is the same."

"I'm not sure I'm following you."

"Salt." Keenan seemed in complete control now. "They can't stand salt."

"I see." Martine relaxed and prepared herself for the joke.

Keenan became very matter-of-fact. "Of course, I didn't forget the beer. Slugs are drawn to beer. I bought many six-packs of imported beer. Then I prepared an enormous barbecue feast—chickens, ribs, pork loin. Casper couldn't hold himself back."

"So you pushed his cholesterol over the top, and he died of a massive coronary."

"Slugs can't overeat. It was the beer. He drank and drank and drank some more, and then he passed out on the patio lounge chair. That was my chance."

"A steak through the heart?"

"Salt. I'd bought dozens of bags of rock salt for this. Once Casper was snoring away, I carried them out of my station wagon and ripped them open. Then, before he could awaken, I quickly dumped the whole lot over Casper."

"I'll bet Casper didn't enjoy that."

"He didn't. At first I was afraid he'd break away, but I kept pouring the rock salt over him. He never said a word. He just writhed all about on the lounge chair, flinging his little arms and legs all about, trying to fend off the salt."

Keenan paused and swallowed the last of the gin. He wiped his face and shuddered. "And then he began to shrivel up."

"Shrivel up?"

"The way slugs do when you pour salt on them. Don't you remember? Remember doing it when you were a kid? He just started to shrivel and shrink. And shrink and shrink. Until there was nothing much left. Just a dried-out twist of slime. No bones. Just dried slime."

"I see."

"But the worst part was the look in his eyes, just before they withered on the ends of their stalks. He stared right into my eyes, and I could sense the terrible rage as he died."

"Stalks?"

"Yes. Casper Crowley sort of changed as he shriveled away."

"Well. What did you do then?"

"Very little to clean up. Just dried slime and some clothes. I waited through the night, and this morning I burned it all on the barbecue grill. Wasn't much left, but it sure stank."

Keenan looked at his empty glass, then glanced hopefully at the empty bottle. "So now it's over. I'm free."

"Well," said Martine, ignoring his imploring gaze, "I can certainly see that you've regained your imagination."

"Best be motivating on home now, I guess," Keenan stood up, with rather less stumbling than Martine had anticipated. "Thanks for listening to my strange little story. Guess I didn't expect you to believe it all, but I had to talk to someone."

"Why not drive carefully home and get some sleep," Martine advised, ushering him to the door. "This has certainly been an interesting morning."

Keenan hung on to the door. "Thanks again, Martine. I'll do just that. Hey, what do you say I treat you to Chinese tomorrow for lunch? I really feel a whole lot better after talking to you."

Martine felt panic, then remorse. "Well, I am awfully busy just now, but I guess I can take a break for lunch."

Martine sat back down after Keenan had left. She was seriously troubled, wondering whether she ought to phone Casper Crowley. Clearly Keenan was drinking far too heavily; he might well be harboring some resentment. But harm anyone…No way. Just some unfunny attempt at a shaggy dog story. Keenan never could tell jokes.

When she finally did phone Casper Crowley, all she got was his answering machine.

Martine felt strangely lethargic—her morning derailed by Keenan's bursting in with his inane patter. Still, she thought she really should get some work done on her sculpture.

She paused before the almost finished marble, hammer and chisel at ready, her mind utterly devoid of inspiration. She was working on a bust of a young woman—the proverbial artist's self-portrait. Martine squared her shoulders and set chisel to the base of the marble throat.

As the hammer struck, the marble cracked through to the base.

Afterword

Not much need be said, actually. Every writer—every creative person—lives in dread of those nagging and inane interruptions that break the creative flow. A sentence perfectly crystallized, shattered by a stupid phone call, never regained. A morning filled with inspiration and energy, clogged by an uninvited guest, the day lost. The imaginative is the choice prey of the banal, and uncounted works of excellence have died stillborn thanks to junk phone calls and visits from bored associates.

After all, a writer doesn't have a real job. Feel free to crash in at any time. Probably wants some company.

Nothing in this story is in any way a reflection upon this one writer's various friends, nor does it in any way resemble any given actual person or composite of any persons known to the author. It is entirely a fictitious work and purely the product of the author's imagination.

It has taken me five days to scribble out this afterword.

There's the door...

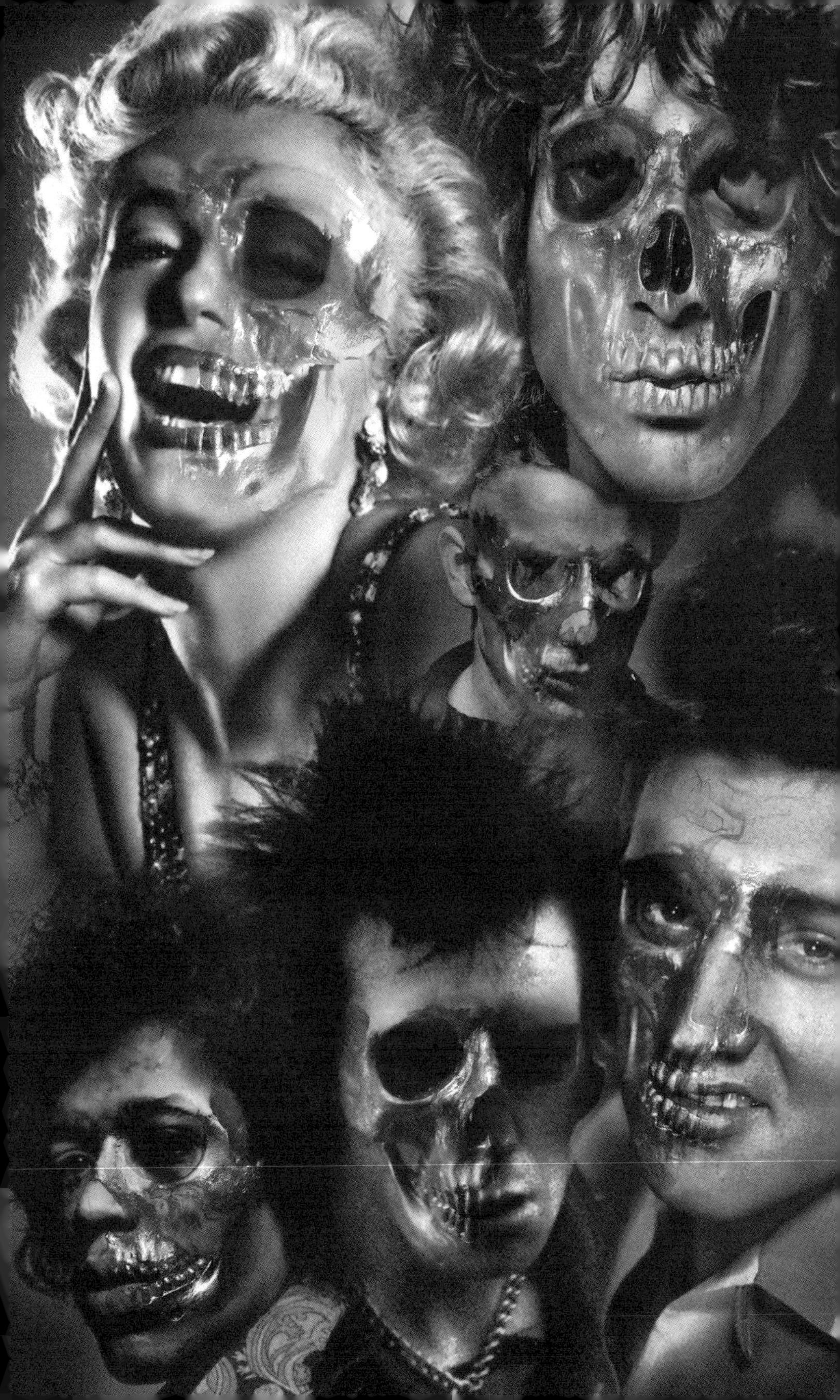

Did They Get You to Trade?

Ryan Chase was walking along Southampton Row at lunchtime, fancying a pint of bitter. Fortunately there was no dearth of pubs here, and he turned into Cosmo Place, a narrow passage behind the Bloomsbury Park Hotel and the Church of St George the Martyr, leading into Queen Square. The September day was unseasonably sunny, so he passed by Peter's Bar, downstairs at the corner—looking for an outdoor table at The Swan or The Queen's Larder. The Swan was filling up, so he walked a few doors farther to The Queen's Larder, at the corner of Queen Square. There he found his pint of bitter, and he moved back outside to take a seat at one of the wooden tables on the pavement.

Ryan Chase was American by birth, citizen of the world by choice. More to the point, he spent probably half of each year knocking about the more or less civilized parts of the globe—he liked hotels and saw no romance in roughing it—and a month or two of this time he spent in London, where he had various friends and the use of a studio. The remainder of his year was devoted to long hours of work in his Connecticut studio, where he painted strange and compelling portraits, often derived from his travels and created from memory. These fetched rather large and compelling prices from fashionable galleries—enough to support his travels and eccentricities, even without the trust allowance from a father who had wanted him to go into corporate law.

Chase was pleased with most of his work, although in all of it he saw a flawed compromise between the best he could create at the time and the final realization of his vision, which he hoped someday to achieve. He saw himself as a true decadent, trapped in the *fin de siécle* of a century far drearier than the last. But then, to be decadent is to be romantic.

Chase also had a pragmatic streak. Today a pint of bitter in Bloomsbury would have to make do for a glass of absinthe in Paris of *La Belle Epoch*. The bitter was very good, the day was excellent, and Chase dug out a few postcards from his jacket pocket. By the end of his second pint, he had scribbled notes and addresses on them all and was thinking about a third pint and perhaps a ploughman's lunch.

He smelled the sweet stench of methylated spirit as it approached him, and then the sour smell of unwashed poverty. Already Chase was reaching for a coin.

"Please, guv. I don't wish to interrupt you in your writing, but please could you see your way toward sparing a few coins for a poor man who needs a meal?"

Ryan Chase didn't look like a tourist, but neither did he look British. He was forty-something, somewhere around six feet, saddened that he was starting to spread at the middle, and proud that there was no grey in his short black beard and no thinning in his pulled-back hair and short ponytail. His black leather jacket with countless studs and zips was from Kensington Market, his baggy slacks from Bloomingdale's, his T-shirt from Rodeo Drive, and his tennis shoes from a Stamford garage sale. Mild blue eyes watched from behind surplus aviator's sunglasses of the same shade of blue.

All of this, in addition to his fondness for writing postcards and scrawling sketches at tables outside pubs, made Chase a natural target for London's growing array of panhandlers and blowlamps. Against this Chase kept a pocket well filled with coins, for his heart was rather kind and his eye quite keen to memorize the faces that peered back from the fringes of Hell.

But this face had seen well beyond the fringes of Hell, and

as Chase glanced up, he left the pound coin in his pocket. His panhandler was a meth-man, well in the grip of the terminal oblivion of cheap methylated spirit. His shoes and clothing were refuse from dustbins, and from the look of his filthy mackintosh, he had obviously been sleeping rough for some while. Chalky ashes seemed to dribble from him like cream from a cone in a child's fist. Beneath all this, his body was tall and almost fleshless; the long-fingered hand, held out in hope, showed dirt-caked nails resembling broken talons. Straggling hair and unkempt beard might have been black or brown, streaked with grey and matted with ash and grime. His face — Chase recalled Sax Rohmer's description of Fu Manchu: A brow like Shakespeare and eyes like Satan.

Only, Satan the fallen angel. These were green eyes with a tint of amber, and they shone with a sort of majestic despair and a proud intelligence that not even the meth had wholly obliterated. Beneath their imploring hopelessness, the eyes suggested a still-smoldering sense of rage.

Ryan Chase was a scholar of human faces, as well as impulsive, and he knew any coins the man might beg here would go straight into another bottle of methylated spirit. He got up from his seat. "Hang on a bit. I'll treat you to a round."

When Chase emerged from The Queen's Larder, he was carrying a pint of bitter and a pint of cider. His meth-man was skulking about the Church of St George the Martyr across the way, seemingly studying the informational plaque affixed to the stucco wall. Chase handed him the cider. "Here. This is better for you than the meth."

The other man had the shakes rather badly, but he steadied the pint with both hands and dipped his face into it, sucking ravenously until the level was low enough for him to lift the pint to his face. He'd sunk his pint before Chase had quite started on his own. Wiping his beard, he leaned back against the church and shuddered, but the shaking had left his hands as the alcohol quickly spread from his empty stomach.

"Thanks, guv. Now I'd best be off before they take notice of me. They don't fancy my sort hanging about."

His accent was good, though too blurred by alcohol for Chase to pin down. Chase sensed tragedy, as he studied the other's face while he drained his own pint. He wasn't used to drinking in a rush, and perhaps this contributed to his natural impulsiveness.

"They'll take my money well enough. Take a seat at the table 'round the corner, and I'll buy another round."

Chase bought a couple packets of crisps to accompany their pints and returned to find the other man cautiously seated. He had managed to beg a cigarette. He eagerly accepted the cider, but declined the crisps. By the time he had finished his cider, he was looking somewhat less the corpse.

"Cheers, mate," he said. "You've been a friend. It wasn't always like this, you know."

"Eat some crisps, and I'll buy you one more pint." No need to sing for your supper, Chase started to say, but there were certain remnants of pride amidst the wreckage. He left his barely tasted pint and stepped back inside for more cider. At least there was some food value to cider in addition to the high alcohol content, or so he imagined. It might get the poor bastard through another day.

His guest drank this pint more slowly. The cider had cured his shakes for the moment, and he was losing his whipped cur attitude. He said with a certain foggy dignity: "That's right, mate. One time I had it all. And then I lost it every bit. Now it's come down to this."

Chase was an artist, not a writer, and so had been interested in the man's face, not his life story. The story was an obvious ploy to gain a few more pints, but as the face began to return to life, Chase found himself searching through his memory.

Chase opened a second bag of crisps and offered them. "So, then?"

"I'm Nemo Skagg. Or used to be. Ever heard of me?"

Chase started to respond, "Yes, and I'm Elvis." But his artist's eyes began filling in the eroded features, and instead he whispered, "Jesus Christ!"

Nemo Skagg. Founder and major force behind Needle—probably the cutting edge of the punk rock movement in its early years. Needle, long without Nemo Skagg and with just enough of its early lineup to maintain the group's name, was still around, but only as a ghost of the original. *Rolling Stone* and the lot used to publish scandalous notices of Nemo Skagg's meteoric crash, but that was years ago, and few readers today would have recognized the name. The name of a living-dead legend.

"Last I read of you, you were living the life of a recluse at someplace in Kensington," Chase said.

"You don't believe me?" There was a flicker of defiant pride in those wounded eyes.

"Actually, I do," Chase said, feeling as though he should apologize. "I recognize your face." He wiped his hands on his trousers, fumbling for something to say. "As it happens, I still have Needle's early albums, as well as the solo album you did."

"But do you still listen to them?"

Chase felt increasingly awkward, yet he was too fascinated to walk away. "Well, I think this calls for one more round."

The barman from The Queen's Larder was starting to favor them with a distasteful frown as he collected glasses from outside. Nemo Skagg nodded toward Great Ormand Street across the way. "They do a fair scrumpi at The Sun," he suggested.

It was a short walk to the corner of Great Ormand and Lamb's Conduit Street, giving Chase a little time to marshal his thoughts. Nemo Skagg. Nova on the punk rock scene. The most outrageous. The most daring. The savior of the world from disco and lame hangers-on from the sixties scene. Totally full-dress punk star: the parties, the fights on stage, the drugs, the scandals, the arrests, the hospital confinements. Toward the last, there were only the latter two, then even these were no longer newsworthy. A decade later, the world had forgotten Nemo Skagg. Chase had assumed he was dead, but now could recall no notice of his death. It might have escaped notice.

The Sun was crowded with students as usual, but Chase made his way past them to the horseshoe bar and sloshed back outside with two pints of scrumpi. Nemo had cleared a space against the wall and had begged another fag. They leaned against the wall of the pub, considering the bright September day, the passing show, and their pints. Chase seldom drank scrumpi, and the potent cider would have been enough to stun his brain even without the previous bitter.

"Actually," Nemo said, "there were three solo albums."

"I had forgotten."

"They were all bollocks."

"I'm not at all certain I ever heard the other two," Chase compromised.

"I'm bollocks. We're all of us bollocks."

"The whole world is bollocks." Chase jumped in ahead of him.

"To bollocks!" Nemo raised his glass. They crashed their pints in an unsteady toast. Nemo drained his.

"You're a sport, mate. You still haven't asked what you're waiting to ask: How did it all happen?"

"Well. I don't suppose it really matters, does it?"

Nemo was not to demur. "Lend us a fiver, mate, and I'll pay for this round. Then Nemo Skagg shall tell all."

Once, at the White Hart in Drury Lane, Chase had bought eight pints of Guinness for a cockney pensioner who had regaled him with an impenetrable cockney accent concerning his adventures during the Dunkirk evacuation. Chase hadn't understood a word in ten, but he memorized the man's face, and that portrait was considered one of his very finest. Chase found a fiver.

The bar staff at The Sun were loose enough to serve Nemo, and he was out again shortly with two more pints of scrumpi and a packet of fags. That was more than the fiver, so he hadn't been totally skint. He brightened when Chase told him he didn't smoke. Nemo lit up. Chase placed his empty pint on the window ledge and braced himself against the wall. The wall felt good.

"So, then, mate. Ask away. It's you who's paid the piper."

Chase firmly resolved that this pint would be his last. "All right, then. What did happen to Nemo Skagg? Last I heard, you still had some of your millions and a house in Kensington, whence sounds of debauchery issued throughout the night."

"You got it right all along, mate. It was sex, drugs and alcohol that brought about me ruin. We'll say bloody nothing about scheming managers and crooked recording studios. Now, then. You've got the whole soddin' story."

"Not very original." Chase wondered whether he should finish his scrumpi.

"Life is never original," Nemo observed. The rush of alcohol and nicotine had vastly improved his demeanor. Take away the dirt and shabby clothes, and he might well look like any other dissipated man in his sixties, although that must be about twice his actual age. He was alert enough not to be gauging Chase for prospects of further largess.

"Of course, that's not truly the reason."

"Was it a woman?" asked Chase. The scrumpi was making him maudlin.

"Which woman would it have been? Here, drink up, mate. Give us tube fare to Ken High Street, and I'll show you how it happened."

At this point Ryan Chase should have put down his unfinished pint, excused himself, and made his way back to his hotel. Instead he drank up, stumbled along to the Holborn tube station, and found himself being bounced about the train beside a decidedly deranged Nemo Skagg. Caught up in the adventure of the moment, Chase told himself that he was on a sort of quest—a quest for truth, for the truth that lies behind the masks of faces.

The carriage shook and swayed as it plummeted through subterranean darkness, yanking to a halt at each jostling platform. Chase dropped onto a seat as the passengers rushed out and swarmed in. Lurid posters faced him from the platform walls. Bodies mashed close about him, crushing closer than the sooty tunnel walls briefly glimpsed in flashes of passing trains and bright bursts of sparks. Faces, looking nowhere, talking in tight bundles, crowded in. Sensory overload.

Nemo's face leered down. He was clutching a railing. "You all right, mate?"

"Gotta take a piss."

"Could go for a slash myself. This stop will do."

So they got off at Notting Hill Gate instead of changing for High Street Kensington; and this was good, because they could walk down Kensington Church Street, which was for a miracle all downhill, toward Kensington High Street. The walk and the fresh air revived Chase from his claustrophobic experience. Bladder relieved, he found himself pausing before the windows of the numerous antique shops that they passed. Hideous Victorian atrocities and baroque horrors from the continent lurked imprisoned behind shop windows. A few paintings beckoned from the farther darkness. Chase was tempted to enter.

But each time Nemo caught at his arm. "You don't want to look at any of that shit, mate. It's all just a lot of dead shit. Let's sink us a pint first."

By now Chase had resigned himself to having bankrolled a pub crawl. They stopped at The Catherine Wheel, and Chase fetched pints of lager while Nemo Skagg commandeered a bench around the corner on Holland Street. From this relative eddy, they watched the crowd stroll past on Kensington Church Street. Chase smelled the curry and chili from within the pub, wondering how to break this off. He really should eat something.

"I don't believe you told me your name." Nemo Skagg was growing measurably more alert, and that seemed to make his condition all the more tragic.

"I'm Ryan Chase." Chase, who was growing increasingly pissed, no longer regarded the fallen rock star as an object of pity: he now revered him as a crippled hero of the wars in the fast lane.

"Pleased to meet you, Ryan." Nemo Skagg extended a taloned hand. "Where in the States are you from?"

"Well, I live in Connecticut. I have a studio there."

"I'd reckoned you for an artist. And clearly not a starving garret sort. What do you do?"

"Portraits, mostly. Gallery work. I get by." Chase could not fail to notice the other's empty pint. Sighing, he arose to attend to the matter.

When he returned, Chase said, with some effort at firmness, "Now then. Here we are in Kensington. What is all this leading to?"

"You really are a fan, then?"

The lager inclined Chase toward an effusive and reckless mood. "Needle was the cutting edge of punk rock. Your first album,

Excessive Bodily Fluids, set the standard for a generation. Your second album, *The Coppery Taste of Blood*, remains one of the ten best rock albums ever recorded. When I die, these go into the vault with me."

"You serious?"

"Well, we do have a family vault. I've always fancied stocking it with a few favorite items. Like the ancient Egyptians. I mean, being dead has to get boring."

"Then do you believe in an afterlife?"

"Doesn't really matter whether I do or I don't, does it? Still, it can't hurt to allow for eventualities."

"Yeah. Well, it's all bollocks anyway." Nemo Skagg's eyes had cleared, and Chase found their gaze penetrating and disturbing. He was glad when Nemo stared past him to watch the passersby.

Chase belched and glanced at his watch. "Yes. Well. Here we are in Kensington." He had begun the afternoon's adventure hoping that Nemo Skagg intended to point out to him his former house near here, perhaps entertain him with anecdotes of past extravagances committed on the grounds, maybe even introduce him to some of his whilom friends and colleagues. Nothing more than a bad hangover now seemed the probable outcome.

"Right." Nemo stood up, rather steadier now than Chase. "Let's make our move. I said I'd show you."

Chase finished his lager and followed Nemo down Kensington Church Street, past the church on the corner, and into Ken High Street, where, with some difficulty, they crossed over. The pavement was extremely crowded now as they lurched along. Tattooed girls in black leather miniskirts flashed suspender belts and stiletto heels. Plaid-clad tourists swayed under burdens of cameras and cellulite. Lads with pierced faces and fenestrated jeans modeled motorcycle jackets laden with chrome. Bored shopworkers trudged unseeingly through it all.

Nemo Skagg turned into the main doorway of Kensington Market. He turned to Chase. "Here's your fucking afterlife."

Chase was rather more interested in finding the loo, but he followed his Virgil. Ken Market was some three floors of cramped shops and tiny stalls—records and jewelry, T-shirts and tattoos, punk fashions from skinhead kicker boots to latex minidresses. You could get your nipples pierced, try on a new pair of handcuffs, or buy a heavy-metal biker jacket that would deflect a tank shell. Chase, who remembered Swinging London of the Beatles era, fondly thought of Ken Market as Carnaby Street Goes to Hell.

"Tell me again," he called after Nemo Skagg. "Why are we here?"

"Because you wanted to know." Nemo pushed forward through the claustrophobic passageways, half dragging Chase and pointing at the merchandise on display. "Observe, my dear Watson."

Ken Market was a labyrinth of well over a hundred vendors, tucked away into tiny cells like funnel spiders waiting in webs. A henna-haired girl in black PVC stared at them incuriously from behind a counter of studded leather accessories. A Pakistani shuffled stacks of T-shirts, mounted on cardboard and sealed in cellophane. An emaciated speedfreak in leather harness guarded her stock of records—empty albums on display, their vinyl souls hidden away. An aging Teddy boy arranged his display of postcards—some of which would never clear the postal inspectors. Two skinheads glared out of the twilight of a tattoo parlor: OF COURSE IT HURTS read the signboard above the opening. Bikers in leather studied massive belts and buckles memorializing Vincent, BSA, Triumph, Norton, Ariel, AJS—no Jap rice mills served here.

"What do you see?" Nemo whispered conspiratorially.

"Lots of weird people buying and selling weird things?" Chase had always wanted to own a Vincent.

"They're all dead things. Even the motorcycles."

"I see."

"No, you don't see. Follow and learn."

Nemo Skagg paused before a display of posters. He pointed. "James Dean. Jim Morrison. Jimi Hendrix. All dead."

He turned to a rack of postcards. "Elvis Presley. Judy Garland. John Lennon. Marilyn Monroe. All dead."

And to a wall of T-shirts. "Sid Vicious. Keith Moon. Janis Joplin. Brian Jones. All dead."

Nemo Skagg whirled to point at a teenager wearing a Roy

Orbison T-shirt. Her friend had James Dean badges all across her jacket. They were looking at a poster of Nick Drake. Nemo shouted at them, "They're all *dead!* Your heroes are ghosts!"

It took some doing to attract attention in Ken Market, but Nemo Skagg was managing to do so. Chase took his arm. "Come on, mate. We've seen enough, and I fancy a pint."

But Nemo broke away as Chase steered him past a stall selling vintage rock recordings. Album jackets of Sid and Elvis and Jim and Jimi hung in state from the back of the stall. The bored girl in a black latex bra looked at Nemo distastefully from behind her counter. Either her face had been badly beaten the night before, or she had been reckless with her eyeshadow.

"Anything by Needle?" Nemo asked.

"Nah. You might try Dez and Sheila upstairs. I think they had a copy of *Vampire Serial Killer* some weeks back. Probably still have it."

"Why don't you stock Needle?"

"Who wants Needle? They're naff."

"I mean, the early albums. With Nemo Skagg."

"Who's he?"

"Someone who isn't dead yet."

"That's his problem then, isn't it."

"Do you know who I am?"

"Yes. You're a piss artist. Now bugger off."

Chase caught Nemo Skagg's arm and tugged hard. "Come on, mate. There's nothing here."

And they slunk out, past life-size posters of James Dean, mesmerizing walls of John Lennon T-shirts, kaleidoscopic racks of Marilyn Monroe postcards. Elvis lip-synched to them from the backs of leather jackets. Betty Page stared wide-eyed and ball-gagged from Xotique's window of fetish chic. Jim Morrison was being born again in tattoo across the ample breast of a spike-haired blonde. A punker couple with matching Sid and Nancy T-shirts displayed matching forearms of needle tracks. Someone was loudly playing Buddy Holly from the stall that offered painless ear piercing. A blazing skull grinned at them from the back of the biker who lounged at the exit, peddling his skinny ass in stained leather jeans.

Outside it was still a pleasant September late afternoon, and even the exhaust-clogged air of Ken High Street felt fresh and clear to Chase's lungs. Nemo Skagg was muttering under his breath, and the shakes seemed to have returned. Chase steered him across traffic and back toward the relative quiet of Ken Church Street.

"Off-license. Just ahead." Nemo was acting now on reflex. He drew Chase into the off-license shop and silently dug out two four-packs of Tennent's Super. Chase added some sandwiches of unknown composition to the counter, paid for the lot, and they left.

"Just here," said Nemo, turning into an iron gate at the back of the church at the corner of Ken Church and Ken High Street. There was an enclosed churchyard within—a quiet garden with late roses, a leafy bower of some vine, walkways and benches. A few sarcophagi of eroded stone made grey shapes above the trimmed grass. Occasional tombstones leaned as barely decipherable monuments here and there; others were incorporated into the brick of the church walls. Soot-colored robins explored wormy crab apples, and hopeful sparrows and pigeons converged upon the two men as they sat down. The traffic of Kensington seemed hushed and distant, although only a glance away. Chase was familiar with this area of Kensington, but he had never known that this churchyard was here. He remembered that Nemo Skagg had once owned a house somewhere in the borough. Possibly he had sat here often, seeking silence.

Nemo listlessly popped a can of Tennent's, sucked on it, ignored the proffered sandwich. Chase munched on cress and cucumber, anxious to get any sort of food into his stomach. Savoring the respite, he sipped on his can of lager and waited.

Nemo Skagg was on his second can before he spoke. "So then, mate. Now you know."

Chase had already decided to find a cab once the evening rush hour let up. He was certain he could not manage the tube after the afternoon's booze-up. "I'm sorry?" he said.

"You've got to be dead. All their heroes are ghosts. They only worship the dead. The music, the posters, the T-shirts. All of it. They only want to love dead things. So easy to be loyal to dead things. The dead never change. Never grow old. Never fade away. Better to drop dead than to fade away."

"Hey, come on." Chase thought he had it sussed. "Sure the place has its obligatory showcase of dead superstars. That's nostalgia, mate. Consider that there were ten or twenty times as many new faces, new groups, new stars."

"Oi. You come back in a year's time, and I promise you that ninety per cent of your new faces will be missing and well forgotten, replaced by another bloody lot of bloody new sods. But you'll still find your bloody James Dean posters and your bloody Elvis jackets and your bloody Doors CDs and your bloody John Lennon T-shirts, bullet holes three quid extra.

"Listen, mate. They only want the dead. The dead never change. They're always there, at your service, never a skip. You want to wank off on James Dean? There he is, pretty as the day he snuffed it. Want head from Marilyn Monroe? Just pump up your inflatable doll.

"*But*. And this is it, Ryan. Had James Dean learned to drive his Porsche, he'd by now be a corpulent old geezer with a hairpiece and three chins like Paul Newman or Marlon Brando. Marilyn Monroe would be a stupid old cow slapping your Beverly Hills cops around—when she wasn't doing telly adverts for adult nappies and denture fixatives. Jim Morrison would be flogging a chain of vegetarian restaurants. Jimi Hendrix would be doing a golden oldies tour with Otis Redding. Elvis would be playing to fat old cunts in Las Vegas casinos. Buddy Holly would be selling used cars in Chattanooga. How many pictures of fat and fading fifty-year-old farts did you see in there, Ryan? Want to buy the latest Paul McCartney album?"

Chase decided that he would leave Nemo Skagg with the rest of the Tennant's, which should keep him well through the night. "So, then. What you're saying is that it's best to die young, before your fans find someone new. So long, fame; I've had you. Not much future in it for you, is there, being a dead star?"

"Sometimes there's no future in being a live one, after you've lost it."

Chase, who had begun to grow impatient with Nemo Skagg, again changed his assessment of the man. There was more in this wreckage than a drunken has-been bitterly railing against the enduring fame of better musicians. Chase decided to pop another Tennent's and listen.

"You said you're an artist, right? Paint portraits?"

"Well, I rather like to think of them as something more than that…"

"And you reckon you're quite good at it?"

"Some critics think so."

"Right, then. What happens when the day comes and they say you aren't all that good, that your best work is behind you, that whatever it was you had once, you've lost it now? What happens when you come to realize they've got it right? When you know you've lost the spark forever, and all that's left is to go through the motions? Reckon you'll be well pleased with yourself, painting portraits of pompous old geezers to hang in their executive board rooms?"

"I hardly think it will come to that." Chase was somewhat testy.

"No more than I did. No one ever does. You reckon that once you get to the top, you'll stay on top. Maybe that happens for a few, but not for most of us. Sometimes the fans start to notice first; sometimes you do. You tell yourself that the fans are fickle, but after a while you know inside that it's you what's past it. Then you start to crumble. Then you start to envy the ones what went out on top: they're your moths in amber, held in time and in memory forever unchanging."

The churchyard was filling with shadows, and Chase expected the sexton would soon be locking the gates. Dead leaves of late summer were softly rustling down upon the headstones. The scent of roses managed to pervade the still air.

"Look." Chase was not the sort who liked touching, but he gave a quick pat to the other man's shoulder. "We all go through low periods; we all have our slumps. That's why they invented comebacks. You can still get it back together."

"Nothing to put back together, mate. Don't you get it? At one time I had it. Now I don't."

"But you can get help…"

"That's the worst part, mate. It would be so good just to blame it all on the drugs and the booze. Tell yourself you can get back on your feet; few months in some trendy clinic, then you're back on tour promoting that smash new album. Only that's not the way it is. The drugs and the booze comes after you somehow know you've lost it. To kill the pain."

Nemo Skagg sucked his Tennent's dry and tossed the can at the nearest dustbin. He missed, and the can rattled hollowly along the walkway.

"Each one of us has only so much—so much of his best—that he can give. Some of us have more than the rest of us. Doesn't matter. Once the best of you is gone, there's no more you can give. You're like a punch-drunk boxer hoping for the bell before you land hard on your arse. It's over for you. No matter how much you want it. No matter how hard you try.

"There's only so much inside you that's positively the best. When that's gone, you might as well be dead. And knowing that you've lost it—that's the cruelest death of all."

Ryan Chase sighed uncomfortably and noticed that they had somehow consumed all the cans of lager, that he was drunker than he liked to be, and that it was growing dark. Compounding his mistakes, he asked, "Is there someplace I can drop you off? I'm going for a cab. Must get back."

Nemo Skagg shook his head, groping around for another can. "It's all right, mate. My digs aren't far from here. Fancy stopping in for a drink? Afraid I must again impose upon you for that."

In for a penny, in for a pound. All judgment fled, Chase decided he really would like to see where Nemo Skagg lived. He bought a bottle of Bell's, at Nemo's suggestion, and they struggled off into the gathering night.

Chase blindly followed Nemo Skagg through the various and numerous unexpected turnings of the Royal Borough of Kensington and Chelsea. Even if sober and by daylight, he'd not have had a clue as to where he was being led. It was Chase's vague notion that he was soon to be one of the chosen few to visit with a fallen angel in his particular corner of Hell. In this much he was correct.

Chase had been expecting something a little more grandiose. He wasn't sure just what. Perhaps a decaying mansion. Nemo Skagg, however, was far past that romantic luxury. Instead, Nemo pushed aside a broken hoarding and slid past, waving for Chase to follow. Chase fumbled after him, weeds slapping his face. The way pitched downward on a path paved with refuse and broken masonry. Somewhere ahead Nemo scratched a match and lit a candle in the near-darkness.

It was the basement level of a construction site, or a demolition site to be accurate. A block of buildings had been torn down, much of their remains carted away, and nothing had yet risen in their place save for weeds. Weathered posters on the hoarding above spared passersby a vision of the pit. The envisioned office building had never materialized. Scruffy rats and feral cats prowled through the weeds and debris, avoiding the few squatters who lurked about.

Nemo Skagg had managed a sort of lean-to of scrap boards and slabs of hoarding—the lot stuck together against one foundation wall, where a doorway in the brick gave entrance to a vaulted cellar beneath the street above. Once it had served as some sort of storage area, Chase supposed, although whether for coal or fine wines was a secret known only to the encrusted bricks. Past the lean-to, Nemo's candle revealed an uncertain interior of scraps of broken furniture, an infested mattress with rags of bedding, and a dead fire of charcoal and ashes with a litter of empty cans and dirty crockery. The rest of the grotto was crowded with a stack of decaying cardboard cartons and florist's pots. Nemo Skagg had no fear of theft, for there plainly was nothing here to steal.

"Here. Find a seat." Nemo lit a second candle and fumbled about for a pair of pilfered pub glasses. He poured from the bottle of Bell's and handed one clouded glass to Chase. Chase sat down on a wooden crate, past caring about cleanliness. The whisky did not mask the odor of methylated spirits that clung to the glass with the dirt.

"To your very good health, Ryan," Nemo Skagg toasted. "And to our friendship."

Chase was trying to remember whether he'd mentioned the name of his hotel to Nemo. He decided he hadn't, and that the day's adventure would soon be behind him. He drank. His host refilled their glasses.

"So, this is it," Chase said, somewhat recklessly. "The end of fame and fortune. Good-bye house in Kensington. Hello squat in future carpark."

"It was Chelsea," Nemo replied, not taking offense. "The house was in Chelsea."

"Now he gets his kicks in Chelsea, not in Kensington anymore," sang Chase, past caring that he was past caring.

"Still," Nemo went on, content with the Bell's. "I did manage to carry away with me everything that really mattered."

He scrambled back behind the stack of cardboard cartons, nearly spilling them over. After a bit of rummaging, he climbed out with the wreckage of an electric guitar. He presented it to Chase with a flourish, and refilled their glasses.

It was a custom-built guitar, of the sort that Nemo Skagg habitually smashed to bits on stage before hordes of screaming fans. Chase knew positively nothing about custom-built guitars, but it was plain that this one was a probable casualty of one such violent episode. The bowed neck still held most of the strings, and only a few knobs and bits dangled on wires from the abused body. Chase handed it back carefully. "Very nice."

Nemo Skagg scraped the strings with his broken fingernails. As Chase's eyes grew accustomed to the candlelight, he could see a few monoliths of gutted speakers and burned-out amplifiers shoved in with the pots and boxes. Nothing worth stealing. Nothing worth saving. Ghosts. Broken, dead ghosts. Like Nemo Skagg.

"I think I have a can of beans somewhere." Nemo applied a candle to some greasy chips papers and scraps of wood. The yellow flame flared in the dark cave, its smoke carried outward past the lean-to.

"That's all right," said Chase. "I really must be going."

"Oi. We haven't finished the bottle." Nemo poured. "Drink up. Of course, I used to throw better parties than this for my fans."

"Cheers," said Chase, drinking. He knew he would be very ill tomorrow.

"So, Ryan," said Nemo, stretching out on a legless and spring-stabbed comfy chair. "You find yourself wanting to ask where all the money went."

"I believe you've already told me."

"What I told you was what people want to hear, although it's partly true. Quite amazing how much money you can stuff up your nose and shove up your arm, and how fast that draws that certain group of sharks who circle about you and take bites till there's nothing left to feed on. But the simple and unsuspected truth of the matter is that I spent the last of my fortune on my fans."

Chase was wondering whether he might have to crash here for the night if he didn't move now. He finished Nemo's sad story for him: "And then your fans all proved fickle."

"No, mate. Not these fans. Just look at them."

Nemo Skagg shuffled back into his cave, picked out a floral vase, brought it out into the light, cradling it lovingly in his hands for Chase to see. Chase saw that it was actually a funeral urn.

"This is Saliva Gash. She said she was eighteen when she hung out backstage. After she OD'd one night after a gig, her family in Pimlico wouldn't own her. Not even her ashes. I paid for the cremation. I kept her remains. She was too dear a creature to be scattered."

Ryan Chase was touched. He struggled for words to say, until Nemo reached back for another urn.

"And this one is Slice. I never knew his real name. He was always in the front row, screaming us on, until he sliced his wrists after one show. No one claimed the remains. I paid for it.

"And this one is Dave from Belfast. Pissed out of his skull, and he stuck his arm out to flag down a tube train. Jacket caught, and I doubt they picked up all of him to go into the oven. His urn feels light."

"That's all right," said Chase, as Nemo offered him the urn to examine. "I'm no judge."

"You ever notice how London is crammed with bloody cemeteries, but no one gets buried there unless they've snuffed it before the fucking Boer War? No room for any common souls in London. They burn the lot of us now, and then you get a fucking box of ashes to carry home. That's *if* you got any grieving sod who cares a fuck to hold on to them past the first dustbin."

Nemo dragged out one of the cardboard boxes. The rotted carton split open, disgorging a plastic bag of chalky ashes. The bag burst on the bricks, scattering ashes over Nemo's shoes and trouser cuffs. "Shit. I can't read this one. Can you?"

He handed the mildewed cardboard to Chase, then poured out more Bell's. Chase dully accepted both. His brain hurt.

"Bought proper funeral urns for them all at first," Nemo explained. "Then, as the money went, I had to economize. Still, I was loyal to my fans. I kept them with me after I lost the house. After I'd lost everything else."

The fire licked at the moldy cardboard in Chase's hand, cutting through his numbness. He dropped the box onto the fire. The fire flared. By its light Chase could make out hundreds of similar boxes and urns stacked high within the vault.

"It's a whole generation no one wanted," Nemo went on, drinking now straight from the bottle. "Only *I* spoke for them. I spoke to them. They wanted me. I wanted them. The fans today want to worship dead stars. Sod 'em all. I'm still alive, and I have my audience of dead fans to love me."

Chase drank his whisky despite his earlier resolve. Nemo Skagg sat enthroned in squalor, surrounded by chalky ashes and the flickering light of a trash fire—a Wagnerian hero gone wrong.

"They came to London from all over; they're not just East End. They told the world to sod off, and the world repaid them in kind. Dead, they were no more wanted than when they lived. Drugs, suicides, traffic accidents, maybe a broken bottle in an alley or a rape and a knife in some squat. I started out with just the fans I recognized, then with the poor sods my mates told me about. After a while I had people watching the hospital morgues for them. The kids no one gave a shit for. Sure, often they had families, and let me tell you, they was always pleased to have me pay for the final rites

Did They Get You to Trade · 185

for the dearly departed, and good riddance. They were all better off dead, even the ones who didn't think so at first, and I had to help.

"Well, after a time the money ran out. I don't regret spending it on them. Fuck the fame. At least I still have my fans."

Nemo Skagg took a deep swig from the bottle, found it empty, pitched it, then picked up his ruined guitar. He scraped talons across the loose strings.

"And you, Ryan, old son. You said that you're still a loyal fan."

"Yes, Nemo. Yes, I did indeed say that." Chase set down his empty glass and bunched the muscles of his legs.

"Well, it's been great talking to you here backstage. We'll hang out some more later on. Hope you enjoy the gig."

"I'll just go take a piss, while you warm up." Chase arose carefully, backing toward the doorway of the lean-to.

"Don't be long." Nemo was plugging wires into the broken speakers, adjusting dials on the charred amps. He peered into the vaulted darkness. "Looks like I got a crucial audience out there tonight."

It was black as the pit, as Chase blundered out of the lean-to. Nettles and thistles ripped at him. Twice he fell over unseen mounds of debris, but he dragged himself painfully to his feet each time. Panic steadied his legs, and he could see the halo of streetlights beyond the hoarding. Gasping, grunting, cursing—he bulled headlong through the darkened tangle of the demolition site. Fear gave him strength, and sadistic fortune at last smiled upon him. He found the rubble-strewn incline, clawed his way up to pavement level, and shouldered past the flimsy hoarding.

As he fell sobbing onto the street, he could hear the roar of the audience below, feel the pounding energy of Nemo Skagg's guitar. Clawing to his feet, he was pushed forward by the screaming madness of Needle's unrecorded hits.

Nemo Skagg had lost nothing.

Little Lessons in Gardening

The benefits of discovering the hanged man were not immediately apparent to Darren Grover.

Shocked, then suspecting a prank, Grover cautiously approached the hanging object. It was not a prank, and Grover was doubly shocked.

Sunlight pierced the wooded glade and dappled the pallid body. It was that of a young man—possibly a student from the nearby university campus. He was quite naked except for some sort of black latex hood stretched tightly over his head, and Grover was relieved that he was spared from seeing his face. A length of cotton rope was affixed to a padded leather collar, looped over the outreaching limb of a large oak, and tied to one gnarled root. Beneath the trunk lay a neat pile of clothes, and inches beneath the dangling toes lay the stained grassy earth. Some distance away a short section of log had rolled.

Although badly shaken, Darren Grover quickly hiked the halfmile trail through the woods to his house and phoned the police.

In the end, the death was ruled accidental—some small consolation to the student's parents. A search of his discarded clothing revealed no suicide note, but did discover a small quantity of crack and attendant paraphernalia. Publications of dubious and pornographic nature were found in his dormitory room, and an alcohol level of .2 was found in his blood. The forest was a short walk from campus and traditionally was an area favored for clandestine and often questionable activities. Whether others had been present at the time of the student's death was never determined.

However, on the basis of the evidence and the absence of other physical restraint, it was concluded that the unfortunate young man had hanged himself accidentally while engaging in a bizarre sexual experience under the heavy influence of drugs and alcohol, either by himself or in conjunction with unknown participants who had fled.

Case closed.

Regardless, it had been an unnerving experience for Darren Grover, a solitary man who enjoyed his salutary walks through the woods. Pine Hill was itself a quiet university town—"a bastion of learning amidst the untroubled fields and forests of the rural South," in the words of William Jennings Bryan at a graduation ceremony. This had been said well before Grover's day, and before the town and university had begun to sprawl across the untroubled fields and forests, but much of this ambience persevered, and it was entirely suited to Grover's tastes.

Darren Grover was professor emeritus of medieval history at the university. Coronary bypass surgery had prompted his early retirement; his health became robust again subsequent to recovery, owing to regulated diet, exercise, medication, and his less stressful schedule. He was a regular at faculty teas, a frequent guest lecturer, and often at work on some scholarly treatise for the journals. Still in his middle sixties, he appeared rather younger: a bit over six feet tall with no trace yet of a stoop, thin and quite wiry now, with much grey in his once bright black hair and beard. His face was long of jaw and nose—the latter capped with bifocals assisting bright brown eyes. He was a temperate man, and after his second and final glass of sherry he would tell the history majors at the faculty smokers about when he and his students had occupied the dean's office in 1968. Until now, this had been his greatest adventure.

A bachelor of the old school, Grover lived in a cluttered and book-laden cottage in a wooded glen, only a brisk walk to the campus where he had spent some thirty years instructing students in the fascinating history of medieval and early modern Europe. Forbidden now his pipe, he still enjoyed his constitutional, weather permitting, in his baggy tweed jacket and shapeless hat, to chat with former colleagues and putter about the university library. Darren Grover was fondly liked by both students and peers, and he was a man at peace with himself and with life. Except for one thorn.

One terrible thorn.

Her name was Clara Perth, and some ten years before she had buried her husband in Passaic, New Jersey and moved south to enjoy the untroubled fields and forests of Pine Hill. Bryan's florid comments had been preserved in real estate ads in *The New Yorker*, and Pine Hill was rapidly becoming a retirement community for acidulous Yankees who wanted a climatic compromise between Northeastern winters and Florida summers. Mrs Perth used her late husband's insurance money to purchase the cottage next door to Grover's.

The grounds of both properties were small. Both landowners liked to garden—Grover was himself quite the amateur botanist. All should have gone well…

Their war began over the English ivy.

Now then: Hargrove Terrace was a wooded cul-de-sac. The street itself ran along the bottom of the glen up to its head, where there was a small turnaround. Some two dozen small houses perched along either slope—most of them two-bedroom brick cottages of similar pattern and built cheaply just after the War. By now most of the houses along Hargrove Terrace were held as investment properties and rented to students and young couples. Groundskeeping was therefore not a high priority, and tenants changed from year to year, and the forest was reclaiming much of its former range.

When Clara Perth purchased her house, its former landlord had bothered with its upkeep about as little as had a succession of student tenants. The grounds were a tangle, the small lawn weedgrown, and the various plantings of shrubbery in a dismal state.

So it was that Darren Grover noted with approval when

Mrs Perth began directing workmen to clear her yard. His own grounds would never make the cover of *Country Living*, but he had a fine mass of shade-loving plants and flowering shrubs that melded pleasantly with the returning forest, and he was delighted to have a fellow gardener as neighbor. True, his several attempts at introduction had been greeted stonily, but he shrugged this off as typical New York manners.

And one bright morning, there she stood on his doorstep rapping at the glass pane.

She said, "I want to know what you're going to do about all that ivy."

Clara Perth was a lumpish, stoop-shouldered thing of sixty-some winters, clad just now in a shapeless grey warm-up suit. Blued curls framed a pinched face set in a perpetual scowl. Her beady eyes, behind thick glasses, radiated suspicious hostility—on the rare occasions when she did make eye contact, and this was one such occasion.

"The ivy?" Grover had just started to ask her in.

"That English ivy you've got growing all across my yard." Mrs Perth turned and led him to the offending vine.

Where their lot lines converged, Grover's side garden was at a higher level by a few feet, owing to excavation at the time their houses were constructed. A lush cover of English ivy grew over the bank and extended into his neighbor's yard. Grover had planted it on his bank years ago to stop erosion. Little else would grow in the poor soil and dense shade. He was quite pleased with its success.

"What's the problem with my ivy?"

"It's full of snakes, and I won't have it growing in my yard."

"All right, then. Have your workmen clear it away."

"Why should I pay to clear away your ivy?"

"Because it's *your* ivy in *your* yard."

"I want it all cleared away." She had that abrasive nasal accent that set his teeth on edge.

"You mean mine as well?"

"Of course! I don't want it growing back into my yard."

"Look," said Grover firmly, thinking of his morning coffee now growing cold. "You do what you like with whatever's in your yard. I'll do as I like with mine."

They did not part wishing one another a good morning. Later workmen ran a string along the property stakes that marked their mutual boundary, and by evening there was only bare earth on Mrs Perth's side of the string.

And so the war began.

The English ivy was not the only innocent martyr. Mrs Perth's gardening was, in fact, a massacre—a bare-earth policy. Granted that some of the shrubbery wanted trimming, the iris and day lilies should be thinned, the roses and azaleas needed feeding…But everything went: chopped down, uprooted, carried away by the harassed workmen—until at last there remained only barren soil and a few fatally over-pruned ornamental evergreens.

Grover watched the destruction in horror. On pleasant days he liked to sit out in his side yard listening to his stereo, and over the years he had grown fond of the haphazard gardening efforts of previous tenants, had come to rely upon the late-blooming azalea set out by a newly-wed couple (Mick and Nora, was it?) a dozen years back, had marked the advent of spring by the naturalized bed of yellow daffodils that had been there since before he had moved to Hargrove Terrace, had admired the tangle of wild rose that sprawled almost into the street. Eradicated. All.

As Grover mourned the murder of old friends, he consoled himself with the thought that his new neighbor was indeed a serious gardener. No sooner was the earth laid bare than she began to replant. Workmen under her sharp-tongued direction planted dozens of flowering trees and ornamental shrubs, bulbs and perennials were set out everywhere, flagstone walks and concrete bird baths appeared, patches of river gravel and clusters of native stone transformed the former unkempt lawn into a sprawling rock garden, tufts of periwinkle and liriope replaced grass and weeds. It was a total transformation, mounted at great expense and considerable energy.

Grover decided that he had misjudged Mrs Perth and that his behavior toward her had been churlish. Quite clearly her intentions were good, albeit she was planting too much and too closely together. Six flowering cherry trees in a ten-foot row would never do. When she began work on her rose garden, Grover felt it only neighborly to give her the advantage of his good advice.

The workmen were at lunch. Mrs Perth, in a shapeless dress and pulled-down straw hat, was regarding their work with disapproval at their progress. She was preparing a bed of tea roses along their mutual property line.

"You've certainly put in a lot of good work here, Mrs Perth," Grover observed. Since the English ivy matter, they had barely spoken.

Mrs Perth favored him with her habitual lowering expression. "I'm paying enough for it."

Undaunted, Grover persisted. "I'm sure you are. That's why I thought I might suggest that you consider a sunnier location for your rose bed. You see, it's dense shade along here. Shame to put all this work into—"

"I'll plant my roses where I please, thank you." Mrs Perth straightened her lumpy body and glared at him. "When you do something about your jungle of a yard, then perhaps I'll ask your advice."

Grover retreated, and the chill set in to stay.

After that, it was an unending series of skirmishes.

The roses, of course, did abysmally in the deep shade. Mrs Perth fed and sprayed and pruned them mercilessly, but by end of season the roses appeared more sickly than when they were unpacked as sticks and roots from the nursery.

A letter to Darren Grover, placed (stampless) in his mailbox: "Will you please remove that thicket of trees at the edge of my lot. It is shading out my rose garden."

Grover had a row of dogwoods, taken from the wild, which he had planted along their lot line. They were now handsome small trees: graceful drooping branches, large white flowers in the spring, bright red berries in the winter. True, their branches overhung Mrs Perth's property. Grover ignored her letter.

Not long after, workmen came and pruned away every branch that violated his neighbor's airspace. It was, after all, the law.

Next season, the roses did equally poorly. In a mass execution, Mrs Perth had them all uprooted and flung into the rubbish heap to be carted away.

She then began work on a dahlia bed. Grover was past explaining to her about shade and drainage, and the dahlias died horribly. Somehow it weighed upon his conscience.

The flowering cherries were too crowded to do well, and they soon shaded out her peonies. Mrs Perth had the lot cut down and uprooted, replacing them with a bed of iris and a great mass of forsythia. The forsythia struggled gamely to please her, but after a few seasons they were ripped up and replaced by flowering quince. The surviving iris gave place to day lilies. The dahlia bed became a tulip bed, which became a row of clematis vines along the newly erected rail fence, which became a rose garden once again.

The shorn evergreens had died that first year.

And so the years passed.

Darren Grover no longer enjoyed sitting out in his side garden, face to face with the glowering lump as she prowled about her grounds wreaking slaughter. He began to think of her as the Wicked Witch of Hargrove Terrace—a malevolent creature constantly setting out innocent vegetation, then summarily executing it. Of course, weeds were her special prey, and she roamed her grounds daily, peering nearsightedly for anything that might be a weed, pulling it up and placing it in her basket. Leaves were also a target. No leaf fell into her yard that Mrs Perth did not hear and find and remove.

It would have been a brilliant garden, if the old witch had any clue as to *how* to garden. Instead she flung plant after plant into the soil, only to cast it forth once it failed to meet her expectations. Grover thought of a bad general hurling his troops against impossible odds, then executing the survivors for cowardice.

All of this leads into the matter of the deaf dog.

The acquisition of the deaf dog came about not long after the murder of the maple.

The tree that Grover prized above all others on his grounds was a large and aged maple, probably well settled in at about the time the American colonials were sniping at British redcoats from behind fencerows here. It was gnarled, sprawling and ungainly, and it had the most wondrous red and gold autumn foliage of any maple in Pine Hill. Of course, Clara Perth hated it. Hated it for the shade it cast upon her garden. Hated it for the leaves it shed across her well-picked yard. Hated it because it was wild and unfettered.

There had been many notes in the mailbox and surly conversations, all to the point that Grover should do something about that half-dead tree. Grover ignored her dire warnings of lawsuit, should the tree topple on to her house, as he ignored the witch in all other matters—having by now forsaken his quiet interludes in his side garden.

When a large branch blew down in a storm and crushed a birdfeeder and a despairing magnolia in her yard, Grover agreed in the out-of-court settlement to pay damages and have the tree removed. The tree fought gallantly for two days, but it had never faced chainsaws before. Mrs Perth watched its dismemberment from a lawn chair.

A stranger in his own yard, Darren Grover sought refuge in his daily walks through the forest. It had been close to a year now since he had encountered the hanged student, and Grover usually avoided that particular wooded glade. On this day his steps were aimless and automatic, and the westering sun found him wandering along his once-familiar path.

As he crossed the glade, Grover paused to study an unfamiliar plant—unusual, in that he could readily recognize most of the local flora. The short-stemmed plant had ovate leaves and bore attractive solitary flowers with a purple bell-shaped corolla. It grew lushly in the loose forest loam and dappled sunlight of the clearing, and it was only after he straightened up from his examination that Grover realized that he was standing beneath the oak limb where the unfortunate student had hanged himself.

In some agitation, Grover hurried back to his house and began to search through his various reference works. While he was a fair amateur botanist, he was a noted medieval scholar, and it required only a short time to interface legend with scientific observation.

The mystery plant was clearly a mandrake—*Mandragora officinarum*— found in southern Europe and northern Africa, not to be confused with the May apple, native to the United States and also called mandrake. No matter: exotic plants often adapted to other climes, and this could easily be a stray from the university's botanical gardens or someone's flower bed.

On the other hand—and this fascinated Grover—according to legend, mandrake was commonly found beneath a gallows—supposedly grown from a hanged man's final ejaculation as the rope wrenched out his breath. A plant spawned of the earth and a dead man's seed. A plant whose root was shaped like a human—legs, torso, arms, its head hidden beneath its foliage. A plant said to hold all manner of magical properties. A plant that uttered a human-like scream when pulled from the earth.

A deafening scream that brought stark madness and death to those who heard its cry.

Darren Grover paged through his books throughout the evening, learning more. Formulating a plan.

It took rather less time than Grover had anticipated. The workers at the local animal shelter were curious as to why Grover wished to adopt a deaf dog. Grover explained that his recently deceased dog had grown deaf during its final years, and that this was a blessing of sorts in that the dog then no longer barked at every odd noise. This kept the neighbors from making complaints and made for a more pleasant companion. Besides, he had grieved so over his pet's passing that he wanted a dog of familiar habits and behavior to replace that loss.

The animal control officers had been prepared to put down the aged bulldog immediately after she was brought to them, but someone remembered the eccentric professor and phoned him. And so Grover acquired a deaf dog.

Her name was Precious, and she was a white English bulldog. Her elderly owners were moving to a retirement condo in Florida (no pets or children allowed), and they had tearfully left her for adoption, not realizing that euthanasia was the usual policy of the local APS. Grover prided himself on her rescue from her politically correct executioners.

Although aged and deaf, Precious retained the ungainly strength of her breed, and the years seemed only to have increased an already voracious appetite. Grover found that his new pet would readily eat anything he offered her, from expensive dogfood to leftovers of any sort. Beef bones or boiled carrots—their fate was certain once dumped in to her bowl. Precious quickly took to her new master and made it a point of honor that the cushions of his favorite chair should not grow cold during his absences. When not eating, the dog usually plopped down and slept close to where her master might be. Grover formed the opinion that Precious's snoring was the cause of her deafness.

More to the point, the bulldog was incredibly strong. On their walks, Grover was virtually dragged along by the panting bulldog as she strained at her leash. Grover was by no means a small man. Once again, fate seemed to have provided him with the proper tool.

And on one moonlit night…

Darren Grover had already soaked the earth about the mandrake. Gingerly he made fast a nylon cord to the base of the plant, scraping away as much loam as he dared. He had not fed Precious all day, and this bothered his conscience.

The bulldog regarded him with curiosity, as he fastened the nylon cord to her leash. Was she meant to stay here? Then why had Master placed her food dish several feet out of reach? That mixture of barbecued chicken and cat food—her very favorites—smelled awfully good. Precious barked loudly as her careless master hurried away. Perhaps he also was growing deaf?

Well, clearly the food was intended for Precious. She dug in her stubby legs, hunched her massive shoulders, and kicked some eighty-five pounds of bulldog into gear. At first there was some resistance. Paws scraped at earth. Muscles strained. Then the leash pulled free. Precious experienced a sudden twinge, but this did nothing to put her off her feed as she plunged into her dish.

Almost home, Grover suddenly felt…*something*. He stumbled

and fell, crouched upon the trail for breath—wondering whether this might be the predicted final heart attack. He supposed he lost consciousness for a moment, as his next clear memory was that of Precious anxiously licking his face. Her breath stank of catfood and the bulldog was dragging an uprooted plant at the end of her lead.

Grover gathered up lead and bare root, and he and Precious fumbled homeward through the dark.

The mandrake root *did* look like a tiny man. Small arms hung down beside a fleshy torso, and the tap root was closely bifurcated. A knobby bit at the bifurcation caused Grover to think of the root as male. A broad tuft of foliage crowned its head.

Grover quickly wrapped the mandrake root in wet towels. Next he selected a gardener's trowel from his shed, and crept with the mandrake root into the bottom of Clara Perth's garden. There, by the light of the moon, he replanted the mandrake, taking care that it blended in with an anemic patch of hosta lilies. Undetected, he returned home to a snoring Precious.

Darren Grover might have relented. It was, after all, just a malicious prank: a harmless experiment, no doubt, based upon foolish legend. Catharsis. It wasn't as though he had laid land mines about her garden— although this thought, too, was pleasant.

A day or so after he had transplanted the mandrake, Grover was accosted by Mrs Perth as he carried letters to his mailbox. He smiled. She returned her fixed querulous grimace.

Clara Perth said, "It's time you did something about all this mess in your yard."

Grover looked quickly about, saw nothing. "Mess?"

"Weeds. Overgrown shrubbery. Ivy everywhere." Mrs Perth pointed in agitation. "Your lot is an eyesore."

"Thank you, but I consider it a naturalized wooded slope with native trees and shrubs pleasingly intermingled with chosen plantings." Grover had used such language before, but always with sympathetic admirers of his grounds.

"Well, it's a jungle of weeds, and it breeds rats. I've already spoken to my lawyers. There's a town ordinance that requires property owners to clean up their premises, in case you didn't know. I can give you the number of the firm that keeps my grounds clean, if you like."

"Thank you, but I can use the exercise," said Grover with studied calmness.

"Just don't be too long about it." Mrs Perth next turned her scowl toward Precious. "And keep that dog away from my yard. She's been fouling it every night. We have a leash law here, you know. I'll phone the animal control people next time I find a pile in my yard."

Grover protested. "But I walk her myself. She's never in your yard. After all, there are a dozen other dogs in this neighborhood."

"One thing more," Mrs Perth had bent the ear of her lawyers that day. "Turn down that stereo of yours. There's a noise ordinance, you know. I moved here expecting a clean, quiet neighborhood, and that's what I'll have."

After that Grover made a token effort at trimming back some wild roses and a row of boxwood. He kept Precious on her lead, and he always walked her on the other side of the street—feeling the baleful weight of Mrs Perth's glare. As the autumn turned the leaves, he returned to his side garden—silently lounging with a book, a tethered Precious snoring contentedly beside his lawn chair.

It took about a week more to happen.

Grover rather wished for a dark and stormy night, or at least a gathering tempest with looming black clouds and the approaching growl of thunder. It was, however, about four on a pleasant, sunny autumn afternoon.

From above the pages of his book, Grover watched. Mrs Perth: shapeless smock, horrid hat, death basket, shears and trowel, on the prowl. He thought suddenly of *A Tale of Two Cities*. Her malignant eyes stabbed each square inch of her yard, as she remorselessly approached the bottom of her garden—snipping and uprooting all that offended her. Another aristocrat's head rolls. And another. Snick, stab, clip, rip.

Grover held his breath as Mrs Perth zeroed in on the mandrake. It had recovered nicely from its uprooting and was clearly at ease amidst the hosta lilies. None the less, it was a weed.

Clara Perth grasped the short tuft of leaves with both hands, braced her stubby legs, and heaved with all of her lumpy strength.

The mandrake easily tore free from its freshly dug planting.

Precious twitched in her sleep.

Clara Perth clasped her hands to her ears, evidently screaming. Bright blood gushed slowly between her clutched fingers and jetted from her mouth. She spun about dizzily—her eyes wide and unseeing. Grover would never forget her face: total horror expressed upon a lifetime wrinkled mass of disapproval.

Mrs Perth staggered several more steps—clawing at the air and mouthing shrieks, as she careened through her garden of martyred plants. She tumbled into the street. For a moment she clutched at the barren asphalt.

A van rounded the curve, honked futilely, and tried to brake in time.

There was an impact, but the coroner's ruling was death by massive cerebral hemorrhage previous to the accident. After all, an elderly lady, straining at the task of her gardening. Moreover, the esteemed Professor Grover had witnessed the attack.

That verdict came later. Just now Darren Grover did two things quickly.

He switched off the Walkman that had plugged his ears. No loud stereo to annoy Mrs Perth. He hated rap music, but it really was deafening.

Then Grover replanted the mandrake in his own garden, patting down the soil with a loving touch.

A Walk on the Wild Side

Leslie Lancaster sat on the edge of the steaming tub, painstakingly shaving his legs with a pink disposable razor. He was not quite nineteen, but his fine blond beard was enough of a problem to require use of an Emulsifying Ointment BP to soften it for a close, smooth shave, and later some Savlon antiseptic cream to soothe the burn. Toweling dry, he wrapped himself in his terry cloth dressing robe and sat down to make up his face.

Leslie Lancaster's parents lived prosperously in Colorado, and they assumed from his cards that their son was enjoying his summer abroad at a youth hostel in London while taking in museums and art galleries and the Changing of the Guard; perhaps a walking tour of the Cotswolds or wherever to perk him up after his nervous collapse at school. In fact Leslie had sublet a small flat in Crouch End for the summer and was supplementing his monthly allowance in a manner his parents could scarcely approve of or understand.

His hair was blond and straight, and Leslie had had it styled in a pert pageboy that fit well beneath a wig if he chose to wear one. Mostly he left off the wig and relied upon his rather pretty features and his skill with the cosmetics his sister had shown him how to use. Lydia was three years his senior and very pretty, and Leslie had burst into tears that day when she had come home unexpectedly and found him dressed in her clothes. She had thought their mother had been shifting her things about.

Dad had taken him to football games in Denver, which Leslie found boring and incomprehensible. When Leslie threw up over the carcass of the deer his father had just shown him how to field dress, Dad had called him Momma's Little Girl. Momma was preoccupied with her church work and often remarked that her life would have been far simpler had Leslie been born a girl and could wear Lydia's hand-me-downs. Lydia had wanted a sister and resented Leslie with all the usual nastiness of sibling rivalry.

When she found him dressed in her clothes, the two held one another and cried much of the afternoon.

After that, she took him shopping for a feminine wardrobe of his own and taught him how to dress up.

Lydia was starting law school now. Leslie was having an educational holiday in London after his little breakdown at school. Next year he would be a senior at Colorado State (his parents had enrolled him in a grade school program for gifted students, making him younger than his class), and this summer he was considering slashing his wrists rather than returning home.

For now, Leslie tied on a semitransparent latex gaff to hide his male bulge. His cock tucked securely away, he pulled on a pair of black silk French-cut knickers and checked the result in his wardrobe mirror. Credible. Perhaps he'd get the operation someday.

The estrogen seemed to be taking some effect meanwhile. Leslie hoped to have real breasts in time. He squeezed his growing breasts hopefully. Maybe soon, with a padded platform bra. For today he struggled into a soft black bra, fastening the hooks in front and then sliding the cups to the front, fitting Spenco Soft Touch Breast Forms into the cups as he shifted them over his own small breasts. He inspected himself in the mirror. The bounce of the breast forms felt real; the darkened areola and preformed nipple protruded from the soft nylon to good effect. Someday silicone implants. Damn the risk.

Leslie Lancaster was slight of build—another failing for which his father had never forgiven him. The 38-C padded bra fit him well, and he could sometimes slither into a size 8 dress. He had been secretly cross-dressing since puberty, for three years now with his sister's help, and he was not a virgin except with a woman. After his breakdown, Lydia had urged him to make the transformation here in London, away from Mom and Dad and Colorado. Long pendant earrings framed his face and made the short pageboy look sexy.

Preliminaries completed, Leslie tugged on a pair of opaque black tights and a very brief black miniskirt. Then a loose black silk blouse that allowed his silicone breast forms to bounce with his gait, and a black cotton jacket with minimal shoulder padding. His shoulders were small, and he looked very sophisticated in an off-the-shoulder party dress. His legs were good, and the jacket and micro-miniskirt made his slim hips less obvious. Black stiletto pumps finished the ensemble, and Leslie had already learned to walk on five-inch heels on London pavement. He examined his face in the mirror, decided a hat wasn't required, and picked up his handbag. No trace of Colorado.

And he was a she.

Leslie usually turned her tricks on Soho when the tourists were about. Arabs paid well. When money was tight, it was Nightingale Lane and Ramsden Road and Oldridge Road and hanging around The Grove. No Arabs in limos. Quickies in side streets. Maybe a beating. Best to work Soho. Or Kensington. Quiet park bench and a knob job. Chase down the come with a half lager at The Catherine Wheel. Ten quid extra without the condom. Sometimes she got extra when the John groped her cock. Sometimes a bloody lip. She carried mint-flavored Mates, not-lubricated, reservoir tip. Kept her breath clean and fresh.

Now then. Leslie Lancaster was sitting inside The Munchkin on St Giles High Street off Charing Cross. The pub had earlier been named The München and had just been renamed The Conservatory, but would always be known as The Munchkin. Leslie had three friends she often met there before strolling over to Soho or wherever.

There was Samantha Starr, a lovely transsexual just beginning to show her age, which was probably twenty-five but old enough to advise Leslie on her chosen path; she was Leslie's best friend and everything Leslie wanted to become. There was Jo Crowther, a slim dyke who had her suspicions about Leslie, but who was too caught up in her abstract paintings to bother pressing further. And there was Philip Anthony, a graying poet, extensively published, peripherally distributed, eternally inebriated, who was clueless about Leslie or he would have been interested. Leslie had met the latter two through Samantha, and she had met Samantha whilst crouched over the toilet with an unsecured door one evening at the Ladies' in the Munchkin. Yes, women are far messier: never sit down on the seat. Samantha had become her mentor and guide, and sometimes Samantha arranged special sessions for better money than the streets.

Samantha said "You're looking very trendy this afternoon. Very much the London office girl." Samantha had on a long blond wig, but was otherwise dressed almost identically to Leslie—thus the joke.

"Yes," said Leslie. "I fear it's catching this season." Her low American accent translated well as a woman's voice to British ears, accustomed as they were to overseas mauling of their language.

"It suits you well," Jo commented, lighting her cigarette. She waved the smoke away, remembering that it made Leslie cough. Jo was Irish and had lovely auburn hair, shorter than Leslie's. They were of a similar size but Jo was wearing a black leather jacket and artfully torn jeans.

"Thank you." Leslie had never made it with another woman, although Samantha had shown her what to do. She sensed mutual interest and made her eyes wide and innocent as she finished her half lager.

Philip stood up and pointed at their glasses. "Same again, ladies?" He and Jo were drinking pints of bitter, Leslie and Samantha half lagers. Philip saw himself as an aging cavalier poet, surrounded by a court of adoring young ladies, and as such he was good always for more than his share of rounds. He was fond of doffing his tweed hat and bowing over their hands, and he was harmless.

Leslie scanned the rest of the patrons. Early in the evening, and mostly the science fiction crowd who hung out here. No money there, although several of the guys had tried to pick her up. Leslie kept it on a business level, although there was the wicked thrill of it. Turn a few tricks every other night or so. Found in the street: over and above her parental allowance. Paid for the flat and a growing wardrobe. On the street she gave only head. No undressing. Unzip his fly, and face in his lap. Quick and easy and out of there. Twenty-five quid for five minutes, ten extra without the condom, swallowed or sprayed over her face. She much preferred a condom. No aftertaste, no sticky mess to ruin her makeup. And no choking. With practice she could now deep-throat an entire cock and hold it there as he ejaculated, feeling the warm spasms of come pulsing into the condom against the back of her throat. She enjoyed the sensation, and the sudden detumescence that meant job over and money in hand. No taxes withheld.

"Here you are, ladies." Philip was back, sloshing glasses. He resumed his chair and lifted his pint. "A toast to the summer solstice, the longest day of the year."

"Is that today?" Leslie could not believe that she had been here in London nearly three months. Two months more, then back to Colorado. She couldn't do it.

"Bad time to be a vampire," Jo said, concerned at Leslie's sudden dismay. "Or to be a Druid sacrifice."

"Oh, the Druids never sacrificed anyone," Philip jumped in, blissfully uninformed as usual. "You know, I'm thinking of joining Wicca. When I was a bit younger, I used to participate in Morris dancing."

"And got hit over the head by a stick." Jo was on a roll, and she got Leslie to giggle.

Leslie got beer up her nose in the process and made for the Ladies'. Samantha followed her in and watched as she fixed her face.

"Look. Do you have any real plans for tonight?" Samantha knew well she hadn't.

Leslie blew her nose. "What did you have in mind?"

"I have an address. Private session." Samantha had dubious connections and had taken Leslie under wing.

"Have you been putting those cards into phone boxes again? The ones that read 'Ultimate Mistress For Lovers Of The Bizarre. Dial 229-something' and that sort? Because the last time you talked me into participating in one of these sessions, I was made to wear a gym slip and to take ten strokes of the cane from a nasty old man—among other things."

"And your share for the evening was fifty knicker."

"I had serious welts for days."

"At five quid a welt. Besides, it was safe sex." Samantha's sex change had been expensive, and her heroin habit wasn't cheap. The weirdos paid well, and she considered their money hers for the taking. Leslie ought to feel more grateful for the work.

"This isn't going to involve water sports, is it?" Leslie drew the line at getting pissed on. Once a geezer had fastened her head in some sort of portable toilet while Samantha squatted over her face. The Brits were a kinky lot, she thought, but then, who was she to talk. She just wanted their money, quick and easy.

"There may be a little B&D, perhaps some spanking. Look, they've seen you with me and asked about you. I told them you were a submissive teenage model who only posed and nothing more. Well, I hinted that you might give a little head for the right knicker. And anyway, I'll be there with you. Safe as houses, and we split two hundred quid plus tips."

"Two hundred quid! That's more than just spanking!"

"Well, there will be several participants." Samantha put her arm around Leslie. "Come on, love. They want the both of us, but I can always phone up another friend."

A woman entered the loo then, so Leslie adjusted her lip gloss while she thought about it. Probably mean a bright red bum in the morning, but a hundred quid plus whatever extra the geezers paid was better than trolling for Arabs in Soho. And Samantha did know the ropes. Literally.

And there was the strapless black leather minidress she'd been dying for in Kensington Market. With the right underwired push-up bra, she'd look smashing in it.

Back at their table, Philip was entertaining Jo with much lurid misinformation about primitive fertility rites performed at the changes of seasons. Jo was very happy to leave Leslie and Samantha to Philip while she bought a round. Philip was a dear old poofter, and at least he hadn't begun to recite his poetry. Yet.

Later, as they were leaving The Munchkin, Jo caught Leslie by the arm. She said in a low voice, "Will you listen to me? Just mind yourself following about Samantha so much. She's wild, and she's, well, clueless."

Jealousy? Leslie wondered. She left the pub with the trace of a blush. She had also had a bit more lager than she'd intended. Philip had recited three of his latest poems, and drink was required.

It was a warm night as they stood out on the pavement for a taxi. Taxis used St Giles High Street as a shortcut, so even this close to nine they had no difficulty. The sky was still bright, owing to the summer solstice, with shadows now dissolving into deeper shadow.

Leslie studied her face in her compact mirror, feeling anxious. "Do they know about me?"

Samantha shared some of her Valiums. She was in a giggly mood. "I just said that you were an American teenage runaway out for a spanking good time!"

That was the funniest line either of them had ever heard, and they hugged one another in a fit of snorting laughter. The driver wondered if they were likely to get sick in his cab. Probably sisters having a reunion, he decided, although the younger one had picked up a slight American accent while abroad.

They got off in Battersea at a pub called the Northcote, as Samantha wanted another half lager and both needed a slash. Also they were early, and the driver couldn't find Auckland Road owing to the car dealership that had obliterated the street sign at this end of Battersea Rise. After, they clopped quickly down the pavement like giddy schoolgirls, clutching their handbags to their middles, laughing away as they talked, paying no mind to their surroundings. Leslie envied the bounce of Samantha's implanted breasts. She'd have hers done at the same clinic.

"Shouldn't we have dressed better for this?" Leslie asked. She had had three of Samantha's Valiums together with the lagers, and she was no longer on Planet Earth.

"I don't think our clothing will long be a factor," said Samantha, starting another run of giggles.

Leslie felt wonderful. Colorado was only a bad dream.

Then Auckland Road began to oppress her. It was a tiny side-street of row houses, brown bricks showing urban decay. Some houses showed diffident potted plants upon the stoop, others appeared abandoned. Leslie could smell curries cooking somewhere. Reggae music thumped in the gathering darkness. The pub at the end of the street looked cheerless and silent.

"Here! They've said two hundred pounds? Look where we are."

Samantha took her arm. "Obviously they've let a flat, love. Hardly discreet to plan their gatherings where their neighbors are all watching, is it?"

They rang a bell near the end of the street. Leslie was reassured when a young man in pinstripes welcomed them inside. The houses on either side were dark and appeared vacant; this house had an empty feel to it, and Leslie told herself that it was one of those places sublet by the hour or night for special needs. Once Samantha had taken her to a sinister flat in Clapham where Leslie had been dressed into a latex maid's costume and required to give head to a similarly clad Japanese gentleman, while Samantha pranced about in a leather corset and whipped them both with a riding crop. Afterward the John had given both of them head. Whips and costumes left with the management. Most hotels did not offer this service.

Leslie sighed as she entered. Just do the trick, take their money, go home. Beats working the burger-doodles in Colorado.

Outside, it was finally dark.

Upstairs, there must have been a dozen people scattered about the large sitting room and kitchen: men and women, mostly well dressed with a few leather-clad punkers. A skinhead in knicker boots handed Leslie and Samantha cups of some hot mulled punch from a bowl in the kitchen.

"God, it's an orgy!" Leslie whispered to Samantha, smiling graciously as she sipped her punch. "Why do they need us? Looks like we're to put on a show for them."

The punch was well laced with rum and probably much more. It hit Leslie between the eyes after the earlier imbibements. She swayed and found herself hanging on to a professional gentleman, who listened to her every word. Samantha was quickly counting fifty pound notes and shoving them into her handbag. She nodded to Leslie and patted her bag, then headed for the loo.

Someone gave Leslie another cup of punch. The walls were decorated with primitive masks and paintings that reminded Leslie of ancient cave drawings. There was a ballet barre standing in the center of the room, sturdily fastened to the floor. A spanking stand, Leslie guessed. The whips and leather gear were likely in another room.

"Just over here," said the professional gentleman, leading her to the ballet barre. "Have you quite finished with your punch?"

"I think I've had a glass too many." Leslie sensed more at work than the alcohol and Valium, and she began to feel panic.

"Just lean against this barre," advised the kindly gentleman.

Leslie placed her hands upon the barre, trying to keep on her feet. Two women were tying her ankles to the uprights of the barre, while the skinhead bound her wrists together to the horizontal bar. One of the women fitted her with a collar and chain, pulling her head down so that she was bent over the barre, legs widespread, ass exposed, and totally helpless. The other woman expertly strapped a rubber ball-gag tightly into her mouth, then thoughtfully rearranged Leslie's hair and earrings over the strap.

She sensed this had been done here before. Often.

Here's where I earn my hundred quid, thought Leslie, wondering why the Brits had this thing about spanking. The school system probably. She looked about for Samantha. People were removing their clothes now. Well, she couldn't give head with this gag in place. Samantha would look after her if things got rough.

"Shall I strip her now?" asked the skinhead.

"Leave that for Him to enjoy," said the professor.

Leslie blinked, trying to stay alert. She tottered in her stiletto heels and would have fallen, but her bonds held her in a fixed position, and she could only slump forward. She felt someone pull up her miniskirt, then hands groped her ass. Someone poured some sort of warm liquid over her tights. Was that blood? It smelled like a goat pen. Sick.

She hoped they wouldn't use canes; that one session had been enough. She chewed on her rubber gag, looking about for Samantha. Everyone was quite naked now, except for Leslie. They were circling about her now. She turned her head. She couldn't see Samantha anywhere. This wasn't Colorado.

Leslie managed to count. There were thirteen of them in the room.

Naked men and women. Someone was drawing a star in a circle about her as she clung to the barre. She supposed the words at the points of the star were Latin, just as she supposed their chanting was Latin — or something else unintelligible. Leslie hadn't a word of Latin, and she knew absolutely nothing about either witchcraft or Satanism; but she had seen horror films, and she couldn't see Samantha. Maybe she was off getting into some dominatrix gear.

They were copulating now as they circled her — women bent over and men riding their backsides like herd animals mating, shuffling all around her, chanting.

It wasn't just a weird orgy with a lot of kinky perverts after all. Through the veil of drugs, Leslie knew real fear.

A moment later, the horned man appeared with the pentacle behind her, and then Leslie *knew real fear.*

She strained helplessly at her bonds, trying to tell herself it was the drugs, that it was only a man with very much body hair and some fake antlers tied to his head. This was like watching *Rosemary's Baby.* Surely the enormous erect phallus was fake — at least a foot in length and dart-headed like an animal's. Leslie caught a glimpse of his eyes and knew none of it was fake. She lowered her face and moaned into her gag. Maybe this was the bad dream.

He snuffled the animal menstrual blood and urine that had been poured over her buttocks. Flat-taloned hands then ripped apart her black tights, shredded her silk knickers, exposing her ass to the chanting coven and its master. Her gaff still concealed her shrinking cock and balls from their sight, and Leslie felt a strange sense of relief that they still hadn't guessed.

The enormous head of the penis rubbed impatiently against her, seeking an opening, skidding across the crack of her ass. Leslie had only been sodomized on occasion—usually by Samantha's double-ended dildo—and she hadn't liked it at all. But needs must when the devil drives.

The room was dimly lit. As the taloned hands pulled her hips closer, Leslie wriggled her ass to meet the questing penis head, felt it lodge in her asshole, and pushed back against it quickly.

She screamed as the pointed head popped suddenly past her overmatched sphincter muscles. She kept screaming as the twelve-inch cock brutally penetrated her rectum, glanced off her prostate and pushed deep inside her colon. She kept on screaming as the horned man began to thrust vigorously in and out of her ass, grasping her hips and grunting with each stroke.

But, of course, that was the reason for the ball-gag.

Only the ropes and the horned man's hands held Leslie from falling. She had bitten deeply into the hard rubber gag, her sobs and gasps replacing her useless screams. She began to echo the horned man's grunts with each thrust, angling her hips as best she could to accommodate his assault. The huge animal phallus was stuffing her, ripping in and out of her insides, as she jolted helplessly in her bonds.

The others were circling them, switching partners, copulating like rutting animals to match the movements of their deity and his virgin bride. Leslie knew she could never pull free from the horned man's grip on her—not until his seed had been spent within her. Despite the terror and the pain, Leslie was joining into their sexual frenzy. She knew Johns. She knew she was giving this one a terrific fuck. She rocked her hips into his loins, wanting every massive inch of him inside her body.

When the horned man came, Leslie screamed anew against her gag—screaming now in passion rather than pain, although the pain was intense. Molten iron seemed to be gushing into her rectum, filling her insides with a rush of inexpressible energy. She thought of an endless cocaine enema, shaking her total being. In that same surge, she felt her own orgasm shudder through her, as her penis jetted spurts into her latex gaff.

As the horned man slowly withdrew from her bleeding ass, Leslie collapsed against her bonds. She was barely conscious when she felt a taloned hand explore her wet gaff, then rip it away. She thought she heard an outraged snarl—like a chainsaw hitting barbed wire in a dead oak.

She was totally unconscious just as the real screaming began.

Dawn came early with the summer solstice, and dawn found Samantha sprawled upon the bathroom floor. The last hit of smack had been over the top after all the rest. She collected her works, amazed to find it all there, and went to look for Leslie.

Leslie was where Samantha had seen her, slumped over the barre. From the look of it, things had become a bit too wild during the night. Samantha untied her, wincing at the blood and semen that had dried on Leslie's torn tights and thighs. She pulled her skirt down to cover her and helped Leslie to a couch, then went into the kitchen for tea. She settled on a bottle of brandy and shared some with Leslie.

"Rough night?" She inquired sympathetically, as the brandy brought Leslie around. They must have all done her ass. Tough on the kid, but it was just a job. Actually they'd only wanted Leslie for the night, but Samantha had insisted on coming along to chaperone and to collect.

"You bitch," said Leslie. She wanted to strangle her but was too sore.

Jo was right: Samantha was clueless. "Look. I told you there'd be a little B&D involved. And now we have our two hundred knicker."

"Half of which you got just to set me up."

"That's still one hundred pounds to your gain. And you're no virgin—though I swore you was. And I meant to help. Really!"

Samantha looked about, unrepentant, still well knackered. "Where did they all go? Look! They've left their clothing all about!"

"I'm certain they're all warm enough without it," said Leslie.

Glancing down into her blouse, she felt her enlarged nipples pressing against her breast forms, pushing them uncomfortably against her tight bra. Her silk blouse, unscathed through it all, was about to burst open. Leslie tugged out the forms, and her breasts filled the bra cups completely.

Her black miniskirt covered her thighs and torn undergarments. Soon Leslie would have to look.

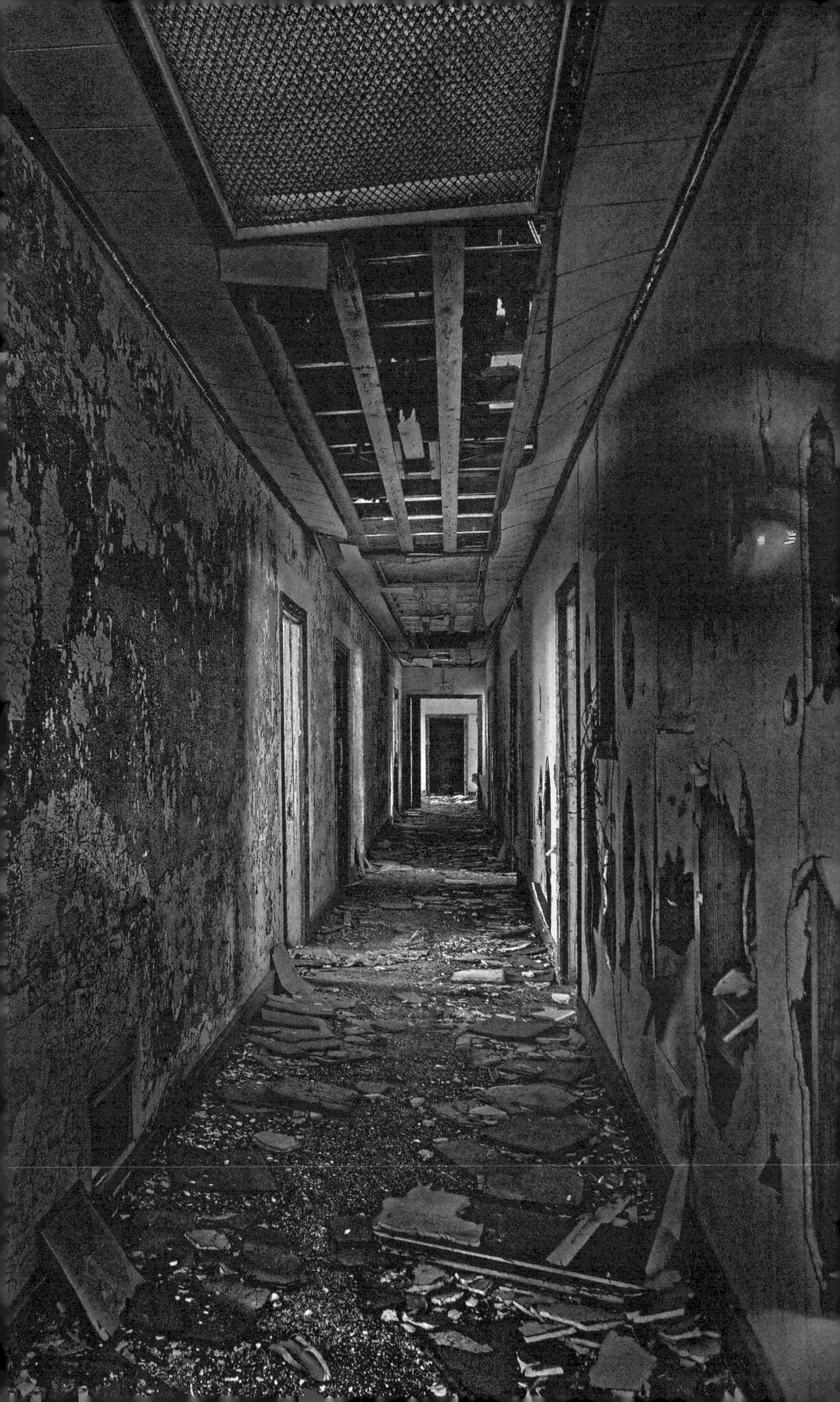

Passages

There were the three of them seated at one of the corner tables, somewhat away from the rest of the crowd in the rented banquet room at the Legion Hall. A paper banner painted in red and black school colors welcomed back the Pine Hill High School Class of 1963 to its 25th Class Reunion. A moderately bad local band was playing a medley of hits from the 1960s, and many of the middle-aged alumni were attempting to dance. In an eddy from the amplifiers it was impossible to carry on a conversation.

They were Marcia Meadows (she had taken back her maiden name after the divorce), Fred Pruitt (once known as Freddie Pruitt and called so again tonight), and Grant McDade (now addressed as Dr McDade). The best of friends in high school, each had gone his separate way, and despite yearbook vows to remain the very closest of friends forever, they had been out of touch until this night. Marcia and Grant had been voted Most Intellectual for the senior class. Freddie and one Beth Markeson had been voted Most Likely to Succeed. These three were laughing over their senior photographs in the yearbook. Plastic cups of beer from the party keg were close at hand. Freddie had already drunk more than the other two together.

Marcia sighed and shook her head. They all looked so young back then; pictures of strangers. "So why isn't Beth here tonight?"

"Off somewhere in California, I hear," Freddie said. He was the only one of the three who had remained in Pine Hill. He owned the local Porsche-Audi-BMW dealership. "I think she's supposed to be working in pictures. She always had a good—"

"—body!" Marcia finished for him. The two snorted laughter, and Grant smiled over his beer.

Freddie shook his head and ran his hand over his shiny scalp; other than a fringe of wispy hair, he was as bald as a honeydew melon. A corpulent man—he had once been quite slender—his double chin overhung his loosened tie, and the expensive suit was showing strain. "Wonder how she's held up. None of us look the same as then." Quickly: "Except you, Marcia. Don't you agree, Grant?"

"As beautiful as the day I last saw her." Grant raised a toast, and Marcia hoped she hadn't blushed. After twenty-five years Grant McDade remained in her fantasies. She wished he'd take off those dark glasses—vintage B & L Ray-Bans, just like his vintage white T-shirt and James Dean red nylon jacket and the tight jeans. His high school crew cut was now slicked-back blond hair, and there were lines in his face. Otherwise he was still the boy she'd wanted to have take her to the senior prom. Well, there *was* an indefinable difference. But given the years, and the fact that he was quite famous in his field…

"You haven't changed much either, I guess, Grant." Freddie had refilled his beer cup. "I remember that jacket from high school. Guess you heart surgeons know to keep fit."

He flapped a hand across his pink scalp. "But look at me. Bald as that baby's butt. Serves me right for always wanting to have long hair as a kid."

"Weren't you ever a hippie?" Marcia asked.

"Not me. Nam caught up to me first. But I always wanted to have long hair back when I was a kid—back before the Beatles made it okay to let your hair grow. Remember *Hair* and that song? Well, too late for me by then."

Freddie poured more beer down his throat. Marcia hadn't kept count, but she hoped he wouldn't throw up. From his appearance, Freddie could probably hold it.

"When I was a kid," Freddie said, becoming maudlin, "I hated to get my hair cut. I don't know why. Maybe it was those Sunday school stories about Samson and Delilah that scared me. Grant—you're a doctor, ask your shrink friends. It was those sharp scissors and buzzing clippers, that chair like the dentist had, and that greasy crap they'd smear in your hair. 'Got your ears lowered!' the kids at school would say."

Freddie belched. "Well, my mother used to tease me about it. Said she'd tie a ribbon in my hair and call me Frederika. I was the youngest—two older sisters—and I was always teased that Mom had hoped I'd be a girl, too, to save on buying new clothes—just pass along hand-me-downs. I don't know what I really thought. You remember being a kid in the 1950s: how incredibly naïve we all of us were."

"Tell me!" Marcia said. "I was a freshman in college before I ever saw even a picture of a hard-on."

"My oldest sister," Freddie went on, "was having a slumber party one night for some of her sorority sisters. Mom and Dad were out to a church dinner; she was to baby-sit. I was maybe ten at the time. Innocent as a kitten."

Marcia gave him her beer to finish. She wasn't certain whether Freddie could walk as far as the keg.

Freddie shook his head. "Well, I was just a simple little boy in a house full of girls. Middle of the 1950s. I think one of the sorority girls had smuggled in a bottle of vodka. They were very giggly, I remember.

"So they said they'd initiate me into their sorority. They had those great big lollipops that were the fad then, and I wanted one. But I had to join the sorority.

"So they got out some of my sisters' clothes, and they stripped me down. Hadn't been too long before that that my mother or sister would bathe me, so I hadn't a clue. Well, they dressed me up in a trainer bra with tissue padding, pink panties, a pretty slip, lace petticoats, one of my fourteen-year-old sister's party dresses, a little garter belt, hose, and heels. I got the whole works. I was big enough that between my two sisters they could fit me into anything.

I thought it was all good fun because they were all laughing—like when I asked why the panties didn't have a Y-front.

"They made up my face and lips and tied a ribbon in my hair, gave me gloves, a handbag, and little hat. Now I knew why sissy girls took so long to get dressed. When Mom and Dad got home they presented me to them as little Frederika."

"Did you get a whipping?" Marcia asked.

Freddie finished Marcia's beer. "No. My folks thought it was funny as hell. My mom loved it. Dad couldn't stop laughing and got out his camera. This was 1955. They even called the neighbors over for the show. My family never let me live it down.

"Pretty little Frederika! After that I demanded to get a crew cut once a week. So now I'm fat, ugly and bald."

"Times were different then," Marcia suggested.

"Hell, there's nothing wrong with me! I was a Marine in Nam. I got a wife and three sons." Freddie pointed to where his plump wife was dancing with an old flame. "It didn't make me queer!"

"It only made you bald," said Grant. "Overcompensation. Physical response to emotional trauma."

"You should've been a shrink instead of a surgeon." Freddie lurched off for more beers all around. He had either drunk or spilled half of them by the time he returned. He was too drunk to remember to be embarrassed but would hate his soul-baring in the morning.

Marcia picked up the thread of conversation. "Well, teasing from your siblings won't cause hair loss." She flounced her mass of chestnut curls. "If that were true, then I'd be bald, too."

"Girls don't have hair loss," Freddie said, somewhat mopishly.

"Thank you, but I'm a mature forty-three." Marcia regretted the stiffness in her tone immediately. Freddie might be macho, but he was a balding, unhappy drunk who had once been her unrequited dream date right behind Grant. Forget it: Freddie was about as much in touch with feminists as she was with BMW fuel-injection systems.

Marcia Meadows had aged well, despite a terrible marriage, two maniac teenage sons, and a demanding career in fashion design.

She now had her own modest string of boutiques, had recently exhibited to considerable approval at several important shows, and was correctly confident that a few more years would establish her designs on the international scene. She had gained perhaps five pounds since high school and could still wear a miniskirt to flattering effect—as she did tonight with an ensemble of her own creation. She had a marvelous smile, pixie features, and lovely long legs, which she kept crossing, hoping to catch the eye of Grant McDade. This weekend's return to Pine Hill was for her something of an adventure. She wondered what might lie beneath the ashes of old fantasies.

"I had—still have—" Marcia corrected herself, "two older brothers. They were brats. Always teasing me." She sipped her fresh beer. "Still do. Should've been drowned at birth."

Her hands fluttered at her hair in reflex. Marcia had an unruly tangle of tight chestnut-brown curls, totally unmanageable. In the late 1960s it had passed as a fashionable Afro. Marcia had long since given up hope of taming it. After all, miniskirts had come back. Maybe Afros?

"So what did they do?" Freddie prodded.

"Well, they knew I was scared of spiders. I mean, like I really am scared of spiders!" Marcia actually shuddered. "I really hate and loathe spiders."

"So. Rubber spiders in the underwear drawer?" Freddie giggled. It was good he had a wife to drive him home.

Marcia ignored him. "We had lots of woods behind our house. I was something of a tomboy. I loved to go romping through the woods. You know how my hair is—has always been."

"Lovely to look at, delightful to hold," said Grant, and behind his dark glasses there might have been a flash of memory.

"But a mess to keep combed," Marcia finished. "Anyway, you know those really gross spiders that build their webs between trees and bushes in the woods? The ones that look like dried-up snot boogers with little legs, and they're always strung out there across the middle of a path?"

"I was a Boy Scout," Freddie remembered.

"Right! So I was always running into those yucky little suckers and getting their webs caught in my hair. Then I'd start screaming and clawing at my face and run back home, and my snotty brothers would laugh like hyenas.

"But here's the worst part." Marcia chugged a long swallow of beer. "You know how you never see those goddamn spiders once you've hit their webs? It's like they see you coming, say 'too big to fit into my parlor,' and bail out just before you plow into their yucky webs. Like one second they're there, ugly as a pile of pigeon shit with twenty eyes, and then they vanish into thin air.

"So. My dear big brothers convinced me that the spiders were trapped in my hair. Hiding out in this curly mess and waiting to crawl out for revenge. At night they were sure to creep out and crawl into my ears and eat my brain. Make a web across my nose and smother me. Wriggle beneath my eyelids and suck dry my eyeballs. Slip down my mouth and fill my tummy with spider eggs that would hatch out and eat through my skin. My brothers liked to say that they could see them spinning webs between my curls, just hoping to catch a few flies while they waited for the chance to get me."

Marcia smiled and shivered. It still wasn't easy to think about. "So, of course, I violently combed and brushed my hair as soon as I rushed home, shampooed for an hour—once I scrubbed my scalp with Ajax cleanser—just to be safe. So it's a wonder that I still have my hair."

"And are you still frightened of spiders?" Grant asked.

"Yes. But I wear a hat when I venture into the woods now. Saves wear and tear on the hair."

"A poetess," remarked Freddie. He was approaching the legless stage, and one of his sons fetched him a fresh beer. "So, Grant. So, Dr McDade, excuse me. We have bared our souls and told you of our secret horrors. What now, if anything, has left its emotional scars upon the good doctor? Anything at all?"

Marcia sensed the angry tension beneath Freddie's growing drunkenness. She looked toward Grant. He had always been master of any event. He could take charge of a class reunion situation. He'd always taken charge.

Grant sighed and rubbed at his forehead. Marcia wished he'd take off those sunglasses so she could get a better feeling of what went on behind those eyes.

"Needles," said Grant.

"Needles?" Freddie laughed, his momentary belligerence forgotten. "But you're a surgeon!"

Grant grimaced and gripped his beer cup in his powerful, long-fingered hands. Marcia could visualize those hands—rubber-gloved and bloodstained—deftly repairing a dying heart.

"I was very young," he said. "We were still living in our old house, and we moved from there before I was five. My memories of that time go back to just as I was learning to walk. The ice cream man still made his rounds in a horse-drawn cart. This was in the late 1940s.

"Like all children, I hated shots. And trips to the doctor, since all doctors did was give children shots. I would put up quite a fuss, despite promises of ice cream afterward. If you've ever seen someone try—or tried yourself—to give a screaming child a shot, you know the difficulty."

Grant drew in his breath, still clutching the beer cup. Marcia hadn't seen him take a sip of it since it had been refilled.

"I don't know why I was getting a shot that day. Kids at that age never understand. Since I did make such a fuss, they tried something different. They'd already swabbed my upper arm with alcohol. Mother was holding me in her lap. The pediatrician was in front of us, talking to me in a soothing tone. The nurse crept up behind me with the hypodermic needle. My mother was supposed to hold me tight. The nurse would give the injection and pull out the needle, quick as a wink, all over and done, and then I could shriek as much as I liked.

"This is, of course, a hell of a way to establish physician-patient trust, but doctors in the 1940s were more pragmatic. If Mother had held my arm tightly, it probably would have worked. However, she didn't have a firm grip. I was a strong child. I jerked my arm away. The needle went all the way through my arm and broke off.

"So I sat in my mother's lap, screaming, a needle protruding from the side of my arm. These were the old days, when needles and syringes were sterilized and used over and again. The needle that protruded from my arm seemed to me as large as a ten-penny nail. The nurse stood helplessly. Mother screamed. The doctor moved swiftly and grasped the protruding point with forceps, pulling the needle on through.

"After that I was given a tetanus shot."

Marcia rubbed goose pimples from her arms. "After that you must have been a handful."

Grant finally sipped at his beer. "I'd hide under beds. Run away. They kept doctor appointments secret after a while. I never knew whether a supposed trip to the grocery store might really be a typhoid shot or a polio shot."

"But you got over it when you grew up?" Freddie urged.

"When I was sixteen or so," Grant said, "I cut my foot on a shell at the beach. My folks insisted that I have a tetanus shot. I flew into a panic, bawling, kicking, disgracing myself in front of everyone. But they still made me get the shot. I wonder if my parents ever knew how much I hated them."

"But surely," said Marcia, "it was for your own good."

"How can someone *else* decide what is *your* own good?"

Grant decided his beer was awful and set it aside. He drank only rarely, but tonight seemed to be a night for confessions. "So," he said. "The old 'identification with the aggressor' story, I suppose. I became a physician."

Freddie removed his tie and shoved it into a pocket. He offered them cigarettes, managed to light one for himself.

"So how'd you ever manage to give anybody a shot?"

"Learning to draw blood was very difficult for me. We were supposed to practice on each other one day, but I cut that lab. I went to the beach for a day or two, told them I'd had a family emergency."

Marcia waved away Freddie's cigarette smoke. She remembered

Grant as the class clown, his blue eyes always bright with ready laughter. She cringed as she remembered.

Grant continued. "Third-year med students were expected to draw blood from the patients. They could have used experienced staff, but this was part of our initiation ritual. Hazing for us, hell for the patients.

"So I go in to draw blood. First time. I tie off this woman's arm with a rubber hose, pat the old antecubital fossa looking for a vein, jab away with a needle, still searching, feel the pop as I hit the vein, out comes the bright red into the syringe, I pull out the needle—and blood goes everywhere because I hadn't released the tourniquet. 'Oops!' I say as the patient in the next bed watches in horror; she's next in line.

"Well, after a few dozen tries at this I got better at it—but the tasks got worse. There were the private patients as opposed to those on the wards; often VIPs, with spouses and family scowling down at you as you try to pop the vein first try.

"Then there's the wonderful arterial stick, for when you need blood gases. You use this great thick needle, and you feel around the inside of the thigh for a femoral pulse, then you jab the thing in like an ice pick. An artery makes a crunch when you strike it, and you just hope you've pierced through and not gouged along its thick muscular wall. No need for a tourniquet; the artery is under pressure, and the blood pulses straight into the syringe. You run with it to the lab, and your assistant stays there maybe ten minutes, forcing pressure against the site so the artery doesn't squirt blood all through the surrounding tissue."

Freddie looked ready to throw up.

"Worst thing, though, were the kids. We had a lot of leukemia patients on the pediatric ward. They'd lie there in bed, emaciated, bald from chemotherapy, waiting to die. By end stage their veins had had a hundred IVs stuck into them, a thousand blood samples taken. Their arms were so thin—nothing but bones and pale skin—you'd think it would be easy to find a vein. But their veins were all used up, just as their lives were. I'd try and try to find a vein, to get a butterfly in so their IVs could run—for whatever good that did. They'd start crying as soon as they saw a white jacket walk into their room. Toward the end they couldn't cry, just mewed like dying kittens. Two of them died one night when I was on call, and for the last time in my life I sent a prayer of thanks to God."

Grant picked up his beer, scowled at it, set it back down. Marcia was watching him with real concern.

"Hey, drink up," Freddie offered. It was the best thing he could think of to suggest.

Grant took a last swallow. "Well, that was the end of the sixties. I tuned in, turned on, dropped out. Spent a year in Haight-Ashbury doing the hippie trip, trying to get my act together. Did lots of drugs out there, but never any needle work. My friends knew that I was almost a doctor, and some of them would get me to shoot them up when they were too stoned to find a vein. I learned a lot from addicts: How to bring up a vein from a disaster zone. How to use the leading edge of a beveled needle to pierce the skin, then roll it one-eighty when you've popped the vein. But I never shoved anything myself. I hate needles. Hell, I wouldn't even sell blood when I was stone broke."

"But you went back," Marcia prompted. She reached out for his hand and held it. She remembered that they were staying in the same hotel…

"Summer of Love turned into Winter of Junkies. Death on the streets. Went back to finish med school. The time away was therapeutic. I applied myself, as they used to say. So now I do heart transplants."

"A heart surgeon who's scared of needles!" Freddie chuckled. "So do you close your eyes when the nurses jab 'em in?" He spilled beer down his shirt, then looked confused by the wetness.

"How *did* you manage to conquer your fear of needles?" Marcia asked, holding his hand in both of hers.

"Oh," said Grant. He handed Freddie the rest of his beer. "I learned that in medical school after I went back. It only took time for the lesson to sink in. After that, it was easy to slide a scalpel through living flesh, to crack open a chest. It's the most important part of learning to be a doctor."

Grant McDade removed his dark glasses and gazed earnestly into Marcia's eyes.

"You see, you have to learn that no matter what you're doing to another person, it doesn't hurt *you*."

The blue eyes that had once laughed were as dead and dispassionate as a shark's eyes as it begins its tearing roll.

Marcia let go of Grant's hand and excused herself.

She never saw him after that night, but she forever mourned his ghost.

In the Middle of a Snow Dream

The costumes were rumored to be genuine Playboy Club surplus, minus the bunny tails and funny ears. Niane Liddell hated them. They were satin or something, heavily boned to pull in the waist and push out the bust, and you needed a friend to help zip you in and out of them whenever you went to the toilet. She had waited topless in bars before, but at least that had been more comfortable than this blue satin torture device. The pawing and patting were about the same either way, but it was cooler topless lugging trays of drinks all about, and at least she could draw full breaths.

This was not the reason why she decided to pour scalding coffee upon her hand.

Niane Liddell actually had just turned twenty-one, although she had claimed to be of that age since she had fled a dying mining town in Campbell County, Tennessee four years before in search of the bright lights of Nashville. Her singing career had not burst upon the country music scene quite as she had expected. After a series of dirty jobs, Niane had saved enough dirty money to afford a bus ticket to Los Angeles. There, she found things dirtier.

Her Nashville agent had promised this and passed her on to a Los Angeles agent who had promised that, but the promises never really came true and neither did Niane's wishes. She slept with the people she was told to sleep with, and she landed a few bit parts in trash films, mostly done directly for videocassette. Niane had a very good body, a naturally pretty face and smile, although she thought her nose too big, lots of shining straight black hair, which she wore Cleopatra style, and an East Tennessee accent that only Nashville should have loved. She took voice lessons, but her film career proved as hopeless as her music career. She could always find work waiting tables in bars, and this she did. Niane took pride in the fact that she hadn't had to turn to the streets, as had so many other crushed hopefuls.

This, despite her growing drug habit.

It had started with a little coke and smack at those parties where she wound up screwing important producers who weren't really producers for important films that never seemed to materialize. And it went on. No stardom. The drugs helped. Niane kept reminding herself that she never took money for screwing on the casting couch. Her only receipts were broken promises and tracks on her arms.

Niane wanted to go home, wherever that was. She saved some money from tips waiting at the topless bars, made a good bit more dancing nude, and, while she refused to admit it to herself, turned a few tricks for customers whom she really did like and who gave her enough money for smack and crack. One night stands was all. She wasn't a prostitute.

Niane was gang-raped one night at a crack house. She was stoned, didn't remember how many and didn't care at the time. She seemed to remember that she owed them some money. Afterward, they gagged her and threw her naked body into a dumpster with her wrists bound and her ankles tied back to a noose around her neck. Then they left her to die in garbage. An example to other bitches.

A bag lady, sleeping inside the dumpster beneath the trash, awoke and found Niane writhing in death throes. She untied her before Niane had completely strangled, and somehow summoned the police.

Niane could tell them nothing. Her only clear memory was of strange dreams as she lay dying in the trash.

Her beating was severe enough to hospitalize her for more than a week. She confessed to her drug addiction as soon as the withdrawal started. They put her on Methadone, Valium and Xanax, and sent her packing once she could walk. Niane was pleased that there would be no scars.

So she hurriedly withdrew her savings—enough for a plane ticket and some to live on—packed whatever she had worth packing, and caught the first flight to Knoxville, Tennessee. The boys at the crack house would be looking for her, this time with bullets to make sure of the job. They wouldn't bother looking as far as Tennessee for a few hundred bucks, and Niane had a girlfriend from Nashville who now worked in Knoxville. Crash space and maybe a job.

Niane's friend worked at Kim's Klub. She was a statuesque black woman named Navonna Wardlow—about three years Niane's senior and above five inches taller than Niane's five-foot-six. Navonna had danced at one of the topless bars in Nashville where Niane had worked the tables. They had stayed in touch after both had left Nashville without stardom. Kim's Klub had opened in Knoxville, and Navonna got a job as waitress/dancer and was in a position to get Niane work there. Good pay, yuppie tips, and crisp bills stuffed into your G-string when you stripped.

Navonna had a bag of bootleg Demerols in her purse, and Niane needed them really badly. But Navonna knew the signs, and Niane was already into her for fifty bucks and her half of the rent money. Niane had been a little overindulgent with her prescriptions. She was running low, trying to stretch them for another few days until she could renew them, and she really needed some Demerols to see her through. And Navonna wouldn't let her have them. And here they'd been pillow mates for several months now. And she'd even let Navonna wear some of her dresses from Los Angeles. The ones she'd worn to auditions. And the red bustier she'd bought at Frederick's of Hollywood. And Navonna was really too tall for Niane's size. It wasn't fair.

It was almost an accident. Niane's hands were sweaty as she filled a carafe from the coffee urn, but she deliberately let it spill onto her hand as it tipped. She screamed. She hadn't known it would hurt this much.

The staff made a fuss. The manager was upset. Navonna sat with her in the employees' rest room and wondered if she might not need to see a doctor for the scald. Niane said there was no need for that, but she could use some Demerol for the pain. Navonna took her back to their dressing room and gave Niane her packet of Demerols. She would look in on Niane in a few minutes.

Marti, a blonde from Crossville, finished her striptease and came in not long after to exchange her G-string for her surplus Bunny corselet. She asked Niane to help her into it. At first she thought Niane was just having a nap. Niane was barely breathing. The Demerols were gone. Marti screamed for help.

Navonna didn't wait for the ambulance. She picked Niane up in her arms, rushed out to one of the taxis that cruised Kim's Klub, and had the driver rush to the nearest hospital emergency room. She performed CPR as best she could as they drove.

The driver had heard many stories of cabbies with women having babies in the back seat on the way to the hospital, but never one of two bimbos in frayed Bunny costumes going at it in a cab. Despite the distraction, he made it to the hospital in time.

Navonna was carrying her in her arms. They were both wearing only their G-strings, but that was OK, as the leaves were stripping from the trees and fluttering down about them. Niane wanted to say something, but Navonna just said, "Hush now, baby," and pressed her breast into Niane's mouth as she carried her along. It was a pathway through wooded mountains—the mountains of Niane's childhood home. She sucked at Navonna's breast, tasting her warm, rich milk.

The fluttering leaves. They weren't leaves. Only made to look like leaves. Camouflage. They were more like tiny flying manta rays of some sort.

Beneath their leaf camouflage they had gills, or gill slits, and tiny sharp teeth in rows within wide mouths. Their bellies were white; their eyes coldly rapacious.

They began to land upon her, biting. Niane tried to warn Navonna, but Navonna only pressed Niane's mouth harder against her breast, walking steadfastly through the attacking flurry of flying creatures. The leaf-mantas were settling all over both of their nude bodies—biting, sucking.

"She's coming around now," Dr Greenfeld told a frightened Navonna. They had given her a white lab coat to cover her costume and told her to wait in the lobby of the ER. Two patients had mistaken her for a doctor.

Dr Greenfeld was a stout, fortyish, very efficient, very much overworked woman. She was a little too aggressive for Navonna's liking.

"Thank God," murmured Navonna.

"Got her here not a minute too soon. Must have been fifty Demerol we pumped from her stomach. Where did she get them?"

"I have no idea. I do know she has prescriptions for Methadone, Valium and Xanax."

"What sort of fool would prescribe that witch's brew!"

"I can't say," Navonna stammered. She hated hospitals. "It was in Los Angeles. She was raped and beaten, left for dead. I think she had been on drugs before that."

Dr Greenfeld's tone softened, but remained brisk. "I see." She glanced at her chart. "And you, Ms Calloway What is your relationship to Ms Liddell?"

"We're co-workers and share an apartment."

Dr Greenfeld had seen their costumes and did not comment. "Next of kin?"

"None that I know of. She's from somewhere in Campbell County. I met her in Nashville when we both had stars in our eyes. Look, I can help cover her bill."

"That's a job for accounting. Just now we'll keep her here under observation until I'm certain that the overdose has cleared her system. After that, I'm signing commitment papers, in as much as she is clearly a danger to herself, if not to others."

"But she scalded her hand, that was all!"

"We'll see that she receives treatment for her substance abuse problems. If she responds well to therapy, I don't expect her to be an in-patient very long. What idiot prescribed her medications! Oh, and we'll need your signature on this."

"Hello, Ms Liddell. I'm Dr Ashford. But please feel free to call me Keith, if that will make you feel more at ease."

"Then please call me Niane. When will I get out of here?"

In the Middle of a Snow Dream

Niane was uncertain, but she guessed she had been on the locked psychiatric ward for about a month. Suicide precautions had been dropped. She had been weaned from her witch's brew of medications and was now coasting along on a minor dose of Mellaril. Someone still seemed to think she needed medication of some sort. She didn't know why.

"I've arranged for a sort of halfway house in the mountains," said Dr Ashford. "It's a sort of old resort hotel, nothing fancy, built in the '20s, and usually rented out to church groups. It's quiet there, and I've already convinced a number of recovering addicts and other patients to spend the week there, sharing experiences, undergoing counseling, before taking the step back to the real world. I feel that this is an excellent therapy opportunity, and, in view of your excellent progress here, I consider you an excellent candidate. This is completely voluntary, of course. What do you say?"

"Excellent," said Niane. She'd kill to get out of this prison.

"Excellent," agreed Dr Ashford.

He was thirty-something, tall and very good looking, with wavy brown hair and neatly trimmed beard. Behind his faux tortoise-rimmed glasses, his eyes were a mild hazel. He wore a loose linen jacket, beige, no tie on a blue button-down collar shirt, and beige cotton Dockers with neat Reeboks. Niane guessed he drove a BMW. She guessed right.

"Can my roommate come along? She's come to visit nearly every day. I don't know how I'd have made it without her."

"Close friends?"

"Very close."

"Then I don't see why not. Others are bringing family members. Perhaps she'd like to participate in group, or just take in the view."

Dr Ashford leaned forward in his chair. "I understand you've had two near-death experiences."

"How did you know that?"

"From your charts, of course. After all, I am a consulting psychiatrist with full hospital privileges. It was by my advice that you weren't given ECT—that shock treatment. Totally uncalled for."

"Just get me out of here."

"I'll see to all the arrangements."

It was a decaying 1920s resort hotel currently named The Brookstone Haven. Staff were minimal—this was off-season—and the place had gone to seed. Sprawling pine logs and cement-chinked construction, bathrooms down the hall. Mountain stream flowing beneath double overhanging verandas. Stream-fed pool that no one would want to jump into even in summer. Just now it was spitting snow.

Niane thought of her mountain home in Campbell County.

Navonna was having a blast. She bounced up and down on their creaky bed. "Hey, we're in a Boris Karloff movie, baby! Just send Bela Lugosi in for me. Man, it's so good to see you out of that place and feeling better. We're going to party here, honey. Then back to work at Kim's Klub until we find something better. We'll do it, girl!"

Navonna hugged her. "God, girl, I've sure missed you."

"I've missed you," said Niane.

Navonna usually wore a wig and had a very short Afro, and that night Niane clung to her hair as best she could, driving Navonna's mouth deep between her thighs. Once she had climaxed, she buried her face between Navonna's legs, loving her frantically. The antique bed creaked and rattled awfully, and they were probably keeping whoever was next door awake, but neither cared. It had been a long time apart.

It was still spitting snow the next morning when Dr Ashford greeted them at breakfast. Scrambled eggs, country ham, red-eye gravy, grits. If you don't want grits, why'd you order breakfast, as the saying goes.

There were Niane and Navonna, somewhat red-eyed as well. Dr Ashford and Dr Greenfeld, both looking cheerful. Niane hadn't realized that Dr Greenfeld was a psychiatrist until several days after her dimly remembered overdose.

The coffee was good. It smelled like Navonna.

There were about a dozen others in the group, some of whom had brought along spouses or friends for support.

Darla King was a burnt-out punker, hostile attitude, who had recently nearly overdosed on smack. Dressed in black, hennaed hair, cute, looked ten years older than she was.

Nathan Morheim was here with his wife. A stroke had left him in a coma for weeks, and his mind had never really recovered. He was a pudgy old man with a happy smile.

Janet Dickson was a chronic schizophrenic, now maintained on Prolixin. When off her medication, she liked to slash her wrists—once nearly fatally. She looked like an aging diner waitress.

Maurice Crossman had come apart in Nam. Parts of his guts were still there. Medics didn't give him a chance, but they dusted him off anyway, and he lived to come back, and he did just fine until the screaming would start again.

Sissy Dexter was a pert blonde teenager. She wasn't wearing a silly helmet when her ten-speed hit an angry Doberman and her head hit the curb. She could joke about getting last rites, and she was through the worst of it.

Jeff Vickery was younger than Sissy. He had a problem with crack, in that he smoked a little too much one night, went into cardiac arrest, and by the time paramedics had him ticking, his brain had taken a licking. His mother was with him.

Alice Shepherd had choked on a bite of steak at a restaurant. By the time someone performed the Heimlich maneuver, she had suffered permanent neurological damage. Her walker and her sister accompanied her.

Daniel Chase was a chronic schizophrenic taking two grams of Thorazine a day. Once, when he forgot his medication, he jumped in front of a bus to tell the driver that he was Jesus. The driver couldn't stop in time to hear the rest.

Tami Malone was a juvenile diabetic. As if acting out her teenage angst, she forgot to take her insulin on occasion in order to get attention. One such occasion had left her near death. Her mother huddled close to her, eating unbuttered toast as an example.

All of this and more Niane confided to Navonna following their first morning group session. Navonna had passed the time reading a Stephen King novel. She had a trailer-load of Demerol hidden in her suitcase, but she wasn't about to let Niane know.

"Let's go for a walk in the snow!" Niane invited. "It really reminds me of home. I'm dreaming of a white Christmas…"

"Yes. Let's do it!" Navonna was so pleased to see Niane back to life once again. That thought stirred another thought, and she thought about that thought as she dressed for outside.

It was a typical east Tennessee snow flurry. Ground frozen enough to hold the flakes, not enough snow to cover the ground. All gone the next day. Unless more came down.

Some of the others were walking about. Niane tried to make snowballs to throw at Navonna, but couldn't scrape up enough of the meager dusting.

They walked giggling along the gravel road, past a series of outbuildings. Garages, storage sheds, individual cabins. All in long disuse. The snow continued to flurry about them.

Niane was determined to make a snowball. She scraped bits of snow from the gravel as they walked.

She stopped suddenly. "Oh! What's this?"

"Roadkill. Yuck!" Navonna turned away.

"But what is it?" Niane carefully picked it up from the snow.

The carcass was flattened and desiccated, about twelve inches in length. Niane at first thought it was a monkey, but this had tiny horns and bat's wings. She flipped it in disgust toward the base of a tall pine tree.

"Squashed prop from *Wizard of Oz*," said Navonna, peeking. "Leave it lay there. Probably some weird kind of bat from these mountains, and bats can carry rabies. Best you go wash your hands."

Niane rubbed her hands on her jeans. That didn't look like any bat she'd ever seen. Endangered species? Escaped from a zoo?

"We need to get back. Dr Ashford has us scheduled for another group session after lunch."

That night, as they nestled together, Niane suddenly said: "I know what the common denominator is here. With the patients."

Navonna was almost asleep. They had wrestled about in a delicious sixty-nine for what seemed like hours. "What denominator? Go to sleep, honey."

Niane sat up in bed and persisted. "We've all of us had near-death experiences."

"Tell me about it in the morning." Navonna rolled over and gave her a reassuring hug, urging her back to her pillow.

Niane had a morning session with Dr Ashford. She hadn't taken any Mellaril since leaving the hospital, so she begged another Demerol from Navonna to steady her nerves. It cleared the furtive movements she kept seeing at the edge of her vision.

Dr Ashford was in his usual positive mood, exuding calm and confidence. "Well, Niane. Please sit down. You seem much more chipper this morning. The mountain air is doing you good, despite this inclement weather."

"Thank you, Dr Ashford."

"Please do call me Keith, if it makes you feel more comfortable. I like to establish an informal rapport with my patients." He was dressed from an L.L. Bean catalogue and very relaxed.

"All right then, Keith."

After the usual preamble, Keith said that Niane was doing very well in group; Niane said that it was a relief to be off drugs and that she had no more suicidal thoughts.

"Let's explore this," Keith suggested. "You were nearly murdered in Los Angeles. What were your final thoughts?"

Niane wanted another Demerol. "I can't really say. I was really stoned before the…the…before it all started. I remember being pulled from a car trunk, then a rope tightening about my throat. It hurt. Then I was thrown into a dumpster. Garbage covered my face. There was laughter. I blacked out. Then there were the police."

Keith studied some notes, made some more. "According to police reports you may have been unconscious for several minutes before the homeless person managed to untie you. You told the police that you had had strange dreams as you were dying. What sort of dreams?"

Niane was definitely getting another Demerol after this session. Navonna had hidden her stash, but she knew where to look. "I was walking naked through the snow, back in Campbell County where I grew up. There were things crawling all about. At first I thought they were sticks or snakes, but then I saw they were more like—what do you call them?—lamprey eels. Like leeches. They had sucking mouths all lined with teeth. They began biting me all over, and I couldn't pull them off!

"Then I could breathe again, and the police came." Niane couldn't stop shaking.

"Yes. Well, I think that's enough for now. We have group just after lunch. Why don't you and your friend have a nice walk through the snow. The exercise is relaxing."

Niane begged another Demerol from Navonna, then they took a nice walk through the snow. The snow was slowly getting deeper, an inch or more. From the clouds, there might be much more on the way. Niane finally made some snowballs. A fight ensued with much shrieking. Niane felt like a teenager again, although she was twenty-one going on one hundred.

She bent down to scrape up another snowball, then screamed:. "Oh my god! Here's another one! And it's alive!"

Navonna rushed to see. "What the fuck!"

It was flopping across the snow. Short brown fur, something like a tailless monkey with membranous wings. It was smaller than a house cat and had tiny horns. Its feet were like an owl's talons. Its muzzle was pointed and had many pointed teeth, which it snapped at them as it crawled across the snow.

Niane bent down to pick it up.

Navonna grabbed her arm and drew her back. "Don't touch it! It's rabid!"

"But it's dying in the snow."

"There's nothing you can do. Leave it!"

"What is it?"

"I think it's a fox bat or a fruit bat, whatever they call them. I can't say. They live in South America."

"Then what's it doing here?"

"Migrating. Someone's pet. I don't know. There may be more of them wintering in these old buildings."

"Bats don't have horns. Or arms."

Navonna dragged at her. "So now you're the expert on bats. Just leave it alone. I'm sure it's rabid."

"We ought to report this to someone."

"Then tell one of the doctors. Will you come on!"

Niane complained about her nervousness that night, but refused to take her Mellaril. Navonna gave in and gave her two Demerol. Then she unpacked their favorite dildo, strapped it on, and soon had Niane too exhausted to complain.

There was more than a foot of snow on the ground by morning. They slept through breakfast. Niane had a morning session with Dr Ashford. She complained that her crotch was too sore because Navonna had been too rough, and Navonna gave her two more Demerols, knowing full well the scam.

At least Niane wasn't pouring coffee on herself. Navonna decided to keep her stash on her person.

Keith was his genial self. Niane was a little stoned.

"Still taking your Mellaril?"

"Yes. But it does make me drowsy." She had flushed it down the toilet yesterday.

Small talk; then: "Let's pick up from yesterday. I think we should explore your recent overdose."

"I scalded my hand. I was already on too much medication. I took a handful of Demerols without thinking what I was doing. It wasn't a suicide attempt. I was just out of control."

"Dr Greenfeld told me you almost died. CPR and quick treatment pulled you through after your heart and breathing stopped. You were clinically dead for several minutes. Very lucky to have pulled through."

"I won't do it again. What's this leading to?"

"What did you experience as you were dying?"

"Again?"

"It's important."

"Navonna was carrying me. We were only wearing our dancer's G-strings. Leaves came fluttering down. Only they weren't leaves. They were like mutated manta rays or something. They settled onto our bare skin, drinking our blood. Surely you have all of this from my hospital records."

"Best to have it from the patient firsthand."

"All of the patients here have had near-death experiences."

"Very observant, Niane. But you are the only one who has died twice. We can help one another to learn."

"About what?"

"About what's on the other side."

"I'm out of here!" Niane stood up.

"Sit down. There's more than a foot of snow outside, and it's still coming down. No road crews here. I doubt you'd get very far. Aren't two death experiences enough?"

Niane sat back down, clenching her fists. "This isn't a retreat or a clinic! What do you want from us?"

Keith folded his hands, trying to look fatherly. "Dr Greenfeld and I have been doing research on near-death experiences. What you and the others have shared with us may answer life's final question: Where do we go after death, and what else is out there?"

"Why this rundown dump of a hotel? Why not a real clinic?"

"Pleasant surroundings. Isolation. Past reports of paranormal phenomena. Conducive to patients' rapport with their buried memories, as you have demonstrated. Dr Greenfeld and I agree that certain points on this earth serve as gateways to other worlds."

This time Niane jumped up for good. "You're no psychiatrist! You're a pair of looney-tunes! Navonna and I are out of here as soon as the snow stops. And I'll tell the others. We'll phone down for a fleet of snowmobiles or something."

"Lines are down," said Keith patiently "Bad storm."

"And you've got bats in your belfry." Niane started for the door, then decided to fire the parting shot. "You really do. Only thing is they live in those old sheds, and they have horns and monkey's arms."

Keith jumped up and grabbed her arm. "What have you seen!"

"Just what I said. Let go of me!" He was very strong.

"Just tell me!"

"I found a dead one in the road when we first got here. Yesterday I found one dying in the snow. Navonna said it was probably rabid and had migrated from South America. Let go of my arm."

Keith's eyes were intense, and he wouldn't let go. "Just show me where you found it. I'll make arrangements for all of us to leave once the snow stops. I promise."

Niane got her coat and pulled a still sleepy Navonna along for protection and confirmation. Keith was waiting impatiently with Dr Greenfeld.

Of course, it was impossible. Niane and Navonna weren't sure just quite where, the bat had still been crawling about, and the snow was approaching two feet in depth. A record blizzard for this area of the Smokies' foothills.

Niane kicked along the gravel road. They'd been at it for hours, and she was freezing. She remembered the large pine tree. There it was, the skeletal one, where she'd flung it, buried under the snow. She scraped away snow.

"Here's one of them."

Keith carefully removed it from the snow. He and Dr Greenfeld examined it in awe.

Keith murmured, "My god, it's really happening!"

The snow was falling so thick that Niane almost didn't see it flying toward them. "Here's a fresh one! Watch out!"

The bat-thing struck Dr Greenfeld, ripping her heavy quilted parka with its teeth. She screamed and slung it off her arm. It flew back into the snow storm, circling.

"Back inside," said Keith. "Quick."

As Niane turned to shuffle back through the snow, she saw a drift move. Something like a lamprey eel peered out. Niane ran as fast as she could, saying nothing to the others.

They passed a clump of reddening snow. Mrs Malone had made a bad decision to have a morning winterland stroll. Keith brushed away enough snow to see the bloated maple-leaf things that feasted upon her.

"The experiment's out of control!" Dr Greenfeld massaged her bleeding arm. "There's too much energy! They're breaking through!"

"Move!" ordered Keith. A stick with teeth shot out of the snow and snapped at his leg, barely missing.

They made it inside and locked the door. For whatever good.

"What's happening!" Niane demanded.

Someone was screaming upstairs. The screams stopped.

"This site is a gateway," Keith said, looking all about. "Sort of a flaw in the universe of the natural human world. The Cherokees knew about it. The whites ignored it. Now things are breaking through."

"You're no psychiatrist," Niane said slowly.

"I am, but I'm also what you might call a sorcerer. Sounds foolish, but we do exist."

"And I'm Elvis in drag. And I'm walking out of here right now. Navonna, come on!"

Keith shrugged. "Doesn't really matter if you believe me. This was to have been an experiment to gather together a group of near-death survivors. I wanted data. I hoped for a possible spiritual manifestation from your combined experiences linking to the gateway here. Nothing like this, however. Together you created too much power. I was only doing research."

"And I was the one locked up in the nut house," Niane said.

Someone else was screaming from the direction of the kitchen. There was the sound of breaking glass. Something hit the front door. Hard.

"You're doing it," Keith said.

"What? What am I doing?"

Keith removed his tie. He seldom wore one. He mopped his forehead with it. "My theory is that when you die, you fall into a universe of absolute evil. Its denizens—demons, if you will—formed by your imagination, descend upon you. No heaven, only hell. When you die and are returned to life, they will try to follow you back into life. You've been dead twice, Niane. And we're standing at a portal. They're following you. They're here. It's all out of control."

Keith whipped his tie around Niane's throat. "I'm sorry, Niane, but this is the only way. I never meant for the experiment to end like this."

Niane clawed at him, gasping for breath.

Navonna rushed to help her, but Dr Greenfeld tackled her. They

In the Middle of a Snow Dream

rolled about on the floor. Niane could hear more screams, but had no breath for her own. Keith ignored her clawing and struggling. He pushed her to the floor, knees on her chest, tightening the tie about her throat. "Third time's the charm, Niane."

Niane lost consciousness. It was all black. It was snowing. She saw a snowman. A very poorly constructed snowman. More like a cone. Its face was covered with icy tentacles. It began to move toward her. Its arms stretched out like thick ropes. It grasped her throat. She couldn't breathe. The darkness thickened.

Niane was able to draw breath again. Navonna was shaking her, her face desperate. "Baby! Baby! Come on, baby! Just hold on for me!"

Niane coughed and sat up. Her throat ached. She gulped air.

Dr Greenfeld was in worse shape. Navonna had crushed her skull with a table lamp.

The door was smashed open.

"Where's Dr Ashford?" asked Niane, holding her throat. She was barely conscious. A tie was wrapped loosely about her throat.

"He's gone. Something broke through the door. I was trying to get away from Dr Greenfeld to help you. All I saw was something like pieces of thick rope reach in and drag Dr Ashford away. Dr Greenfeld turned to look, and I hit the bitch with that lamp. I think I may have killed her."

A frosted tentacle snaked through the broken door, curled about Dr Greenfeld's leg, dragged her into the snow.

Navonna was still too stunned to know panic. "Girl, we've got to get out of here." She said it as if she were speaking of leaving a bad singles bar. There were more screams from upstairs. Navonna didn't seem to hear. Her nose and lips were bleeding, unheeded. She just hung on to Niane, out of it.

"We'll never make it just now in the snow," Niane said. "We'll lock ourselves in our room. I think they won't harm me."

"Who?"

"My death fantasies. They only followed me from the other side. The others lacked the power to escape them. Let's hurry. I think I can protect us both now."

They huddled together throughout the evening and a sleepless night, hearing an endless barrage of screams and crashing sounds.

"From ghoulies and ghosties and things that go bump in the night, dear Lord preserve us." Navonna must have said that prayer a hundred times as they clutched each other and shuddered at every sound. Niane seemed much calmer now and kept reassuring her. Navonna gave them both some Demerols.

By daybreak it had all stopped. Except the snow. Just flurries.

They crept out cautiously. The smell of death hung over the decaying hotel. There were no sounds.

"Are they all dead?" Navonna wondered.

"Do you want to look?" Niane fussed with the telephone. Yes, the lines really were down. She begged a Demerol off of Navonna.

"All right. We'll hike it to town. Maybe we can hitch a ride once we hit the highway, if it's clear. I'm not staying here another moment." Niane tugged on her coat.

"Are those…those things gone?" Navonna worried.

"Let's not wait to find out. I think they got what they came for. For now. Come on!"

The wind had blown the dry snow into drifts, clearing much of the gravel road. They had trudged along for about a mile before Navonna fell back and noticed that Niane was leaving no footprints in the snow. Nor a shadow.

Probably just the snow in her eyes and the glare. She hurried to keep up.

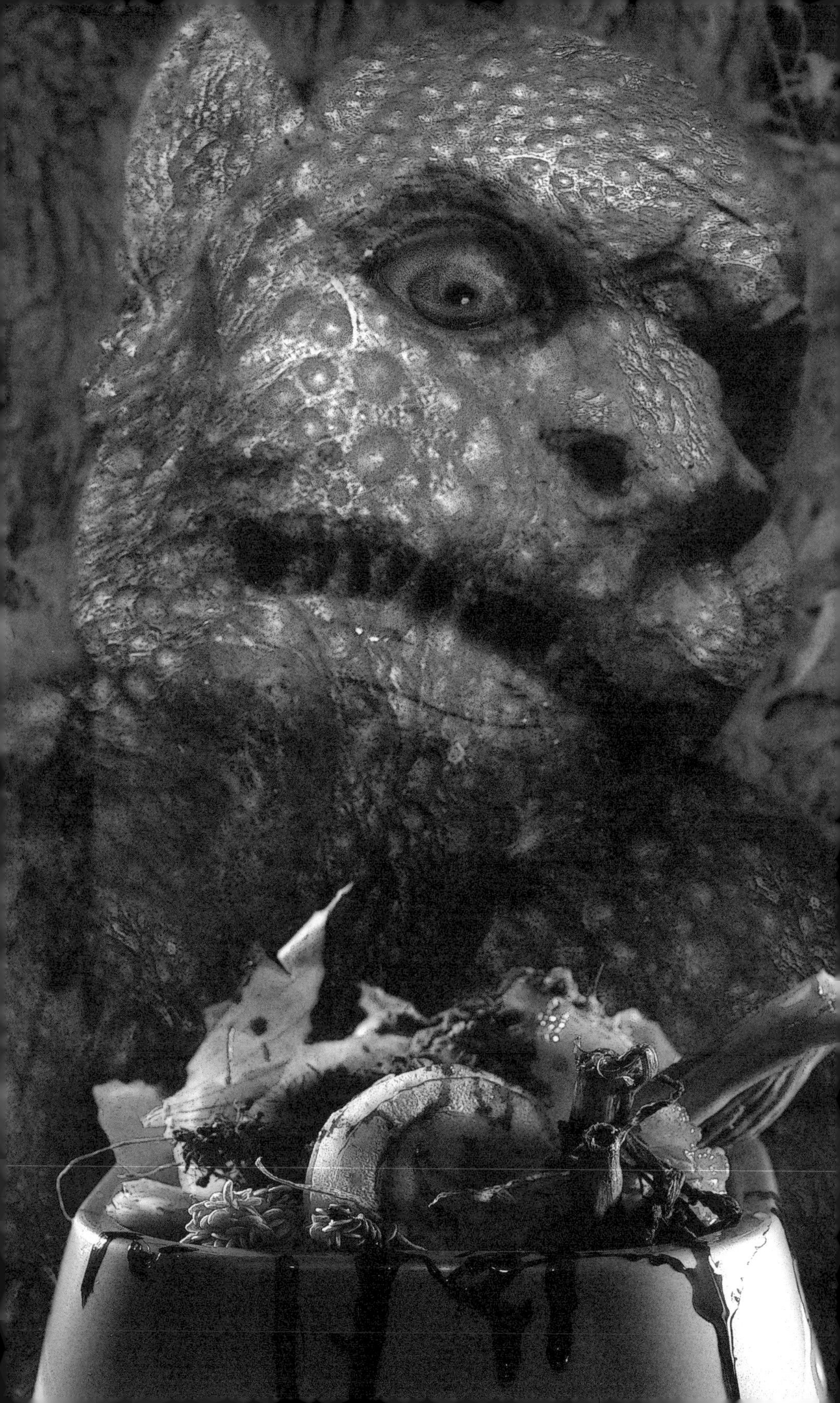

Gremlin

Once upon a time in a village not unlike your own, there lived a kindly old author, who, although he worked very hard, was always poor...

Blaine Adams was a writer of good intentions but minimal abilities, and he liked his gin. That he ever managed to publish at all was primarily due to his prolific output and to his persistence. Given skin thick enough and time, he could usually find some second-rate publisher who would accept his third-rate novels for bottom-list rates. He wrote equally well in all categories — Gothics, mysteries, westerns, science fiction, swords-and-sorcery, bodice rippers, horror, whatever markets were receptive at the moment. It's just that he never wrote very well. Once Edmond Hamilton, a venerable pulp writer, had told him, "No writer is a hack if he enjoys what he's doing." Within these parameters, Blaine Adams was not a hack.

When his wife left him for an androgynous artist with an attitude and good coke connections, Blaine Adams' world caved in upon him.

Blaine Adams lived in a small cottage in the deep, deep woods. It was a small frame house, actually, and it was on the edge of a state forest preserve. He enjoyed walks in the woods with his dog, a shaggy mutt named Buford, as exercise after hours of abusing his typewriter. Karen, his wife, was a potter, and she plied her wares from a mall shoppe in the nearby university town. Buford died not long after she left him, and he couldn't decide which emptiness was the more painful.

His had been a simple life. Hours at his typewriter—he planned to purchase a word-processor whenever he got a really big advance. Boring lines at the post office waiting to mail manuscripts and collect rejected ones sent out weeks before—he really hoped to find a good agent soon. Chores about the house and unkempt yard while his wife was in town, plying her trade, and then start dinner. Adams was as good a cook as writer—enthusiastic, undaunted, and incompetent. At night, some cable and a cold cuddle; he suggested that she see a doctor about her headaches. Anyway, there was the gin to keep him company.

Blaine Adams was really only thirty-something, but he appeared older due to a receding hairline and a bookish nature that peered out from behind bifocals. Given that, he was tall, had once been rangy, but was now showing an incipient double chin from beneath his craggly black beard where grey hairs were beginning to show through.

The walks in the woods kept him fit, despite his sedentary occupation. When the state had purchased the sweep of ridges, they had enclosed a number of old farming settlements—abandoned since the Depression or earlier, and now little more than tree-grown foundations, forest-claimed fields, and collapsed barns. Here and there yellow daffodils, orange day-lillies, and purple cemetery vine still bloomed beside old homesites and forgotten stones of weed-covered family cemeteries. Buford used to hunt here in vain for slow-moving squirrels.

Blaine Adams had published thirty-something books—almost half of them under his own name—but none were ever reprinted.

For weeks he waited for Karen to return, numb from shock and disbelief. After some months, he stayed numb from gin, still hoping against his blurred reality. He tried to force himself to write, but even he saw the hopeless mediocrity of his efforts. Bills began to accumulate, and Tanqueray became Gordon's became generic gin. Enough royalties trickled in to keep him afloat—his lifestyle was a modest one—and he might have made it had not his companion of sixteen years died one horrible night.

He buried Buford in the yard.

And he could no longer bear to walk in the woods.

Loneliness and depression set in with killing certainty. Blaine Adams stumbled through his gin-fogged days in utter isolation, staring dumbly at his typewriter without inspiration, feeding himself without thought.

It is difficult enough to cook for one person, harder still when there is little appetite. Adams left barely tasted pots of chili, overdone meatloaves, half-eaten hamburgers, meal after wretched meal—all to moulder in his refrigerator. Somehow Adams always thought he would get around to finishing his leftovers, but, of course, these held even less appeal to his appetite than they did when freshly cooked. But Blaine Adams was a frugal man, and he hated to let anything go to waste.

A manuscript entitled Wire Edge awaited Adams the next morning. The opening chapters of the novel bore some minimal resemblance to House of the Hungry Dead. The manuscript for the latter had been neatly torn into quarters—all 372 pages at once—and dumped into the wastebasket. There were stains of barbecue sauce on the torn pages. Adams sniffed cautiously. There was also the faint odor of dirt and ancient decay. Of mildew and mould.

Of a neglected graveyard.

Blaine Adams remembered his walks through the forest preserve, with its tumbled-down farmhouses and forgotten family cemeteries. His mind refused to accept it, but his writer's imagination whispered mad thoughts that he could not flee from.

Adams drank gin-laced coffee all afternoon. That evening he filled Buford's bowl with rancid collard greens, a stone-hard chunk of pound cake, the scrapings of a container of jalapeño and bean dip, half a bag of stale corn chips, and the smoldering last of another ill-fated pot of chili. Then he waited quietly.

The wind began to stir about midnight. Adams kept the television blasting as usual, and pretended to sleep through the

Val Lewton flick on AMC. He could see the screen door from his chair, and, despite the wind and the television, he could hear the sound of the crockery food dish being pushed about on the porch. He remembered how Buford used to push the bowl across the floor in a feeding frenzy, rasping his teeth to chew the last crumbs from the edges.

Silence, then the lapping of water. Adams thought he heard a soft belch.

The screen was securely latched, but the hook flipped open as a small hand reached through the torn screen. The hand that touched the door was about the size of a child's hand, but thick-fingered and with spadelike stubby claws.

It entered the kitchen confidently, gazing briefly at Adams in his chair. Adams had kept his eyes lowered, and now he clamped them shut.

It was somewhere between a toad and a dwarf. As a writer, Adams had read too much about elves and fairies and trolls and goblins. His guest was a hobbit from Hell. It was just over four feet in height, and it was almost human in shape, but the coarse scales interspersed with tufts of grey fur that covered its body were proof it wasn't human — even without looking at its face. Large, toad-like eyes, yellow and slit-pupiled, peered from above flattened nostrils and a wide, wide mouth with thin lips and very many pointed yellow teeth. Pointed ears poked through the long tufts of fur that hung down from its scaly scalp, and a short pair of crooked horns grew out of the top of its skull. Its arms were too long, its legs were too short, and its feet were narrow and taloned. A pronounced pot-belly hung out over a dirty pair of cut-off houndstooth check slacks — these last missing from Adams' clothesline many weeks back.

It's a gremlin — that was all Adams could think. My God, I've got a gremlin. He cracked open his eyelids.

The gremlin had opened his refrigerator. Pleased, it nodded and ran a long black tongue over its thin lips. Then, moving almost noiselessly, it quickly entered Adams' study and sat down at his desk. For a moment it shuffled papers about, then it stretched its stubby fingers, cracked its knuckles. Leaning forward, it began to type.

The clawed fingers seemed to rush across the keyboard too fast to follow as page after page spun out like magic. The gremlin was composing final copy faster than a word processor could print out. And the only noise from the typewriter was a soft strumming sound. Adams was right: it was magic.

After about an hour, the gremlin stopped typing. It read through the new chapters of *Wire Edge*, nodded and placed them in a neat stack—then stretched languidly and got up. Rubbing its belly happily, it beamed a horrible smile at Adams in his chair, and let itself out by the kitchen door.

Adams did not fall asleep until dawn.

He remembered the fairy tale about the elves and the shoemaker. And in his fumbling efforts at research, he had read about the little people in the myths of many cultures. Sometimes friendly, sometimes mischievous, sometimes inimical. In days gone by, peasants would leave out bowls of milk or meal as offerings to win their favor. Sometimes the little people would repay them with acts of kindness. Sometimes it just held them at bay.

Blaine Adams had no illusions as to his culinary skills. Only a gremlin could love the dismal messes he left out. And he'd been adopted by a gremlin.

Where had it come from? There were miles of forest, the ruins of old settlements, the forgotten graveyards. Had some immigrant brought the creature here, or was it native to these woods? Useless to attempt to explain magic. Gin and exhaustion called a halt to Adams' speculations.

Go with the flow, Adams decided, and the next night he lavished half a bottle of Tabasco sauce on the dreadful failure of short ribs and dumplings he had seen the gremlin eyeing in his refrigerator.

Wire Edge came in at about 200,000 words a few weeks later. The contract had called for only 75,000 words, but Adams' editor was basking in the praise for having brought in a potential year's best seller for a mere $5,000 advance. She generously sent him a small bonus check and another three-book contract, but a hungry agent had got wind of her new discovery, and he tracked Blaine Adams down.

Negotiations. Contracts. Mega bucks. Mega hype. Hardcovers. Film options. Cover blurbs from the genre's finest.

The Calling was rushed into print amid a flurry of extravagant reviews and enthusiastic reader reception. The publisher promised more Blaine Adams shock classics in the near future, and the public grabbed up copies of *Stalker* as fast as the news-stands could stock them.

It was all happening very fast.

By nature shy and reclusive, Blaine Adams left everything to his new agent. He was content to bank his checks, and he refused to appear on talk shows or to do a signing tour.

The elves had abandoned the shoemaker after they realized he had discovered them. Adams did not stray from his routine. Each night he set out leftovers. As the contracts for new books came in, he foraged through his boxes of rejected manuscripts and hopeless starts—leaving them on his desk when required.

Life was good. For both of them.

And then a local bookstore insisted on having a meet-the-author signing party.

Adams should have refused, but the proprietor was an old friend.

He was seated at a table laden with hot-off-the-press copies of *Wire Edge* when the screaming started.

Fans lined up before his table suddenly bolted for exits. Wine glasses shattered on the floor; a buffet table went crashing. Some, suspecting a publicity stunt, crouched behind shelves of books. Adams stumbled to his feet, staring in horror.

The gremlin moved complacently through the scene of panic, pausing briefly to swallow a handful of chicken wings. It wiped its fingers on the remains of the tattered and mouldering antique tuxedo it wore, then hurried over to where Adams stood frozen.

"Sorry I'm late," the gremlin apologized, "but it took me awhile to dig up this tux: for the occasion."

Adams guessed where it had dug up the tux, but he was past shuddering.

The gremlin climbed into his vacated chair and beamed over the stacks of books at what remained of its fans. It slung a long arm affectionately around the slumping Blaine Adams.

"Hey, I love this guy!" the gremlin proclaimed. "And just wait till you read his cookbook!"

Prince of the Punks

The aged cemetery in Battersea had been in disuse for some years. Weeds grew thickly, cut back only at long intervals by uncaring caretakers. Vandals had knocked over some of the tombstones, broken off bits from the statues of angels. A number of the graves had been opened and robbed. Modern graffiti—some of it Satanic—sprawled across many a Victorian mausoleum.

It was a typical London autumn afternoon. Spitting rain, cold, overcast. Inspector Blount considered himself a fool for trudging along through this mess. Detective Sergeant Rollins gave him reproachful glances but kept silent; he was a tall, sour man in his thirties, ambitious for promotion. Dr Hoffmann led the way vigorously, despite his aged legs. He must be all of eighty. Detective Sergeant Rollins carried his heavy leather bag.

"It's just a short matter of finding his tomb," called back Dr Hoffmann.

Inspector Blount cursed himself for venturing out on this lunatic outing. He was rotund and graying, too old for this sort of thing. Still, Dr Hoffmann might lead them to some manner of clues. Anything would help this investigation.

Six unsolved deaths in two months, all with linking modus operandi. All of them teenagers, found within a few miles of this vicinity, puncture wounds to the throat, bodies drained of blood. The tabloid press was filled with screaming headlines of Satanic rituals and vampiric sacrificial killings. More quietly and more firmly, orders came down to solve the mess quickly.

Which was why Blount and Rollins were following a probable senile lunatic through a forgotten Victorian cemetery in the rain. He might know something. He might even be their killer.

"I have made a lifetime study of vampires," Dr Hoffmann had said, when he presented himself in Inspector Blount's office. "Your murders are clearly attacks by a vampire. I think I can find him. And destroy him."

Inspector Blount had just been upbraided with the others for lack of progress. He was having his tea and thinking of retorts he wished he had dared make. His assignment was to explore the Satanic youth gang element to the murders. Thus Dr, Hoffmann was sent to his office, and Inspector Blount was in a testy mood.

"A vampire? How many sugars?" He poured a cup for Dr Hoffmann. A nut case just might know something worth following with regard to other loonies of his acquaintance. Any sort of lead just now.

"Two, please. Yes, a vampire. Obvious, isn't it." Dr Hoffmann sipped his tea. "If I'm correct, and I think I am, judging from the localities of the deaths, it's one Giles Ashton, entombed within the family crypt, St Martin's, Battersea, in 1878. Months later, they opened his coffin clandestinely and drove a stake through his heart. There had been numerous deaths such as these in the vicinity. Described as anemia. Ashton had been known to explore the black arts. Died under strange and unspecified circumstances. After that, the deaths ceased."

Inspector Blount finished his tea and wished it were a cup of single malt. At least he was pursuing his assignment by listening to this mad geezer. "How do you know all this, then?"

"I've spent my life studying vampirism."

"Oh, yes. I forgot. So then. Why is this Giles Ashton suddenly on the prowl after all these years?"

"I think it's those young punk would-be Satanists, raiding unfrequented cemeteries and robbing graves for skulls and other human remains. I think some of them broke into the Ashton crypt, opened his coffin, saw the stake through his heart, and removed it to see what would happen. It would have released him."

"I see."

Dr Hoffmann examined his watch. "Just past midday. I have wooden stakes and mallet, garlic, crucifix, holy water, and consecrated host. We can find his crypt before darkness and destroy him before he kills again."

Inspector Blount had just received a severe reprimand to produce results right now. His position was in jeopardy. The man was a senile fool, but if he did have any knowledge of Satanic rites near the murder scenes, Blount could truthfully report that he was following every lead. Perhaps the geezer might lead him to something important.

So Inspector Blount summoned Detective Sergeant Rollins, and the two of them followed Dr Hoffmann off into the rain and the weeds and the vandalized graves.

"Here it is!" Dr Hoffmann pointed to the mausoleum. It had been blemished with spray-paint graffiti; the door had been forced. In eroding marble letters, the name of Ashton could still be read upon the cornice.

Inspector Blount envisioned a gang of depraved teenagers, high on drugs, performing Satanic rituals here. Drinking the blood of their spaced-out sacrifices, leaving their bodies close by, too crazed to think of hiding them. This might be the break.

"Vampires sleep by day," Dr Hoffmann said. "Giles Ashton will be resting in his coffin."

Inspector Blount had seen the movies. Let the old geezer go on about with it. He and Rollins should find evidence here. It was a large mausoleum, ideal for cult activities. In the semidarkness, Blount observed with disgust empty cans of Tennent's Super, broken syringes, used condoms, dirty blankets, more graffiti. A large pentagram painted on the floor. Blount suspected that it wasn't actually paint.

"Over here!" Dr Hoffmann pointed to a vandalized coffin. It

bore evidence of having been forced open recently, and a verdigris-covered bronze tablet read: GILES ASHTON. 1830–1878. MAY HE REST FOREVER.

"Quick! Hand me my bag!"

Rollins did so, feeling like an idiot.

Dr Hoffmann removed a sharpened wooden stake and a mallet. "Now then. Remove the coffin lid, and you'll find your killer."

My God, the man is serious, thought Inspector Blount. Best to humor him, then get on with the serious detective work. He and Rollins lifted the coffin lid, as Dr Hoffmann stood poised to strike.

The coffin was empty.

Dr Hoffmann stared at the empty coffin. "They must have hidden his body!"

A figure stepped out from the deepest shadows at the back of the crypt.

"After so long a sleep," said Giles Ashton, "I find I have insomnia."

He also had a sawed-off shotgun.

(The original version of this story was written
in collaboration with John Mayer.)

The Picture of Jonathan Collins

The advert had promised "Psychic Consultations" and listed an address in Chelsea.

Jonathan Collins stood before the door of this address, still considering. He was a slightly built man, apparently just nearing thirty. He was clean-shaven, had neat but longish black hair, bright brown eyes, very good features and wore a dark blue pin-striped suit—de rigueur for a middle management position at the largish London hotel where he worked. He had on tight black leather shoes, neatly laced. At a glance, he was a handsome young man on the way up.

He sucked in his breath and rang the bell.

The door opened.

"Yes?"

"Miss Starlight?"

"Yes?"

"I'm Jonathan Collins. I arranged for a consultation."

"Please, do come in."

Victoria Starlight appeared to be somewhat older than Collins. Her hair was a mass of brown elflocks bound with a tangerine scarf. She wore a shapeless black smock, many necklaces, bracelets and rings, and gold-framed granny glasses straight from the late sixties. Her flat was cluttered with books and objets d'art, but meticulously dusted. She had four cats that were visible.

She ushered Collins to a small table. The table was set with a deck of Tarot cards and a crystal ball. Collins felt like a fool.

"Fancy some jasmine tea? I've just put the kettle to boil."

"Not just yet."

"I read tea leaves as well."

"My nerves can't manage tea just now."

The kettle was at a boil. Victoria saw to it and returned with her cup of tea. She sat across from Collins, waiting for him to speak.

Collins sighed and decided to get on with it. "Miss Starlight, I collect pornography."

"What?" She seemed poised to throw the teacup.

"Not modern smut," Collins said hastily. "My interest is only in material from the turn of the century—antique French postcards, art studies, that sort of thing. Somehow I seem to identify myself with that period. I hope this doesn't offend you."

"That you have an affinity for the *fin de siècle* does not. Pornography does. Why are you here?"

"It's these." Collins reached into his suit-coat pocket and produced two aging photographs. "I obtained these at an estate auction as part of a collection. I should warn you that they are explicit."

Victoria examined them with distaste. They appeared to be late-Victorian photographs.

The first was of two young men. One was wearing a garland, woman's black stockings and white silk knickers with lace and ruching, open at front and back. He was crouching upon a hassock. The other young man was standing, wearing black stockings with ribboned garters and a petticoat, which he was holding high above his waist as he thrust his cock deep into the other man's ass. The crouching man was looking back to watch the action.

The second photograph was similar, with the same two men, but shot against a different backdrop. One young man was standing bent over, holding his knees. He wore a garland and a lacy dress and black stockings with garters; the dress and petticoats were pulled above his hips. The other young man was wearing black stockings with ribboned garters and a black corset. He stood behind his partner, his cock thrusting into the other's ass. Their faces were cherubic with pleasure.

"Why show me this trash?" Victoria threw the photographs back to Collins.

Collins spread them out on the table. "Look closely. That's Oscar Wilde. I've verified that from other photographs."

"So sell it to *The Sun*. I'd always heard that Wilde was dead butch."

"And the man wearing the garland looks all too much like me."

Startled, Victoria reexamined the photographs, studying Collins's face. "He *does* look like you. A relative? Or coincidence? Or is this a hoax?"

"Not a hoax. As to the rest, I was hoping you might be able to tell me."

"Perhaps you may have had a gay ancestor. Perhaps he did have a fling with Oscar Wilde or someone who resembled him. Does this make you uncomfortable?"

Collins peered at the photographs. "I think that may be *me* wearing the garland. See? Even the same mole over the left cheekbone."

Victoria sipped her tea. She was not actually a psychic, but she had a smattering knowledge of the occult. The loonies who consulted her kept her off the dole. This man was a megaloony.

"Right, then. Are you telling me that you are over a century of age, and that you were photographed being buggered by Oscar Wilde in drag?"

"I don't know what to think. Not for certain." Collins pocketed the photographs. "I was in London during the Blitz. All of my records were destroyed in the course. Evidently I was buried in the rubble when my house took a direct hit. I lay in a coma for more than a week. No one could say how I survived. After, I had no memories. I had to learn to walk and speak all over again. But there were no scars."

Victoria reached for a cigarette. She was trying to quit, but… "So you're going on sixty-something. You're certainly keeping fit."

The Picture of Jonathan Collins · 259

"I put it to good diet and regular exercise," said Collins. "But after I discovered these photographs, strange memories of a life before the War began to haunt me."

"Memories of a previous life?"

"Of this same life."

Victoria glanced at her mantel clock. She usually booked sessions for one hour, but this time she must find a way to cut it short.

Collins went on: "You've read Oscar Wilde's *The Picture of Dorian Gray*?"

"I have," she said carefully.

Collins withdrew the photographs and looked at them again. "I believe that the premise of the story is true. And I believe that Wilde based the character Dorian Gray on me."

"I'm sorry." Victoria was pouring herself more tea. "You believe that you are Dorian Gray?"

"No. Just a model for his character. I was young and pretty. Wilde used me like a woman. I think one of his set *did* paint a portrait of me — a portrait that aged through the years, whilst I've remained the same."

"And why have you just now come upon this conclusion?" Victoria had two Tarot readings scheduled for the afternoon, then an evening crystal gazing.

"I told you: these photographs," said Collins, still fumbling with them. "Memories came back. Began to distill."

Likely distilled single malt whiskey, Victoria thought. "What is it you wish me to do?"

Collins seemed desperate. "If this is true, then I have to find my portrait so that I can protect it."

"Didn't it go up with that bomb?"

"No. Of course not. Otherwise I wouldn't be here."

Victoria composed herself. Loonies paid. "What you need to do, Mr Collins, is to channel your thoughts back to the last century. By doing so, you may follow the path of your portrait and rediscover your lost years. I have some gems and crystals that will assist you — aquamarine, black tourmaline and rose quartz. They are pendant to a silver chain which you must wear as you meditate upon these thoughts. You may need to reenact past experiences of profound emotional energy to help the crystals lead you back."

And she took him for fifty quid, mainly for the baubles, and after Collins left, she made doubly certain of the bolts.

Victoria Starlight then picked up her favorite cat, a monstrously obese gray tabby, and cradled her. "Oxfam, that was bloody well the craziest git we've ever let into our flat."

Jonathan Collins actually had held a number of positions since the War. He was very good at middle management, but shifted positions frequently—banks, hotels, brokerage firms—before he actually reached boardroom level. He was generally well liked by his fellow workers, who gossiped that he dyed his hair, lied about his age and worked out regularly. The latter two were correct. He was a quiet, polite man, something of a womanizer, seldom drank, but would stand a round or two. When the subject of conversation turned to Collins, it was agreed that he was one of the last of the old school, born out of his age. Only a few associates, mainly female, had ever seen his collection of *fin de siècle* pornography.

To the best of his knowledge, Jonathan Collins had never had or considered having a homosexual experience of any sort. Then he discovered the photographs. Strange and disturbing memories began to overwhelm his dreams. Why could he remember the taste of Oscar Wilde's come when he awoke?

Collins tried to meditate with the stones. He only grew bored, then fell asleep. After several such failures, he decided that either he didn't know how to meditate or the woman was no more than a well-paid fake. Nonetheless, she had advised him that he might need to reenact past experiences of profound emotional energy in order to channel.

Collins waited another week, then explored the phone boxes. His dreams had become disremembered fantasies, leaving him with only a sleepless haze of uncertainty. His fellow workers at the hotel expressed concern about his health. Collins explained it all as a bout of flu. It was going around.

The phone boxes in the West End were festooned with daily supplies of cards advertising sexual favors of any sort and including a phone number. Some were nicely illustrated. Collins passed over the spanking, schoolgirls in uniform, water sports and the usual. After three or four boxes, he selected one which read: "Stern TV Wardrobe Mistress Seeks Submissive Slaves for Training."

After three or four days, he phoned the number.

Collins was given an address near Baker Street. Desperate by now, he presented himself at the door of the flat promptly as scheduled. He was certain that any minute his hair might be thinning and that his teeth probably were loosening in their gums. His nails seemed to be pulling away from the quick, and his digestion was not good. He had to find the painting.

A tall blonde in a tight, long velvet dress answered the bell. Her features were quite feminine, heavily made-up and very stern.

Collins almost stuttered. "Good evening. I'm Mr Collins. I believe I have an appointment."

"Get inside." She practically dragged him past the doorway "I am Mistress Gwen. You will always address me as Mistress Gwen. You will answer only to Miss Joan. And why are you wearing those ridiculous clothes, Miss Joan?"

"I…"

Her riding crop smacked his backside. "No excuses! Show me your forty quid, and I'll soon see that you are properly attired for a young lady."

Collins pulled out the two photographs from his suitcoat pocket, along with his wallet. "This is what I want."

Mistress Gwen looked at the pictures, then looked shrewdly at Collins. No, not from the police. Some twisted Yuppie out for a night's thrills. She didn't usually perform sex—most clients just liked to dress up and be dominated, then wank off. But…

"That's another forty quid."

Collins paid her and was led into a large bedroom.

Mistress Gwen smacked her riding crop. "Out of those clothes. All of them. Right now."

Collins hesitated over his boxer briefs, but a smack from the riding crop made him drop them with the rest of his clothes.

"Good," said Mistress Gwen. "You please me when you obey.

If you're a good little Miss Joan, perhaps I won't have to cane you. Now, then, put on this condom. I won't have you soiling my wardrobe."

Mistress Gwen unzipped her dress. Beneath it she was wearing a black leather corselet with six suspenders attached to black seamed hose, and black six-inch stiletto pumps. The corselet showed some cleavage, but the bulge in her black knickers revealed that she was a he. Mistress Gwen began choosing things from her chest of drawers.

"These should fit you, Miss Joan."

Mistress Gwen helped Miss Joan put on a black bra with foam rubber falsies, then a pair of black tap pants over a black suspender belt and black seamed hose. After that came a black corset, laced tight, and a pair of ankle-strap stiletto shoes. She made Miss Joan sit at the dressing table whilst she applied makeup to her face and lips, then fitted her with a curling black wig.

Miss Joan minced around the room, getting lessons in deportment and frequent whacks from the riding crop.

"Now it's time for the rest of your training," said Mistress Gwen. "Get on your knees on the bed. Now!"

Miss Joan did as she was told. Mistress Gwen had pulled down her knickers, revealing a formidable erection. She rolled on a lubricated condom, then yanked down Miss Joan's knickers and climbed up behind her on the bed.

Miss Joan gasped for breath as Mistress Gwen's cock pressed into her. She pushed her face and padded breasts into the bed pillows, stifling a moan as the head pierced her and the rigid length slid in behind. Mistress Gwen began to thrust quickly, lovelessly. Her hand reached around for Miss Joan's cock and stroked it.

Mistress Gwen was deliberately brutal as she fucked her. She stroked Miss Joan's cock as if she were trying to pull it off. Mercifully soon, Miss Joan felt Mistress Gwen's cock pulse and strain inside her ass; then came her own orgasm.

Miss Joan passed out upon the pillows…

• • •

Collins was crouched upon a hassock. He was wearing lacy open knickers and black stockings. Oscar Wilde, clad in black stockings, his petticoat upraised, was buggering him soundly.

"Hold that!" someone called out.

Wilde paused, his cock partially withdrawn. There was a bright flash, then a plume of burned powder. Collins turned his head. The photographer was removing the glass plate, inserting a new one.

Wilde resumed sodomizing him, thrusting slowly. "We'll have these to show to select friends to see how pretty you are now," Wilde said. "You'll treasure these photographs when you are old and decaying."

Collins glanced up at the windows, shuttered from outside. Lettering there read: "J. MacVane. Photographic Studio."

Wilde surged deeply into him, coming in violent spurts. There was another flash of light…

Miss Joan was lying across a bed, and someone was shaking her. She opened her eyes and found that she was in drag with a filled condom on her drooping cock and a sore ass. She groaned and sat up.

Mistress Gwen was watching her with concern. All she needed was a dead John on her premises. "You feel all right? You were passed out for a minute or so there. You got a condition of some sort?"

"I just was carried away," said Miss Joan.

"Yes. Well, you gave me a fair start. Now, change your clothes and be off. I have another client in an hour." Mistress Gwen considered telling Miss Joan not to come here again, but eighty knicker was eighty knicker, and she was a good fuck. Responsive. Perhaps too responsive.

Collins tried the directories, on the one chance in a million that the firm of J. MacVane might still be doing business. It wasn't. Not under that name, at least. Countless wasted phone calls told him nothing. He realized that he was only assuming that the studio had been in London.

He phoned the auction house whence he had obtained the photographs. They furnished no useful information. The lot of photographs was merely an item from an estate: the deceased was not to be named.

After a week of blind ends and disturbing dreams, Collins made another appointment with Mistress Gwen.

Mistress Gwen received Collins with mixed feelings. She knew he wasn't police, and a regular at eighty quid was too good to turn away. But that fainting spell: if it happened again, she might have to reconsider.

The session went much as before. This time Mistress Gwen was dressed mainly in black latex and leather gear. She soon had Miss Joan wigged and corseted, with red latex spanking knickers, open at the back, and matching latex shoulder-length gloves and stockings. She added a slave collar with a lead, then instructed Miss Joan sternly, often using her riding crop on Miss Joan's exposed bottom.

Having put Miss Joan through her paces, Mistress Gwen ordered her to stand before the white bedroom wall. She took out a Polaroid camera from a drawer, demanding that Miss Joan pose for her.

Miss Joan protested. "You could use these for blackmail."

Mistress Gwen worked the camera. "These are Polaroids. No negatives. Yours for a keepsake. Something to remember how pretty you are, Miss Joan, and where to come to be pretty again at any time. Besides, I think you rather enjoy being photographed. You really do like to pose."

Mistress Gwen took ten shots of Miss Joan in various poses, set the photographs aside, then said, "These will be another ten quid."

Watching her clock, Mistress Gwen next commanded Miss Joan to kneel upon the bed, then undid the zip of her leather knickers. She rolled on a lubricated condom, gave Miss Joan's bottom a few more whacks to improve her own erection, then mounted her. She pressed her cock into Miss Joan's rectum as quickly as she could force it, anxious to complete the session, and began to move her hips furiously. She had let an aging queen in maid's costume give her a blow job earlier that day, and this second ejaculation would take time. Time was money.

The Picture of Jonathan Collins

Miss Joan was rocking from the ceaseless drilling she was getting. She moved her hand back to her cock, hard and throbbing beneath the latex spanking knickers. She was about to come...

Collins was standing beside a plaster mock-up of a Greek column. Behind him was a backdrop of a Doric temple. Collins wore a garland in his hair and nothing else. The studio was quite warm.

"Just a moment, Jack."

Oscar Wilde rose from his chair. He was also naked, and Collins remembered being sodomized by him only minutes ago. Wilde stroked his cock, bringing Collins to full erection.

"Much better, Jonathan. Take the photograph, Jack."

Again a flash and a puff of smoke. Collins blinked.

"That was a beautiful pose, dear boy," said Wilde. "Your body perfect, your lovely penis saluting the flag and your face aglow from a good buggering. I think I shall have this one mounted and framed."

"I wish I could stay like this forever, if it pleases you."

Wilde smiled. "Go on and toss yourself off. I want to see it."

Collins began to jerk his rigid cock. He hadn't come during his buggering, and he was close to ejaculation. "I would give my soul to remain forever young as in that photograph."

His come spurted from him as Wilde watched thoughtfully. There was another flash...

"Wake up!" Mistress Gwen slapped Miss Joan's bottom with her crop and shook her roughly.

Miss Joan opened her eyes, trying to recognize her surroundings. Her latex knickers were sticky with come; the condom had either slipped or burst.

"Good. Do you make it a habit of passing out when you reach your orgasm?"

"Perhaps this corset is too tightly laced."

"Well, then, let's just unlace you. Then clean yourself and get into your clothes. And don't forget your photographs."

Mistress Gwen again considered telling Miss Joan to stay away, but she reckoned she might hit her for a hundred quid next session. Perhaps add some bondage, a good spanking, a gym slip instead of a corset, a pair of schoolgirl's knickers she must wear home. Miss Joan had all the marks of a regular and profitable client.

Besides, the man was clueless.

Collins asked for a week's holiday from the hotel. Despite short notice, it was readily granted. The staff had commented for some weeks that Mr Collins appeared to be under some stress. A holiday was well overdue.

He had previously obtained a pass to the library at the British Museum, and he spent the first days researching any material regarding the life and times of Oscar Wilde. Wilde's notorious affairs were discussed with varying degrees of discretion. Nowhere was there mention of anyone named Jonathan Collins or a photographer named Jack MacVane. But then, such matters as these had been strictly clandestine in that era.

Collins phoned Victoria Starlight for an appointment. He told her that he had twice been able to channel. She told him to keep at it and hung up. He left several messages on her answering machine, but none were returned.

Collins phoned Mistress Gwen, who did pick up her phone for him. "I want to do some shopping," he said resolutely, "and I shall need your assistance. I wish to acquire a woman's costume of approximately 1890 — original if possible."

Mistress Gwen was already consulting her filofax. A dead Thursday until ten. "Is this for you to wear?"

"Yes. Of course, I'll pay you for your time and expertise — and as before."

"Won't come cheap." Mistress Gwen left that open-ended. "I do know all the shops, and I suppose I can cancel a few sessions. Come round with a taxi as quick as you can, and we'll shop for your wardrobe." And mine as well, she thought as she hung up the phone. It wasn't going to be a dull Thursday after all.

Mistress Gwen was modestly dressed in black tights and minidress, stilettos and a chained and studded motorcycle jacket when Collins came to her door. They got into the taxi, and Mistress Gwen gave an address near Portobello Road. As the day progressed, Mistress Gwen would give many addresses.

They found several petticoats, some open knickers with lots of lace, a chemise and a camisole, and two corsets—Collins insisted that Mistress Gwen must have the black one—at the vintage clothing shops. Mistress Gwen insisted upon high-buttoned shoes with five-inch heels, and a shop that catered to transvestites supplied these for them both, along with black silk stockings and ribboned garters. The dress took some doing, but after a search, a shop in Camden Passage had a lovely ball gown which Mistress Gwen judged would fit Miss Joan once she was tightly laced. She picked out a pair of twenties vintage silk camiknickers for herself and included them with the sale. Collins stopped at a florist's and, after some doing, managed a floral garland.

Well laden, they arrived back at Mistress Gwen's flat by midafternoon. Mistress Gwen had also had an excellent luncheon at Collins's expense; she saw prospects of yet more knicker and was in the very best of spirits. The man must be made of money. She poured two glasses of sherry.

"Now, then, Miss Joan. Shall I help you try on your new wardrobe? You should be very pretty."

Collins reached into his suit coat and withdrew one of the photographs. It was the one of the young man in drag, skirts thrown up, standing bent over as the other man in a black corset and stockings sodomized him.

"I want it just like this."

Mistress Gwen dealt with clients obsessed with their fetishes every day. She returned the photograph. "Then let's get dressed properly."

"I want it just like this," Collins repeated. "No wigs, no makeup, no falsies, no condoms. Just like the picture." He handed the photograph back to Mistress Gwen. "Does your camera include a timer?"

"It does."

"I want a photograph of the two of us, just like that."

"This will all cost a little more, of course," said Mistress Gwen.

She set up her camera on a tripod as Collins undressed. She did get frequent requests from clients for photographs of the two of them together. She removed her wig and makeup, brushed up her short black hair, then got out of her clothes. Miss Joan was struggling into her new garments and required assistance. They laced each other into the corsets, and Mistress Gwen finally settled Miss Joan into her dress. It was a good fit.

Miss Joan bent over, pulling her skirts over her hips. "Is this like in the photograph?"

Mistress Gwen checked her camera for frame and took a shot. "Very much so. You even look like the boy you're dressed up as. Let's try another."

Mistress Gwen was wearing just the corset, stockings and garters, and her new shoes. She applied lubricant to her cock, set the timer, then stood behind Miss Joan. She guided her cock just past the head into Miss Joan's ass as the camera flashed. Withdrawing, she collected the photograph and showed it to Miss Joan, along with the Victorian picture. "It's a very close match."

"Take another to be sure." Miss Joan was tottering on her five-inch heels. Her hands were braced on her knees.

Mistress Gwen reset the timer, then moved behind Miss Joan, reinserting her cock a short way. "Are you all right?"

"Yes. It feels good. Now smile for the camera."

The flash went off, and Mistress Gwen plunged her cock all the way into Miss Joan's ass, grasping her hips to keep her from falling. "Just try not to faint on me this time. I don't want you dangling from my dick." She began to work her hips slowly back and forth against Miss Joan's lace-circled ass. Mistress Gwen was enjoying herself; no need to rush a good fuck. Many of Miss Joan's fifty-quid notes would be hers soon enough…

Collins was sitting on the edge of a bed, his dress soiled and his face running with tears. Oscar Wilde had finished getting dressed and was laying five pounds upon the dressing table.

"Please, let's not have further histrionics. You surely must have known that you were only a passing infatuation."

The Picture of Jonathan Collins · 269

"You used me like a girl," Collins sobbed. "Now you're paying me as if I were a prostitute."

"I'm certain that you will find other men," said Wilde, moving toward the door. "By the by, if you pop round to Soho, Jack should have some photographs for you. Keep them and remember your beautiful youth."

"I never want to see them!"

"That's not what you said short days ago. And what's said is said." Wilde adjusted his hat and left the room...

"It's not a painting. It's a photograph," Miss Joan murmured.

"Of course," panted Mistress Gwen. "I just took them." Miss Joan was about to fall over, but Mistress Gwen held her hips tightly and made several more deep, quick thrusts as her orgasm jetted into Miss Joan. It was one of the best, and a pity she had to charge for such pleasure. Miss Joan had been silent during most of her screwing; there was semen running down her stockings, so Mistress Gwen assumed she had been quietly tossing herself off beneath her heaped petticoats. At least she hadn't fainted. Mistress Gwen let her spent cock slip out of Miss Joan's ass, pulled down Miss Joan's skirts and helped her to sit down on the bed.

"It's a photograph!" Miss Joan did seem a bit scattered.

"Yes?" Mistress Gwen collected the last photograph she had shot. Very good, indeed. A close reenactment of the Victorian original, and Miss Joan's resemblance to the buggered boy in the dress was uncanny.

"That bastard!" Miss Joan pointed to the original. "He fucked me for a few weeks, paid me off as if I were a whore, then wrote a book about me!"

"I think a glass of sherry will do you good," said Mistress Gwen. "Settle you down a bit."

Collectors know other collectors, whether they collect coins, stamps, books, old cars, whatever. They make acquaintances and sometimes friends with those of similar interests.

Having exhausted all other avenues, Collins thought of phoning fellow collectors of vintage pornography. Secretive by nature and necessity, only a few others were well enough known to him personally to phone for assistance: any information on one Jack MacVane, photographer with studio in Soho, circa 1890.

On his fourth call, Collins got lucky. The call was to an acquaintance, Herbert Musgrave, an established dealer in antiquarian and esoteric books. His tastes in other matters were also esoteric.

"Yes, dear boy. J. MacVane. Yes, I have a number of pieces of his work. Bit of a decadent by all accounts. Yes, I heard about your luck at that estate auction recently. Look, why not pop by here this evening, say about sixish? You show me yours, and I'll show you mine. Excellent. Cheers!"

Herbert Musgrave had a semi-detached house in Crouch End and a small bookshop in Kensington which specialized in deluxe bindings, antiquarian books and other sorts, if you asked properly. He was a short man, putting on flesh, somewhere past fifty, with graying hair and beard, and bifocals. He and Collins often met at book fairs, exchanging pleasantries over a glass of wine and sometimes exchanging wrapped parcels.

Collins arrived at half-past six, owing to traffic. Musgrave greeted him enthusiastically. He was wearing a smoking jacket, and he had set out sherry, cheese and biscuits.

Once settled: "Well, give us a look at your find." He examined the two photographs with keen interest. "Oh, yes. These are the work of J. MacVane. That's his studio. Quite rare. Excellent find! I have a few others from these sets, but not these two. Would you consider selling them?"

"Sets?"

"Yes. For the elaborate staging as seen here, photographers often took a dozen or more plates, selling the best in packets of six to ten sequential photographs. Here, let me show you."

Musgrave had already set out a photo album. He quickly turned through it. "Yes, here they are. Some others in the sets."

There were six photographs. Of the first pair, one was of the young man in the dress, assisting the other with his corset; the next portrayed him giving the other man a blow job. The next four were from the other set. The first showed the two men dressing each other; next, the man in the petticoat smiling as he guided his cock into the other's mouth as he crouched upon a hassock; another, with his cock completely engulfed in his bent-over ass; the last, with the man in open knickers lying on his back on the hassock, legs high in the air, while the other man stood between his legs, fucking him as if he were a woman.

"MacVane's work is rather scarce," said Musgrave, reaching for the sherry. "I can offer you a good price."

"What do you know of the man?"

"Very little. He had a studio in Soho for a short time, took very good photographic portraits. He mingled with the most decadent of the artists and writers, that sort of thing. Said to have been intimate with Aleister Crowley and that lot. Most of his work was done on private commission—largely just nude studies of all ages and gender, but he also did a good bit of what you see here. Again, mostly on private commission. However, some prints got into circulation, and a scandal resulted. MacVane left London a jump ahead of the police and set up shop again in Paris. After photographing some memorable postcards, he was found dead in his studio. Talk was that he was poisoned, but the inquest ruled natural causes—he was a notorious drunkard—and so the matter and MacVane were soon forgotten."

"I think that's Oscar Wilde in the photographs."

Musgrave adjusted his glasses and peered closely. "No, no, no, dear boy. Of course not. Some resemblance, certainly, but if you'll pardon my saying so, the other man looks far more like you than does his lover resemble Oscar Wilde."

Musgrave sipped his sherry, for which he had a weakness, and studied Collins's handsome face, for which he also had a weakness. Thinking about it, he decided there really *was* an astonishing resemblance to the young man in the photograph. Musgrave wondered if Collins might have had a gay ancestor. Might it run in the family…?

"I have a few of his nude studies over here." Musgrave pulled down a larger album. "Got them as part of a larger lot of Victorian photography at Sotheby's some years back. It was an unsorted jumble, so I had it quite cheaply."

Collins paged through the album. There was a buxom woman, another buxom woman, a girl of about ten, a boy of about the same age, another buxom woman, a boy in his teens, a muscular man of about twenty-five, another buxom woman, a girl of perhaps five, two buxom women embracing.

"This next is my favorite," said Musgrave, sliding closer.

Collins stared at the photograph of himself, standing nude beside a plaster Doric column, against a Grecian backdrop. His mouth felt dry, and he reached for his sherry.

"The same dear boy as in those other photographs. And he *does* look very much like you, Jonathan. At least the face does."

"I really must have this," Collins said.

"There's another pose on the next page that shows him wanking off."

"I'll trade you my two photographs."

Musgrave shook his head.

"And add to that one hundred pounds."

Musgrave considered. The offer was really a very good one. But Collins seemed very interested in this one photograph. The sherry had gone to Musgrave's head and made him reckless. Besides, he hadn't known that Collins was interested in male pornography. Still waters.

He looked again at Collins's two photographs. "Acts like this. Between two men. I mean, have you ever…?"

The next morning Collins phoned for a taxi. Musgrave saw him out, still in his dressing robe, and invited Collins to come again soon. Collins left without his two photographs, short by a hundred pounds, with Musgrave's come due to meet somewhere between his stomach and his rectum. But he had *the* photograph wrapped securely and in his hands.

As he got into the taxi, Collins wondered if he hadn't played the fool all along. The man in the picture should have aged whilst he stayed young. Neither of them had aged. Perhaps there actually had been a painting. Perhaps the aging portrait was only Wilde's embellishment. Musgrave had been all over him throughout the night. He was too wrung out to want to think of his next possible move. Perhaps another session with Mistress Gwen.

After kissing Collins good-bye, Musgrave lit a cigarette and poured a glass of sherry. An enchanting but exhausting night; he was pleased that today was Saturday, so that his young assistant would be there to open shop. A shame to have taken such advantage of young Jonathan, but experienced collectors must learn never to permit their eagerness to acquire an object to reach the attention of its owner.

Besides, Musgrave had also purchased the glass negatives as part of the auction lot. He would have a new print made straightaway. Collins could still boast of having the original.

Climbing to his attic, Musgrave rummaged around and found the box of glass negatives, barely glanced at after the auction. Yes, it should be here. He carefully sorted through the plates. All of these were promised to be of the prints in his album. Here was the young man tossing off by the Greek column. Perhaps Collins would come back for that one.

The last plate was of a hideous, bloated old man, bald and toothless, sagging belly, covered with scars and blotches.

"Bloody hell! What was MacVane thinking when he took this!" Musgrave complained. "On one of his binges when he had this creature pose!"

He set the plate aside with a shudder. Two careful searches through the glass negatives did not reveal the plate he wanted.

"Cheated again!" Musgrave said angrily. In vexation he snatched up the offending glass negative, carried it downstairs all the way to the back, then hurled it into the dustbin at the back wall.

The glass negative shattered impressively. Musgrave felt somewhat better.

The taxi driver heard the scream from the back seat, turned his head to look, screamed himself. He went over the curb and struck a lamppost. He was still screaming when passersby pulled him out, head bloody and smashed against the steering wheel.

There was no point in pulling out his passenger, if that was what it was.

It was still clutching in one rotting hand a parcel which was found to contain an old photograph of a nude young man. As the police pulled the parcel away, the crumbling hand, still clutching, broke away.

The driver had a concussion and no memory of the morning.

The body had crumbled into broken bits and dust.

The police suggested some bizarre prank. The inquest reluctantly concurred. There simply could be no other explanation.

The picture disappeared into police archives.

Jonathan Collins was never found.

Locked Away

It was a small gold locket, late Victorian, shaped as a heart, usual period embellishments, pendant from a heavy gold chain. The locket came as part of a lot of estate jewelry for which Pandora had just made a successful bid. She was quite pleased with her purchase, although she had had to bid very high. She generally did well on her buying trips.

Pandora Smythe—she had taken back her maiden surname—owned and managed an antique shop in Pine Hill, North Carolina, a sort of sleepy college town now overrun with development, yuppies employed by the numerous white-collar industries, and retirees from up North. Pandora was English by birth and couldn't complain about newcomers, especially since they enjoyed spending too much money for antique furnishings to grace their new town houses and condos, erected where a year before all had been woodland.

Her shop was, not unsurprisingly, named Pandora's Box, but it did a very good trade, and Pandora employed three sales assistants, one of whom she would take with her on buying trips. Pandora Smythe had a peaches-and-cream complexion, angular but pert features, was rather tall, jogged daily to preserve her trim figure, was blond and green-eyed and nearing thirty. Her two vices were an addiction to romance novels and sobbing through vintage black-and-white tear-jerkers on rented videocassettes.

She wished she were Bette Davis, but instead she was a sharp businesswoman, and she had made only two mistakes of note: She had married Matthew McKee and stayed with him for most of a loveless year despite his open philandering and drunken abuse of her. She had bought a locket.

It had been a good day at the shop. Doreen and Mavis had managed very well; Derrick had seen to the packing and delivery of the larger auction items—some very good and very large Victorian furnishings and a few excellent farmhouse primitives, which would be stuck in the back of Volvo wagons before the week was out. Pandora carried back the case of jewelry herself, chiding herself for having paid too much, but that bastard Stuart Reading had been keen for the lot as well. Probably would have fetched far more as individual pieces, but the day was long, and most of it was costume, worth more as antique pieces rather than any intrinsic value.

"Ooh! I love those jade earrings!" Mavis was peering over her shoulder as Pandora sorted through her trove across her desk.

"Take them out of your salary, then." Pandora gave them a quick look. "I'll want fifty dollars for them. About turn of the century. And that's green jasper, not jade."

"Then I'll only give you thirty dollars."

"Forty. That's gold."

"Staff discount. Thirty dollars. And I have cash."

"Done." Pandora passed the earrings to Mavis. She could have had the fifty easily from a shopper, but she liked her staff, liked Mavis, and there was more here to turn a handsome profit than she had thought. Eat your heart out, Stuart Reading.

"Here's the thirty." Mavis had dashed for her handbag.

"A sale. Put it in the cash drawer." Pandora was sorting the cheaper bits from items which might demand a professional jeweler's appraisal. Of the latter there were a few.

"Here. I quite fancy this." Pandora lifted the golden locket. An inscription in Latin read *Face Quidlibet Voles*.

Mavis examined it. "Late Victorian. Gold. Yours for a mere two hundred dollars."

"I've *already* purchased it, Mavis." Pandora fussed with the gold chain. "Give us a hand with the clasp."

Mavis worked the clasp behind her neck. "You going to keep it for yourself?"

"Maybe just wear it for a few days. How does it look?"

"Like you need a poodle skirt to go with it."

Pandora faced an antique mirror and arranged her hair. "Feels good. Think I'll wear it for a bit. As you said, should fetch two hundred dollars. Solid gold. Look at the workmanship."

Mavis peered into Pandora's cleavage. "I can't make out what the lettering means. Face something voles? That's silly. Voles are cute. Got them in my garden. Industrious little rodents. Better than having squirrels chewing up the bird feeders."

Pandora studied her reflection. "Problem with gold. A well-worn locket. And I haven't had Latin since a schoolgirl."

"Let's open it up and see what's inside!" Mavis fumbled with the catch. "Should be a lock of hair or some old portraits." She tried again. "Shit, it won't open."

"Stop tugging!" complained Pandora. "I'll manage once I'm at home."

Pandora took a long shower, wrapped herself in towels and terry cloth robe, made a small pot of tea, added cream, two sugars, and a bit of lemon to her cup, flicked on the television, curled up on her favorite couch, snuggled under a goose down comforter, and waited for her hair to dry. Her hair was too straight for her liking, so she preferred not to use a blow dryer.

The television was boring. The tea was good. She fiddled with the catch on the gold locket—she hadn't been able to work the chain clasp before showering. The hot water had done the trick. The locket snapped open.

Inside, nothing. Pandora was somewhat disappointed.

Feeling the fatigue from her buying trip, she set aside her teacup and fell into sudden sleep.

She was wearing a schoolgirl's gym slip. Two of the sisters were holding her arms, as she was bent over a desk. A third sister flipped up Pandora's skirt and yanked down her chaste white cotton knickers. Sister brandished a wooden ruler. The other girls in the classroom stared in frightened anticipation.

"You were seen touching yourself," said sister.

"I'm an adult businesswoman! Who the hell are you?"

"You've only made it all the worse."

The ruler smacked her bottom. Pandora yelped in pain. Again and again the ruler came down. Pandora began to cry. Her classmates began to titter. The ruler continued to whack her reddening buttocks. Pandora screamed and tried to escape the tight grip of the other two sisters. The beating continued.

She felt a rush of orgasm.

Pandora gasped and sat up, almost overturning her teacup. Dizzily she finished it, noticed the locket had closed. Must have done it while asleep. No more strong tea at bedtime. She removed the towel from her head and brushed out her hair. Strange dream. She had never attended a Catholic school. Her parents were C of E, she was secular humanist, in currently politically correct jargon.

Her buttocks hurt. In the mirror she saw welts.

By morning there was nothing to remark upon. Pandora shrugged it off to lying on a rumpled bathrobe and an agitated imagination. She let her staff run the shop, while she sifted through the classifieds and notices of upcoming sales. Doreen got an easy seven hundred dollars for the heart-of-pine table, poorly restored and purchased at a tenth of that. Pandora began to feel better, but still made an early day of it. She thought of Doreen and Mavis as Bambi and Thumper from that James Bond film. Derrick was perhaps James Bond. They could mind the store.

She put on a pink baby-doll nightgown—she had a weakness for fifties nostalgia—curled up in her bed and began reading *Love's Blazing Desire* by David Drake, her favorite romance author. She fidgeted with her locket.

It opened.

Pandora was wearing a white cone bra and a white panty girdle attached by garters to beige stockings. Her party dress was somewhere in the back seat of a '56 Chevy, and she was on her knees on the cemetery grass.

Biff and Jerry were in a hurry, as the cops patrolled this strip looking for teenagers getting their thrills. They'd just dropped their jeans and Y-fronts. Standing beside the car, they were letting Pandora give them double head.

She couldn't take them both all the way into her mouth at once. She gave each cock a quick deep throat, alternating by sucking in both heads, tonguing them rapidly, while she jerked them off separately, fingering her cunt from outside of the tight chastity belt of her panty girdle. She'd told the boys that she was on the rag, because neither had thought to buy rubbers.

Biff was yelling, "Gawd! Gawd! Gawd!"

Jerry said, "Shut up, douche bag! You'll get the cops on our ass!"

Pandora said nothing, making only slurping and sucking sounds. She couldn't completely close her lips over both cocks, and saliva was drooling down her chin and onto her bra.

Jerry grunted, and Biff repeated, "Gawd!" Their come gushed into Pandora's mouth faster than she could swallow, spraying over her face. She gobbled down the sticky, salty tide, sucking in both cocks as they grew limp, all the while rubbing her fingers against her cunt outside the elastic barrier of her panty girdle. Her orgasm came just as she accepted both flaccid cocks all the way into her throat.

Pandora choked and sat up in bed, still cradling the romance novel. She had never even ridden in a '56 Chevy, had no real idea as to what one looked like. Saliva covered her cheeks and chin. She wiped it with a tissue. It smelled like semen. It tasted like semen. It was semen.

The locket had closed.

Pandora was useless at the shop the next day. She went home at lunch, complaining about a touch of flu. Her workers expressed sympathy; she hadn't looked well. Mavis reminded her of a country auction this coming Saturday, which Pandora and Derrick meant to attend, and said that Stuart Reading had phoned before she got in. Pandora said that Stuart Reading could get stuffed, and then she went seeking a warm shower. Perhaps she was coming down with flu.

The shower was just what she needed: hot, steaming, relaxing taut muscles. Toweling off, her fingers brushed her locket. It clicked open.

Pandora was in a steamy men's locker room, and she was wearing only a jockstrap. White, elastic, no bulge over her crotch. Not so for the others in the locker room: male hunks, dripping sweat, jockstraps bulging.

Pandora yipped as one of them flipped her on the ass with his rolled towel. "So, if you want to play football with the big boys, then you have to bend over."

They forced Pandora to kneel onto a weight bench. Seconds later a soapy cock was pressing into her ass. Pandora cried out as the head popped into her, and its length was stuffed in brutally to the balls. The man began to thrust into her ass violently, urged on by cheers from the others. Pandora gasped but endured the pain. After a few minutes she felt his cock strain and pulse, spurting come into her rectum.

The second entry was not as painful, and the man came quickly after a few rapid thrusts. The third cock was thick and long; the man fucked her ass slowly while the others yelled for him to hurry up. The fourth man seemed to come forever. The fifth was in and out of her ass in a minute. The sixth took his time and paused to drink a beer. By the seventh her ass was sore and bleeding, but he reached into the pouch of her jockstrap and massaged her pussy. The eighth followed suit, playing with her clit. By the ninth Pandora finally had her orgasm.

She was lying across her bed. The locket was closed. Her ass was in agony. She stumbled onto the toilet seat in extreme urgency. There was a little blood and a great spewing of mucus from her ass as she sat down on the seat. Later she cleaned herself, then tugged off her jockstrap. She did not own a jockstrap. To the best of her knowledge.

Pandora made an emergency call to her therapist, scheduling

an appointment for the next day. Dr Rosalind Walden had been very supportive during the dark months of her broken marriage. Pandora felt she could help her understand this series of nightmares—if nightmares they were.

Dr Walden was a trim brunette, with rather short hair (a salon cut), close to Pandora's height, and looked more a successful career woman than a psychiatrist. Today she was wearing a loose business suit ensemble of dark linen and black hose. Pandora felt comfortable with her and gratefully sank onto her couch.

Later, Dr Walden said, "So you think these dreams are associated with this antique locket. Why not then just get rid of it?"

"I think I may enjoy these fantasies," Pandora confessed.

"You are recovering from a dysfunctional marriage, during which your former husband physically and sexually abused you. I think there may be a part of you that enjoys being the victim. We need to explore these repressed needs. But now, let's have a look at this locket."

Dr Walden bent over her, fumbling with the catch. Pandora liked the brush of her hands against her bosom. "I can't work it."

"Let me." Pandora clicked open the locket.

Rosalind was already leaning over her. She bent her head closer and kissed Pandora softly on the lips. In a moment their tongues were wriggling together.

Breathless, Rosalind broke off their kiss and turned to pull off her panties. Pandora was surprised to see that she wore a black garter belt. She tossed the lacy black panties onto the floor by the couch, then quickly sat astride Pandora's face. She raised her skirt, looking into Pandora's eyes. "You want my pussy. You know you want my pussy. Tell me that you want my pussy."

Rosalind had shaved her crotch for a thong bikini line. It smelled of musk and faint perfume. Her pussy lips were already engorged and spreading.

"I want your pussy."

"Say it louder! You won't be able to beg in another second!"

Pandora shouted. "Yes! Please! I want to eat your pussy!"

Rosalind lowered herself onto Pandora's face, silencing her

with a gag of flesh. Pulling her skirt to her breasts, she watched Pandora's face as she rocked back and forth against her tongue. She squeezed her breasts as she rode Pandora's face, shoving her clit against her nose.

Almost smothered, Pandora worked her tongue twirling around Rosalind's clit and into her vagina. Her pussy was salty but sweet with juices. It excited her. She could feel her own pussy growing wet. She felt Rosalind come onto her mouth, almost choking her. After a brief spasm of ecstasy, Rosalind began to ride her face all the harder. Pandora's cunt grew hotter and wetter. She tried to masturbate herself, but Rosalind's legs restricted her arms, and she could not reach inside her skirt.

The second time Rosalind came was violent enough to trigger Pandora's own orgasm.

Pandora sat up from the couch. The locket was closed.

Dr Walden was making a few notes. "Repressed sexual fantasies are common to all of us, and it's not unusual for patients to experience them involving their therapist.

"Oh, would you like some coffee? You fell asleep for a moment there."

"I'm all right."

"Well, are you sure you can drive? I've written out a prescription here for something that will help you sleep at night. Most likely job worries and travel stress have created sleep deprivation, causing these repressed fantasies to emerge in REM sleep. Try these for a week. If they help, I'll renew the prescription. If not, we may need to consider an antidepressant. In any event, don't hesitate to call me at any time."

"Thank you." Pandora recovered her handbag from the floor beside the couch. There was a pair of lacy black panties lying beside her bag. She quickly slipped them into her bag as Dr Walden wrote out her prescription.

Derrick Sloane was at her door at six in the morning. Pandora pulled on her robe and let him in.

Derrick looked embarrassed. "You'd said to come around at six, and I hadn't heard different. So. Here I am. Right on time. Are you feeling all right? Flu can be nasty. If you want to sit this one out, I can go wake up Mavis and let Doreen keep shop while we're at the auction."

"No. It's just that my shrink gave me some sleeping pills. I'll just get dressed. Would you please make the coffee?"

"Didn't even know you saw a shrink."

Derrick was familiar with her kitchen and had a cup waiting for her when Pandora finished dressing.

"Thanks. This will help. I can't miss this auction."

Derrick made better coffee than Pandora could. He was taller than she was, in his twenties, well versed in antiques, and very well built. Ideal for lifting and loading heavy pieces at auctions and moving them about the shop. He was darkly handsome, and Pandora rather fancied him, but suspected he was gay. At least, he'd never made a move on her or the others at her shop, and Mavis was to die for.

It was a bright spring morning, and Pandora felt much better with the coffee. She had pulled on some faded blue jeans and scuffed Reeboks, a T-shirt advocating saving whales, and a denim jacket. Derrick had buttered toast for her, and she munched this as she carried her plastic mug to the van.

Derrick had on black Dockers, a Graceland T-shirt, and a light jacket of black leather. That would get hot once the sun was high. Pandora glanced at her watch. They were running a bit late, but should be there in fine time for the viewing.

Derrick moved the van along swiftly. Pandora admired his shoulders. Yes, they reached the pre-auction viewing with good time to spare. It was an 1880s farmhouse whose heirs wished to liquidate along with all properties, and Pandora knew for a fact that the house was a treasure trove.

Of course Stuart Reading was there, mingling with the other dealers and the mundanes. He sidled up to Pandora. He was a balding, sixty-something with a paunch and reek of pipe tobacco.

"Sorted out that lot of jewelry from the Beales' estate yet? I see you're wearing her locket."

"Whose?"

"Tilda Beale. You outbid me for the lot, inasmuch as I was only interested in a few of the pieces. I can offer you a very good price on the few I'm interested in. The jasper earrings?"

"Jade. Already sold."

"Chrysolite, actually. Do you still have the necklace of carnelian and bloodstone? The matching earrings? Come, give me a good price and I won't bid against you on that pokeberry-dyed spindle bed you have your eye on. And I do have a buyer in mind for them, so you can get the bed without my overbidding, and we'll both profit."

Reading peered at the locket, pulling it away from Pandora's bosom, much to her distaste. "*Face Quidlibet Voles.* Do what thou wilt. Aleister Crowley. Where on earth did she acquire this? Wore it always. Probably family motto. Consider selling it?"

"The necklace and earrings are for sale, of course. Not the locket. What do you know of Tilda Beale?"

"You should do your homework, my dear, if you're to stay afloat in this business. She was a maidenly spinster who never had an impure thought. A matriarch of our church." Reading was a Southern Baptist. "Passed on at age one hundred three. Wonderful woman. Won't be any more like her."

"No impure thoughts?"

"If she ever had any, which I doubt very much, she kept them locked away in her heart. Hey, they're about to start. Will we cut a deal?"

They did, and Derrick and Pandora carried off the heirloom spindle bed in triumph.

After unloading the bed and the rest of Pandora's purchases, Derrick suggested that they stop off at his place for some champagne, which he'd been saving since his team lost the Super Bowl. Pandora was in high spirits after a successful auction and from selling the necklace and earrings to Stuart Reading at an exorbitant price—his buyer must be daft.

"Super!" she said. Was Derrick making a move? Perhaps she had been wrong about him.

Derrick actually had several bottles of champagne in his fridge. They went through the first one rather quickly with some Brie cheese and Ritz crackers—Derrick apologizing all the while. He said he'd run out of peanut butter and Velveeta. They both exploded into laughter. Derrick opened a second bottle.

"This locket," said Pandora, after a glass too many. "What do you make of it?"

"Still wearing that? Woman's picture and a lock of hair. Saw it at the auction with the rest of the lot last week."

"But it's empty."

"Mistake somewhere. Doesn't matter. Let's have a look." Derrick fumbled with the clasp.

"Let me," said Pandora, and the locket opened.

By the end of their kiss, Derrick was pulling off her T-shirt. She pulled off his. She was wearing a bra, he wasn't. He removed that as well as her jeans, she followed suit, and after minimal fumbling, their clothing was all in a pile and so were they.

"Do you mind if I tie you?" Derrick asked.

"What?" Pandora was dazzled by the champagne.

"Just a little gentle bondage. A real turn-on. It helps me drive you to new heights of passion."

Bad line from one of her romance novels, but Pandora was ready for anything now. Derrick's cock was starting to straighten, and she realized she had been wrong in considering him gay. There must be ten inches there, if she helped him along.

"Sure. If it pleases you."

Derrick opened a drawer full of many ropes and things. Pandora obediently stood with her hands crossed behind her back as he tied them.

"Let's see how close these elbows can come together."

"That hurts!" Pandora whimpered, as another rope pulled her arms together brutally. Another rope passed around her back and breasts, pinching them cruelly.

"You'll get used to it," said Derrick. He had passed a length of rope in several turns about her waist, tightly cinching a few turns through her cunt and ass. "Your pussy is already getting wet, so you know you enjoy this. Now, walk into the bedroom and lie down on the bed."

Derrick tied her ankles together and then her knees. He rolled her onto her stomach and tied a short length of rope between her ankles and wrists, drawing them together in a tight hog-tie.

Pandora was clutching her ankles and in some pain. Her back was bowed, her breasts raised from the bed. This wasn't gentle bondage, but she had gone too far now.

"But how can you screw me like this?"

"Down the throat, babe. Open wide, bitch, if you ever want to be untied." He stood beside the bed and grabbed her hair.

Derrick's huge erection was suddenly bouncing against the back of her throat as Pandora tried to engulf it. She thought of the movie she'd seen about Mr Goodbar or something. She was completely helpless. Maybe this was all in fun.

Derrick was excited and came very quickly, filling her throat with his long blasts of come. He grabbed her head and slammed her face again and again against his crotch, yelling obscenities at her all the while.

When she had sucked out the last drops of come, he withdrew from her mouth. Pandora was in real pain from the brutal hog-tie. "I think this game has gone on long enough. Please untie me."

"I think you talk too much." Derrick was rummaging through their clothes. He folded her panties into a neat wad, soiled crotch leading as he pushed them into her mouth and tied them there tightly with her bra.

"Just to keep the come inside while I plan the rest of our evening."

Pandora rocked back and forth on the bed, helpless, only able to make muffled grunts.

Derrick rolled her onto her side. He wound another long length of rope around her back and encircling her breasts. He tied the ropes in a tight tourniquet around each breast. Pandora's breasts quickly swelled from the stricture. Derrick seemed pleased by the effect of her bulging, reddening breasts. Then he clamped clothes pins onto her nipples.

Pandora made muffled sounds through her gag.

Derrick watched her writhe about while he smoked a cigarette. Rising, he rubbed the cigarette out on her ass. Her screams were lost in the panty-bra gag. Derrick lit another cigarette.

"Like that, bitch? Here's another game we'll try."

Derrick brought a candle from his dinner table, lighted it, and began to drip hot wax onto Pandora's tortured breasts. She made frantic sounds through her gag.

Her pain turned Derrick on, and his cock hardened quickly. He stroked it over her breasts and face as the wax dripped onto her red and swollen breasts. "I think I'll come up your nose and see if you can breathe come."

Pandora's eyes pleaded. The gag was already choking her.

"Maybe later. Let's see how you like this." Derrick ejaculated onto her agonized breasts, following the spurts of come with hot candle wax, sealing it to her flesh. "Which is hotter, bitch?"

Derrick rolled her back onto her belly, then violently jabbed the burning candle stub into her ass, wedging it between the ropes that bound her crotch.

"If you lie still and don't make a fuss about the hot wax running over your ass and slit, maybe I'll blow it out before it burns all the way down."

He pushed his cigarette against her other ass cheek, lit another, and sat back to watch. He took a large knife from the drawer and tried its edge.

Pandora was in agony, but she wriggled her body against the rope that ran through her cunt, rubbing her clitoris as hot wax dripped into the crack of her ass. The flame scorched her wrists as the candle burned down. Soon it would be scorching her ass cheeks. She writhed harder, rubbing her clit against the rope. The flame had reached her ass.

It look forever to reach orgasm, but she did.

The locket was shut.

Pandora staggered from Derrick's sofa.

Derrick was carrying a tray of tea things. "Hope you like herbal teas. This one is one of my favorites. Do you take honey? This will help you wake up. You've been out for an hour. You really shouldn't mix auctions with flu."

Derrick was wearing an apron. He set the tea tray down on the table beside the sofa and began to pour. "Oh. And this is my friend, Denny. He came home while you were in slumberland."

Denny was a handsome, muscular blonde of just past twenty, perhaps. He waved and said the usual pleasantries as he accepted a cup of herbal tea. Then he said, "Derrick told me you've been at it since six this morning. No wonder the nap."

"Glass of chablis helped," said Derrick, sipping his tea. "And Pandora shouldn't have insisted upon helping with the lifting—women's lib or not."

"We'll see you safely home once you've finished. You really do need to take a few days off from the shop. We guys can run it. We worry about you. Flu can be much worse than just a bad cold."

Derrick drove Pandora home. Pandora thanked him and Denny, locked her door, undressed, broke away the wax that still clung to her breasts, took a pill, then passed out on her bed.

It was Sunday, so she slept through. By dusk she was stumbling about the house in her robe, stirring a mixture of black coffee, sugar, and brandy to wash down the aspirin. She followed that with a straight brandy, then collapsed onto her favorite couch.

Probably flu. Her joints ached. As if she'd been tied in severe restraint. Flu. Lifting. Overwork. Fresh as a daisy come Monday morning. Maybe take the day off, as Derrick had suggested. Probably made a fool of herself passing out like that. More vitamins, more jogging, no champagne. Chablis?

There had been no champagne. Derrick had only stopped at his place to check his mail and feed the cat, and Pandora had wanted to make a phone call. Glass of chablis? Maybe.

Blackout. Whatever. Flu. Overwork. Losing it.

Pandora felt the urge and plopped very carefully onto the porcelain throne, for her ass was very painful. After some straining, she felt much better. Then she noticed the candle stub floating in the bowl. She flushed and fled her bathroom as she was still screaming.

"Bitch! Bitch! Bitch! Sanctimonious Baptist bitch!" Pandora

tugged at the gold chain of the locket as she stumbled naked into her bedroom.

"Bitch! You locked all your sexual fantasies away in your heart! Bitch! Bitch! You just waited! You fucking bitch!"

Pandora was in no state to work the clasp. After several tries she managed to snap the chain, chafing her neck in the process. She threw chain and locket onto the floor. The locket snapped open. She started to smash it with her bare foot, but it was only a locket with a lock of hair and a portrait of a young woman of another century.

Pandora sat down on her bed. She covered her face in her cradled hands. "Wasn't you. It's me. I'm losing it. Can't hold back my fantasies any longer. Don't even want to. I won't be like you."

Pandora washed away the thin string of blood from her neck. Looking into her mirror, she admired the red tattoo of a heart upon her left breast. She had blocked it out of her mind, but now she remembered getting a little tight, walking past the tattoo parlor, feeling daring, feeling the needle drilling into her skin. She wondered what else was missing from her blackouts and where the fantasies began. The last beating her husband had given her put her in the hospital for three days. Dr Walden had told her it was a severe concussion.

It was growing late, but the singles bars were open and sure to be hot. Pandora carefully dressed herself in black hose and garter belt, black panties and platform bra, and a clinging black tube dress and black stiletto heels. The low cleavage and push-up bra showed her heart-shaped tattoo to good advantage. She hadn't felt at all embarrassed when she purchased all of this, she now remembered: She'd felt brazen and had smiled at the clerk in a way that had made the girl nervous.

This was the first time Pandora had worn the ensemble. At least she thought it was.

She carefully put on her makeup, brushed her hair, as she wondered what to do next. There was a small stain like an old scab on the hem of her dress, but she cleaned that away without much trouble. Maybe she should wear the red outfit instead.

Dr Walden had said to call at any time. After the singles bar, perhaps. She could ask Dr Walden for her opinion. Tonight or another night.

She opened a drawer and popped the switchblade into her black sequined handbag. Frowning, she removed it, pressed the release button: mechanism well oiled and functioning, blade sharp and clean. Satisfied, she returned the switchblade to her handbag. She remembered buying it as a part of a carton of bric-a-brac at an estate auction. Like with the locket. She remembered cleaning off the blood last time she put it into the drawer. Or was that just another fantasy?

The knife was real.

Derrick might be fun. Later.

And Mavis. Delicious.

No more the victim.

I've Come to Talk with You Again

They were all in the Swan. The music box was moaning something about "everybody hurts sometime" or was it "everybody hurts something." Jon Holsten couldn't decide. He wondered, why the country-western sound in London? Maybe it was "everybody hurts somebody." Where were The Beatles when you needed them? One Beatle short, to begin with. Well, yeah, two Beatles. And Pete Best. Whatever.

"Wish they'd turn that bloody thing down." Holsten scowled at the offending speakers. Coins and sound effects clattered from the fruit machine, along with bonks and flippers from the Fish Tales pinball machine. The pub was fusty with mildew from the pissing rain of the past week and the penetrating stench of stale tobacco smoke. Holsten hated the ersatz stuffed trout atop the pinball machine.

Mannering was opening a packet of crisps, offering them around. Foster declined: he had to watch his salt. Carter crunched a handful, then wandered across to the long wooden bar to examine the two chalk-on-slate menus: Quality Fayre was promised. He ordered prime pork sausages with chips and baked beans, not remembering to watch his weight. Stein limped down the treacherous stairs to the Gents. Insulin time. Crosley helped himself to the crisps and worried that his round was coming up. He'd have to duck it. Ten quid left from his dole check, and a week till the next.

There were six of them tonight, where once eight or ten might have foregathered. Over twenty years, it had become an annual tradition: Jon Holsten over from the States for his holiday in London, the usual crowd around for pints and jolly times. Cancer of the kidneys had taken McFerran last year; he who always must have steak and kidney pie. Hiles had decamped to the Kentish coast, where he hoped the sea air would improve his chest. Marlin was somewhere in France, but no one knew where, nor whether he had kicked his drug dependence.

So it went.

"To absent friends," said Holsten, raising his pint. The toast was well received, but added to the gloom of the weather with its memories of those who should have been there.

Jon Holsten was an American writer of modest means but respectable reputation. He got by with a little help from his friends, as it were. Holsten was generally considered to be the finest of the later generation of writers in the Lovecraftian school—a genre mainly out of fashion in these days of chainsaws and flesh-eating zombies, but revered by sufficient devotees to provide for Holsten's annual excursion to London.

Holsten tipped back his pint glass. Over its rim he saw the yellow-robed figure enter the doorway. He continued drinking without hesitation, swallowing perhaps faster now. The pallid mask regarded him as impassively as ever. An American couple entered the pub, walking past. They were arguing in loud New York accents about whether to eat here. For an instant the blue-haired woman shivered as she brushed through the tattered cloak.

Holsten had fine blond hair, brushed straight back. His eyes were blue and troubled. He stood just under six feet, was compactly muscled beneath his blue three-piece suit. Holsten was past the age of sixty.

"Bloody shame about McFerran," said Mannering, finishing the crisps. Carter returned from the bar with his plate. Crosley looked on hungrily. Foster looked at his empty glass. Stein returned from the Gents.

Stein: "What were you saying?"

Mannering: "About McFerran."

"Bloody shame." Stein sat down.

"My round," said Holsten. "Give us a hand, will you, Ted?"

The figure in tattered yellow watched Holsten as he arose. Holsten had already paid for *his* round.

Ted Crosley was a failed writer of horror fiction: some forty stories in twenty years, mostly for nonpaying markets. He was forty and balding and worried about his hacking cough.

Dave Mannering and Steve Carter ran a bookshop and lived above it. Confirmed bachelors adrift from Victorian times. Mannering was thin, dark, well-dressed, scholarly. Carter was red-haired, Irish, rather large, fond of wearing rugby shirts. They were both about forty.

Charles Stein was a book collector and lived in Crouch End. He was showing much grey and was very concerned about his diabetes. He was about forty.

Mike Foster was a tall, rangy book collector from Liverpool. He was wearing a leather jacket and denim jeans. He was concerned about his blood pressure after a near-fatal heart attack last year. He was fading and about forty.

The figure in the pallid mask was seated at their table when Holsten and Crosley returned from the bar with full pints. No need for a seventh pint. Holsten sat down, trying to avoid the eyes that shone from behind the pallid mask. He wasn't quick enough.

The lake was black. The towers were somehow behind the moon. The moons. Beneath the black water. Something rising. A shape. Tentacled. Terror now. The figure in tattered yellow pulling him forward. The pallid mask. Lifted.

"Are you all right?" Mannering was shaking him.

"Sorry?" They were all looking at Holsten. "Jet lag, I suppose."

"You've been over here for a fortnight," Stein pointed out.

"Tired from it all," said Holsten. He took a deep swallow from his pint, smiled reassuringly. "Getting too old for this, I imagine."

"You're in better health than most of us," said Foster. The

tattered cloak was trailing over his shoulders. His next heart attack would not be near-fatal. The figure in the pallid mask brushed past, moving on.

Mannering sipped his pint. The next one would have to be a half: he'd been warned about his liver. "You will be sixty-four on November the eighteenth." Mannering had a memory for dates and had recently written a long essay on Jon Holsten for a horror magazine. "How do you manage to stay so fit?"

"I have this portrait in my attic." Holsten had used the joke too many times before, but it always drew a laugh. And he was not going on sixty-four, despite the dates given in his books.

"No. Seriously." Stein would be drinking a Pils next round, worrying about alcohol and insulin.

The tentacles were not really tentacles—only something with which to grasp and feed. To reach out. To gather in those who had foolishly been drawn into its reach. Had deliberately chosen to pass into its reach. The promises. The vows. The laughter from behind the pallid mask. Was the price worth the gain? Too late.

"Jon? You sure you're feeling all right?" Stein was oblivious to the pallid mask peering over his shoulder.

"Exercise and vitamins," said Holsten. He gave Stein perhaps another two years.

"It must work for you, then," Mannering persisted. "You hardly look any older than when we first met you here in London some ages ago. The rest of us are rapidly crumbling apart."

"Try jogging and only the occasional pint," Holsten improvised.

"I'd rather just jog," said Carter, getting up for another round. He passed by the tattered yellow cloak. Carter would never jog.

"Bought a rather good copy of *The Outsider*," said Foster, to change the subject. "Somewhat foxed, and in the reprint dust jacket, but at a good price." It had been Crosley's copy, sold cheaply to another dealer.

Holsten remembered the afternoon. Too many years ago. New York. Downstairs book shop. Noise of the subway. Cheap shelf. *The King in Yellow*, stuffed with pages from some older book. A bargain. Not cheap, as it turned out. He had never believed in any of this.

The figure in the pallid mask was studying Crosley, knowing he would soon throw himself in front of a tube train. Drained and discarded.

"Well," said Holsten. "I'd best be getting back after this one."

"This early in the day?" said Mannering, who was beginning to feel his pints. "Must be showing your age."

"Not if I can help it." Holsten sank his pint. "It's just that I said I'd meet someone in the hotel residents' bar at half three. He wants to do one of those interviews, or I'd ask you along. Boring, of course. But…"

"Then come round after," Mannering invited. "We'll all be here."

But not for very much longer, thought Holsten; but he said: "See you shortly, then."

Crosley was again coughing badly, a stained handkerchief to his mouth.

Jon Holsten fled.

The kid was named Dave Harvis, he was from Battersea, and he'd been waiting in the hotel lobby of the Bloomsbury Park for an hour in order not to be late. He wore a blue anorak and was clutching a blue nylon bag with a cassette recorder and some books to be signed, and he was just past twenty-one. Holsten picked him out as he entered the lobby, but the kid stared cluelessly.

"Hello. I'm Jon Holsten." He extended his hand, as on so many such meetings.

"Dave Harvis." He jumped from his seat. "It's a privilege to meet you, sir. Actually, I was expecting a much older…that is…"

"I get by with a little help from my friends." Holsten gave him a firm American handshake. "Delighted to meet you."

The tentacled mouths stroked and fed, promising whatever you wanted to hear. The figure in its tattered yellow cloak lifted its pallid mask. What is said is said. What is done is done. No turning back. Some promises can't be broken.

"Are you all right, sir?" Harvis had heard that Holsten must be up in his years.

"Jet lag, that's all," said Holsten. "Let's go into the bar, and you can buy me a pint for the interview. It's quiet there, I think."

Holsten sat down, troubled.

Harvis carried over two lagers. He worked on his cassette recorder. The residents' bar was deserted but for the barman.

"If you don't mind, sir." Harvis took a gulp of his lager. "I've invited a few mates round this evening to meet up at the Swan. They're great fans of your work. If you wouldn't mind…"

"My pleasure," said Holsten.

The figure in tattered yellow now entered the residents' bar. The pallid mask regarded Harvis and Holsten as Harvis fumbled with a microcassette tape.

Holsten felt a rush of strength.

He mumbled into his pint: "I didn't mean for this to happen this way, but I can't stop it."

Harvis was still fumbling with the tape and didn't hear.

Neither did any gods who cared.

Final Cut

No one gets well in a hospital.

Dr Kirby Meredith had forgotten who had said that to him, but he hadn't forgotten the words. He was a prematurely aging attending psychiatrist at a large hospital in Pine Hill, North Carolina. He had graduated from the medical school here, gone through his residency, attained his present senior status. Talk was that he would go a long way, perhaps chairman of the department when the time was right.

Dr Meredith was a non-intimidating, rather dumpy man of thirty-something, with sandy hair and grey in his frizzy beard. He wore the same striped ties he had worn for years, button-down collar shirts, and cotton Dockers. Still wore tight black leather dress shoes, and he pulled on a rumpled tweed jacket whenever he thought the occasion called for it: weekly court commitment hearings held here at the center; patient's family inquiring as to family member's progress. Shrinks do not wear white. Bad for patient rapport.

He hated wearing ties. If he ever set up a private practice, it would be T-shirts and maybe a sweater. A cardigan. No, just the T-shirt. Or some jogging sweats. Not that he ever jogged. Assume the air of informality. Patient at ease. Dream on.

Dr Meredith had just completed his rounds, was making medication adjustments to his charts, making mental notes regarding his students and staff, and considering journal club that evening, where he hoped his residents finally would be brought up-to-date on lithium therapy. There was a fine line between maintaining a manic-depressive and killing him, and the foreign resident who had confused q.o.d. with q.i.d. was going to speak at length upon the subject. In broken English.

"Dr Meredith." The nurse knew better than to interrupt him needlessly, and Meredith felt the tension. "He says he's your cousin, and it's urgent."

"Thank you." Meredith picked up the phone. He shouldn't be receiving personal calls here, unless from his wife or daughter. He worked hard, did not like to be interrupted. Once at home, he could find time for friends and family.

"Kirby!" said the voice over the phone. "It's your favorite cousin, Bob. I got a problem, maybe. Janice told me how to reach you at the hospital."

"What's the problem, Bob?" Meredith thought Cousin Bob sounded drunk. He'd rarely seen him sober. Bob Breenwood lived about half an hour's distance from Pine Hill and ran a small hardware business in a small town. They got together regularly to go fishing. Bob was always drunk. His wife and staff ran the business.

"Just started vomiting. Blood. Can't stop it."

Meredith froze for a moment. "How much blood?"

"I don't know. I was cooking a steak on the charcoal grill, and then it just started."

"Is it bright red, or is it sort of like dark and clotted, like it's coming from your gums or sinuses, and you've maybe swallowed it and choked it up?"

"It's bright red, and there's more of it coming up. All the time. Oh, shit! I got to hit the toilet!"

Meredith was very firm. "Have your wife call 911. Emergency. Get over here without delay. You're likely bleeding to death from ruptured esophageal varices. Do it now. I'll be here. For you. There's no time to waste. You'll be dead in an hour."

Possibly putting it a little too strong, but Meredith phoned 911 himself, with frantic details. Maureen Breenwood had already called. Meredith hovered about the Emergency Room, getting in the way, while explaining why an attending shrink was in the way. He was well liked, and the staff were ready when the ambulance arrived.

Bob's hematocrit was down to 10, for someone who liked to take down record lows. Typed and crossmatched, the units of blood finally flowed into his arm. He did not go into shock, by some miracle. A balloon was inserted past his esophagus, reducing the bleeding, and his blood pressure finally stabilized at 105/90 from 60/45. He should have been dead.

Dr Meredith observed, but stayed out of the way. He wouldn't want two or three other shrinks all giving therapeutic advice as he interviewed his patient, and he respected professionalism. Instead he made frequent visits to Maureen, who had left the waiting room for the chapel, and reassured her as she spoke with the priest. Dr Meredith was an atheist, but therapy was therapy. Janice was coming over to be with her.

Cousin Bob was fully stabilized by three in the morning and off to Intensive Care. Dr Meredith checked Maureen into a nearby hotel and promised to phone if there were any complications, then returned to his office in the psychiatric wing and fell asleep on his couch.

Meredith woke up about seven, very groggy but too concerned to go back to sleep. He brushed his hair and brushed his teeth, washed his face and sprayed his armpits, put on a fresh shirt and tie from his file cabinets. He wondered why he bothered to pay a monstrous mortgage for their home. He phoned his wife to see if she might stay with Maureen a few hours while Ashley was at school, and to say privately to Janice that things weren't going well — she knew that — and that he'd be home for dinner on time — she doubted that. Hell. This hospital was home.

Dr Meredith knocked back a cup of coffee at the administrative office, had another, tossed a buck into the coffee fund. He hated coffee. About time for morning rounds, and then he had group at eleven. He wished he were as young as his med students, or even the residents. Youth and enthusiasm. Hell, he wasn't that old. He wished he had learned to play an electric guitar. Joined a rock band. Better the devil that you know. He poured another cup of coffee, then went to rounds.

Bob Breenwood was asking for him from the Intensive Care Unit as soon as they removed the balloon from his esophagus. Meredith delayed an outpatient appointment and went to see him instead of taking a late lunch. He wasn't hungry.

Cousin Bob was a year and a half older than Meredith, something he wouldn't let Meredith forget when they went skinny dipping together and Bob was growing hair on his crotch and Meredith was too young. Much later, Bob got him laid for the first time, double-dating in Bob's family's Nash Rambler with the fold-down front seat and a friendly high school girl and a convenient cemetery.

Meredith sat down on one of those uncomfortable plastic chairs at the bedside. Bad practice to sit down on the bed.

Maureen was sniffling, holding Bob's hand. She was a stout brunette with acne scars, but a good cook, which is why Meredith reckoned Bob had married her, because she couldn't keep house and the rest was none of his business.

Bob was as chunky as his wife: blue eyes, blond hair, rather short, no tattoos. Meredith had always thought them a good match. Happy, harmless couple. He was waiting for dozens of clueless offspring to appear.

Instead.

"Maureen," said Bob. "Could you let me talk to Kirby in private? Just for a few minutes. After all, he's a shrink."

"Sure." Maureen left the room.

Cousin Bob glanced around the Intensive Care Unit. There was fear in his eyes. Understandably.

"Liver's gone, they say."

Dr Meredith had read the charts. "Always a chance for a repair. This is 1973, after all."

"Kirby, they're saying I'm just a drunk. I don't think they really give a damn."

"I'm here for you. I'm staff."

"Did you know that I had TB years back?"

"No. You never told me."

"Friend of mine got it doing time in some shithouse reform school. We'd pass cigarettes and beers back and forth. They found some spots on my lungs after he'd been diagnosed. Put me on their two-drug therapy. Public health shits coming by to make sure I took all my pills. Isoniazid and something, I forget. Took them for ten years or so at their lawful command. Turns out that the combination wipes out your liver long-term."

"Shit." Meredith was familiar with the situation, but could think of nothing more profound to say. He wished he'd known about Bob in time.

"So now I'm here with a trashed liver, wiped out by the best medicine you can offer, told that I'm an alcoholic, serves me right. And they want to operate. Womak procedure, I think they call it. What do you think? I'm ready to walk."

Dr Meredith had read his cousin's chart. "Well, for whatever reasons, you are in liver failure, and you're bleeding internally. Very badly. It will start again and maybe not stop. I'm a shrink, and your surgeon can explain it far better. Basically, they'll remove your spleen and the region of your stomach and lower esophagus where these varices—knotted-up-blood-vessels—lie. The liver can take a lot of abuse, and only a small portion need recover. There's work on liver transplants. I don't see it happening soon, but you're buying time."

"Then you think I should do it? The surgery?"

"I don't see any real choice. I mean, if you start bleeding again…"

Bob grabbed his hand, weakly. "Kirby, I'll go for it on your word."

It was a nonelective case, and surgery was under way by lunchtime the following day. Meredith bought a stale ham sandwich from a machine, munched on it, phoned his wife. She wasn't home. He fumbled around his desk and found some Maalox. By the time he'd had sessions with a few patients, it was growing dark and Cousin Bob had made it through surgery. Meredith spoke to him in the recovery room. He phoned his wife. She wasn't home. Meredith went back to his house. He microwaved a low-cal dinner, ate part of it.

Bob seemed to have come through it all very well. Maureen was at his bedside. Meredith persuaded Janice to visit with her when Janice could spare the time.

"I had a dream, Kirby," Bob told him two days post-op. "I'm not sure it was a dream."

"Do you want to talk about it?"

"I'd climbed out of my bed, pulled out the IVs. I was fumbling my way along all these corridors. Lost. Just trying to get out. Go home.

"I was somewhere in the basement—I don't know how. I pushed open a door, thinking it led out. Only I was in the hospital morgue. Two doctors were doing an autopsy on a man. I think the man was me. I must have fainted, but I remember someone taking me back to my room. I'm afraid, Kirby."

Dr Meredith considered. He decided to be reassuring. "Near-fatal illness. Major surgery. Anesthesia. Pain medication. Not an uncommon sort of nightmare. Just rest and let your body heal. Just ask the nurse to call me if you have any more bad dreams."

He examined the charts, just in case, and found nothing out of the ordinary.

All of this was at the end of June. July brought in a new crop of interns, freshly graduated from med school and eager to excel. Dr Meredith lost a few of his residents, gained a few more, none of whom seemed promising, but that was his task—to bring them around. When he closeted himself in his office, he studied travel brochures.

Cousin Bob was now five days postop and starting to take semisolid foods.

He choked on the cherry Jell-O. Maureen pounded his back and shouted for help. By the time the nurse arrived, Bob's breathing passage was clear, but the spasms had opened some sutures, and this was causing pain and some bleeding. The nurse called for an intern.

The intern had only just arrived at the medical center, knew nothing about his patient, saw the postop abdominal incisions and fresh bleeding, obvious severe pain—and ordered a liberal injection of morphine to quell pain and agitation. He hadn't thought to check the charts for liver function, but he had been told that the patient in 221 was a hopeless drunk. Whatever. Who cares.

Cousin Bob died before Dr Meredith could rush over from the psychiatric wing. Janice came to be with Maureen. Meredith followed the body to the basement morgue. There would be an autopsy, although it was obvious to most idiots in white coats that a patient with minimal liver function had been massively overdosed.

"Shit! He's back again!" The chief pathologist was breaking in another pale and trembling med student. Meredith suspected he enjoyed this sort of thing or he'd leave this to residents.

"What do you mean?"

"Patient stumbled in here a few nights back. Guess he just couldn't wait."

"Nothing in his chart about that."

"One of your patients? Well, orderlies don't like to report a fuss when there's no harm done."

"No harm done."

"Looks bad for the hospital."

No one ever gets well in a hospital.

Dr Meredith wandered from the basement morgue, seeking his office.

The oppressive walls soaked with pain and rage pressed down on him. He thought of a thousand Cousin Bobs—slowly, painfully killed by the best efforts of modern unfeeling medicine. No one ever gets well in a hospital.

Tomorrow he would clear out his office.

Tomorrow couldn't come soon enough.

Brushed Away

As a teenager in the 1950s, Maurice Tarwater was considered by his peers to be hopelessly square, strictly from hunger, and probably queer. Perhaps it was because he wore his older brothers' out-of-fashion hand-me-downs. Perhaps it was his acne. Perhaps it was his funny name.

He couldn't dance. He listened to classical music instead of this new rock and roll. He couldn't drive a car. His father insisted that a boy must be at least eighteen to begin driving lessons. He was hapless in sports. He didn't smoke cigarettes at lunch break, and he didn't touch a drop of smuggled beer at the few parties he attended. He was seldom invited. He was hopeless at dating.

In grade school he was the target of playground bullies. This continued. In high school phys-ed he wore his jock strap over his white cotton Y-fronts, afraid to expose his tiny dick and almost hairless crotch. When the gin-soaked coach forced him to take a shower, the rest of the boys made jokes about the size of his dick and its fringe of pale blond hair. Then they'd flap his ass with rolled up rat-tail towels as he struggled back into his Y-fronts.

He was born on the cusp for school admission, perpetually almost a year behind his dark-haired classmates. A year is important when you're growing up.

It peaked when he was forced under threat of a beating to suck dicks in the shower room while the others watched. They were hairy. He hated hairy crotches. There were painful thrusts up his ass by soapy dicks. They were most of them virgins, although they bragged about back seat conquests, and came almost instantly. Just masturbating into a hairless wimp. A laugh riot. Rites of adolescence.

Five minutes or so in the shower room, over with, towel off, find white cotton Y-fronts, find algebra class, find snickers and stares, then find the bus home.

Word spread. Coach caught them eventually, and broke the crowd up. Maurice was expelled for a week and sent for psychological therapy. The rest got detention hall for rowdy behavior.

They beat him up after school when he returned.

Maurice never had any luck in dating after that. Not that he'd had much before. Somehow he graduated.

His grades were good. Maurice was quite intelligent, but because of his record as a sexual pervert who had been undergoing therapy (your record will follow you everywhere, he was warned), no college would accept him. His parents said that they would support him for another year. His family was strict Southern Baptist, and he had never been forgiven for his wanton deviant behavior. He never forgave them.

Maurice landed a job as file clerk at a hospital in Los Angeles. Far from home. He was very competent. Before long he was promoted to a minor supervisory position. His immediate superior occasionally gave him curious looks, but all went well for a time.

It was 1961.

Except for the shower room rapes, Maurice was still a virgin. And he was twenty-one.

Maurice had been enjoying an active sex life, however, on his own. It suited his needs. It *had* suited his needs.

He frequented the sleazy newsstands, as he had done since high school. *Playboy* and all the rest, even the sleaziest magazines. Bare tits and ass, panties, bras and lingerie. Not a hair showing of a cunt. At age twenty-one, Maurice Tarwater had never even seen a photograph of a cunt, much less seen one in the flesh. Once, in high school, he had put his hand on his date's breast, outside her dress. She had slapped him, called him a creep, and the party chaperons had told his parents.

A cunt was all a great mystery. His parents never explained or spoke about it, and his classmates all knew he was a queer.

He knew they didn't have dicks. Somehow or other they still managed to pee. And have babies. He wondered if babies came out of their ass. That must be it. The pictures never showed it all.

This was because Maurice most enjoyed nudist magazines, sold from under the counter. He'd paged through them as a teenager—once he could find a newsstand dealer who would sell them to him—then masturbate frantically into rubbers he had bought with great stealth at a local hamburger joint. Saved and washed, he could get a dozen or more jerk-off fantasies at two for a quarter before they burst. His parents never caught him. He was lucky in this.

The nudes in the nudist magazines were always air-brushed. Cunts and pubic hairs all whisked away. Nothing but a smooth V between groin and thighs. Where then was this furry cunt that the boys at school had talked about? Probably they were making it all up to confuse him, like the time in the shower when they told him to pick up the soap and then goosed him with more than a finger.

Some of the book stores in Los Angeles had very large and very expensive books of classical art, mostly of nudes. Maurice bought several. Little help. He had known that women had breasts; their hands or something else was always in the way of their mysterious V. The men usually had something obscuring their genitalia as well: Maurice recalled his Baptist upbringing and decided it was usually a fig leaf. He bought some art books, described as studies of nude models for the budding artist. He discovered Betty Page in one, airbrushed like all the rest. Just the blank V. Was that all?

For some months Maurice contented himself by jerking off over photographs of air-brushed nudes and demure works of art. Isolation had been bred and beaten into him.

He had grown to love the smooth, clean lines of an air-brushed crotch. No wonder women could wear clinging nylon panties in those magazines, while he had to wear the baggy cotton Y-fronts his mother still bought for him. No dick to bulge out from under *their* skirts. No wonder they laughed at him.

Maurice bought a jock strap from a sports shop and a fig tree from a nursery. He glued a fig leaf to the pouch, then tried the jock strap on. He posed before his mirror. The costume did little for him and only brought back memories of the high school locker room. He had pretty features, a slight build, and not enough muscle to pose as Adonis or David. Well, it was worth the try. Smooth and clean, just like the pictures in the art books. No guilt. Very little bulge.

After a month he worked up the courage to purchase some panties in various sizes. "For my wife," he said to the girl at the register, his face reddening. She only nodded, neither knowing nor caring.

Maurice tried them all on. Still a bulge. Tight or loose. No airbrush. He compared his reflection to his magazines. No bulge in *their* panties. Where did it go? Air-brush? Fig leaf? Nothing there at all? No dick of *any* sort? All smooth and clean? Nothing nasty?

Maurice had to know. No one could tell him, if they would. It was 1961, and Maurice was twenty-one.

He looked young and innocent enough for the bartender to ask for ID, just in case Maurice might be a part of some cop sting. The bartender served him a rum and Coke. Maurice seldom drank. He nursed his drink at the bar. The place had sleaze engrained through the plastic decor. Maurice had scouted it out carefully, He had taken a few weeks of courage to work up to this point.

She was wearing a blonde wig and a tight black sheath dress. She was not all that much older than Maurice, and she sat down beside him, gave him the eye, wondered if he might buy her a drink, and the usual fell into place.

They had several drinks, as Maurice needed to buck up his nerve. Eventually they left for a hotel room, and Maurice put down some money. She said her name was Gale, and that was good enough as she undressed. Maurice had never seen a woman undress before. He was frozen.

"Here, let me help you." Gale was stripped to her bra and panties, quickly done from long practice. She pulled off Maurice's shirt while he fumbled with his shoes and socks, then got him out of his trousers.

"Big one," she said, massaging his crotch. "You'll be fun." She pulled down his Y-fronts, giving him a quick kiss on his dick.

Moving back, Gale removed her bra and panties—this John was petrified—then spread herself out on the bed. "Well, come on."

Maurice stood still, gaping at her outspread cunt. His cock was only half erect. He continued to stare.

"First time, honey? Well, come on. It won't bite you."

Maurice continued to stare at the hairy monster. There was a slit between her thighs beneath the fur. Nothing like an air-brushed photograph. Women had a hole where a dick should be. His father had been right when he told him that women were dirty vessels of sin. At least she couldn't hurt him. Not like the boys.

Gale rolled about seductively. "Look, if you'd rather have a blow job, that's ten bucks extra."

Shower room flashback.

Maurice instantly came, spurting long streams onto the bed.

Gale had seen it all. "Still have to pay, kiddo. See me again when you're not so nervous. Don't feel bad. Happens to lots of men." She began to dress.

Maurice spent a lot of nights worrying if he really were queer, just like his classmates had jeered. He bought some muscle magazines, looked at photos of young men in posing straps, bought some posing straps for himself, tried them on, posed in front of his mirror, tried masturbating while looking at the magazines. Not even an erection. He was pure.

The only sex that was good for him was to jerk off over those pictures of air-brushed cunts. No hairy slits. Clean and pure. Nothing dirty.

Not the hairy bullies in the shower room. Not being slammed back and forth until he knelt and opened his mouth.

There was nothing wrong with him.

Nothing dirty.

Not like the hairy slit in women. He'd never seen one until now, but the other boys had said that they had and described it, lying all the while. It had to be some aberration, like the few boys in the shower room whose dicks hadn't been circumcised.

A clean, smooth V. That was what the nudist magazines showed. That had to be right.

There was nothing wrong with him.

Nothing dirty.

Clean and smooth. A fig leaf. Panties. No bulge.

No genitalia. Trust the magazines.

Nothing dirty.

There was nothing wrong with *him*.

Maurice Tarwater bought a nice attaché case, and he filled it with things that he needed. It was easy to get them at the hospital, even for a file clerk. It was all very clear to him now. The photographs were correct. Cameras don't lie.

He found Gale easily enough at the same bar, and they went to the same hotel. Surprisingly, she did remember him, probably because he had left her a good tip to cover his embarrassment that night. A few drinks, off they went.

Gale was first to undress, figuring that this was going to be another thirty-second trick, and there were more Johns out there. She left on her garter belt, stockings and heels. Saved time, and most Johns enjoyed the thrill. She made come-to-bed sounds.

Maurice had undressed and was pulling on some sort of G-string thing with a leaf attached to the pouch.

"What's that?" Gale had seen some weirdos before.

"A fig leaf."

"Whatever gets you hard." At least he wasn't wearing women's underwear like the trick two nights ago. "Come on, Adam. Eve's waiting."

She spread her legs. No bulge. Hairy monster. Wet slit. No dick at all. It was worse than he'd remembered. His father had warned him.

"Want some cognac?" Maurice drew a flask from his case. "Helps to calm me down."

"Sure. It's your dime, remember."

Eve drank. Adam pretended to sip.

Once the barbs had taken effect, Maurice gave her an injection of pilfered Demerol. It would be morning, if ever, before she recovered consciousness.

He removed a razor and shaving cream from his case, and he painstakingly shaved off every bit of hair from Gale's crotch. Smooth as a baby's bottom. But still that annoying slit.

He took out a suture kit and tightly laced her labia together. It demanded some work, as this was his first time, but it was almost right. There was some minimal bleeding. He dabbed at that with some cotton.

Using a lot of thick pancake make-up, Maurice filled in the furrow of her cunt, then smoothed it all down. A Vee. Clean and smooth. No hair. No nasty slit. Just like in the pictures.

His cock grew rigid as he looked at her. He pulled down the posing strap, then masturbated onto her air-brushed cunt, reaching the best orgasm he had ever known. He left the fig leaf over her cunt.

He thought about smothering her with a pillow, but murder was a sin and a crime, and no one gave a shit about a roughed-up whore. She could have the stitches out tomorrow. He left an extra twenty on the nightstand and decided to move on.

Maurice laid low for a few weeks. As expected, no interest in a roughed-up hooker. Cool. He bought some more posing straps, some more magazines of muscle boys posing in posing straps. Nothing. Penis not erectus. He was OK, all right, normal. Fucking lies from high school. He could scatter come all across a whore's cunt. They'd never done that. Even to their wives.

He shot off rubbing himself through the nylon while wearing a pair of panties and reading a girlie magazine and looking at a girl's big butt stretching against red transparent panties similar to his own. But that was normal enough. All the guys in the locker room did it. Jerk off. Every day. Didn't admit it.

Used him for their secret fantasies. Soapy dicks. Goosing. Laughter. Penises shoving. Jock straps. Coaches. One day he'd get back at them all. Just now he knew he could get hard looking at girlie magazines. Normal.

He wiped himself clean and threw the damp panties into the laundry bin. The bra was still fresh, and he placed it into his lingerie drawer before going out for the night. There was nothing wrong with *him*.

Los Angeles sprawls for miles and miles and miles. Maurice found another, more distant bar.

He was soon dancing with Lana, who wanted a career in movies. Maurice said that he did too, and that he had some connections, but nothing definite. They had a few drinks and went to Lana's apartment, to talk over prospects.

It was the sort of cheap lodgings that see too many Hollywood hopefuls come and go. Lana apologized for the apartment, Maurice poured her a drink from his case, and Lana went quickly to sleep. Then the syringe. Barbs and Demerol. Then the razor and the shaving cream.

Maurice undressed her carefully She had a lovely body and probably really was nearly eighteen. He shaved her crotch carefully, not wanting to hurt her.

Then he stitched her labia together tightly, smeared it all with pancake make-up until it was a perfect air-brush. Maurice changed into his posing strap and then pulled down his fig leaf. He hadn't thought he could come this hard so soon again, but after much pumping he spurted all over her airbrushed cunt.

Feeling a little guilty, he left her there on the bed. There were worse lessons to be learned in Los Angeles. At least he hadn't raped her.

There was Ashley. Runaway from Ohio.

There was Jessica. Needle tracks all over.

There was Terri. Already shaved. A model.

There were others.

They were just hookers. Loose women cruising the singles bars. He always paid, and he didn't hurt them much.

Maurice kept moving. Los Angeles is a big load of a town. Lots of loose women. His father had warned him. Cops don't care much about what happens to hookers and wannabes and runaways. Yes, they had an MO and some descriptions that might fit a few thousand men. Whores and drifters, ER takes out the stitches, no permanent harm, probably asked for it. Who cares?

Better work to do. Teenage gangs. Pot dealers. Underage drinkers. Car wrecks. Racing on Mulholland. If you got paid for kinky sex, then don't come crying to us. You got what you asked for. Go back to Ohio where you belong.

Maurice was doing very well under this climate of opinion. He considered moving to San Francisco. Perhaps there he could find the perfect air-brushed companion of the night.

It really was time to move on, but Maurice had changed his hair style, grown a mustache, changed apartments, changed his wardrobe to resemble a rising corporate executive, and was doing very well at climbing into middle management, although his fellow workers thought he'd let success go to his head prematurely. There was talk about how he gained his promotions. Fuck 'em. Maurice had already secured a position as senior supervisor in San Francisco.

Maurice met Kim—or she met him—at a rather posh singles bar (they were just coming into vogue) and had the usual brief come-on. Kim was a trim brunette, very much into the Jackie Kennedy look. She was a surgical nurse at one of the hospitals, trying to sound very professional, and very much on the make. As a rule, Maurice would have left her alone, preying on the usual hookers and bar-flies, but he was transferring to the San Francisco job shortly And she *was* on the make. Nurse Floozie.

Perhaps a little casual dalliance. Nothing that could create difficulties. She had a beautiful smile. Probably gave good blow jobs. Wine and dine, then slam bang, thank you ma'am. If she kept her panties on, so he didn't have to see that horrible hairy slit, he could probably come right into her face. She looked like she might like that. He would.

He gave her a false name, said he was an intern at another hospital. Always a good ploy with nurses. So it went as planned. A few more drinks than planned, but they were eventually in Kim's apartment. A bit seedy, but then, nurse's salary. Kim made them both drinks from her bar, then said she was going to slip into something more comfortable. Perfect. He'd soon slip her out of it.

Maurice finished his drink as he listened to her changing. Pleasant rustlings of women's clothes, shifting off and on, on and off. He could smell her perfume. Probably putting on a baby doll nightie. The drink was a strong one.

Maurice passed out very suddenly.

When Maurice awoke, he was gagged and tied spread-eagled to Kim's bed. He was naked, lying across a rubber sheet. Kinky. He was still floating on drugs, and there were needle marks sullen against his arm.

Kim was removing latex surgical gloves. They were covered with blood.

Gale was at the bedside. As was Lana. And Ashley. And Jessica. And Terri. And others.

Maurice gurgled helplessly.

"All finished," said Kim. "And he's coming around. No more Demerol. Let him enjoy it." She set aside his suture kit.

Along with Kim, the others also were all naked. They all must have recently shaved one another, but their filthy slits were open and wet again, showing only a few scars from his surgery. He must remedy that. It was all some sort of hallucination.

Maurice was still too groggy to move on the bed, or to feel pain. Kim was handed a Kotex napkin, and she strapped it firmly over his crotch, securing it in place with lots of surgical tape. It fit perfectly. No bulge. Just like in the retouched photographs in the magazines.

They'd shaved him. No ugly pubic hair. Just a perfect V between his thighs. There was some blood on the Kotex.

"Let's just leave him like this," said Kim. "I only rented this place for the week. Registered as May West. Can you believe? The maid will find him in the morning. He won't be pressing charges. He won't be pressing anything. Maybe flowers."

They each bent over him and showed him their clean, smooth crotches. Just like his. The scars were nice. They needed to be stitched and air-brushed once again.

Maurice struggled with the ropes as they dressed and left him. He was still too far under the Demerol to grasp the situation.

He stared drowsily at his air-brushed crotch, wishing to masturbate. A smooth, clean Vee. Airbrushed. No bulge. His dick would rise soon beneath the Kotex.

Then he realized the nature of the gag that was taped inside his mouth. Somehow he still managed one final orgasm.

Old Loves

He had loved her for twenty years, and today he would meet her for the first time. Her name was Elisabeth Kent, but to him she would always be Stacey Steele.

Alex Webley had been an undergraduate in the mid-1960s when *The Agency* premiered on Saturday night television. This had been at the height of the fad for spy shows—James Bond and imitations beyond counting, then countermoves toward either extreme of realism or parody. Upon such a full sea *The Agency* almost certainly would have sunk unnoticed, had it not been for the series' two stars—or more particularly, had it not been for Elisabeth Kent.

In the role of Stacey Steele she played the delightfully eccentric-— "kooky" was the expression of the times—partner of secret agent Harrison Dane, portrayed by actor Garrett Channing—an aging matinee idol, to use the expression of an earlier time. The two were employed by an enigmatic organization referred to simply as The Agency, which dispatched Dane and Miss Steele off upon dangerous assignments throughout the world. Again, nothing in the formula to distinguish *The Agency* from the rest of the pack—except for the charisma of its co-stars and for a certain stylish audacity to its scripts that became more outrageous as the series progressed.

Initially it was to have been a straight secret agent series: strong male lead assisted by curvaceous ingenue whose scatterbrained exploits would provide at least one good capture and rescue per episode. The role of Harrison Dane went to Garrett Channing—a fortuitous piece of contrary-to-type casting of an actor best remembered as the suave villain or debonair hero of various forgettable 1950s programmers. Channing had once been labeled "the poor man's James Mason," and perhaps the casting director had recalled that James Mason had been an early choice to portray James Bond. The son of a Bloomsbury greengrocer, Channing's Hollywood-nurtured sophistication and charm seemed ideal for the role of American super-spy, Harrison Dane.

Then, through a casting miracle that could only have been through chance and not genius, the role of Stacey Steele went to Elisabeth Kent. Miss Kent was a tall, leggy dancer whose acting experience consisted of several on-and-off-Broadway plays and a brief role in the most recent James Bond film. *Playboy*, as was its custom, ran a pictorial feature on the lovelies of the latest Bond film and devoted two full pages to the blonde Miss Kent—revealing rather more of her than was permitted in the movies of the day. It brought her to the attention of the casting director, and Elisabeth Kent became Stacey Steele.

Became Stacey Steele, almost literally.

Later they would say that the role destroyed Elisabeth Kent. Her career dwindled miserably afterward. Some critics suggested that Miss Kent had been blackballed by the industry after her unexpected departure from the series resulted in *The Agency*'s plummeting in the ratings and merciful cancellation after a partial season with a forgettable DD-cup Malibu blonde stuffed into the role of female lead. The consensus, however, pointed out that after her role in *The Agency* it was Stacey Steele who was in demand, and not Elisabeth Kent. Once the fad for secret agent films passed, there were no more roles for Stacy Steele. Nor for Elisabeth Kent. A situation-comedy series flopped after three episodes. Two films with her in straight dramatic roles were noteworthy bombs, and a third was never released. Even if Elisabeth Kent succeeded in convincing some producer or director that she was not Stacey Steele, her public remained adamant.

Her only film appearance within the past decade had been as the villainess in a Hong Kong chop-fooey opus, *Tiger Fists Against the Dragon*. Perhaps it lost some little in translation.

Inevitably, *The Agency* attracted a dedicated fan following, and Stacy Steele became a cult figure. The same was true to a lesser extent for Garrett Channing, although that actor's death not long after the series' cancellation spared him both the benefits and the hazards of such a status. The note he left upon his desk: "Goodbye, World—I can no longer accept your tedium" was considered an enviable exit line.

The Agency premiered in the mid-1960s, just catching the crest of the Carnaby Street mod-look craze. Harrison Dane, suave super-spy and mature man of the world though he was, was decidedly hip to today's swinging beat, and the promos boldly characterized him as a "mod James Bond." No business suits and narrow ties for Harrison Dane: "We want to take the stuffiness out of secret agenting," to quote one producer. As the sophisticated counterpart to the irrepressible Miss Steele, Dane saved the day once a week attired in various outfits consisting of bell-bottom trousers, paisley shirts, Nehru jackets, and lots of beads and badges. If one critic described Harrison Dane as "a middle-aged Beatle," the public applauded this "anti-establishment super-spy."

No such criticism touched the image of Stacey Steele. Stacey Steele was the American viewing public's ideal of the Swinging London Bird—her long-legged physique perfectly suited to vinyl mini-dresses and thigh-high boots. Each episode became a showcase for her daring fashions—briefest of miniskirts, hip-hugging leather bell-bottoms, see-through (as much as the censors would permit) blouses, cut-out dresses, patent boots, psychedelic jewelry, groovy hats, all that was marvy, fab and gear. There was talk of opening a franchise of Stacey Steele Boutiques, and Miss Steele became a featured model in various popular magazines seeking to portray the latest fashions for the Liberated Lady of the Sixties. By this time Elisabeth Kent's carefully modulated BBC accent would never betray her Long Island birthright to the unstudied ear.

Stacey Steele was instant pin-up material, and stills of the miniskirted secret agent covered many a dorm wall beside blow-ups of Bogie and black-light posters. Later detractors argued that *The Agency* would never have lasted its first season without Stacey Steele's legs, and that the series was little more than an American version of one of the imported British spy shows. Fans rebutted such charges with the assertion that it had all started with James Bond anyway, and *The Agency* proved that the Americans could do it best. Pin-up photos of Stacey Steele continue to sell well twenty years after.

While *The Agency* may have been plainly derivative of a popular British series, American viewers made it their favorite show against formidable prime-time competition from the other two networks. For three glorious seasons *The Agency* ruled Saturday nights. Then, Elisabeth Kent's sudden departure from the series: catastrophe, mediocrity, cancellation. But not oblivion. The series passed into syndication and thus into the twilight zone of odd-hour reruns on local channels and independent networks. Old fans remembered, new fans were born. *The Agency* developed a cult following, and Stacey Steele became its goddess.

In that sense, among its priesthood was Alex Webley. He had begun his worship two decades ago in the TV lounge of a college dorm, amidst the incense of spilled beer and tobacco smoke and an inspired choir of whistles and guffaws. The first night he watched *The Agency* Webley had been blowing some tangerine with an old high school buddy who had brought a little down from Antioch. Webley didn't think he'd gotten off, but when the miniskirted Miss Steele used dazzling karate chops to dispatch two baddies, he knew he was having a religious experience. After that, he watched *The Agency* every Saturday night, without fail. It would have put a crimp in his dating if Webley had been one who dated. His greatest moment in college was the night when he stood off two drunken jocks, either of whom could have folded Webley in half, who wanted to switch channels from *The Agency* to watch a basketball game. They might have stuffed Webley into a wastebasket had not other *Agency* fans added their voices to his protest. Thus did Alex Webley learn the power of fans united.

It was a power he experienced again with news of Elisabeth Kent's departure from the series, and later when *The Agency* was cancelled. Webley was one of the thousands of fans who wrote to the network demanding that Stacey Steele be brought back to the show (never mind how). With the show's cancellation, Webley helped circulate a petition that *The Agency* be continued, with or without Stacey Steele. The producers were impressed by such show of support, but the network pointed out that 10,000 signatures from the lunatic fringe do not cause a flicker on the Nielsen ratings. Without Stacey Steele, *The Agency* was out of business, and that was that. Besides, the fad for overdone spy shows was over and done.

Alex Webley kept a file of clippings and stills, promotional items, comic books and paperbacks, anything at all pertaining to *The Agency* and to the great love of his life, Elisabeth Kent. From the beginning there were fanzines—crudely printed amateur publications devoted to *The Agency*—and one or two unofficial fan clubs. Webley joined and subscribed to them all. Undergraduate enthusiasms developed into a lifelong hobby. Corresponding with other diehard fans and collecting *Agency* memorabilia became his preoccupying outside interest in the course of taking a doctorate in neurobiology. He was spared from Viet Nam by high blood pressure, and from any long-term romantic involvement by a highly introverted nature. Following his doctorate, Webley landed a research position at one of the pharmaceutical laboratories, where he performed his duties efficiently and maintained an attitude of polite aloofness toward his coworkers. Someone there dubbed him "the Invisible Man," but there was no malice to the *mot juste*.

At his condo, the door to the spare bedroom bore a brass-on-walnut plaque that read *HQ*. Webley had made it himself. Inside were filing cabinets, bookshelves, and his desk. The walls were papered with posters and stills, most of them photos of Stacey Steele. A glass-fronted cabinet held videocassettes of all *The Agency* episodes, painstakingly acquired through trades with other fans. The day he completed the set, Webley drank most of a bottle of Glenfiddich—Dane and Miss Steele's favorite potation—and afterward became quite ill.

By now Webley's enthusiasm had expanded to all of the spy shows and films of the period, but old loves die hard, and *The Agency* remained his chief interest. Webley was editor/publisher of *Special Assignment*, a quarterly amateur magazine devoted to the spy craze of the '60s. *Special Assignment* was more than a cut above the mimeographed fanzines that Webley had first begun to collect; his magazine was computer-typeset and boasted slick paper and color covers. By its tenth issue, *Special Assignment* had a circulation of several thousand, with distribution through specialty bookshops here and abroad. It was a hobby project that took up all of Webley's free time and much of his living space, and Webley was content.

Almost content. *Special Assignment* carried photographs and articles on every aspect of the old spy shows, along with interviews of many of the actors and actresses. Webley, of course, devoted a good many pages each issue to *The Agency* and to Stacey Steele—but to his chagrin he was unable to obtain an interview with Elisabeth Kent. Since her one disastrous comeback attempt, Miss Kent preferred the life of a recluse. There was some dignity to be salvaged in anonymity. Miss Kent did not grant interviews, she did not make public appearances, she did not answer fan mail. After ten years the world forgot Elisabeth Kent, but her fans still remembered Stacey Steele.

Webley had several years prior managed to secure Elisabeth Kent's address—no mean accomplishment in itself—but his rather gushing fan letters had not elicited any sort of reply. Not easily daunted, Webley faithfully sent Miss Kent each new issue of *Special Assignment* (personally inscribed to her), and with each issue he included a long letter of praise for her deathless characterization of Stacey Steele, along with a plea to be granted an interview. Webley never gave up hope, despite Miss Kent's unbroken silence.

When he at last did receive a letter from Miss Kent graciously granting him the long-sought interview, Webley knew that life is just and that the faithful shall be rewarded.

He caught one of those red-eye-special flights out to Los Angeles, but was too excited to catch any sleep on the way. Instead he reread a well-worn paperback novelization of one of his favorite

Agency episodes, The Chained Lightning Caper, and mentally reviewed the questions he would ask Miss Kent—still not quite able to believe that he would be talking with her in another few hours.

Webley checked into a Thrifti-Family Motel near the airport, unpacked, tried without success to sleep, got up, showered and shaved. The economy flight he had taken hadn't served a meal, but then it had been all Webley could manage just to finish his complimentary soft beverage. The three-hour time change left his system rather disordered in any event, so that he wasn't certain whether he actually should feel tired or hungry were it not for his anxiousness over the coming interview. He pulled out his notes and looked over them again, managing to catch a fitful nap just before dawn. At daylight he made himself eat a dismal breakfast in the motel restaurant, then returned to his room to shave again and to put on the clothes he had brought along for the interview.

It was the best of Webley's several Harrison Dane costumes, carefully salvaged from various Thrift Shops and yard sales. Webley maintained a wardrobe of vintage mod clothing, and he had twice won prizes at convention masquerades. The pointed-toe Italian boots were original to the period—a lovingly maintained treasure discovered ten years before at Goodwill Industries. The suede bell-bottoms were custom-made by an aging hippie at an aging leather crafts shop that still had a few psychedelic posters tacked to its walls. Webley tried them on at least once a month and adjusted his diet according to snugness of fit. The jacket, a sort of lavender thing that lacked collar or lapels, was found at a vintage clothing store and altered to his measurements. The paisley shirt, mostly purples and greens, had been discovered at a yard sale, and the beads and medallions had come from here and there.

Webley was particularly proud of his Dane Cane, which he himself had constructed after the secret agent's famous weapon. It appeared to be a normal walking stick, but it contained Dane's arsenal of secret weapons and paraphernalia—including a radio transmitter, recording device, tear gas, and laser. Harrison Dane was never without his marvelous cane, and good thing, too. Alex

Webley had caused rather a stir at the airport check-in, before airline officials finally permitted him to transport his Dane Cane via baggage.

Webley still clung to the modified Beatles haircut that Harrison Dane affected. He combed it now carefully, and he studied his reflection in the room's ripply mirror. The very image of Harrison Dane. Stacey Steele—Miss Kent—would no doubt be impressed by the pains he had taken. It would have been great to drive out in a Shelby Cobra like Dane's, but instead he called for a cab.

Not a Beverly Hills address, Webley sadly noted, as the taxi drove him to one of those innumerable canyon neighborhoods tottering on steep hillsides and the brink of shabbiness. Her house was small and featureless, a little box propped up on the hillside beside a jagged row of others like it—distinguishable one from another chiefly by the degree of seediness and the cars parked in front. Some cheap development from the 1950s, Webley judged, and another ten years likely would see the ones still standing bought up and the land used for some cheap condo development. He felt increasingly sad about it all; he had been prepared to announce his arrival to some uniformed guard at the subdivision's entrance gate.

Well, if it were within his power to do so, Webley intended to bring to bear the might and majesty of *Special Assignment* to pressure these stupid producers into casting Elisabeth Kent in new and important roles. That made this interview more important than ever to Webley—and to Miss Kent.

He paid off the cab—tipping generously, as Harrison Dane would have done. This was perhaps fortuitous, as the driver shouted after him that he had forgotten his attaché case. Webley wondered how Dane would have handled such an embarrassing lapse—of course, Dane would never have committed such a blunder. Webley's case—also modelled after Dane's secret agent attaché case, although Webley's lacked the built-in machine gun—contained a bottle of Glenfiddich, his notes, cassette recorder, and camera. It was essential that he obtained some photographs of Miss Kent at home: since her appearance in the unfortunate *Tiger Fists* film, current photos of Elisabeth Kent were not made available. Webley had heard vicious rumors that the actress had lost her looks, but he put these down to typical show biz back-stabbing, and he prayed it wasn't so.

He rang the doorbell, using the tip of his cane, just as Dane always did, and waited—posing jauntily against his cane, just as Dane always did. The seconds dragged on eternally, and there was no response. He rang again, and waited. Webley looked for a car in the driveway; saw none, but the carport was closed. He rang a third time.

This time the door opened.

And Alex Webley knew his worship had not been in vain.

"Hullo, Dane," she said. "I've been expecting you."

"How very good to see you, Miss Steele," said Webley. "I hope I haven't kept you waiting."

And she was Stacey Steele. Just like in The Agency. And Webley felt a thrill at knowing she had dressed the part just for the interview—just for him.

The Hollywood gossip had been all lies, because she hardly looked a day older—although part of that was no doubt due to her appearance today as Stacey Steele. It was perfect. It was all there, as it should be: the thigh-length boots of black patent leather, the red leather minidress with LOVE emblazoned across the breastline (the center of the O was cut out, revealing a daring glimpse of braless cleavage), the blonde bangs and ironed-straight Mary Travers hair, the beads and bells. Time had rolled back, and she *was* Stacey Steele.

"Come on in, luv," Miss Steele invited, in her so-familiar throaty purr.

Aerobics really can do wonders, Webley thought as he followed her into her living room. Twenty years may have gone by, but if *The Agency* were to be revived today, Miss Kent could step right into her old role as the mod madcap Miss Steele. Exercise and diet, probably—he must find some discreet way of asking her how she kept her youthful figure.

The living room was a close replica of Stacey Steele's swinging London flat, enough so that Webley guessed she had removed much of the set from the Hollywood soundstage where the series was actually shot. He sat down, not without difficulty, on the inflatable day-glo orange chair—Dane's favorite—and opened his attaché case.

"I brought along a little libation," he said, presenting her with the Glenfiddich.

Miss Steele gladly accepted the dark-green triangular bottle. "Ah, luv! You always remember, don't you!"

She quickly poured a generous level of the pale amber whisky into a pair of stemmed glasses and offered one to Webley. Webley wanted to protest that it was too early in the day for him to tackle straight Scotch, but he decided he'd rather die than break the spell of this moment.

Instead, he said: "Cheers." And drank.

The whisky went down his throat smoothly and soared straight to his head. Webley blinked and set down his glass in order to paw through the contents of his case. Miss Steele had recharged his glass before he could protest, but already Webley was thinking how perfect this all was. This would be one to tell to those scoffers who had advised him against wearing his Harrison Dane costume to the interview.

"Here's a copy of our latest issue..." Webley hesitated only slightly "...Miss Steele."

She took the magazine from him. The cover was a still of Stacey Steele karate-chopping a heavy in a pink foil spacesuit. "Why, that's me! How groovy!"

"Yes. From 'The Mod Martian Caper,' of course. And naturally you'll be featured on our next cover, along with the interview and all." The our was an editorial plural, inasmuch as Webley was the entire staff of *Special Assignment*.

"Fab!" said Miss Steele, paging through the magazine in search of more photos of herself.

Webley risked another sip of Glenfiddich while he glanced around the room. However the house might appear from the outside, inside Miss Kent had lovingly maintained the ambiance of The Agency. The black lights and pop-art posters, the psychedelic color schemes, the beaded curtains, the oriental rugs. Indian music was playing, and strewn beside the vintage KLH stereo Webley recognized early albums from the Beatles and the Stones, from the Who and the Yardbirds, from Ultimate Spinach and Thirteenth Floor Elevator. He drew in a deep breath; yes, that was incense burning on the mantelpiece—cinnamon, Miss Steele's favorite.

"That's the platinum bird you used in 'The Malted Falcon Caper,' isn't it?"

Miss Steele touched the silver falcon statuette Webley had spotted. "The very bird. Not really made of platinum, sorry to report."

"And that must be the chastity belt they locked you into in 'The Medieval Mistress Caper." Again Webley pointed.

"One and the same. And not very comfy on a cold day, I assure you."

Webley decided he was about to sound gushy, so he finished his second whisky. It didn't help collect his thoughts, but it did restore a little calmness. He decided not to argue when Miss Steele refreshed their drinks. His fingers itched for his camera, but his hands were trembling too much.

"You seem to have kept quite a few props from *The Agency*," he suggested. "Isn't that the steel mask they put over your head in 'The Silent Cyborg Caper'? Not very comfortable either, I should imagine."

"At times I did find my part a trifle confining," Miss Steele admitted. "All those captures by the villains."

"With Harrison Dane always there in the nick of time," Webley said, raising his glass to her. If Miss Steele was in no hurry to get through the interview, then neither was he.

"It wasn't all that much fun waiting to be rescued every time," Miss Steele confided. "Tied out in the hot sun across a railroad track, or stretched out on a rack in a moldy old dungeon."

"'The Uncivil Engineer Caper,'" Webley remembered, "and 'The Dungeon To Let Caper.'"

"Or being strapped to a log in a sawmill."

"'The Silver Scream Caper.'"

"I was brushing sawdust out of my hair for a week."

"And in 'The Missing Mermaid Caper' they handcuffed you to an anchor and tossed you overboard."

"Yes, and I still have my rubber fishtail from that one."

"Here?"

"Certainly. I've held on to a museum's worth of costumes and props. Would you like to see the lot of it?"

"Would I ever!" Webley prayed he had brought enough film.

"Then I'll just give us a refill."

"I really think I've had enough just now," Webley begged.

"Why, Dane! I never knew you to say no."

"But one more to top things off," agreed Webley, unable to tarnish the image of Harrison Dane.

Miss Steele poured. "Most of it's kept downstairs."

"After all, Miss Steele, this is a special occasion." Webley drank.

He had a little difficulty with the stairs—he vaguely felt he was floating downward, and the Dane Cane kept tripping him—but he made it to the lower level without disgracing himself. Once there, all he could manage was a breathless: "Out of sight!"

Presumably the downstairs had been designed as a sort of large family room, complete with fireplace, cozy chairs, and at one time probably a ping pong table or such. Miss Kent had refurnished the room with enough props and sets to reshoot the entire series. Webley could only stand and stare. It was as if an entire file of *Agency* stills had been scattered about and transformed into three-dimensional reality.

There was the stake the natives had tied her to in "The No Atoll At All Caper," and there was the man-eating plant that had menaced her in "The Venusian Vegetarian Caper." In one corner stood—surely a replica—Stacey Steele's marvelous VW Beetle, sporting its wild psychedelic paint scheme and harboring a Porsche engine and drivetrain. There was the E.V.O.L. interrogation chair from "The Earth's End Caper," and behind it one of the murderous robots from "The Angry Android Caper." Harrison Dane's circular bed, complete with television, stereo, bar, machine guns, and countless other built-in devices, was crowded beside the very same torture rack from "The Dungeon To Let Caper." Cataloging just the major pieces would be an hour's work, even for Webley, and a full inventory of all the memorabilia would take at least a couple days.

"Impressed, luv?"

Webley closed his mouth. "It's like the entire *Agency* series come to life in one house," he finally said.

"Do browse about all you like, luv."

Webley stumbled across the room, trying not to touch any of the sacred relics, scarcely able to concentrate upon any one object for longer than its moment of recognition. It was all too overpowering an assault upon his sensory mechanisms.

"A toast to us, luv."

Webley didn't remember whether Miss Steele had brought along their glasses or poured fresh drinks from Harrison Dane's art nouveau bar, shoved against one wall next to the mind transfer machine from "The Wild, Wild Bunch Caper." He gulped his drink without thinking and moments later regretted it.

"I think I'd like to sit down for a minute," Webley apologized.

"Drugged drinks!" Miss Steele said brightly. "Just like in 'The Earth's End Caper.' Quick, Dane! Sit down here!"

Webley collapsed into the interrogation chair as directed—it was closest, and he was about to make a scene if he didn't recover his balance. Automatic cuffs instantly secured his arms, legs, and body to the chair.

"Only in 'The Earth's End Caper,'" said Miss Steele, "I was the one they drugged and fastened into this chair. There to be horribly tortured, unless Harrison Dane came to the rescue."

Webley turned his head as much as the neck restraints would permit. Miss Steele was laying out an assortment of scalpels and less obvious instruments, recognized by Webley as props from the episode.

"Groovy," he managed to say.

Miss Steele was assembling some sort of dental drill. "I was always the victim." She smiled at him with that delightful madcap smile. "I was always the one being captured, humiliated, helplessly awaiting your last-minute mock heroics."

"Well, not all the time," Webley protested, going along with the joke. He hoped he wasn't going to be ill.

"Are these clamps very tight?"

"Yes. Very. The prop seems in perfect working order. I think I really ought to stretch out for a while. Most embarrassing, but I'm afraid that drinking this early…"

"It wasn't enough that you seduced me and insisted on the abortion for the sake of our careers. It was your egotistical jealousy that finally destroyed me. You couldn't stand the fact that Stacey Steele was the *real* star of *The Agency*, and not Harrison Dane. So you pulled strings until you got me written out of the series. Then you did your best to ruin my career afterward."

"I don't feel very good," Webley muttered. "I think I might be getting sick."

"Hoping for a last-second rescue?" Stacey Steele selected a scalpel from the tray, and bent over him. Webley had a breathtaking glimpse through the cut-out of LOVE, and then the blade touched his eye.

The police were already there by the time Elisabeth Kent got home. Neighbors' dogs were barking at something in the brush below her house; some kids went to see what they were after, and then the police were called.

"Did you know the man, Miss Kent?"

Miss Kent nodded her double chins. She was concentrating on stocking her liquor cabinet with the case of generic gin she'd gone out to buy with the advance check Webley had mailed her. She'd planned on fortifying herself for the interview that might mean her comeback, but her aging Nova had refused to start in the parking lot, and the road call had eaten up the remainder of the check that she'd hoped would go toward overdue rent for the one-storey frame dump. She sat down heavily on the best chair of her sparsely furnished living room.

"He was some fan from back east," she told the investigating officer. "Wanted to interview me for some fan magazine. I've got his letter here somewhere. I used to be in films a few years back—maybe you remember."

"We'll need to get in touch with next of kin," the detective said. "Already found the cabbie who let him out here while you were off getting towed." He was wondering if he had ever seen her in anything. "At a guess, he waited around on your deck, probably leaned against the railing—got a little dizzy, and went over. Might have had a heart attack or something."

Elisabeth Kent was looking at the empty Glenfiddich bottle and the two glasses.

"Damn you, Stacey Steele," she whispered. "Goddamn you."

Lacunae

They were resting, still joined together, in the redwood hot tub, water pushing in bubbling surges about their bodies. Elaine watched as the hot vortex caught up streamers of her semen, swirled it away like boiled confetti, dissipating it throughout the turbulence.

I'm disseminated, she thought.

Elaine said: "I feel reborn."

Allen kissed the back of her neck and brushed her softening nipples with his fingertips. "Your breasts are getting so full. Are you stepping up the estrogens?"

His detumescent penis, still slick with Vaseline, tickled as it eased out of Elaine's ass. Allen's right hand moved down through the warm water, milked the last droplets of orgasm from Elaine's flaccid cock. Gently he turned Elaine around, kissed her lovingly—probing his tongue deep into her mouth.

"Here," said Allen, breaking their kiss. He pushed down on Elaine's shoulders, urging her beneath the foaming surface. Elaine let her knees bend, ducked beneath the water that swirled about Allen's hips. As Allen's hands cupped her head, Elaine opened her mouth to accept Allen's slippery cock. She tasted the sweet smear of her own shit as she sucked in its entire length. Suddenly swelling, the cock filled her mouth, hardening as it pushed deep into her throat.

Elaine gagged and tried to pull back, but Allen's hands forced her head hard into his pubic hair. Water filled Elaine's nostrils as she choked, bit down in an uncontrollable reflex. Allen's severed cock, bitten free at the base, wriggled inward, sliding past the back of her throat and down into her windpipe.

Elaine wrenched free of Allen's hands. Blood and come filled her lungs—spewed from her mouth in an obscene fountain as her head pushed toward the surface. But her head could not break through the surface, no matter how desperately she fought. There was a black resilient layer that separated her from the air above, closed like wax over her face, pushed the vomit back into her lungs.

A vortex of blood and semen sucked her soul into its warm depths.

The first thing she heard was a monotoned *shit-shit-shit*—like autumn leaves brushing the window. She became aware of an abrupt pressure against her abdomen, of vomit being expelled from her mouth. She was breathing in gasps.

She opened her eyes. The layer of clinging blackness was gone.

"Shit goddammit," said Blacklight, wiping vomit from her face and nostrils. "Don't ever try that alone again."

Elaine stared at him dumbly, oxygen returning to her brain.

Beside her on the carpet lay the black leather bondage mask—its straps and laces cut. The attached phallus-shaped gag, almost bitten through, was covered with her vomit. A spiked leather belt, also slashed, was coiled about the mask.

"Jesus!" said Blacklight. "You OK now?"

He was wrapping a blanket around her, busily tucking it in. There was a buzzing somewhere, in her head or in her pelvis—she wasn't sure. Memory was returning.

"I dreamed I was a man," she said, forcing her throat to speak.

"Fuckin' A. You nearly dreamed you were dead. I had a buddy from Nam who used to do this kinda shit. He'd been dead two days before they found him."

Elaine looked upward at the chinning bar, mounted high across her entrance hall doorway. The leather mask with its padded blindfold and gag—sensory deprivation and sensual depravity—cutting out the world. The belt, looped around her neck, free end held in her hands as she kicked away the stool. The belt buckle should have slipped free when she fainted from lack of oxygen. Instead its buckle had become entangled with the complex buckles of the bondage mask, not releasing, nearly suffocating her. Friends who had shown her how to experience visions of inner realities through this method had warned her, but until now there had been no problems. No worse than with the inversion apparatus.

"I heard you banging about on the floor," Blacklight explained, taking her pulse. He had been an army medic until he'd Section-Eighted—no future for a broad six-foot-eight medic in the paddies. "Thought maybe you were balling somebody, but it didn't feel right. I busted in your door."

Good job through two dead-bolts and a chain, but Blacklight could do it. Her neighbor in the duplex loft had split last week, and the pizzeria downstairs was being redone as a vegetarian restaurant. Elaine might have lain there dead on the floor until her cats polished her bones.

"I dreamed I had a cock," she said, massaging her neck.

"Maybe you still do," Blacklight told her. He looked at his hands and went into the bathroom to wash them.

Elaine wondered what he meant, then remembered. She reached down to flick off the vibrator switch on the grotesque dildo she had strapped around her pelvis. Gathering the blanket about herself, she made it to her feet and waited for Blacklight to come out of the bathroom.

When she had removed the rest of her costume and washed herself, she put on a Chinese silk kimono and went to look for Blacklight. She felt little embarrassment. Between cheap smack in Nam and killer acid in the Haight, Blacklight's brain had been fried for most of his life. He was more reliable for deliveries than the Colombians, and old contacts supported him and his habit.

Blacklight was standing in the center of her studio—the loft was little more than one big room with a few shelves and counters to partition space—staring uncertainly at an unfinished canvas.

"You better look closer at your model, or else you got a freak."

The canvas was wall-sized, originally commissioned and never paid for by a trendy leather bar, since closed. Blacklight pointed. "Balls don't hang side by side like that. One dangles a little lower. Even a dyke ought to know that."

"It's not completed," Elaine said. She was looking at the bag of white powder Blacklight had dropped onto her bar.

"You want to know why?"

"What?"

"It's so they don't bang together."

"Who doesn't?"

"Your balls. One slides away from the other when you mash your legs together."

"Terrific," said Elaine, digging a fingernail into the powder.

"You like it?"

"The thing about balls." Elaine tasted a smear of coke, licking her fingertip.

"Uncut Peruvian flake," Blacklight promised, forgetting the earlier subject.

Elaine sampled a nail-full up each nostril. The ringing bitterness of the coke cut through the residues of vomit. Good shit.

"It's like Yin and Yang," Blacklight explained. "Good and Evil. Light and Dark."

One doesn't correct a large and crazed biker. He was wrestling his fists together. "Have you ever heard the story of Love and Hate?"

Across the knuckles of his right fist was tattooed *LOVE*; across those of his left: *HATE*.

Elaine had seen *Night of the Hunter*, and she was not impressed.

"An ounce?"

"One humongous oh-zee." Blacklight was finger-wrestling with himself. "They got to be kept apart, Love and Hate, but they can't keep from coming together and trying to see which one's stronger."

Elaine opened the drawer beneath her telephone and counted out the bills she had set aside earlier. Blacklight forgot his Robert Mitchum impersonation and accepted the money.

"I got five paintings to finish before my show opens in SoHo,

OK? That's next month. This is the end of this month. My ass is fucked, and I'm stone out of inspiration. So give me a break and split now, right?"

"Just don't try too much free-basing with that shit, OK?" Blacklight advised. He craned his thick neck to consider another unfinished canvas. It reminded him of someone, but then he forgot who before he could form the thought.

"Your brain is like your balls, did you know that?" He picked up the thread of the last conversation he could remember.

"No, I didn't know that."

"Two hunks rolling around inside your skull," Blacklight said, knotting his fists side by side. "They swim in your skull side by side, just like your balls swing around in your scrotum. Why are there two halves of your brain instead of just one big chunk—like, say, your heart?"

"I give up."

Blacklight massaged his fists together. "So they don't bang together, see. Got to keep them apart. Love and Hate. Yin and Yang."

"Look. I got to work." Elaine shook a gram's worth of lines out of the baggie and onto the glass top of her coffee table.

"Sure. You sure you're gonna be OK?"

"No more anoxic rushes with a mask on. And thanks."

"You got a beer?"

"Try the fridge."

Blacklight found a St Pauli and plinked the non-twist-off cap free with his thumb. Elaine thought he looked like a black-bearded Wookie.

"I had a buddy from Nam who offed himself trying that," Blacklight suddenly remembered.

"You told me."

"Like, whatever turns you on. Just don't drop the hammer when you don't mean to."

"Want a line?"

"No. I'm off Charlie. Fucks up my brain." Blacklight's eyes glazed in an effort to concentrate. "Off the goddamn dinks," he said. "Off 'em all." There were old tracks fighting with the tattoos, as he raised his arm to kill the beer.

"Are you sure you're gonna be OK?" He was pulling out a fresh beer from behind the tuna salad.

Elaine was a foot shorter and a hundred pounds lighter, and aerobicise muscles weren't enough to overawe Blacklight. "Look. I'm all right now. Thanks. Just let me get back to work. OK? I mean, deadline-wise, this is truly crunch city."

"Want some crystal? Got a dynamite price."

"Got some. Look, I think I'm going to throw up some more. Want to give me some privacy?"

Blacklight dropped the beer bottle into his shirt pocket. "Hang loose." He started for the door. The beer bottle seemed no larger than a pen in his pocket.

"Oh," he said. "I can get you something better. A new one. Takes out the blank spots in your head. Just met a new contact who's radically into designer drugs. Weird dude. Working on some new kind of speed."

"I'll take some," said Elaine, opening the door. She really needed to sleep for a week.

"Catch you later," promised Blacklight.

He paused halfway through the door, dug into his denim jacket pocket. "Superb blotter," he said, handing her a dingy square of dolphin-patterned paper. "Very inspirational. Use it and grow. Are you sure you're gonna be okay?"

Elaine shut the door.

Mr Fix-it promised to come by tomorrow, or the next morning after that, for sure.

Elaine replaced the chain with one from the bathroom door, hammered the torn-out and useless dead-bolts back into place for her own peace of mind, then propped a wooden chair against the doorknob. Feeling better, she pulled on a leotard, and tried a gram or so of this and that.

She was working rather hard, and the air brush was a bit loud, although her stereo would have drowned out most sounds of entry in any event.

"That blue," said Kane from behind her. "Cerulean, to be

sure—but why? It impresses me as antagonistic to the overdone flesh-tones you've so laboriously mulled and muddled to confuse the faces of the two lovers."

Elaine did not scream. There would be no one to hear. She turned very cautiously. A friend had once told her how to react in these situations.

"Are you an art critic?" The chair was still propped beside her door. Perhaps it was a little askew.

"Merely a dilettante," lied Kane. "An interested patron of the arts for many years. *That* is not a female escutcheon."

"It shouldn't be."

"Possibly not."

"I'm expecting my boyfriend at any minute. He's bringing over some buyers. Are you waiting for them?"

"Blacklight contacted me. He thought you'd like something stronger to help you finish your gallery collection."

Elaine decided to take a breath. He was big, very big. His belted trenchcoat could have held two of her and an umbrella. A biker friend of Blacklight's was her first thought. They hadn't quite decided whether to be hit-men for the Mafia or their replacements in the lucrative drug trade. He was a head shorter than Blacklight, probably weighed more. There was no fat. His movements reminded Elaine of her karate instructor. His face, although unscarred, called to mind an NFL lineman who'd flunked his advertising screentest. His hair and short beard were a shade darker than her hennaed Grace Jones flattop. She did not like his blue eyes—quickly looked away.

"Here," said Kane.

She took from his spade-like hand a two-gram glass phial—corner headshop stuff, spoon attached by an aluminum chain.

"How much?" There was a can of Mace in the drawer beneath the telephone. She didn't think it would help.

"New lot," said Kane, sitting down on the arm of her largest chair. He balanced his weight, but she flinched. "Trying to recreate a lost drug from long ago. Perfectly legal."

"How long ago?"

"Before you'd remember. It's a sort of super-speed."

"Super-speed?"

Kane dropped the rest of the way into the chair. It held his weight. He said: "Can you remember everything that has happened to you, or that you have done, for the past 48 hours?"

"Of course."

"Tell me about 11:38 this morning."

"All right." Elaine was open to a dare. "I was in the shower. I'd been awake all night, working on the paintings for the show. I called my agent's answering machine, then took a shower. I thought I'd try some TM afterward, before getting back to work."

"But what were you thinking at 11:38 this morning?"

"About the showing."

"No."

Elaine decided it was too risky to jump for the phone. "I forget what I was thinking exactly," she conceded. "Would you like some coffee?" Scalding coffee in the face might work.

"What was on your mind at 9:42 last night?"

"I was fixing coffee. Would you like some...?"

"At 9:42. Exactly then."

"All right. I don't remember. I was flipping around the cable dial, I think. Maybe I was daydreaming."

"Lacunae," said Kane.

"Say, what?"

"Gaps. Missing pieces. Missing moments of memory. Time lost from your consciousness, and thus from your life. Where? Why?"

He rolled the phial about on his broad palm. "No one really remembers every instant of life. There are always forgotten moments, daydreams, musings—as you like. It's lost time from your life. Where does it go? You can't remember. You can't even remember forgetting that moment. Part of your life is lost in vacant moments, in lapses of total consciousness. Where does your conscious mind go? And why?

"This," and he tossed the glass phial toward her, "will remove those lost moments. No gaps in your memory—wondering where your car keys are, where you left your sunglasses, who called before lunch, what was foremost in your mind when you woke up. Better than speed or coke. Total awareness of your total consciousness. No more lacunae."

"I don't have any cash on hand."

"There's no charge. Think of it as a trial sample."

"I know—the first one is free."

"That's meant to be a mirror, isn't it." Kane returned to the unfinished painting. "The blue made me think of water. It's someone making love to a reflection."

"Someone," said Elaine.

"Narcissus?"

"I call it: *Lick It Till It Bleeds*."

"I'll make a point of attending the opening."

"There won't be one unless people leave me alone to work."

"Then I'll be getting along." Kane seemed to be standing without ever having arisen from the chair. "By the way, I wouldn't shove that. New lab equipment. Never know about impurities."

"I don't like needlework anyway," Elaine told him, dipping into the phial with the attached spoon. She snorted cautiously, felt no burn. Clean enough. She heaped the spoon twice again.

She closed her eyes and inhaled deeply. Already she could feel a buzz. Trust Blacklight to steer her onto something good.

She was trying another spoonful when it occurred to her that she was alone once again.

Blacklight secured the lid of the industrial chemical drum and finished his beer. The body of the designer drug lab's former owner had folded inside nicely. Off to the illegal toxic waste dump with the others. Some suckers just can't tell which way the wind blows.

"Did you really land in a flying saucer? he asked, rummaging in the cooler for another beer.

Kane was scowling over a chromatogram. "For sure. Looked just like a 1957 Chrysler 300C hubcap."

Blacklight puzzled over it while he chugged his beer. The prettiest girl in his junior high—her family had had a white 300C convertible. Was there a connection?

"Then how come you speak English so good?"

"I was Tor Johnson's stand-in in *Plan 9 from Outer Space*. Must have done a hundred retakes before we got it down right."

Blacklight thought about it. "Did you know Bela Lugosi?"

Kane jabbed at the computer keyboard, watching the monitor intently. "I've got to get some better equipment. There's a methyl group somewhere where it shouldn't be."

"Is that bad?"

"Might potentiate. Start thinking of another guinea pig."

At first she became aware of her hands.

It was 1:01:36 am, said the digital clock beside her bed. She stepped back from the painting and considered her hands. They were tobacco-stained and paint-smeared, and her nails needed polish. How could she hope to create with hands such as these?

Elaine glared at her hands for 43 seconds, found no evidence of improvement. The back of her skull didn't feel quite right either; it tingled, like when her Mohawk started to grow out last year. Maybe some wine.

There was an open bottle of Liebfraumilch in the refrigerator. She poured a glass, sipped, set it aside in distaste. Elaine thought about the wine for the next 86 seconds, reading the label twice. She made a mental note never to buy it again. Stirring through a canister of artificial sweetener packets, she found half a 'lude, washed it down with the wine.

She returned to *Lick It Till It Bleeds* and worked furiously, with total concentration and with mounting dissatisfaction, for the next one hour, 31 minutes and 18 seconds.

Her skin itched.

Elaine glowered at the painting for another 7 minutes 19 seconds.

She decided to phone Allen.

An insomniac recording answered her. The number she had dialed was no longer in service. Please...

Elaine tried to visualize Allen. How long had it been?

Her skin itched.

Had she left him, or had he driven her out? And did it really matter? She hated him. She had always hated him. She hated all that she had previously been.

Her body felt strange, like a stranger's body. The leotard was binding her crotch. Stupid design.

Elaine stripped off her leotard and tights. Her skin still itched. Like a caterpillar's transformation throes. Death throes of former life. Did the caterpillar hate the moth?

She thought about Allen.

She thought about herself.

Love and hate.

There was a full-length mirror on her closet door. Elaine stared at her reflection, caressing her breasts and crotch. She moved closer, pressed herself to the mirror, rubbing against her reflection.

Making love to herself.

And hating.

Pressed against her reflection, Elaine could not ignore the finest of scars where the plastic surgeon had implanted silicone in her once-flat breasts. Fingering her surgically constructed vagina, Elaine could not repress the memories of her sex-change operation, repress the awareness of her former maleness.

Every instant remembered. Of joy. Of pain. Of longing. Of rage. Of hatred. Of self-loathing.

Of being Allen.

Her fists hammered her reflection, smashing it into a hundred brittle moments.

Blood trickled from her fists, streamed along her arms, made curling patterns across her breasts and belly.

She licked her blood, and found it good. It was shed for herself.

Gripping splinter shards of mirror, Elaine crossed to her unfinished painting. She stood before the life-sized figures, loving and hating what she had created.

Her fists moved across the canvas, slashing it into mad patterns.

Take. This is my body. Given for me.

Blacklight was finishing a cold anchovy and black-olive pizza. He considered his greasy sauce-stained hands, wiped them on his jeans. Stains were exchanged, with little disruption of status quo. He licked his tattooed knuckles clean.

It was raining somewhere, because the roof of the old warehouse leaked monotonously away from the light. He watched Kane. Maybe Lionel Atwill's caged gorilla on the loose in the lab. Maybe Rondo Hatton as Mr Hyde.

"So what are lacunae?"

Kane was studying a biochemical supply catalogue. "Gaps. Cavities. Blank spaces."

"Spaces are important," Blacklight said. He knotted his pizza-stained fists and rolled their knuckles together.

"Do you know how atomic bombs work?"

"Used to build them," Kane said. "They're overrated."

"You take two hunks of plutonium or something," Blacklight informed him. "Big as your fist. Now then, keep space between them, and it's on safety. But…" and he knocked his fists against one another "…take away the spaces, slam 'em together. Critical mass. Ker-blooie."

He punctured the lecture with an explosive belch. "So that's why there's always got to be spaces in between," Blacklight concluded. "Like the two halves of your brain. Id and Ego. Yin and Yang. Male and Female. Even in your thoughts you've got to have these gaps—moments to daydream, to forget, to be absent-minded. What happens when you fill in all the lacunae?"

"Critical mass," said Kane.

The mirror was a doorway, clouded and slippery with the taste of blood. Clutching angry shards of glass, Allen and Elaine waited on opposite sides, waited each for the other to break through.

The Truth Insofar As I Know It
by David Drake

Karl Wagner died during the morning of Friday, October 14, 1994.

Karl was an alcoholic. He'd destroyed his liver before reaching age forty-nine (his birthday is December 12). He'd gone off to England for three weeks. I saw him the Tuesday of his return and realized he was dying of congestive heart failure. Edema, shortness of breath, extreme weakness, chest pains—it wasn't, as he would say, a subtle diagnosis.

When Karl's liver shut down in England, he stopped excreting fluids. They filled his tissues and body cavity, squeezing the heart and raising his blood pressure. Nothing else appearing, his heart would eventually have stopped, but instead an artery in his gut burst. He lost blood for a day or two and eventually fainted while he was standing in his bathroom. He fell over backward into the tub and finished dying there.

Think of Karl the next time you have a glass of Jack Daniel's.

He'd told a friend in England that he knew his liver was gone and that he was dying, but he insisted to me and others here that he was just tired because of the trip and the walking he'd done in London. He refused to let us take him to the hospital; and, realistically, there was little that doctors could have done for him by that point.

I miss Karl more than I can say, but the Karl I miss died a long time ago, at the height of his commercial and critical success, while he was married to a beautiful woman who idolized him.

I met Karl in late January of 1971 shortly after I'd returned from 'Nam to Duke Law School in Durham, NC, from which I'd been drafted two years before. One of my army buddies had mentioned the year before that he'd spent part of his embarkation leave in Chapel Hill, very close to Durham, "...dropping acid with my old Kenyon College roommate..."

That was Karl. I'd met Manly Wade Wellman in Chapel Hill on my embarkation leave, so I recognized Karl as the guy Manly had described as "a young friend in medical school here who's sold a novel. It's Robert E. Howard stuff."

While the buddy and I were in Cambodia in 1970 he got a copy of that novel: Karl's first book, *Darkness Weaves*. This was in its Powell Publications format. It had been cut from 70,000 to 50,000 by an apparently random excision of words, with amazing misspellings and additional editorial meddling that beggars comprehension.

It was still a hell of a good book. My buddy said that soon after he got back to the World he'd be seeing Karl, and that he'd arrange for all of us to get together after I got back (a couple weeks later).

He did. Karl and I became close friends.

Karl had dropped out of medical school after the authorities told him he would have to repeat his third year. His grades were fine, but they didn't like his attitude. Karl's parents had been supporting him through med school. They agreed to continue the same level of support through two years of writing full time, with the proviso that if Karl wasn't self-sufficient by the end of that period he would go back and finish med school.

Powell (a pornography publisher that was trying to break into SF) had contracted to pay $500 for *Darkness Weaves* and actually paid about $400 before the company went bankrupt. On the strength of that sale, however, Karl had sold to Paperback Library a collection of novellas, *Death Angel's Shadow*, and an unwritten novel, *Bloodstone*. The advance for the collection was $1,200; I think the novel may have been $1,500. That success convinced

The Carcosa Boys: David Drake, James Gray Groce, and Karl Edward Wagner, 1976. Commercial Photograph taken for The Fourth World Fantasy Convention Program Book, 1979. Photo courtesy of C. Bruce Hunter.

Karl that he had a real career as a writer.

The first task was to write *Bloodstone*. He dived into it with enormous energy. All his life Karl did his rough drafts in pencil on a legal pad, edited them in longhand, and then typed up the final copy. I sat on the floor of his bedroom/study proofreading the final pages as they came out of the typewriter. He sent the book off to Paperback Library.

It came back by return mail, unread, with a letter from his editor saying that the house had decided to drop SF. She hoped they would still publish the collection.

Knowing a little more about the business now, I wonder what kind of contract Karl had signed that gave Paperback Library the right to do that with no payment whatever. In any case, a kill fee wouldn't have made a great deal of difference in the longer term.

For the remainder of 1971 and the following year Karl

Manly Wade Wellman and Karl Edward Wagner, 1975. Photograph by David Drake.

energetically shopped *Bloodstone* and began work on other projects. He had a beer downtown with Manly every Wednesday afternoon, and the three of us (with Frances Wellman and my wife Jo) got together regularly for dinner and to read to one another the latest things we'd been writing.

In addition to short fiction about Kane, Karl read the opening to a straight western, *Satan's Gun* (an attempt to break into another genre) and the opening chapters of *In the Wake of the Night*, a Kane novel he'd started before I met him. It was to be over a hundred thousand words long, a very big book for the day.

Nobody bought *Bloodstone*. One rejection that sticks in my mind was that of Fred Pohl (then at Ace, I believe), who said that he "…couldn't get a handle on the book."

Karl sold "In the Pines," a present-day fantasy novelette written several years before, to *F&SF*, but the magazine returned his new Kane novelette "The Dark Muse" with copy editor's markings already on it. The decision against publishing had been made at a very late stage…

Stu Schiff started *Whispers*, paying a penny a word and probably doing more to keep horror alive in the '70s than any

Joanne Drake, E. Hoffmann Price, Barbara Wagner, and Karl Edward Wagner in Karl's living room in 1975. Photograph by David Drake.

other single factor. *Whispers* published some of Karl's best fiction, including "Sticks"—written for the magazine—but the $81 payment didn't cover rent and groceries for the time it took Karl to write the story.

Unless you've been there yourself you can't really understand how frustrating all this is. Karl handled it as well as anybody could. He never gave up, but he did have to go back to med school. He graduated after two years and took a residency position (psychiatrists don't have to intern) as the only psychiatrist at the state mental hospital in Butner who was a native English speaker.

Karl started Carcosa, a small press publishing house, in 1972, in partnership with me and a former roommate of Karl's named Jim Groce (by then a practicing psychiatrist). It was entirely Karl's baby, though the initial capital came from Jim and me.

Our original intention was to republish *Varney the Vampire*, a Victorian penny dreadful which Manly said was available on microfilm from the British Library. We actually got the microfilm—I wonder what happened to it?—but fortunately

Lee Brown Coye, Karl Edward Wagner, Barbara Wagner, and James Gray Groce at the burial vault in the Hamilton, New York Cemetery in 1975. Photograph by David Drake.

that was the only money we'd sunk into the project before Arno Press announced their three-volume edition. (Dover later came out with a much more readable text in two volumes.)

Plan B was to publish a collection of Manly's fantasies under the title Manly had proposed for an Arkham House edition in the late 1940s: *Worse Things Waiting*. The Arkham project was a casualty of small-press business conditions at the time and perhaps also a falling out between Manly and Mr. Derleth over whether the latter had anything to teach the former about writing. The Arkham House and Carcosa contents were largely different.

Carcosa and particularly *WTW* proved extremely frustrating. We were honest but very ignorant; among other things we believed the dates our printer (in Lakemont, Georgia) gave us. We ran a year late.

Others were doubtful about our honesty. The letter from Gerry de la Ree accusing us of being another fan press rip-off was particularly hurtful; but we were, after all, holding his money.

James Gray Groce and Karl Edward Wagner in Lee Brown Coye's garage workshop in 1975. Photograph by David Drake.

One afternoon I dialed Karl by accident. He'd just talked to the printer and said to me, "I'm frankly suicidal." I took the afternoon off work and we went to bookstores in Raleigh.

Worse Things Waiting is a wonderful book in every respect. It was probably worth what it cost. But it *did* cost, all of us and especially Karl.

Things slowly started to work out. Paperback Library did publish *Death Angel's Shadow*. The company was bought by Warner Communications and restarted its SF line, including *Bloodstone*. Karl got a hustling young agent, Kirby McCauley, who instantly improved the terms of the new contract and sold an unwritten Kane novel, *Dark Crusade*, for $2,000.

The Robert E. Howard boom of the 1970s was getting well under way. Kirby sold to Zebra Books a package of non-Conan REH fiction which included a provision for Karl to write novels about the character Bran Mak Morn at $2,500 apiece. Karl was convinced he could write four Bran novels annually; on the strength of that contract he quit his residency after one year.

Karl Edward Wagner, 1976. Photograph by David Drake.

Writing didn't go as fast as Karl hoped. The first Bran novel, *Legion from the Shadows*, was long overdue and the occasion of many calls to Karl by his editor (which didn't help).

Dark Crusade was later yet, but by 1976 Karl turned it in. Kirby then got Karl a three-book contract from Warners at excellent money for the time: $2,500 for a Kane collection, *Night Winds*, $4,000 to republish the complete version of his first novel, *Darkness Weaves*; and $10,000 for a new novel, *In the Wake of the Night*, which was already begun.

Then Kirby secured one of his brilliant coups: he got Karl a contract to write three Conan novels for Bantam at a base U.S. price of $60,000/book. Karl would only clear $40–45,000 per

David Drake & Karl Edward Wagner at the 1987 World Fantasy Convention, Nashville, Tennessee. Photograph by John L. Coker, III.

book of the U.S. money, but there were extensive sales of foreign rights which brought his share well up above the U.S. price.

And that's when it stopped.

Karl finally managed to turn in one of the three Conan novels, *The Road of Kings*, in 1978. Karl sent in two-thirds of the novel, claiming it was the whole thing; worked over the weekend and sent in most of the remaining portion, claiming it had been left out of the envelope by mistake; and sent in the last chapter after another all-nighter. Conan Properties, the owner of the rights, canceled the other two (they were assigned to Poul Anderson and Andy Offutt at, I'm told, much less money).

The Road of Kings is a very good novel. It's the last novel Karl ever wrote. In fact, he made only one more serious attempt at writing a novel: the 22,000-word fragment that appears in the KEW special issue of *Weird Tales*. All the other novel fragments that Karl published here and there date from before the collapse.

Kirby with his usual brilliance sold a horror novel, *The Fourth Seal*, to Bantam (for $65,000, with $25,000 on signing) in 1987 without an outline or a word on paper. Karl started the book only to the extent of writing two pages describing the heroine's lingerie.

I don't know what happened. I was there the whole time, seeing Karl five or six days a week, and I don't have a clue.

Karl always claimed he was writing and that the problems were external. Neither statement was true. In the mid-1980s, a number of genuinely bad things happened to him: Manly Wade Wellman, our friend, died; Karl's wife left him; and his parents had serious health problems. Karl blamed his delays on all those things, but the collapse had come long before. (While I have no use at all for Karl's ex-wife, she was not primarily responsible for the problems with the marriage nor for its final dissolution.)

Friends who knew Karl in undergraduate and medical school tell me that though he always drank, his alcohol intake increased greatly in the later 1970s. That was my feeling also, but since I don't drink myself I don't have a good way to judge how much somebody else is putting down. (There's no "Fix me one while you're in the kitchen" for a yardstick.) It's my suspicion that Karl drank because he couldn't write rather than the reverse, but I don't know.

In his later years Karl wrote a number of short stories, some of which were brilliant (here I'm thinking particularly of "Neither Brute Nor Human"). In his last year or so his output increased significantly, though I wouldn't put the quality of those stories against that of his early work.

Karl proved unable to finish even the large fragments from his productive period. He completed one fragment as a novelette, "Blue Lady, Come Back." I found its depiction of Manly to be both false and offensive, and the result lame by any standards. (Karl, Manly and I had together visited the haunted house of the story.)

Karl did a screenplay for a third Conan movie. That got him money ($30,000) and some anecdotes about Hollywood, but the screenplay was rejected before the studio shelved the project. He did a treatment for a film about the Asian culture-hero Monkey, for Japanese backers. They liked his work, but they ultimately picked another writer who had experience in animation when they decided to go that route. Those were the only film/TV writing projects for which Karl was paid, though he occasionally received option money and himself worked on spec on ideas which didn't get funded.

A local artist had done half a dozen pages of art for a graphic novel, *Tell Me, Dark*, but he wasn't himself a writer and came to Karl for a script. They sold the project to DC on the strength of artist's name for very good money (Karl's share was $15,500).

Karl wrote *Tell Me, Dark* with four "tracks," as he called them, of text. Material from any or all tracks might be in a given panel. I asked Karl how DC could make that intelligible in a comic format; he replied, "That's their problem."

DC ultimately solved the problem by rejecting Karl's script. Another writer wrote the book (with Karl's permission) from the art, with no reference to Karl's text. At the insistence of both the artist and the actual writer, Karl was allowed to keep the whole advance and DC kept Karl's name on the book. None of the published text is Karl's.

There's one more story about Karl that deserves to be told here. After Karl's death another friend and I were emptying Karl's house of material that the family didn't have to know about. I was pulling things out of a closet and the friend was tossing them into a garbage bag to be taken to the dump.

I tossed out a padded envelope containing three porno novels. The friend looked more closely at them: they were three copies of the same 1973 Beeline Book, *The Other Woman*, credited to "Kent Allard"—the name Karl generally used in his fiction for the character representing himself. There was a typed slip from the publisher identifying them as author's copies.

During a time when I saw Karl very frequently, and when we frequently talked in our desperation of trying porn despite the extremely low rates of pay (about $300 for all rights), he'd written a porn novel of which I knew nothing. That sort of sums up Karl: I probably knew as much about him as anybody else did, but nobody knew—or knows—the whole truth. Particularly the truth about the really basic question: why?

He was so much. He could have been so much more.

—David Drake

Acknowledgements

All stories by Karl Edward Wagner have been reprinted by permission of the Karl Edward Wagner Literary Group.

"Various Encounters with Karl" copyright Peter Straub 1983. Originally published in *In a Lonely Place*. Reprinted by permission of the author.

"The Last Wolf" copyright Karl Edward Wagner 1975. Originally published in *Midnight Sun* #2, Summer-Fall 1975.

"Into Whose Hands" copyright Karl Edward Wagner 1983. Originally published in *Whispers IV*.

"More Sinned Against" copyright Karl Edward Wagner 1984. Originally published in *In a Lonely Place*.

"Shrapnel" copyright Karl Edward Wagner 1985. Originally published in *Night Visions 2*.

"Silted In" copyright Karl Edward Wagner 1987. Originally published in *Why Not You and I?*.

"Lost Exits" copyright Karl Edward Wagner 1987. Originally published in *Why Not You and I?*.

"Endless Night" copyright Karl Edward Wagner 1987. Originally published in *The Architecture of Fear*.

"An Awareness of Angels" copyright Karl Edward Wagner 1988. Originally published in *Ripper!*.

"But You'll Never Follow Me" copyright Karl Edward Wagner 1990. Originally published in *Borderlands*.

"Cedar Lane" copyright Karl Edward Wagner 1990. Originally published in *Walls of Fear*.

"The Kind Men Like" copyright Karl Edward Wagner 1991. Originally published in *Hotter Blood*.

"The Slug" copyright Karl Edward Wagner 1991. Originally published in *A Whisper of Blood*.

"Did They Get You to Trade?" copyright Karl Edward Wagner 1992. Originally published in *MetaHorror*.

"Little Lessons in Gardening" copyright Karl Edward Wagner 1993. Originally published in *Touch Wood: Narrow Houses Volume Two*.

"A Walk on the Wild Side" copyright Karl Edward Wagner 1993. Originally published in *The Ultimate Witch*.

"Passages" copyright Karl Edward Wagner 1994. Originally published in *Phobias*.

"In the Middle of a Snow Dream" copyright Karl Edward Wagner 1994. Originally published in *South From Midnight*.

"Gremlin" copyright Karl Edward Wagner 1995. Originally published in *Beyond* #1, April/May 1995.

"Prince of the Punks" copyright Karl Edward Wagner 1995. Originally published in *100 Vicious Little Vampire Stories*.

"The Picture of Jonathan Collins" copyright Karl Edward Wagner 1995. Originally published in *Forbidden Acts*.

"Locked Away" copyright Karl Edward Wagner 1995. Originally published in *Dark Love*.

"I've Come to Talk with You Again" copyright Karl Edward Wagner 1995. Originally published in *Dark Terrors: The Gollancz Book of Horror*.

"Final Cut" copyright Karl Edward Wagner 1996. Originally published in *Diagnosis: Terminal, An Anthology of Medical Horror*.

"Brushed Away" copyright Karl Edward Wagner 1997. Originally published in *Exorcisms and Ecstasies*.

"Old Loves" copyright Karl Edward Wagner 1985. Originally published in *Night Visions 2*.

"Lacunae" copyright Karl Edward Wagner 1986. Originally published in *Cutting Edge*.

"The Truth Insofar As I Know It" copyright David Drake 1995. Originally published in *Exorcisms and Ecstacies*. Reprinted by permission of the author.